RADWINTER

by

LOIS ELSDEN

'Radwinter' is dedicated to my family, stretching back across the generations, to Essex and Suffolk, to Cambridge and Littlehampton, to Wintzenheim and Colmar, London and Hobart.

'Radwinter' is dedicated to my ancestors who had to flee their homes, who worked on the land as agricultural labourers, who worked in wood yards on the docks, who were slop collectors, who scrubbed floors in convents, who worked on the railways and in the train sheds and as engine drivers, who were landlords of pubs and who went to Tasmania as traders.

'Radwinter is dedicated to my sister Andy Elsden, and to the memory of my mum Monica Matthews Elsden and my dad Donald Elsden.

With many thanks to my friends who have helped me with this book, Isabel Lunn, Sveta Wadowska and Barbara Czerny.

This book is self-published on Amazon; it is self-edited and I apologise for any errors which have escaped my notice, or which have been mischievously inserted when I wasn't looking by the grammar gremlins.

All my characters are fictitious and their stories imaginary, and although I have used some names from the distant past, they do not portray any real person or event. Any similarity to a real person or event is entirely coincidental. Polish soldiers did come ashore in Portsmouth, and you can visit their memorial in Kingston Cemetery Portsmouth.

COPYRIGHT

Copyright ©Lois Elsden 2017

RADWINTER

My name is Thomas Radwinter; I'm just really ordinary, and nobody would really notice me... I'm about five foot ten... well, maybe five foot nine, reddy-brown hair, and hazel eyes. I've grown a beard because everyone said I was baby-faced and when you're thirty-two and look like a giant baby it's a bit ridiculous.

Apart from my brothers and my cousins, I don't know anyone else called Radwinter, but I'd never really thought about that until my brother Paul unexpectedly rang me. He's invited me and Rebecca round to meet his new fiancée. I hadn't even realised he was going out with anyone. I know he has girlfriends but I didn't think he was interested in anyone in particular. He has four boys, the oldest is eighteen and the youngest, Tom, is twelve. I'm his godfather; I was really pleased when Paul asked me, even though I had to tone it down because Rebecca was put out that she wasn't asked to be god-mother. I wasn't surprised about it; we weren't married at the time; she was my girl-friend, that was all.

I have three brothers, Marcus who's the oldest and a bit scary; he brought me up really because my dad disappeared, when I was about four I think. He's fifty-four, so a lot older than me. Paul is forty-eight, and John is forty, so I'm the baby by quite a bit.

I'm always criticised for being absent minded and forgetting things, which is why I write everything down... except I don't write things down, I start writing but then wander off into writing something else and get involved in what I'm writing, not what I was trying to remember.

I'm writing this down because Paul wants us to meet Ruthie, his fiancée, and also he wants to find out about the family tree... he's asked me to make some notes about it... I don't know what he means because I don't know anything, so I started with writing about me and the family, but I've wandered off a bit.

My father's name is or maybe was, Edward, I don't remember him, and my mum was Sylvia; she died when I was eighteen, just before I went to University. I went to Strand Uni because that's all we could afford, so I lived at home with Marcus and his wife; my two other brothers had left by then. I know my mum had two sisters, and my dad had a brother and a sister so I have some Radwinter cousins, but I don't know any more. Maybe Paul will ask them about the family... they're bound to know more than me. I don't understand why he's asked me anyway.

Friday, September 27th 2013, evening

I knocked on Paul's door and I must admit I felt rather glum; I shouldn't have been surprised that Rebecca had something else to do which involved the car, so I'd had to catch the bus. I'd asked if she could drop me off, but she said as we live on one side of Strand and Paul lives on the other, it wasn't convenient as she was going in the opposite direction. I was so cross I didn't even ask where she was going, and it was only as I sat on the number 403 that I wondered.

We live in one of the flats near the sea; from the upper floors you can either look out over the sea, or look inland towards the hills. We live on the first floor, so we see the hedge of larches out of the bedroom windows, and the road and houses from the front room and kitchen. The larches do look lovely when they change colour in the autumn, but I'd rather see the sea... and I would quite like a garden, although Rebecca says she's glad we haven't got one because I'm so lazy I would never cut the grass.

Paul's front door is set under an arched porch, and as usual there were football boots, and wellies and stuff piled on one side. I had my hand up to knock again, wondering if I'd got the day wrong, when the door was flung open by Tom.

"Thomas!" he cried as if he was delighted to see me. "It's Thomas!" he yelled back into the house.

I stepped inside and he flung his arms round my waist and hugged me. What a nice boy he is! I hugged him back and said how much he'd grown, and he had, I didn't have to bend to him even though he's still smaller than me. I expect he'll grow tall like his father and Marcus. He asked to take my coat, so grown up, and as I rescued my wallet I found a fiver which I slipped him. I was rewarded by a beaming grin and another hug.

"I'm off to Scouts now," he said. There was a knock at the door and he opened it to a boy about the same age. Tom grabbed his jacket, gave me a wave and disappeared. "Tell Dad I've gone with Sam!" he called then the door slammed and I was alone in the hall.

The hall was large and well-lit and despite being an all-male household, Paul manages to keep it neat. He has a cleaner who comes in several times a week, but Paul is just a neat bloke. Everything he does is precise, and he always looks tidy, unlike me. Rebecca told me I just look like a bundle of clothes, well, a fat bundle of clothes she said to be accurate. Considering she buys all my things that's hardly my fault… but she says I'm fat so maybe that's my fault… but then she moans if I don't eat what she's cooked… and she is a very good cook so I like eating her meals…

I stood in the hall not quite knowing what to do, dithering, Rebecca would say; the house was quiet although there was music coming from somewhere, and the sound of a guitar being played from somewhere else, and what sounded like gun fire from someone playing a computer game.

Should I knock on the sitting room door? But that would be silly, knocking in my own brother's house. Or maybe they were eating a late dinner, there was a sweet caramelly smell…unless it was an air-freshener, Rebecca had one once that smelt like strawberry bootlaces… the long sweetie things which I still sometimes secretly buy…

Or maybe they were in the kitchen… what to do? I stood dithering and suddenly the kitchen door was flung open…

Paul's family do a lot of door flinging, they are always so cheerful and exuberant... very different from Marcus's two.

"Tommy!" only Paul calls me that, well, John does too sometimes. He looked pleased to see me, well, he looked delighted which always surprises me when anyone does and why anyone should. "What are you doing, lurking here?! Come through to the kitchen, we're in here."

My hair colour has been described as mouse, and when Rebecca is cross with me and I don't answer back, she calls me a mouse... I guess it's being brought up by Marcus which has made me restrained... inside I feel like yelling at her, bellowing at the top of my voice, shouting at her to shut the fuck, shut the fucking fuck up... but something about this restrained violence almost frightens me, so I button it down.

I received a second hug, bone-crunching and unusually I also got a smacking kiss on my cheek. Paul looked very well; he's taller than me, and big too, but unlike me he doesn't look fat. Maybe it's the clothes he wears, he always looks smart and modern, and fashionable, which considering he's nearly fifty and a single dad who has to work hard is a lesson to me, when I'm younger and married with no children... children... that's another story...

Marcus has grey hair, and Paul has gone grey early, and not just the pressure of his work and the family. You can see it in pictures of him in his twenties, that there's silver running through his dark hair. I think it is a family thing because John, who's only forty has a lot of grey in his brown hair ... Paul is very handsome, well, all my brothers are, the handsome gene passed me by somehow...

"Tommy, come and meet Ruthie! I've been telling her all about you!" and he pulled me through to the kitchen.

"All about me? Well, that didn't take long," and I gave my nervous laugh. I know it's a nervous laugh; someone at work was recording someone's leaving speech and in the background was this tittering, which I belated realised was me laughing.

A tall woman rose from sitting at the kitchen table and came to me with her arms out to embrace me. Like Paul, her hair was white, but she was obviously younger than him… she was slim, but not too slim… and she was… well, she was just lovely. My heart gave a little lurch as she hugged me and kissed my cheek on the same place Paul had.

"Thomas, I've heard so much about you! How nice to meet you at last!" and she did look as if she meant it.

"Hello, Ruthie, I'm afraid Paul has been remiss, he's told me nothing about you," I replied and Paul laughed and clapped me on the shoulder and asked what I was drinking.

"Let's stay in the kitchen, Paul," Ruthie said. "I want to keep an eye on that gingerbread." The kitchen was full of delicious smells, the caramel that I'd smelt in the hall and now the spiciness of ginger and molasses.

"Something smells good," I said and blushed as I heard the nervous laugh escape.

"You will be my guinea pig," and Ruthie sat me down and put a plate of millionaire's shortbread in front of me.

The door opened and Django came in, Paul's eldest son; he was christened David Django but as soon as he was old enough he insisted on being Django. No doubt it was his guitar I'd heard.

He greeted me and then swooped on the shortbread.

"Can I have one, Ruthie," he asked, taking one, and I noticed how pleasant and casual he was towards her. If she was to be his step-mum he obviously didn't mind.

"Yes, and call your brothers, I want to know what you think. It's a new recipe, strawberry millionaire's shortbread," she said.

It was like eating heaven; still slightly warm, the short bread was soft and melting with pieces of strawberry, the caramel was not too sickly with a faint trace of orange somewhere in the gooey sweetness, and the dark chocolate was not too bitter with a bit of a zing…

"Is there ginger in the chocolate?" I asked indistinctly. "There's something… some flavour…"

"Well done you for spotting it, you've obviously got the Radwinter palate!"

Django, his mouth full, was at the door yelling for his brothers.

"Ruthie! Cake!" he yelled and before long Luke and Otis bounded into the kitchen. Like Tom they'd all grown and I felt overwhelmed by big cheerful youths, all eagerly scoffing the strawberry millionaire's shortcake.

Paul stood back, arms folded, the usual glass of wine in his hand, looking like nothing more than an enormous, very pleased, and almost smug, silver lion.

Rebecca was home when I got in; I'd thought she was going to be out late, so I'd sat in Paul's warm and comfy kitchen, eating too many pieces of shortbread and then too many more pieces of ginger bread which had different spices in… and chilli… and when I asked Ruthie whether she liked hot things, everyone laughed and I blundered on saying I meant did she like hot stuff, then there was even more laughter, but it was at what I'd said, not at me. Paul said I was a star and his favourite brother, news to me, but I made some facetious remark in response which was greeted by more hilarity and Paul poured more wine.

It was a wonderful evening, one of the best in my life I think. Tom came home and his friend Sam came in too, he was stopping over, and Paul asked if I wanted to stay too… but of course I had to get back to Rebecca.

"What a shame she couldn't come, I'm looking forward to meeting her… another time soon, I hope," said Ruthie as she hugged me.

Paul had insisted I took a taxi which was a good idea since I'd drunk such a lot of his velvety wine.

"Hiya, Thomas," said the taxi driver as I got in. "It's me, Shohib, we went to school together."

I was pleased to meet him again; we'd been sort of close until year 11, then he'd gone college and I'd stayed on at school. We were both outsiders, I think looking back on it. He had a big family and they were all very sporty, mostly cricket, but he had twin brothers a year younger than us who were a fearsome pair of forwards, about the only Asian lads who played rugby.

So, I'd had a nice ride back home and Shohib and I swapped phone numbers, and I was in a really happy place until I got in and Rebecca started moaning because I was late, and because I was drunk, and I became a bit huffy and grumpy and went to bed.

Saturday, September 28th 2013

The next evening curiosity overcame Rebecca and she asked about Ruthie.

"She's lovely!" I exclaimed and went on for a couple of minutes about the shortbread and ginger bread, until I realised that Rebecca was frowning.

"What does she look like?"

It amazes me that Rebecca is so often so jealous when she is also so critical of me.

"Um..." I felt as if I was blushing, which was silly. "Um, I guess she's quite tall, um, and she's not too slim..." I tried to remember. I remembered her sparkling eyes and her dimples and the beaming grins she flashed at Paul. "Um she's about Paul's age I think and she's got grey hair..."

"Grey hair?" Rebecca looked more cheerful. "That doesn't sound like Paul's type, young and tarty is more his style."

"Oh, she's definitely not young and tarty," I replied which made her sound old and frumpy.

We had a pleasant dinner; Rebecca is a very good cook and she'd made something different with mushrooms and prawns and cream and tomatoes.

We both had work to do so we sat with our laptops and Rebecca had East Enders on; she was sitting so I couldn't see her screen so I guessed she was actually playing some game she likes where she has to buy furniture for her mansion, I think... and she chats to the neighbours, not our real neighbours but neighbours of her on-line mansion.

I had some reports to redraft but before I did I checked my emails. I nearly deleted one from Ruthie because I didn't recognize her address and the subject line was 'family tree' which made me think it was an advert for a genealogical site.

Why would Ruthie be writing to me? Last night was a bit of a blur now... I just remember laughing a lot and eating and drinking a lot, and feeling... happy.

"Hi Thomas, great to meet you at last!" At last? As if she'd been wanting to meet me? She was probably being polite. *"We had such a good time that we didn't really talk about the other reason I wanted to meet you... I guess you know Paul is really interested in finding out about the Radwinters, and where you come from etc."* No, actually, I didn't know that; he mentioned it when he rang to ask me and Rebecca round. *"Well, he wants to know about the family, but actually he isn't really interested in the finding out, and anyway he's so busy with his business and the boys. He was thinking of asking one of these professional people to research, but that would cost a lot I think, and anyway it's my hobby... genealogy I mean. So I offered to see what I could do... I'm not a professional or anything, I just do it for fun, but I've been doing it for about seven years now and have got quite far back in my own family..."*

I must have made some sort of puzzled noise because Rebecca looked up.

"Paul's fiancée has written to me," I explained. "About the family tree."

Rebecca looked suspicious.

"Paul's Googled Radwinter but just comes up with a village in Essex; he went on some genealogical sites but he didn't make much progress... in fact he made no progress at all... anyway, to cut a long story short, he said you'd be the ideal person to help because you're the cleverest in the family and have a memory like an elephant..."

I looked up at Rebecca who was still gazing at me.

"I don't know what to make of this, Becca; Paul wants me to help find out about the family tree... I can't think why."

I hoped I wasn't blushing, but with the low energy bulbs we have now to save energy the light is so dim she probably couldn't see. *The cleverest in the family? Memory like an elephant?* Really? Is that what he thinks?

"Perhaps it's because you're a solicitor. Do you think he's hoping to find some money that's been left... you know, like in 'Heir Hunters'?"

"Maybe... Yes, that must be it..." that didn't sound likely at all, but Rebecca went back to her game, and then went into the study to Skype someone who was also playing.

Our flat is quite a decent size, purpose built, with a small hall leading in from the corridor and lifts, a largish sitting room with a fire with mock coals, a nice dining area, a very good sized kitchen, and two bedrooms, one of which we - well Rebecca mostly, uses as a study cum office. It means she can be private when she's playing her game – and not disturb me, not that it does disturb me...

"If you're not interested, or are too busy, don't worry... but I did enjoy meeting you and thought it would be fun to have someone to help with this... Paul says none of you know anything about the family, but I bet there might be

some names or places which ring bells once we start digging!"

It did sound intriguing; I've always felt a little detached despite having my brothers and nieces and nephews and cousins. I guess it was Dad disappearing and Mum... well, Mum...

*"Let me know, but I won't be offended if you're not interested. Looking forward to meeting Rebecca,
Love
Ruthie
PS I haven't started doing anything yet, apart from looking up the Radwinter Village web-site.*

I sat and thought about it. Perhaps I needed a coffee. I went to the study and knocked lightly, the door was open, Rebecca wasn't being secretive, it was just she wanted to get away from the TV that I wasn't watching.

"Should I help Paul, do you think?" I asked when she took off her headphones. "And would you like a coffee?"

"Yes, coffee, please... and yes, why not help Paul, you never know what we might get out of it, and if you're in at the beginning you can make sure you get your fair share!"

*"Hi Ruthie, Thomas here, yes it sounds fun; I'll look at the village site and then tell me what else you want me to do.
Love
Thomas"*

Love Thomas? It sounds fun? Really?

Rebecca works as the manager of a care home for the elderly; whatever she is like with me, with the residents she is amazing. She is actually an administrator and has to deal with finance and planning and staffing and all sorts of things which to me sound really boring. She is good at her job, she enjoys it, and she makes time to go round and visit the residents, join in their activities, of which there are loads, check the staff are where they should be, and never shirks when it's necessary to change a bed, or wipe up a mess, or sort out someone's hygiene… she's amazing! She's energetic, enthusiastic, organized, and well-liked…. Maybe she spends so much of her energy and care on the residents of the Willows, that there isn't much left when she comes home.

Maybe we were too young when we got together; maybe I should have stepped back from feeling grateful that someone liked me enough to have sex with me, and who said that they loved me. Maybe, when she contrived a scenario when I proposed to her, I should have thought about it a little more and maybe, as kindly as I could, change my mind.

Sunday, September 29th 2013

Radwinter. Radwinter is a small village in Essex. I've looked on the village website which is interesting and full of information, and I've looked at other sites, including a history site which had a list of women's marriages from 1813 right up to 1958 and there were no Radwinters; there were no doubt lovely young women called Raven, Read, Reader and Reeve, and handsome grooms named Rands, Reeves, Reynolds, Richardson… but no Radwinters. I looked at baptisms, just in case, but no Radwinters. So I guess that despite the name, our family didn't come from the Essex village of Radwinter. Oh, and I looked at burials… no surprises there, Rash, Raven, Rayner, Reader and Redhouse… but no Radwinters.

So what do I know about our family? My dad is... heck! I don't even know if he has a middle name! I don't know anything about him, he's never mentioned and on the odd occasion that I've asked for some reason, there was such a smudged answer that I sometimes wonder if he's dead... I think I had to give his and Mum's names when I got my passport... did I have to when I got married? I can't remember, and I don't remember any other names than Edward Radwinter and Sylvia Magick (yes really, Mum was Magick before she married Dad)

My name is Thomas Marcus Radwinter... my middle name is after my big brother... as I think about it now, I think he is Marcus Edward... Paul is Paul Quillen (P.Q.R. – I wonder if that's significant...? I'm beginning to read all sorts of things into the family now) John is John Magick Radwinter. I've never really thought about names before, my first name is so ordinary, my last name is so unusual.

Maybe on this quest I should write down all I know, before I add anything else I find out.

- Edward Radwinter m Sylvia May Magick –
- Marcus Edward m. Jill? – Sarah and Paula
- Paul Quillen m. Susan? – David Django, Luke Dylan, Samuel Otis and Tom Bowie
- John Magick m. (1) Eleanor? (2) Fiona Roberts
- Thomas Marcus m. Rebecca Smith

I don't remember the surnames of Marcus's wife, or Paul's ex or John's ex number one; I only know Fiona Roberts because she was in my class at school. As you can see, Paul and Sue gave all their boys ordinary first names but then interesting second names, and that's what Django and Otis call themselves... Luke and Tom see quite happy being Luke and Tom...

My dad had a brother, Uncle James who died a few years ago; he and Aunty Mo had two sons and a daughter, my cousins, Max, Tony and Sammy... they've all got children... Aunty Angela married and had children but I'm a bit muddled by their names, Brian is one I think, but they moved away and I don't remember any of them... but do I need to write them down here? Is it relevant? Not at the moment... I guess I'll have to talk to everyone to see what they remember, thinking about what Ruthie said about ringing bells...

"What are you smiling at?" Rebecca seemed irritated, sometimes she is after playing her game, perhaps she falls out with her 'neighbours'.

I remember her complaining once that someone hadn't mowed their lawn and had planted trees too near her fence... I was quite confused until I realised that it was an imaginary lawn and pretend trees planted next to a virtual fence.

"Come and have a look," I said. "I'm trying to do the family tree, come and see if you remember any of the names I've forgotten."

And to my surprise, she sat down beside me, took the laptop and had a look at my attempts at the family tree. I'd closed down this bit, so all I had was the tree on an ordinary Word doc. She asked some good questions too... who were my grandparents, where did they live, where were Edward, James and Angela born...

And I suggested a glass of wine, and even though it was a Sunday and she was on an early tomorrow, she agreed, and we had quite a nice evening together.

I thought I'd start with Radwinter village... yes, I know, there are no Radwinter connections, but it just seems odd that our unique name is the same as a place... or maybe it is just a coincidence, or maybe Radwinter is a corruption of something else...

In Radwinter there is the Church of Saint Mary the Virgin and on the history site there are some wonderful photos of the reredos within the church, but it was bought and put there in the 1880's; the church itself is over seven hundred years old. I'd like to go and visit and see it for myself; I'm not religious but I do like visiting churches... I wonder if Marcus would be interested as he's a vicar? As well as the church it mentions chapels... are they different? I don't know much about religion, despite Marcus... Primitive Methodists... what are they? Baptists... I really don't know.

Looking at the history of the village it seems as if it was a busy place at one time; I really would like to go and see what is there now. According to the website there were blacksmiths, and many different shops including two butchers and two bakers (no mention of candlestick makers... *stop it Thomas, don't be silly*... Rebecca is always telling me off for my childish sense of humour) there were sweetie shops, a fish mongers, general stores and even a tobacconist, and many different craftsmen such as cobblers and tailors and lots of other businesses.

No surprise that there are pubs, including the Plough and the Red Lion, and windmills... I guess it's a farming area...

Essex, that's a farming county, isn't it, and isn't it by the sea too? I don't know anything about Essex, apart from it being an overspill area for London, but it can't all be like that. I've never been there... maybe I should look at a map... There were four windmills, it says... definitely a farming community, and a prosperous one too. Didn't Constable paint pictures in Essex, or have I imagined that?

I'm onto the history page... Neolithic skeleton, bronze Celtic warrior, Roman roads and coins... medieval tile kiln and fishponds... once it was Great Radwinter and Little Radwinter, perhaps that's me, little Radwinter... 1066, Doomsday, a lord of the manor named Frodo... *what? Really?*

This page also tells me the village is near Saffron Walden and on the road to Haverhill, and on the River Pant... I must look at a map.

Onto the Radwinter Records page... a war memorial with no Radwinters on it, but how sad to see the same names cropping up, three men called Andrews, five men named Halls, two Potts, two Ruses, three Swans and two Thakes... so sad... I don't think I'm old but I bet they were younger than me... maybe some of them as young as my nephew Django... it doesn't bear thinking about.

Radwinter seems an interesting place... I really want to visit... I wonder if Rebecca would like to go for a weekend there... probably not, she likes shopping and going on holiday to somewhere sunny.

In 2006 there was a talk by someone called Fiona Wells; it sounds really interesting, about the history of the villager and area, called 'Rooted in the Soil – a glimpse at the landscape history of Radwinter'. As well as the history of the different manors and farms, Ms Wells mentions medieval industry, bricks and tiles made from local clay, and the production of potash used in bleaching… the things I'm finding out! … but nothing about anyone called Radwinter… as usual I'm getting distracted, but I think Ruthie wanted me to look at this, otherwise why did she send me the link?

The last thing is the 1881 census; there are many names I've become familiar with on this site, but no-one called Radwinter.

Well… that's it with the websites… I'll make some proper notes, but I don't think there is a link, just a coincidence.

So back to Google… hmmm, Wikipedia doesn't have much to add, but here is an entry for Doomsday, all about taxable units and their value, households and plough land, plus other resources which are things like meadows and woodland… The taxes are all in geld, the value in pound, and I'm shocked to see that as well as villagers and smallholders there are also slaves! I thought there were peasants and serfs, I didn't know there were slaves! Livestock is what you'd expect, cattle, pigs, sheep and goats … and bees! Well, beehives. There are no horses except for two cobs which I discover are small horses, so who pulls the ploughs across the plough land – cattle? *Slaves*?

I have a right old chuckle over the names of the lords and tenants! It really is like something out of Lord of the Rings! Ordgar, Algar and Frodo, yes Frodo! brother of Abbot Baldwin. Aelfric and Wulfwin son of Alfwin and then a bloke who sounds like half a glass of white wine, Demiblanc…. How about this - Guthroth of Radwinter! Tihel of HellÈan!

So there we are, Frodo... but no hobbits... the films were terrific... but Rebecca didn't like them, and after Sean Bean was killed in the first one, she didn't want to watch any more.

Friday, October 4th 2013

I think Rebecca wanted to see Ruthie which was why she came with me to Paul's party. She didn't usually come, some excuse, often work related, and when she did come I felt even more awkward than when she didn't. It was a party for the family; I hadn't heard any more from Ruthie and since I hadn't found out anything and didn't know what to do next, I hadn't got in touch with her. I wondered if she'd be asking everyone about the family at the party, but she and Paul just seemed so very happy, chatting, laughing, usually with their arms round each other or holding hands, I'd never seen him look so content, so proud and pleased with himself in a good way.

Ruthie was sparkling too. She was wearing a long black tunic thing with a diamond necklace and black trousers. She had a silver glittery belt, and she just looked amazing. I don't mean I fancied her, well, I did sort of, but not like I wanted to do anything about it... she has such a strong personality she rather terrifies me, in a nice way.

The boys were all there, Django had his guitar out, and a friend was on a cajón, and another lad was playing the harmonica. It was better than having CDs playing, more friendly somehow. My cousins Max and Tony were with their wives; their children were young and not with them. I chatted to them while Rebecca stood silently beside me; she is so sociable at work, I've seen her at parties, talking and laughing with the residents and their families, even people who have problems speaking so it's difficult to understand them, she would chat away, all smiles.

Somehow with my family she isn't like that; maybe because there are so many men.

I asked Max and Tony about the family, but they didn't know anything; Uncle Jim had been in the RAF and was stationed all over the world so it was only when they were older and living back in the area that we got to see them much… after Mum had died, actually, now I come to think about it.

I noticed John standing talking to a woman with red hair; I hadn't seen him arrive so I went over, and he introduced me to Laura but he didn't say, 'girlfriend' so I didn't know if she was with him, or maybe was a friend of Ruthie's.

"Is Marcus coming?" I asked John; he laughed.

"I don't think so, shame really, being a family affair."

Of all my brothers, John is the one I felt closest too, and least intimidated by, but somehow things have changed with Paul, and I'm seeing a different side to him.

"Rebecca, I think I've met you before," said Laura pleasantly. "I work at Maple Lodge and some of our team came to visit the Willows to see your good practice. You probably don't remember me, but I remember you; you gave us an inspirational talk, and we were so impressed with what you do. We've tried to implement some of your ideas at Maple."

John looked politely surprised. I wasn't; everyone spoke highly of Rebecca in her professional role. Rebecca thawed immediately and began to chat to Laura and I could tell John was even more surprised.

"Rebecca, you haven't got a drink, let me get you one," he said; John is always so kind and thoughtful, in a quiet unassuming way.

"It's alright, Thomas will get me one, white wine, please." For some reason she wanted me to go, so I trotted off obediently.

Paul stopped me as I was about to go into the kitchen and asked me to find some more peanuts and olives; his boys had disappeared and he had to get some more wine.

I went into the kitchen but there was no obvious sign of nuts and olives and I began to explore the cupboards. There was a pantry by the back door and I guessed I might be successful there. The door was stiff and I yanked it back and somehow as I wrenched it open I lost my balance and sort of fell into the cupboard and the door shut behind me. I was in the utter dark apart from a tiny line of light round the door. I felt for a catch or a light switch feeling very foolish.

There was a burst of laughter and I could hear women's voices. I knocked gently on the door and was about to call out, feeling really stupid, when I heard them mention Rebecca's name.

They were standing very near the pantry, no doubt getting drinks from the counter beside it. It would be too embarrassing to knock or call out again now.

"They are such an odd couple, aren't they?" I think it was Amelia, Tony's wife.

"They're so old-fashioned, like an old aunty and uncle from a different generation; anyone would think he was older than Paul!" that was Andrea, Max's wife. Rebecca would be appalled, she always thinks she's so fashionable and she spends enough money on clothes!

"I don't mind her, I suppose" said one of them and I waited, blushing, waited for her to say that she *did* mind me. "But why on earth Thomas married her I cannot imagine. He is such a sweetheart, he's gorgeous, why doesn't he ditch her and get someone who would appreciate him?"

"I know, he's utterly adorable, I love him! He's so funny, and when he puts on those sad puppy eyes, well, who could resist him!"

There was a crash as one of them dropped an empty bottle into the box beneath the counter and I jumped, knocking something from the shelf which miraculously I caught. Their voices moved away and I heard a man say something and I banged on the door and called out.

The door opened and I almost fell over Django's cajón playing friend. I mumbled something and thanked him as he laughed at me and I rushed out of the kitchen which was suddenly full of people.

"Where have you been? And where's my wine?" it was Rebecca, still with Laura although John had disappeared. "And what have you got those chickpeas for?"

I looked down; I was still holding the bag of chickpeas which I'd knocked off the shelf and caught.

"Hummus," and I hurried back to get her wine and to see if someone knew where the nuts and olives were. *Sweetheart? Adorable? Puppy eyes?* Unbelievable.

Monday, October 7th 2013

I'm a solicitor, and for the most part it's just ordinary stuff, conveyancing, making a will, legal advice... nothing exciting at all. I'm not sure if I like that, but it's a good job and I feel comfortable.

Several things have been playing on my mind; Ruthie, I mean Ruthie telling me what Paul thought of me, and Paul himself, he seems so warm towards me... not that he was ever cold, he was just big brotherly as if I was a little kid and we had nothing in common. Always pleasant, always friendly, always the big bear hug, but it was almost as if it was because that was what brothers do. When I went to meet Ruthie, and when I went back with Rebecca for the party he was different; in fact at the party we had quite a long chat about nothing in particular, just conversation.

I didn't ask him about the family tree stuff, I didn't ask him about his business, he's a wine merchant; I asked him about the boys because I'd quite lost track of them. I always remember their birthdays because that is something Rebecca is very good at; she has an app where she lists all the family birthdays with reminders in advance so we can get a card organized and signed, and some money put in for the nephews and nieces.

I realised that much as I like the boys, I knew hardly anything about them apart from the fact that Django loves music, and the order in which they come. So I found out that he was going to take a year out before Uni, so would I like to have a chat with him about it as I probably knew more than Paul did. As Django wanted to do music and performing arts, or English, I wasn't sure I was the right one, but I agreed eagerly. Luke was getting on alright with his A levels but he wasn't sure he was taking the right subjects; he'd stick with them until the end of term and see how his assessments went, then maybe think again. He was taking sciences and geography, but he was very good at languages, and wondered if he should swap to them. Otis was doing fine at the start of his GCSEs, and

Tom was doing great in his second year at secondary school.

I asked about Ruthie and said how much I liked her; Paul was pleased and told me all about her, then called her over as she was passing with a tray of little pastry things like upside down umbrellas filled with sea food. So she stood and chatted and Paul disappeared with the tray, leaving me with a pastry thing in each hand.

Ruthie was between jobs; she had worked in a bookshop and deli in Strand, doing a lot of the cooking and catering, but she had come into some money and left to go travelling. Now she was back, and was thinking about writing a cookery book…. Another cookery book, the shops were full of them, would there be room for one more, she said? But she was writing a very successful blog and an on-line food column so that was what she was doing at the moment.

So it hadn't seemed right to ask her about the family tree with all the bustle going on around us… but it had been on my mind quite a lot for some reason.

Another thing playing on my mind was my marriage, but I can't even say what I was thinking, just muddly, dissatisfied, grumpy thoughts.

I was at my desk at work, reading through some tedious documents when Ruthie texted me. Did I fancy getting together for a proper chat about the FT… *FT*? Family tree! She was free tonight as Paul was at a wine fair in Birmingham. I could come to Paul's, or she could come to me, or we could meet somewhere.

I had a panicky feeling and felt a little wheezy and wondered if I had my inhaler.

I texted back and said I'd have to check with Rebecca... Oh Lord, what on earth could I say to Rebecca?

My phone bipped again but it wasn't Ruthie, it was my wife. She had a meeting tonight; she would be very late as there were several of them going somewhere. Could I get my own dinner, there was plenty in the fridge or freezer.

I texted back; did she mind if I went out for a bite, just for a change.

Her message came back almost instantly. *Good idea xxx*

Really?

Greek food... well I've been to Greece a few times, Rebecca likes it, and I like Greek food, I like it a lot, but Rebecca says I like all food a lot which is why I'm so fat. Periodically she puts me on diet, but I'm not very good at dieting I keep forgetting; but I am quite an expert *on* diets, the latest is the 5:2 Diet, but it doesn't seem to be working with me. Anyway, Greek food... I like Greek food so when Ruthie suggested we meet at the meze bar by the harbour in Strand that sounded nice; I'd not been there before which is why I didn't realise it was a Lebanese place.

It was very nice, though; we sat downstairs but there was an upstairs posh restaurant, Ruthie told me. I felt really comfortable with her; I'm usually a bit stuttery and nervous and say silly, things, make jokes that aren't funny, but somehow with Ruthie I just felt normal and myself.

She liked food too... well, obviously it's her job so she was really interested in the menu and seemed really pleased when I was keen to try everything. She suggested the mixed mezze so I just let her choose; some places you go to and you have mixed starters and it's just a set thing... here you could choose any eight dishes from the menu for £18.99, which seemed very reasonable.

"Are you feeling peckish, Thomas, should we order a couple of extras?"

I was all for that, and when Ruthie realised I wasn't driving because Rebecca had the car, she was delighted that we could have a really nice bottle of wine "or two" (or two? I'd be legless!) So she looked down the menu, and ticked off what she wanted on the handy mezze order form on the table. Hummus awarma, baba ghanouge, fava beans, moujadara, kalaj, sojok, calamari, maghmour...

"Does that sound alright? We've got hummus, aubergine, beans in garlic and coriander, lentils and coriander – that sounds a bit like dhal, haloumi cheese in flatbread, lamb sausage in a pomegranate sauce, squid and aubergines and chick peas... hang on, two lots of aubergine, let's get rid of the baba ghanouge and have rojack... sounds a bit like Kojak, are you old enough to remember him? Rojack crispy lamb filled rolls... sounds like spring rolls, sounds lovely!"

Did she mean something by the Kojak remark; did she think I was a child? But wait, what did it matter, Ruthie is Paul's fiancée and I'm married too, we can just be friends, age doesn't matter... I tuned into what she was saying to the waiter.

"And we'll have an extra tabouleh and some fatoush... oh and I think we ought to have some olives while we're waiting, and let's kick off with the Chateau Musar Jeune," she beamed at the waiter, then beamed at me. "Is that OK Thomas?"

It sounded wonderful! We chatted for a little, it was so easy… I asked her about the millionaire's strawberry shortbread, she'd tried it again with cherries and some almonds in the biscuit and flaked almonds on top… the olives and wine arrived, Ruthie tasted it and said it was lovely, and so it was…

I have such a sweet tooth I told her I'd liked the strawberry shortbread.

"Perhaps you could do a range, the strawberry one, and the cherry, and then… well the caramel made me think of banoffee… so could you do a banana one?" then I felt stupid because she went glazed.

She pulled out a note book and began to scribble furiously. "Don't mind me, I just have to write it down while it's in my head! Brilliant idea, Thomas, any other thoughts?"

"Well not every one's got a sweet tooth… how about a cheese one?" the thought just leapt into my head and out of my mouth and I blushed at how stupid it sounded.

She stared at me as if I was mad. She grabbed her wine and took a swig then went back to her notebook.

"Genius, you are a taste genius," she said scribbling madly.

"So, Thomas," said Ruthie a little later as we surveyed the ruins of the meal… and what a meal, I didn't know what I'd liked best, it all tasted delicious, and yet somehow simple, the flavour of the ingredients standing out and not all merged together. "Any Radwinter thoughts?"

I told her what she knew already, about the village in Essex, and the total lack of people with our name. She burrowed in her bag and produced a sheet of paper which she handed me. It was a copy of an old document; the document was two facing pages, and you could see where it had been looped together by string or thread, and the pages had been attached to each other. The pages were numbered 11 and 12 and at the top of the right page, hand written beside 'County or borough of', were the words 'County of Essex', and below that beside 'Parish or township of', it said 'Radwinter'. Finally it said 'Enumerator schedule'.

Each of the two pages was sectioned out in a table; across the head of the columns was written Place, 'HOUSES' (subdivided into 'Uninhabited or building' and 'Building'), 'NAMES of each person who abode therein the preceding night',' AGE and SEX' (subdivided into male and female) 'PROFESSION, TRADE, EMPLOYMENT or of INDEPENDENT MEANS', 'Where Born' (subdivided into 'Whether Born in same County' and 'Whether Born in Scotland, Ireland or Foreign Parts').

There were twenty five rows and then at the bottom was a row 'TOTAL in page', and the left hand page was 21, but in the right hand page 60. There were entries to about halfway down page 21, all hand written

"Is this from the census?" I asked. 1841, She told me.

She passed me another sheet; this was obviously the front sheet of the document. It was printed but the details had been written in by hand.

At the top it said 'ENGLAND AND WALES'

Enumerator's Schedule:

- County of *Essex* (parliamentary division)
- Hundred, Wapentake, Soke or Liberty of *Freshwell*
- Parish of *Radwinter (part of)*
- City, or Borough, or Town, or County Corporate of
- Within the Limits of the Parliamentary Boundary of the City or Borough of
- Within the Municipal Boundary of.
- Superintendent Registrar's District of
- *Saffron Walden*
- Registrar's District *Radwinter*

No. of Enumeration District *1*

Description Ditto... *All that part of the parish of Radwinter, that lies on the north and south east side of the High Road leading from Saffron Walden to Hempsted*

I took a little sip of wine and saw there was a second bottle on the table; I'd been so engrossed that I hadn't noticed.

I looked back at the original sheet she'd given me, and looked down the list of names.

- Mary Francis abt. 1791, Thomas Francis abt. 1816 - Well, I guess Mary was the mother
- The Kittridge family, William and Caroline and baby Julia
- The Mosses, Thomas and Susan and baby Mary

Then -

- John Morris abt. 1791
- Joseph Saward abt. 1761
- Rose Bush abt. 1826

... Rose Bush... did she get teased at school?

- James Swan abt. 1771

- James Swan abt. 1821
- Mary Swan abt. 1821
- Robert Swan abt. 1826

The Swans, old James, seventy years old and his family, husband wife and brother, or sister and two brothers?

- Thomas Radwinter abt. 1815

I gasped out loud and I think I must have shouted something because the waiter came hurrying over. I smiled and said everything was fine, wonderful… but… I looked at Ruthie. I was in a state of shock.

"It's Thomas!" I exclaimed. I drank some more wine and my hand was shaking. She filled my glass with some from the new bottle and I stared distracted at the label. 'Chateau Musar Bekaa Valley, Lebanon 2005'.

I ate another rojack, my heart was thumping… how stupid to have this reaction.

"Is he my ancestor?" I asked at last, wiping my fingers.

"I'm not sure, I don't know yet," she replied. "I've been a bit busy with food and writing so I haven't had a real lot of time to find out. But he is the only Radwinter anywhere in the census for England and Wales, but look at what it says about him."

I looked at Thomas, my namesake; I looked all across his information. There was a mark in the first column of the record, and I looked up to see that it was the column marked 'Houses', and the sub-column 'Uninhabited or Building'. What did that mean, was he sleeping in a barn, was he sleeping rough? He was younger than me, twenty-six… sleeping rough? I looked all the way across to the very last columns where there was another mark.

'Whether Born in Scotland, Ireland or Foreign Parts'… so he could be Scottish, or Irish, or from foreign parts… how intriguing!

I suddenly felt very excited and raised my glass of Chateau Musar Bekaa Valley.

"Cheers! Here's to Thomas!"

There was no proof, yet, that he was my ancestor, but I just felt he *was*!

Thursday, October 10th 2013

"You're very grumpy today," Kylie was never shy of the honest opinion… which in a way I prefer.

I once overheard Julie and Vicky who hadn't seen me as I was on the floor picking up the paperclips I'd managed to throw into the air and sprinkle everywhere. They'd come in after lunch and were talking about 'the firm' as they called the solicitors, as opposed to 'the office' which was the administrative staff. By some fluke they just happened to be talking about me… I was alright, one said, but I had no inter-personal skills.

I stayed crouched beside the filing cabinet until I heard one say she needed to go to the Ladies, and the other say she would take the letters to the Post Office across the road. On that occasion it was Kylie who'd found me still on my hands and knees feeling angry and upset… what was wrong with my interpersonal skills?

"What's wrong with my interpersonal skills?" I asked Kylie now as the paper-clip incident jumped into my head.

"Yer what?"

I'd spoken without thinking, as so often happens and now I blushed and stuttered and became more grumpy as I asked her about some papers I wanted.

"Can I be honest?" said Kylie, once I'd finished snapping at her.

I sagged... Rebecca had said that last night... *Can I be honest? Well, no, not if you're going to say something I don't want to hear.*

"You're just an awkward git," Kylie said. "I don't mean awkward like you want to be difficult, I mean awkward that you don't know what to say and get all embarrassed and blurt things out and then get more embarrassed."

I could feel that I was red to the tips of my ears now. I shuffled some papers around and looked at the computer screen which I hadn't switched on yet.

"Can I be even more honest?" Kylie went on. "You need to do something daring – do a parachute jump, or go on the Trans-Siberian railway, or have an affair!"

"Affair!" I spluttered. "I'm married!"

"Exactly!" and with that Kylie flounced off.

It's impossible to describe my feelings at that moment.

Since the wonderful meal at the Lebanese restaurant, and since I'd found out about Thomas, the other Thomas, born nearly two hundred years ago, my head had been in a whirl... I felt unsettled and irritable and happy, and silly... I felt discontented with my life, and I found myself worrying about the twenty-six year old who on the night of the census had been living in 'a building'.

I didn't know how censuses worked; did the fact that Thomas was mentioned next to the Swan family mean that the building belonged to them? Were they farmers with a barn, was it just a shed, a place for chickens and cattle? Was it an abandoned cottage? When was the census? Was he cold? Was he hungry? Where was his family... his family were in 'Scotland, Ireland or Foreign Parts'.

I somehow didn't mention to Rebecca that Ruthie had been with me at the Lebanese restaurant, and I don't know where she was with her colleagues. I told her what a nice menu it was and suggested we went there some time, our anniversary maybe?

She seemed to like the idea and got out one of her cookery books which had some of the recipes I told her about. I also told her about Thomas and showed her the papers Ruthie had given me, but she wasn't very interested really, certainly not very excited as I was. She thought Paul had sent them to me, and I didn't make any other comment.

A couple of days later she made kufte to start with, then a sort of makanek, which at the restaurant had been a chicken and coriander sausage, but she just did it with pieces of chicken in the lemony sauce. She is such a good cook it was delicious, and we just had rice and a salad to go with it. I opened a bottle of wine which we don't often do during the week.

We had a very pleasant evening, and she didn't go on her game at all, and I didn't do any work, although I should have done.

Later as we lay in bed, about to go to sleep, I asked something which had been on my mind for a few days... well, a bit longer, actually, since Paul had first mentioned the family.

"Becca, do you think we should start a family?" I asked. I'd loved being in Paul's house with his boys, the party had been great with the cousins as well, it just seemed like the right idea. We would have to move of course... the flat wasn't big enough... a garden would be lovely... perhaps I could learn how to grow vegetables... John was good at that.

"What did you say?" she asked sleepily.

"I was just wondering, I was just thinking, maybe it's time we should have a family."

She jerked awake.

"What's brought this on?" she was definitely taken aback... had she not thought about it? One of the care staff at the Willows had a baby and brought it in, and Becca had picked it up and wandered about with it showing it to all the residents, a lovely smile on her face.

"I've been thinking about it for a while... I thought you might have been too," I tried to sound affectionate but a panicky sensation was gripping me again... these strange anxiety attacks were happening more frequently after years of not bothering me.

"Let's not discuss it now," she said and rolled onto her side, her back to me, but not moving away from me as she did when we'd had words.

I let it go... until the next evening when I mentioned it again because now it was on my mind. One of the women at work, Vicky had come in today and told us she was pregnant. I was delighted for her and actually hugged her. I don't know who was more surprised, her or me; she was one of the ones who'd said about my interpersonal skills.

I was taken aback by Rebecca's reaction; she seemed horrified at the thought, a baby? Having a baby now? It seemed an ideal time, we were comfortably off and secure in our jobs, and I made the mistake of saying she didn't want to leave it too late...

Too late? *Too late?* What the hell did I mean by that? What was I implying? That she was old? That she was middle-aged?

I admit we did have a bit of a row; I was more upset than I expected and it ended up as if I was demanding she got pregnant. I went into the kitchen and made a cup of tea neither of us wanted, and when I came back she was in the study with her headphones on, playing her game. I put her tea beside her and mouthed 'sorry'. She gave a tight smile...

So Kylie was quite right to say I was grumpy, I *was* grumpy. And I couldn't think of any worse idea than that of having an affair.

Monday, October 14th 2013

John rang me and asked if I fancied a beer. I'd never been so popular! First Paul, now John... you never know, Marcus might ring me up next... actually, no he wouldn't. Rebecca was on a late shift so it was perfect. We'd been polite with each other since the row and I daren't talk about babies again... not yet, but I would. Maybe Kylie was right, but not an affair, a family.

I met John at the Bolton Spanner; I'd been in there a couple of times before, but not recently. As with Paul, I was surprised how easy it was to chat to him. What had changed? Nothing that I had done, nothing that I could think of.

I asked about Laura and he gave a rueful smile; she wasn't quite as keen as he was and had suggested they let things cool. He asked about Rebecca and I responded cheerfully as if everything was alright. Well it was alright, it was the same as ever it was, but *I* wasn't quite right somehow.

John looks like a slim, brown version of Paul; Paul is silver, John is brown, a naturally tanned skin, very blue eyes; he looks ten years younger than he is, not because he's trying to, he just does. He usually wears black, and so he was this evening, black t-shirt, black jeans, and a black fleece draped over the chair.

"So what's the secret of a happy marriage, bro?" he asked.

"A happy marriage?" I was perplexed.

"You and Becky seem solid, you seem happy, what's the secret? I hoped Laura might be third time lucky..."

I gave a deep sigh... I seemed to be on a switchback as if I was a teenager, really happy, then down in the dumps... that's a quaint phrase, but that's where I was now, down in the dumps. Paul's kitchen, happy place, home a ho-hum place, Pauls party, the Lebanese restaurant, happy, home and work...

"Are things not ok?" John asked because I hadn't replied. He's grown a beard, a little goatee, and it makes him look like a picture I had of Mr Tumnus from Narnia.

"I don't know... don't say anything to anyone, don't say anything to Paul... well, I just feel as if it's time we had a family and Becca doesn't."

John looked thoughtful. He was older than me, did he want a family too?

"Doesn't think it's time, or doesn't at all?"

That thought hadn't struck me... maybe she didn't want a family at all!

"I don't know... I just feel, sort of unsettled... maybe it's Paul and Ruthie, they seem so happy..."

"I know," John finished his pint in a long swig and went to the bar and I realised how crass I was ... fancy mentioning the happy couple when John had just told me he and Laura had finished! Kylie had said I was awkward...

I apologised when he came back, but he smiled in his friendly way and said it didn't matter, it was alright. He is such a nice man; when we were children I'd known him best out of the three of them; Paul and Marcus had gone by the time I remember anything, although Marcus came back when things were bad with Mum, but for a lot of the time it was John and his little kid brother, me.

"How are you getting on with this family tree thing?" John asked and I told him what I'd found out about the village in Essex, I visited the site constantly, reading and rereading the information and I showed him the census information, and he laughed at the name Thomas Radwinter.

"So do you think we're Scottish or Irish? Should we be McRadwinter, or maybe O'Radwinter?" John laughed. "Anyway, I've been having a think since Paul mentioned it, and I've written out what I know... but Marcus is the one to ask. Ring him up, or go and see him, he'd know. He might even have some papers, you know like old letters or birth certificates, that sort of thing. I know Ruthie has gone back to the beginning, but maybe we should come from the other direction too?"

That sounded sensible. John gave me a couple of sheets of A4 covered in his microscopic writing; it was too dark in the Spanner to make it out, and anyway it would be better if I looked at it without having drunk rather more beer than I should have.

"How did Ruthie get this census material?" he asked. She was on some sort of genealogical site; she paid a subscription and could get copies of stuff. "What's she on to now?"

I had no idea… she seemed rather taken up with millionaire's shortbread at the moment. Maybe I could do some exploring if she told me what the site was.

My phone rang, and to my surprise it was Rebecca; she was coming through town, did I want a lift rather than the bus? She'd never offered before… but maybe she'd forgiven me, maybe she wanted to make it up to me. I texted back immediately and finished my beer. John said he was staying in town, there was a band on at Needles that he wanted to catch…

I put the papers in my bag; I'd have a look at them later.

Tuesday, October 15th 2013

I dithered over whether to ring Ruthie; she's given me her number, but I'm not always very good on the phone, so maybe I should I text her but that seemed a bit abrupt so I emailed her and spent a long time dithering again over whether to say '*hi*' or '*hello*' or '*dear*'. I settled on 'hi' and just briefly mentioned the Lebanese meal, then asked about the shortbread and suddenly I found I'd written a whole paragraph about it. I'd become a bit fixated on the idea of a savoury millionaire's shortbread; the shortbread part was ok, cheese, nuts, mustard, seeds, that was fine... but what about the caramel?

You couldn't have a savoury caramel, unless you put peanut butter in it which is popular... I'd had some really nice peanut butter ice-cream at a food fair Rebecca and I went to. But supposing you just took the idea of having a sweet layer... maybe quince jelly, maybe a sort of syrupy chutney? Maybe a pomegranate sort of jelly stuff? But then what could you do with the top... it has to be chocolate... but chocolate and cheese? Chocolate and peanut butter and cheese? It doesn't sound right even if you use chilli chocolate... so I was stumped on the chocolate, but I'd give it some more thought.

I'd written a whole long paragraph without even mentioning why I was writing. I told her how exciting it was, how excited *I* was at finding Thomas... and what should I do next? Should I look at the next census which was ten years later – but I guessed she might have already done that... or were there other things she could look at, or I could look at if she told me how? And how did I get on this genealogical site, it sounded really interesting and useful...

I wasn't sure I wanted to find out about my mum's family... A few issues there, but the name Magick must be quite unusual, I'd never come across anyone else with that surname. And how could we find if Thomas was related to us? I felt as if I'd be really disappointed if he wasn't, but even if he wasn't, it was nice to think about someone else with my name, even though I worried about him in the building that night… when was the census? If it was in the summer then he'd probably be OK, but if it was in the winter, sleeping in a building… and a building from the 1840's might only be a shack, mightn't it? I didn't know…

I'd written another enormous paragraph… she wouldn't want to read all this… I hadn't even asked how she and Paul were… usually letters begin with it.

I apologised for rambling and asked after her and Paul and the boys… had she any brothers and sisters, I hadn't asked her… did she have a big family… how far had she got with her tree… were there any other Ruthies… and then I realised I didn't even know her surname or even if her name was really Ruthie or just Ruth which was a name I liked…

I stopped writing… if Rebecca and I had a little girl we could call her Ruth… that would be a nice gesture to Ruthie, and it was a nice name, Ruth Radwinter… that sounded lovely… but supposing he was a boy… he couldn't be Thomas again, but maybe he could have Thomas as a middle name… I wouldn't want him to have my father's name, or maybe Paul, because he'd been so kind to me, but Marcus had helped me when I was a kid, and John, I was closest to John… well, unless I had four boys… four boys! Like my family, like Paul's family! Four! Would we be able to afford it? Well we'd move, obviously, we'd move if we had one baby, a child needed a garden to run around in and a washing line to put the nappies on… or maybe we would have those disposable nappies… but that never seemed very nice, putting dirty nappies in the rubbish…

"Thomas!" it was Gerald, one of the partners.

"Oh, sorry, sorry, Gerald!"

We had a meeting, well of course we did, it was Tuesday and we always have a meeting on Tuesday. Was I late? No, but it was time to move.

I quickly wrote, 'Love to you and Paul from Thomas and Rebecca' and sent it before I realised what a lot of nonsense I'd written...

I was blushing as I went through to Gerald's big office where the five of us had chairs round his lovely old desk. It had been his great-grand-father's, the great-grand-father who was the son of the original Mr Gerald who'd started the firm.

"Do you know anything about your family tree, Gerald," I asked as I drew up a comfortable chair.

He might have looked startled for a second, as I was from having asked it.

"Well, yes, quite a bit actually; my wife is a member of the local family history group, she's done a lot of work... goes right back to the fifteenth century."

He seemed pleased I'd asked and spoke about it a little before we got down to business.

Ruthie emailed me.

Hi Thomas! Does anyone ever call you Tom? I just wondered because really I'm Ruth-Ann but I've been Ruthie all my life, but I've never heard anyone call you anything other than Thomas, only Paul when he's talking to you, but not when he's talking about you. Oh dear, that sounds as if he's gossiping, I don't mean that, I just mean when he told me about you when we first got together... God, I'm rambling.

Hey, you're a genius with food! Give up being a solicitor and become a food-person! Can you cook – do you cook? Seriously though, I was really impressed and grateful for your suggestions. I've been having a go at the banoffee idea you had and now I'm plunged into cheese shortbread... would you and Rebecca like to come round some time and be a taste panel for my stuff... I would really value your opinion, you've got a great palate, must be a Radwinter thing!

Well, that was a surprise... unless she was just being polite, but I didn't think she was the sort of person to just be polite... I suddenly felt a sort of smug happiness.

I'm really sorry Thomas, I haven't done any work on the family tree... I have been up to my ears in cooking, writing, and I've been doing some demos.... Nothing exciting, there were two for the WI and then one for the U3A and I went into the sixth form college on a taster day... except I was doing the cooking not the tasting! I did your gingerbread – you know you suggested I use coriander and star anise and dried pear, well it's just magic, so thanks for that idea!

Had I said that? I vaguely remember waffling on in Paul's kitchen about the spices I thought would be nice in gingerbread and telling Ruthie that Rebecca had made a cake with pears, but I thought dried pears might be nicer because the fresh pears were very wet being so juicy... Fancy her remembering, fancy her trying it!

The family tree site I go on is MyTimeMachine... there are lots of other sites, I guess one of the biggest is Ancestry, *there's also* GenesReunited *and Find My Past*

If you wanted to go on MyTimeMachine you could start your own tree etc., or I could give you my password and you can look at my stuff... but the only trouble is then you'd have all my family tree which I don't think you'd be interested in... we're Jordans, by the way, that's my name, Ruthie Jordan.... So it's up to you.

I've looked in parish records for Thomas Radwinter.... They go back before the census started, some of them way back to the sixteenth century, but I can't find a single Radwinter and I can't find any in any Scottish records. I haven't got access to any detailed Irish stuff, but I've had a quick trawl through what I can get to and nothing has come up...

So my thoughts on where Thomas came from... all I can think of is that he was a beggar child with no name and someone in the village 'adopted' him or at least took him in, and he was given the name Radwinter after the place, just so he had a name... and maybe even given Thomas as well by the family, if it was a family name.

My other thought is he might be a gypsy child... but I don't know much about gypsies, so you might explore that, or finally my other other thought that he might be an illegitimate child of someone in the village, and given the name Radwinter to conceal whose child he really was. Does that make sense? Do you get what I mean?

"What's the matter with you?" it was Rebecca. She'd been frosty with me since we'd had our 'discussion' about having children.

"Nothing... it's just some of this family tree stuff about Thomas – you know, I told you about the other Thomas Radwinter who was born in 1815," I pointed at the screen so she could see what Ruthie had written.

Rebecca wasn't interested really, though.

"You look like you've lost a shilling and found a sixpence," and then she laughed. "My grandma used to say that, I haven't thought of that since I was a kid. It's you going on about the family tree I expect!"

"No, I mean, yes... I'm just trying to find out where Thomas came from, he just seems to have arrived in Radwinter."

"There's a place called Radwinter?" I'd already told her, she'd obviously not remembered.

"Yes, it's in Essex, I wondered if we might go there one weekend?"

She used to watch a programme called 'The Only Way is Essex', so the thought obviously didn't appeal.

"I think the countryside is beautiful round there, and it's near a place called Saffron Walden which is really, really lovely!" I'd looked at a lot of places in Essex recently. "It's got a turf maze which is really unusual, and castle ruins, and lots of lovely medieval houses!"

Rebecca prefers shopping malls and retail outlets to castle ruins and old houses... so going on an expedition to Radwinter was pretty unlikely... I would like to go all the same.

I went back to Ruthie's email. She suggested that I try to find Thomas on the 1851 census, and also see if he married and had children; later censuses also had more detail, such as where people were born and their occupations... on the page she'd given me, some of the people had occupations, most of the Swans seemed to be carpenters, and some of the others were Ag Labs, agricultural labourers, but later records had more precise information.

She finished by mentioning again that she'd like to get together with me and Rebecca, and she wouldn't force us to try her shortbread!

I sat back, smiling at the invitation, but with a niggle of anxiety about Thomas... a beggar child, a gypsy child, an unwanted and unacknowledged illegitimate child?

Thursday, October 17th 2013

I joined MyTimeMachine, and it was fascinating... I spent a few days playing with it when I had a spare moment. I could find all sorts of things in births deaths and marriages, I avoided my own immediate family, I didn't really want to think too much about my mum and dad, but I looked up famous people, Charles Dickens, that sort of thing... and somehow I was avoiding looking up Thomas.

Kylie had accused me of being cheerful and asked if I was having an affair and then she laughed in a really silly way when I got cross and said of course I wasn't. Gerald gave me an email address for the family history group that his wife belonged to, but also told me they met on a Tuesday afternoon so really that wasn't much good because obviously I'm at work. He suggested I might get in touch anyway; if I became a member, even if I couldn't go to the meetings it would be somewhere I could ask questions if I got stuck in my researches. He asked me how far I'd got, and I said I was stuck on someone in 1841 who didn't seem to have been born anywhere, nor have any parents.

He seemed interested and said he would ask his wife if she had any ideas, which was very kind.

I'd had a few sporadic looks on the net to find stuff about life in Essex in the 1840's and it seemed pretty hard for poor people, and I guess Thomas was poor. I wondered if I could find any trace of him before 1841 but when I accidentally came across a record for the assizes and some poor man was sentenced to be whipped, and another sentenced to death, it rather shook me.

So one evening when Rebecca was on her game in the study with the door closed, and I'd finished all the stuff I had to do for work, I took the plunge and looked to see if Thomas had got married... I don't know why I'd messed around for so long not looking, either he got married and had kids, or he wasn't the right person and just disappeared.

I found the search, marriage, and typed in Thomas Radwinter... it was kind of strange writing my own name... I clicked search, the little thing went round and round and then, bingo! But, what? Three Thomas Radwinters? Then I realised one was me and I felt a little silly, but odd because there was a record of my marriage to Rebecca.

I sat and looked at it for a little while thinking about things, and then clicked on the earliest one, 1845, Thomas would have been thirty... Thomas Radwinter married either Rebecca Swan or Thirza Downham... Rebecca Swan? There were Swans in Radwinter... did he, like me, marry a Rebecca, but unlike me, he married a swan? I've just reread that last sentence and noticed I'd missed the capital on Swan which made me think that it looked as if I'd married the ugly duckling...

Rebecca is quite attractive, she has shoulder length, wavy very dark hair, dark eyes, glasses and quite a serious face but she looks lovely when she smiles. She thinks she is fat, well, I suppose she isn't slim, but she is tallish and has long legs so she doesn't look fat, just rounded in a nice way. Anyway I am fat, well, stout, so I have a warped perspective, as she once told me. Marcus is very lean, and so is John, Paul is more sturdy, but he never looks it because of the smart way he dresses; his jeans always look new, and his shirts always look crisp and freshly ironed.

Thinking about the way my brothers look, anyone seeing them together could tell they're brothers even though superficially they look different; it is something about their eyes. The Radwinter eyes are very blue and very piercing; Marcus always makes me feel nervous as if he can read my mind and see into my heart, and he is quite cold, well, cool in the way he looks at you. Paul can look like that too, but not as cold, but perceptive; he is a mind and heart-reader too, but to know the truth, not to find fault... but then Paul has this lovely crinkly smile which makes his eyes twinkle and look mischievous. John's eyes have a softer, kindly look; he's nearly always smiling, not in a mocking way, but in a friendly way; even when he is serious, his eyes are kind, and he seems to read my mind in a different way, as if he understands me rather than being critical of me.

I don't have Radwinter eyes, I'm the one in the family with hazel eyes... what had Andrea or Amelia said, *'sad puppy eyes'*... really?

Rebecca Swan was born in 1822, and another Rebecca Swan was born in 1826. There are 20 Swans in Radwinter in 1841, Isaac and Elizabeth and baby Charles; old James, young James, Mary and Robert, another family - William Swan, aged fifty-five, and possibly his son Robert, daughter or daughter in-law Sarah, then maybe another son Charles and then five year old Ann. There is another family, William Swan, b1801, Susan Swan b 1793, *Rebecca* Swan b 1827, Eliza Swan b 1830, William Swan b 1833 and little George Swan born two years before the census in 1839. Then all on her own, below the Giblins is another Rebecca, born in 1822.

I'm feeling a little more confident with MyTimeMachine, and I've looked up Rebecca who appears below the Giblins; Mr Giblin, Frederik, aged sixty, is a farmer who lives at Bendysh Hall with his wife, Mrs Giblin, Elizabeth aged fifty, and his children, Emma, twenty, Clara, fifteen, Julia, fifteen, and Charles, fifteen and Ellen, thirteen…. Wait a minute, triplets? In 1826? That must have been most unusual! Maybe there were twins and another born ten months later… I went to school with the Armsteads, all three in my class, Kai, and then Sia and Sha who were twins…

Back to Bendysh Hall; little James Chapman aged nine (m.s. – male servant) Eliza Woollard aged fifteen (f.s. – female servant) and nineteen year old Rebecca Swan also a servant. Poor little James, only nine and a servant.

I don't even know if Rebecca married Thomas Radwinter; his name isn't mentioned in one of the records I found when I double checked Rebecca Swan's marriage… but I note the date is 1847, and the option on the bridegrooms is Edward Nash, George Cox and would you believe it,

Josiah Swan! I don't really understand the way the names are options... I must ask Ruthie.

I looked back at the Radwinter history page where the names of grooms had ended with Charles Ketteridge and Louisa Atherton had married... and realised I'd not looked at page 2! Idiot! And there between the marriage of William Purkiss, bachelor of Hempstead and Alice Osborn, spinster of Radwinter parish, and Thomas Rands, bachelor of Barrow and Alice Mary Mascall, spinster of Radwinter, there, there was Thomas Radwinter, bachelor foreign, and Thirza Downham, spinster of this parish!

So it seems as if maybe, Thomas didn't marry a Swan but a Downham... Thirza... what a strange name, I've never heard it before, although I notice that there are other Thirza's in Radwinter in 1841... I've made a spread sheet of all the people in Radwinter at the time of the census, all five hundred and seventeen of them.

Little baby Thirza Savill was born in 1840, and Thirza Richardson was born in 1829, so Thomas's Thirza, if she is, was the oldest. Thomas and Thirza... Thirza Radwinter... mmmm, I'm not sure I'll call my little girl that! For a start Rebecca wouldn't like it, she would like names like Amy, or Emily, or Katie... I'm not sure what names I like... there are some unusual names in 1840's Radwinter, for girls, Lillah, for example, or Lydia, Julia, Selina, I like all those names...Lillah Radwinter, Julia Radwinter... but not Thirza!!

Something strange has just happened... Rebecca brought me a cup of coffee and I was trying to show her what I'd found, but I'm still not very good at MyTimeMachine and I somehow jumped onto census information for Thirza

Downham and she appears in 1851 and every year until 1881.

"So? She's on the census, what's wrong?" Rebecca asked, I think she's trying to be interested. "Isn't that good that she's there?"

"Well, if she married Thomas in 1845, she would be Thirza Radwinter, wouldn't she? I don't think women kept their own names then, in fact, I'm sure they didn't… and she wouldn't have got divorced would she? Did people get divorced then?"

Rebecca gave me a slightly suspicious look, but it might have just been the light reflecting on her glasses… she sometimes thinks I'm thinking things that I'm not.

"Well look up Thirza Radwinter, then… perhaps there were two Thirza Downhams and the other one married him… it doesn't seem likely… they both seem quite unusual names," she was staring at the screen as I looked at the 1851 census.

"Well, there are three other Thirzas, and eight other people called Downham in 1841," I told her and flashed to the spread sheet to show her.

"Well look for Thomas again," she said… but for some reason I was a little nervous, as if I was meeting someone and wasn't sure whether they liked me… but that was just stupid!

I looked at the 1851 census… I just had a feeling about Thirza…

In 1851 Thirza was living in Red Oaks Hill, Ashdon, Saffron Walden; she was living with her father James Downham who was seventy-two years old and a farmer owning thirty acres and employing a man and a boy. I have no idea how big thirty acres is. I walked through to the study where Rebecca was back on her game, she was Skyping someone but as I came in she immediately closed down the screen... maybe her friend was in her pyjamas or hadn't done her hair!

I asked her about acres but she hadn't a clue and seemed annoyed that I thought she might know; her father has some land the back of their house so I thought she might have known how big it was. I went back to the census; also living with Thirza was her brother Richard, a year younger than her and working on the family farm.

I found the 1861 census and looked up Thirza again.

I had a bit of a shock... and then thought that I'd obviously made a mistake somewhere because when I saw Thirza's information it plainly said she was unmarried; not widowed, or divorced, but unmarried. She was now a housekeeper, and her date of birth was now 1823... which reminded me, I wanted to ask Ruthie about the triplets, and also the fact that I'd noticed there were lots of children apparently born in the same year, and then several years without them being born... maybe the date was when they were baptised or something...

The census return said Thirza was living now at Little Brockholds, and she was employed by an elderly widower, Edmund Emson, who was born in the marvellously named Helions Bumpstead... is there really such a place? He was a farmer of one hundred and thirty acres, over four times what her father had had, and he employed eight hands and fifty-one boys. Edmund's son, Robert, was also on the farm, unmarried and aged forty-six. There are two young servants, Emma Kitteridge and Arthur Kittingbock the groom. Kittingbock... I've looked at a copy of the original form and indeed it looks like

Kittingbock, but surely it can't be! I've checked Helions Bumpstead and it really does exist, about five miles from Radwinter.

In 1871, still unmarried, and now forty-eight, Thirza is still at Little Bockholes; old Edmund has died but Robert still owns the farm, although there is no mention of it still being a farm; he has a lodger, Thomas Andrews, and another servant, Susan Baines who's sixteen.

In 1881 Thirza is living alone, head of the household, a household of one; she is back in Radwinter at 39, Golden Lane… and I have just looked on Google maps and Golden Lane still exists.

"You're not still looking at that are you?" Rebecca made me jump and I wondered how long I'd been puzzling over the different census returns and the muddled information I had about Thirza… and I wasn't even sure she'd married Thomas anyway, why was I worried about her?

There was a Thirza who was buried in Radwinter in 1888, but she was aged seventy-two, born in 1815… not the right person. There was a baby Thirza Downham born in 1860, so obviously Thirza was a Downham family name… but tragically she was buried February 1st the following year, not even a year old. (There was also a Sarah Thirza Selina Downham, born and died in 1847, and Eveline Thirza Downham born 1888 and died 1893 in Monmouthshire… any connection? How can I find out? Does it matter?)

Feeling rather gloomy, I shut down the computer and went to the bathroom to get ready for bed.

Monday, October 21st 2013, morning

"I guess you've heard then," said Kylie, putting a cup of coffee down. She has a way of sounding rude even when she isn't.

"What do you think about savoury millionaire's shortbread? Sort of cheesy?" I asked.

"You what?" I wanted to write 'yerwot' because that's what it sounded like.

"You know millionaire's shortbread, sort of like a shortbread biscuit with caramel and then chocolate on top? What about a savoury version?"

"You're mental!"

It was only as she was walking away I called her back to ask her what I'd heard because I didn't think I'd heard anything.

"Well you've got a face like a slapped arse!" and she turned to go.

"I don't know what you're talking about!" I said... I really didn't.

I was fed up again... I just felt so unsettled for some reason... I was puzzled about Thirza, I wanted to go on MyTimeMachine all the time at work – but of course I didn't, and I kept thinking about babies... women were supposed to do that. I really would have to snap myself out of this, it was ridiculous!

"You really haven't heard? You don't know?" she looked round. Our office is long and thin, and I'm at the very end. Vicky was at her desk, headphones on, pounding away at some report, Julie was on the phone, Sandra was with Gerald and Martin and Gordon, the two other solicitors, were having an earnest discussion about some documents they were looking at.

"Come outside for a fag," Kylie said in a mysterious voice.

"I don't smoke!"

"I know you don't, you idiot." And she stalked away and I heard her say 'fag-break' to Julie as she marched past.

I sipped my coffee, then overcome with curiosity I followed.

"Going to the shop, Tommo? Get us some doughnuts!" Gordon said. I hate being called Tommo. "You know the big bags of a dozen! Ta, mate!"

Tommo… hmmm.

I hurried outside and wished I'd grabbed my coat. I didn't know where people went to smoke so I was standing looking around thinking I ought to get the doughnuts when I heard a bellow of 'oy!' and Kylie waved at me from the doorway of the exit to the cinema in the building next to where we worked.

"Doughnuts!" I called.

I received a 'yerwot' and I pointed to my mouth. I could almost hear her thoughts *'for fuck's sake, you idiot'* and she came stomping over to me. Did she ever walk normally?

"Doughnuts," I said. "I have to get some doughnuts."

"Have you got an eating disorder?" she asked, walking beside me in sort of normal way as I hurried round to the supermarket. Just because I am a bit overweight, she thinks I have an eating disorder. "You're not diabetic or something and have to have sugar?"

"What are you talking about?"

"They're moving to Castair," she said jumping from eating disorders to a completely different topic.

I hadn't a clue what she meant; Castair was a place I hadn't been too very often, and when I had I hadn't liked it. Dreary, miserable, post-industrial, uninteresting, characterless. Rebecca and I had looked at houses there before we got the flat because they were cheaper, but not cheap enough to persuade us to want to live there.

Maybe I was doing it wrong; maybe if we moved to a house with a garden and more bedrooms then Rebecca would see that having children would be a great idea! I'd have to think about this!

"I don't think I'd like to live there, even though the property's cheap," I waited while she ground out her cigarette before we went into the supermarket. "I like being here in Strand, but Easthope is quite nice, and it's an easy journey from there."

"Well, it's about the same distance, isn't it?" she put some Mars bars in the basket I'd automatically picked up.

"Well it's nearer where I'm living now, but from Easthope would be OK, Rebecca could drop me off when she's on a day shift."

"But you live in those flats over beyond the prom, don't you?" Kylie put some Lucozade in my basket. "It's even further from there than from Easthope, at least in Easthope you're on the right side of Strand."

The girl's an idiot; I hadn't a clue what she was talking about.

"Well, I won't be able to," she said. "There's no way I could get over to Castair for quarter to nine, not with the buses, and Castair Station is miles out of town."

"Why do you want to go to Castair," I was totally confused, about as confused as I was standing looking at the doughnut display. There were big bags alright, but custard filled, jam filled, chocolate sauce... what did Gordon want? I'd have to ring him.

"I don't *want* to go to Castair; I'm going to have to take redundancy if they offer it."

I turned away from the doughnuts. "Kylie, can you tell me what you're going on about?"

"When they move to Castair; I won't be able to get there... no way, not unless I leave about six in the morning."

"Who's moving to Castair?"

"Fairfield and Dunbar."

"But we're Fairfield and Dunbar ..." I was beginning to get a sick feeling.

"You don't know do you? Fairfield and Dunbar are merging with Lyon Abrams... they're moving into that big new office block on the other side of Castair, you know, where they pulled down the polythene factory."

It was lucky I'd decided to carry my inhaler; I'd been getting anxious about getting anxious, afraid of having a bad attack, although I'd not had one for years. I pulled it out and took a big breath.

"Do you want to sit down, shall I ask them to get a chair?" Kylie was concerned.

I looked at her properly. I don't think I ever had before. She had golden curly hair which she sometimes wore in corn rows and a light brown skin; her father came from Tobago she'd once told me, and she'd made some remark about being Black British to Julie who'd been asking in her nosy roundabout way where she was from. Kylie had green eyes and was rather fierce.

"Are you sure? No one's told me," I was suddenly angry.

"Well no-one knows, only Gerald and Monty," Gerald Dunbar and Monty Fairfield, the sons of the original families. "Don't tell anyone you know... I just thought you must know because you've been such a grumpy git recently, and even more wacky than usual. Don't tell anyone! It's top secret! I'll get the sack if they find out I know!"

I took a few deep breaths.

"I won't say anything, Kylie... I need to think about this..."

"You won't tell anyone will you?" for once *she* looked anxious. "I know I won't be able to keep my job, but I want a decent pay-off and a good reference which I won't get if someone goes blabbing."

Meaning me. "Honestly, Kylie, you can trust me, I know I'm a buffoon sometimes, but you can trust me."

"I trust you, Thomas, of course I do... you're sound... so come on grab the doughnuts before they start gossiping about us."

"Gossiping?" I grabbed a bag of double filled jam and custard doughnuts and we headed for the check-out, my mind was reeling... moving to Castair, merging with Lyon Abrams? Good heavens!

I paid for the Mars bars, Lucozade and doughnuts then handed her the bag.

"They're for you," she said, she was smiling in a normal way at me, which made me suspicious. "Cos of your diabetes."

"I haven't got diabetes," why on earth did she think I had? "And why on earth would they be gossiping, and who are they?"

We were hurrying back; it was beginning to rain and it was a cold, nasty rain.

"Cos I fancy the pants off you!" she winked and grinned as I held the door open. She waltzed in and I stood there, door in hand staring after her. "Buffoon!" she called and then ran up the stairs.

Monday, October 21st 2013, evening

I was bursting to tell Rebecca about Lyon Abrams; luckily I hadn't had time to think about it because there was a sudden rush. Someone had made a mistake on a big contract and there was masses of work to do to unpick the problem. Luckily it wasn't my mistake, and I would have been surprised if it was because I'm very, very careful about my actual work. I know I'm a bit of a dream, as Rebecca tells me... 'oh, he's off in his head' she says, not 'off my head' but 'off *in* my head'... but when I'm doing work I'm a bit obsessive... and even Gerald asks me to check things sometimes because he knows I'm so meticulous.

Rebecca picked me up after work which was good because the cold drizzle had turned into cold rain, and there were even a few bits of sleet, and it wasn't even November. It was really cold and I didn't fancy waiting in the bus station.

I'd waited outside the cinema for her, almost bouncing with impatience, I had to spill it all out! My worries and anxieties… moving to Castair… should we get another car… should we move to somewhere between here and there, one of those funny little villages, Bethel or Lebanon… but supposing, like Kylie, they didn't want me…

…. And what had Kylie meant, she fancied the pants off me? Stupid girl! What an unkind thing to joke about! She'd been working with Gordon for the rest of the day as we all pounded away at our computers or huddled over printouts, Gerald pacing round the office, chivvying us. Once Kylie brought me tea.

"Doughnut!" and if anyone could be rude and suggestive with a single word Kylie could. She actually sniggered out loud as she walked off and I pounded the keyboard even more furiously and was even more furious to see I'd made some ludicrous spelling mistakes. Spellcheck offered me 'amigo' instead of 'making' and 'weevil' instead of 'view'… I sat back and ate my doughnut, squirted jam down my shirtfront and ended up cross and anxious and had to use my inhaler again… twice in one day… maybe I ought to see the doctor.

I got in the car and Rebecca launched into one of her tirades… not against me, thank goodness, but about the family of one of the residents. She is so passionate about her work, she cares so much for the people she works with… and somehow I couldn't interrupt her to tell her about Lyon Abrams or Castair… and I didn't know the details anyway... this was just gossip from Kylie... maybe she'd got it wrong, maybe she'd misunderstood... there'd been not a whisper about Castair as far as I knew... how did she know? I'd have to overcome my annoyance with her and ask her about it.

We'd stopped at some traffic lights and Rebecca was using a tissue because she was so upset and I pattered her arm and made some comforting remarks.

"Thank goodness you're always the same, Thomas," she said sniffing. "You're always the same."

It was a bit of a back-handed compliment but she was upset.

"I am, Rebecca, and I'll always support you, you know that... and if you want to chuck the job and do something else, that's fine, we'll manage!"

"I didn't mean I want to chuck the job, I love it!" she was snappish, which actually was a good sign, it meant she was feeling less emotional. "I can't see me ever wanting to give it up... You're not thinking about a family again, are you?"

"No, no, of course not, I understand how you feel, but I just meant... well, if things go wrong, it's not the end of the world if we have to do something else, even if we have to move!" I was testing the water here... we might have to move....

"Thank you... but my job is safe and it's what I want to do, what I love doing... but maybe we should start thinking about moving... maybe the flat is getting a little small for us..."

I was so excited I could hardly speak, so I wisely said nothing. My phone bipped and it was Paul; was I free, would I like to come round? Ruthie had a surprise for me!

Tentatively I asked Rebecca if she'd like to come to Paul's. He hadn't mentioned her, but I wanted her to meet Ruthie properly... and maybe seeing the family all happy together would find a little chink in her no-family-for-us armour!

"After the day I've had," she negotiated a bus which had suddenly stopped... oh well, I would go on my own, brave the foul weather on the bus and maybe get a taxi home. "You can drive and I can drink your brother's wine."

Despite everything, I suddenly had a happy feeling again.

I was fidgety and restless; perhaps I'd eaten too many shortbreads... I did feel slightly queasy but I thought it was things on my mind rather than the banoffee one and then the stilton and date (what an inspiration... but did I like stilton and fig better?)

At Paul's I'd had nothing to drink at all; Paul had said a little glass would be alright, surely, but I said with regret that I wouldn't. I got the feeling they were trying really hard to be welcoming to Rebecca... They are welcoming, but when I was there before it had all seemed very laid back and normal, now it seemed as if we were guests rather than family.

Paul had talked to me a lot, and Ruthie talked to Rebecca; she seemed a little cool towards me, but maybe that was just me being sensitive, or maybe she had caught the slight attitude Rebecca sometimes has when other women talk to me... I think I said before that she gets jealous, but why on earth would she... or should she?

"Adorable," and I'd said it out loud as I remembered what Amelia had said...or was it Andrea?

"Adorable? This shortbread is adorable?" Paul burst out laughing, and soon everyone was laughing, and Otis and Tom screeched and then ran round shouting *'adorable shortbread! Adorable shortbread!'* and as usual I'd felt an idiot but tried to smile as if I thought I was funny too.

Ruthie was busy scribbling on her pad again; she'd been making notes all evening as we commented on the shortbread and she'd glanced up at me and winked so perhaps she wasn't being cool, perhaps she was just trying to be friendly to Rebecca.

Now I couldn't sleep.

"Why don't you get up and have a drink," Rebecca mumbled. I was disturbing her by squirming around trying to get comfortable. We'd made love and usually I slide into sleep all warm and smiley, but now I just felt as if there were crumbs in the bed. Or ants, and thinking of ants made my skin crawl so I did get up, pulled on my dressing gown and went and got a drink of milk.

I wandered about the sitting room, wondering whether to watch TV. I was wide awake; should I tell Rebecca what Kylie had told me? But suppose it wasn't true –I don't mean that Kylie had lied, she wasn't like that, too brutally honest if you ask me! But supposing she'd misunderstood something? Or supposing it was only an idea that didn't come to anything, or supposing it was just some gossip... Or supposing the firm *was* moving?

Would they want to take all of us? I was the junior solicitor, there were the three others, Martin, Gordon, Sandra and me, then Julie and Vicky and Kylie who were office, and above us all was Gerald and the invisible Monty; he only came out of the closet or out of the woodwork when we were out for the office 'do'. Would all of us be able to move? How many admin staff did Lyon Abrams already have? Would they want three more? Would Kylie lose her job? And how many solicitors were there? Would they need four more plus Gerald and Monty?

I Googled Lyon Abrams and went to their home page:

The firm of Lyon Abrams & George Pitiris LLP celebrated their third anniversary this year after their amalgamation in 2010 of the two successful and well-regarded law firms of T. Lyon & T. Abrams of Castair and George Pitiris & F. Smith of Coventry. We have offices in Castair, Coventry and Harrogate with over sixty experienced staff, familiar with a wide range of legal matters; we are able to provide a full and professional service in all the common aspects of legal work and have specialists available for specific needs. Our services include dealing with all aspects of Residential Property, Will and Probate, Family and Matrimonial and Civil Litigation...

And so it went on... so the nine of us would be gobbled up by the mighty Lyon Abrams with offices in Castair and Coventry... sixty experienced staff... would they need nine more?

On the other hand, Kylie might be wrong...

I went on MyTimeMachine; I went on the 1851 census and searched for Thomas. My heart stood still.... There was no Thomas Radwinter b1815... had he died? Was he not my ancestor? Was he nothing to do with us, just a coincidence?

I went back to search and changed the date of birth from within two years (which is what was suggested) to within five years… and still no Thomas… I went to deaths and burials and typed his name in again… There was one other Thomas Radwinter whose death was registered, but not born anywhere near the date that my Thomas was.

I closed the site and wandered back into the kitchen. We'd had such a nice evening, Rebecca had seemed to enjoy herself and I'd managed to forget my anxiety about work… Now I was back on the switchback and plunging down into the gloomy place.

I didn't want any more milk. I got a glass and poured myself a whisky and went back to the computer. I had a glance at my emails; some work stuff and an email from Ruthie.

"Hi Thomas! Great evening, nice to meet Rebecca properly, thanks for all the comments about the shortbread and once again you have been an absolute saviour. I'm seriously thinking of marketing my shortbreads through on-line ordering, maybe find some retail outlets later but before I can go ahead, I need to have a name… I have been absolutely stumped, and been driving Paul and the boys mad with trying to come up with something and lo and behold, thanks to you I have it! Adorable Shortbread! Doesn't that sound just amazing? Isn't just the best name! You are so brilliant, such a star!"

The switchback began chugging up hill and I had a big swig of the whisky, then another, then went and poured another measure.

"I'm so sorry, that having told Paul I'd help with tracing the Radwinters I've been such a dud, all this cookery stuff is really taking off! My blog is having an amazing number of hits, and has been reblogged on some really cool sites... My Twitter stuff is really taking off too, I'm still hopeless but Luke has been my saviour, he's the Twitter wizard here! I haven't got a discrete website, but he's going to do me one... I know he's only a kid but he is so clever – he has a real talent for this techie stuff... he's in a bit of a turmoil about his A-levels, I think Paul told you; he's thinking of switching to languages but now he's wondering whether to do CAD too... I can't help... maybe you could talk to him... I know you're not in education, or in the things Luke's interested in, but you always see things so clearly... must be the lawyer in you!

"Let me know how you're getting on with the FT stuff... and I really will try and have another go at it sometime!

Love to you both and grateful hugs!

R and P xxx"

I went back to MyTimeMachine, called up the 1851 census and just put Radwinter into the search, no other name, no birth date.

'There are 4 results for "Radwinter" in 1851 England, Wales & Scotland Census' it said and then there were five columns before the little icon that you could click to see either a transcription or the record itself. The first column was the name and the fact it was found in the census for 1851, then a column showing it was Great Britain and England, then county, year of census, birth year, age and registration district.

Four results, but none of them Thomas... however... there were no other Radwinters anywhere, so maybe these people were our family, maybe Thomas was an erroneous red herring? All four of the results were in Surrey, all in the registration district of Godstone which I'd never heard of and didn't know where it was… Was it near Godalming, was Godalming in Surrey? I'd heard of Godalming…

- Tolluk Radwinter, born 1845, age 6
- Robert Radwinter, born 1848, age 3
- Thirza Radwinter, born 1850, age 1
- Lamy Radwinter born 1828, age 23

Thirza… I was excited to see the name Thirza again… but mystified as well… and Lamy… that rang a bell… I looked back at my notes; there was a Lamy Coote living with a family in Radwinter in 1841, the Newells… there were other Cootes in the village too, so maybe she was just having a sleepover… but surely they didn't have sleepovers then? Don't be ridiculous, Thomas, you're drinking your whisky too quickly.

If there were little boys who were servants aged nine, then probably Lamy Coote aged thirteen, living with the Newells was a little servant girl too. Yes, F.S., Lamy was a female servant to the Newells, Benjamen Newell aged forty, Susanna Newell aged twenty-five, then Alfred, twelve, William Newell, five, Elizabeth Newell, three and Osman born in 1840.

I stared and stared at the page; Susanna was too old to be Benjamen's daughter, but probably too young to be his wife as Alfred was twelve… unless the first Mrs Newell had died and Susanna was the second wife, with a step-son and three of her own children. If Lamy was the daughter of the Cootes who were above the Newells on the register, James and Ann who had five children under the age of nine, and James Coote as an Ag Lab, Agricultural Labourer, they were probably pleased that their eldest, Lamy, was working with the Newells.

I looked at the 1851 census for the Newells; they'd moved to somewhere called Thaxted and they now had more children, Robert who was twenty-one but who hadn't been on the previous census, Osman, Edwin, Fanny, Cecilia, Emma and Clarissa... no Lamy looking after them. They are harness makers... not many of them about these days!

Why am I faffing about with the Newells...once again I am putting off looking at the real thing... the Radwinters... side-tracked by stuff... Back to Godstone, back to Tolluck, Robert, Thirza and Lamy...

The register of the census has now changed: there are five parts across the top, Parish (or Township, crossed out) of Blechingley, Ecclesiastical District of, City or Borough of, Town of, Village of – all these last four crossed out, so this is for the parish of Blechingley... never heard of it.

Then there are nine columns

- No. of householder's schedule (I think, it's tricky to see)
- Name of Street, Place or Road, and Name of No. of House
- Name and Surname of each person who abode in the house on the Night of 30th March 1851
- Relation to Head of Family
- Condition
- Age of – sub-divided into Male/Female
- Rank, Profession or Occupation
- Where Born
- Whether Blind or Deaf-and-Dumb

Tolluck is living at 168 Stychens (??) with Thomas and Jane Charlwood, aged forty-five and forty-two; Thomas Charlwood is a Gravel Digger Labourer, and he and his wife were both born in Surrey Godstone. There are four children, Thomas Charlwood aged seventeen, who is also a Gravel Digger (it says uncle, but I think it must mean he is Thomas senior's nephew), George fourteen, Charles five who is a scholar and little Emily aged just two. In their house at 168 Stychens is Tolluck Radwinter, and in the Relation to Head of Family column it says, lodger… aged 6? A lodger? He is also a scholar and he was born… in Radwinter….

I feel hot, I feel cold, I feel strange. I get up, have another whisky, make a cup of tea, drink the tea, sit back down with the whisky.

- Tolluck… what an unusual name, I've never heard it before… He was born in 1845 the same year that Thomas Radwinter married either Rebecca Swan or Thirza Downham.
- Robert Radwinter… I find little Robert and baby Thirza and Lamy all on the same page, living in the same place, in Blechingley… the Union Workhouse… I sit literally shivering…
- Robert Radwinter, inmate, 3, son of pauper, born Epping, Essex
- Thirza Radwinter, inmate, 1, daughter of pauper, born Lambeth London
- Lamy Radwinter, inmate, 23, pauper general servant, born Radwinter Essex

This can't be a coincidence… I want to print off what I've found but it might wake Rebecca; I save it into my Time Keeper's Cabinet as the site so quaintly calls where you save your documents. I drink my whisky and go to bed. Rebecca stirs and mumbles that I'm cold. I won't be able to sleep, my head is spinning... I sleep.

Tuesday, October 22nd 2013, morning

Rebecca was on a later shift so I walked down to the bus stop; it was very cold but at least it wasn't raining. I'd woken up at the normal time despite the interrupted night, and despite the amount of whisky I'd put away, which I discovered when I looked at the level in the bottle. I felt very sober... sober in many ways. Thomas had vanished but I had no doubt that the children and Lamy in Blechingley were his, the names were too coincidental. Tolluck was a mystery, but there'd been many strange names which I'd found in the censuses, lots of Biblical ones, Jabez, Job, Jeremiah... Harriet spelled Harriot...

As I stood at the bus stop I found myself putting some of the names I'd come across with Radwinter, a little Radwinter looking up at me as I held her. Lillah Radwinter, Isabella Radwinter... the bus came and I showed my pass and went and sat in my usual place, and at the next stop Jessica got on and came and sat next to me. We're bus buddies; we met on the bus and have never met anywhere else, but over the last couple of years we usually sit together.

We chat about all sorts of things, at quite a superficial level really, I don't tell her any secrets and I'm sure she doesn't tell me any... In a strange way, and this does sound very strange, she's a very close friend... I can't think of anyone else I see as regularly or talk to as much as I do to her. So we talk about work, she's an accountant for a farm machinery company which has an office in Strand;

she's married to David, no kids, her parents live in Easthope, his live in Oak, she has a sister called Rachel… and I tell her about me and Rebecca.

She sat down today as if she was tired and we exchanged the usual pleasantries.

"Are you OK, you look a little peaky, Jessica, you've not got a cold coming have you?" There was a cold-thing going round our office; so far I hadn't any symptoms. When I'd mentioned it to Rebecca she started giving me Vitamin C drinks and told me to eat extra fruit.

Jessica said she was fine and asked after the shortbread… I guess I'd been boring everyone about it. I remembered Ruthie's email… *Adorable Shortbread!*

"Is she going to do a Christmas range?" Jessica asked… hmmm, a Christmas range… "I'd buy some! In fact I could eat some right now… gosh I'm starving!"

I laughed… I'd had a good breakfast, porridge with goji berries… I'm not that keen on them, but Rebecca thinks they're good for me.

"I don't suppose you've got any to try, have you, I actually am really hungry," she looked very pale suddenly.

I hadn't got any, sadly, but I got out my lunchbox and made her eat my sandwiches because she did look as if she was going to faint. I was a bit surprised that she took them with very little persuasion… we weren't really that sort of friend usually, just bus-buddies.

She asked how the family tree research was going, and I bored her with the ins and outs of it… I had it all in my head at the moment, but I would need to get it down on paper in more than just the scribbled notes I'd made for reference of pages I'd looked at.

She seemed really interested and much more cheerful since she'd demolished my sandwiches as if she was starving. She'd offered to give me money so I could buy lunch later, but I refused with mock indignation which made her laugh. The colour had come back into her face now; I wondered if actually she'd had a row with David because when she'd got on the bus she almost looked as if she'd been crying, her eyes were a little red and her nose was pink... and not just with the cold.

We got off the bus and walked together until she had to turn off Little Street to get to where her office was.

"I say, Thomas, can I tell you something?"

I had a sudden flash-back to Kylie '*being honest*' and I felt a quiver of nerves.

"Please don't tell anyone... well, obviously you won't, you don't know anyone...but I'm pregnant!" she absolutely glowed.

I hugged her with delight.

"Jessica! That's wonderful! Oh, congratulations! I'm so happy for you!" I could see now, she was absolutely radiant! Her eyes were sparkling and her skin glowed. "Oh, really, I'm so pleased, really, really pleased!" I hugged her again, more gently, gave her a kiss on her warm cheek and feeling mightily cheered, and very envious of David, I set off up the hill towards the cinema.

"Oy!" there could only be one person to 'oy' me, Kylie on the other side of the road, scowling, her face like thunder.

She crossed over, giving a V-sign to a driver who hooted her, and a finger to a taxi who wouldn't let her cross from the middle.

"She's not your wife!" she scowled. What the hell had it to do with her, Jessica could be my sister for all she knew.

"No, she's not, she's my bus-buddy," I snapped, I was getting fed up with Kylie.

"Bus-buddy? You twat," she stalked along beside me. She had long legs and I had to hurry to keep up with her.

"Do you want to know the latest on shortbread?" I asked, panting a little, patting my pocket to check my inhaler.

"Shortbread? You are an idiot!"

"But a loveable idiot!" I replied remembering what John had once said to me.

Kylie wrenched open the door as if she wanted to take it off its hinges.

"Twat," she said but in a nice way.

She usually bounded up the stairs; I think she did it to wind up the repressed receptionist, an older man with a lecherous eye but a timid tongue. Today she got in the lift with me; I stood against the wall rather nervously, who knows what this mad girl would do.

"Sorry," she said, looking at the display panel. "I'm just really wound up about my job."

I felt very sorry now, and sorry for her. I didn't know much about her but I'd heard that she'd come off the estate at Hope Village and she'd been to what is now called *'The Hope Academy… Gateway to the Stars'*. Yes really. It really is called that.

"I'm sure it'll be ok," I said. "Perhaps you're mistaken… perhaps they're not going to merge… I looked at Lyon

Abrams' web-site, they're a big firm already... why would they want to take over us?"

She shrugged, still looking at the display.

"And anyway, they'd want an office here in Strand."

"Too much competition since Medley, Medley and Medley took over those other offices."

That had been a bit of a worry a year or so ago when we'd heard M, M and M had been seen talking to Monty. It all came to nothing, but perhaps Monty and Gerald had their own agenda... The lift stopped but the doors remained closed.

"But you'd soon get another job, you're intelligent, clever, loads of personality," I tried to sound encouraging, I'd never seen her look so despondent.

The doors opened and the cleaning ladies, Irina and Sonia, and the one cleaning man, Pyotr, waited for us to get out, greeting us cheerily.

"Loads of personality," said Kylie and managed a half-powered smile.

Now Kylie had put it into my mind, I was suspicious of everything. Gerald seemed really busy, his office door firmly shut which is unusual, he has a very literal open-door policy. Sandra was with him half the morning and Julie was with him the whole morning. We were all busy doing our usual things, seeing clients, ringing people, doing the paperwork, and I wondered if I imagined a strange tension. Gordon and Martin kept going over to each other's desks and talking in low voices...

I was probably imagining it.

Thursday, October 24th 2013, lunch time

The shops were full of Christmas displays already, and in my lunch hour I wandered round, wondering what to get Rebecca; I'd had to come into town since Jessica had eaten my lunch. I was smiling thinking about it, how happy I was for her. Vicky at work was obviously pregnant now but it didn't seem to bother her, she always looked well and worked just as hard and for just as long a day as usual. It would be her first child but she seemed very laid back about it. I couldn't talk to her about having kids, but now I might be able to ask Jessica.

Somehow things didn't seem quite right between me and Rebecca, but I have no idea what I even mean by that. We'd been married for nine years, it would be our tenth anniversary next April, we ought to do something special to celebrate… Rebecca has always been particular about things, she's always been the dominant one, and has sometimes seemed critical of me, and gets fed up with me because I'm so useless at things… but we rub along OK. It wasn't just me thinking about having a family, it was before I was even aware of that… It sort of became apparent after I went to Paul's and first met Ruthie and was sitting in his kitchen… I'd arrived on his doorstep feeling dull and a bit sad for no reason, and went home really cheerful.

Would Rebecca like some jewellery? She has quite a lot of nice things, her parents often buy her expensive stuff… clothes and perfume are too boring, but I would probably get her perfume anyway, as well… as well as what?

My phone rang and it was Rebecca; what a surprise.

"You sound very cheerful," she said as if I usually sounded miserable… did I?

"Well, I'm just doing a little Christmas shopping, if you know what I mean!"

She seemed pleased and then asked an unexpected thing; first, Ruthie had mentioned that she did demonstrations to schools and places, did I think she would do something for the residents of The Willows? Then, did I think Ruthie and Paul would like to come round for dinner one night?

This was staggering! We'd had Paul, and John, round for dinner on occasions, when they were with their ex-wives, but not recently. The evenings had been such hard work, and although they'd thanked us, and had reciprocated with asking us round to them, the occasions hadn't been among the best in my life.

I had no idea about the cookery demonstration, I told her, but I was sure they would like to come for dinner, and I thanked her for being so considerate, and said I thought it was a great idea. She suggested a couple of dates and then rang off, and I felt warm and happy and my eyes fell on a Lebanese cookery book, 'The Lebanese Kitchen', by Salma Hage. I would go round to see John in his bookshop and get a copy from him!

I remembered the last time I'd seen John, he'd given me some things about the family tree... I hadn't even looked at them; how stupid of me, and how rude not to have got in touch with him about it! I was so obsessed with Radwinter, and now Blechingley (I must find out where that is) that I've not thought about us in our generation... maybe because that would involve me thinking about my dad, which I didn't want to do, and my mum, which I didn't want to do either.

I wouldn't go round to his shop today, I would look through what he'd given me tonight and I'd go and see him tomorrow and see if he had the Lebanese cookery book… I texted him, asking if he would be in the shop tomorrow lunchtime and he texted right back as if he had his phone in his hand, saying he couldn't do tomorrow but he'd like to meet for lunch, so where did I fancy eating? He gave me a couple of lunchtimes he was free and I suggested that as the harbour was ten minutes away, why didn't we go to the Lebanese place again, and I could try some of the things I hadn't last time.

I texted Paul with the dates Rebecca had given me for dinner, then thought about texting Ruthie about the cookery demonstration at The Willows; I was standing beside the Christmas display as I waited for the text to Paul to send. There was an arrangement of German cookies and gingerbread… the flat biscuity sort of gingerbread, not like our English gingerbread, our Parkin sort of gingerbread, all sticky and gingery and treacly…

I texted Ruthie: *Hi Ruthie, Thomas here. Rebecca wonders if you do cookery demos for places like where she works, The Willows full of old folk, some of them a bit wandering and also have you thought about gingerbread? Like the adorable shortbread but gingerbread?*

I caught sight of the time, and set off back to work, feeling quite pleased with myself. I felt quite organised, I'd texted John, sorted one of Rebecca's Christmas present, got 10th anniversary plans in my mind, texted Paul, texted Ruthie… now back to work.

I went back to the 1851 census and stared at the sad little entry for the children… where was Thomas, and why was little Tolluck living with the gravel digging Charlwoods?

I Googled Blechingley and came up with Bletchingley with a 't'; when I checked a little Wiki map popped up telling me that Bletchingley is a village in Surrey, on the A25; it's east of Redhill and west of Godstone... so that was it.

I looked at a Google map and street view of Bletchingley; there was no trace of a Workhouse, but after a hundred and sixty years, that's not surprising I guess. I did however find Stychens; I was quite excited. Stychens Lane was off the main A25, it was Castle Street (was there a castle in Bletchingley?) before it became the High Street which ran through the main part of the village.

I Googled Godstone Union and came across a site all about workhouses... it was fascinating and I was tempted to look up Strand, but no, I must stay focussed on my task and look up Godstone. The site was called 'The Workhouse... The Story of an Institution...', and I made a note of it and saved it to my links in my Time Keeper's Cabinet.

There was a page with two maps, one of the village, and one a plan of the workhouse itself. Apparently there was a workhouse in Bletchingley recorded in 1777, for up to fifty 'inmates'... inmates, how cold that sounds. The Godstone Poor Law Union where Lamy was with Robert and Thirza was 'officially formed' in 1835, on October 31st, with a Board of Guardians, eighteen men (I guess they would be men) who oversaw fourteen parishes, Bletchingley, Caterham, Chelsham, Crowhurst, Farlelgh, Godstone, Horne, Limpsfield , Oxted, Tandridge, Tatsfield, Titsey, Warlingham, Woldingham. It was actually built four years later, it says, north of Bletchingley and cost £3,850... that sounds an awful lot of money for those days...

The site then describes the building, U-shaped with an open entrance to the east. There was a separate school block built as well, so at least the little paupers could be educated.

I looked at the Google map again and saw the church; I went on street-view and down Church Street... the church is the Church of Saint Mary the Virgin... St Mary the Virgin! Exactly the same as in Radwinter! I continued along Church Lane but there's no sign of any trace of a workhouse, only some new houses.

Bletchingley looks a pretty little village; I wonder how pretty Thomas's family thought it, looking out from the windows of the Workhouse?

I'd made a spread sheet of Radwinter parish in 1841, and I set about making a similar one for Bletchingley, a mighty task because it was a bigger parish. I didn't know how long the family stayed there, but it had been useful having all the names from Radwinter as I was checking things... I'm sure there is a much quicker and easier way of finding your ancestors, but I'm a very amateur amateur and I'm just doing what I can. I will have a good look at Bletchingley at some time, find out about its history etc... I wonder how the family had ended up there... it was a long way from Essex, via London where little Thirza was born.

I found the registrations of the birth of the four children; Tolluck, spelt Tolik here, was born in Radwinter in the fourth quarter of the year. Thomas and Thirza had married in the fourth quarter too, October, November or December, so little Tolluck would have been born just before or after their marriage... I was convinced without proof that Thirza was his wife, not Rebecca Swan.

Tolluck… what would Rebecca think of us calling our little boy Tolluck… not even worth mentioning it…

I printed off the four documents, and put them in the file I was building up.

So where was Thomas in 1851… he didn't appear in any census record for that year. Perhaps he'd gone back to where he'd come from; I remembered the 1841 census, 'Scotland, Ireland or Foreign Parts'. Perhaps he'd gone home to his family, abandoned Lamy and the children. I wasn't sure he'd married Lamy, even though she had his name, there was no marriage record…

The phone rang and it was Paul; he was delighted at the invitation, and he gave me a date. He handed the phone to Ruthie. She would be pleased to go to the Willows, but she'd like to talk to Rebecca to find out what would be best for the residents, how much they could manage to do themselves, or would they just be watching her cook? She'd like to do some cooking *with* them, if that was possible, she said.

She asked me what I meant about the gingerbread; there was a laugh in her voice and I hoped she wasn't thinking I was an idiot. I told her about the displays of German gingerbread I'd seen which was the dry biscuit sort, which was OK, but always tasted more of cinnamon than ginger to me. I told her about real gingerbread, like Parkin and wondered if she could do squares of it, like she did her shortbread, but decorate it in a Christmassy ways… gold leaf maybe, or candied fruit, or glazed nuts, or edible glitter… I'd seen edible glitter when Rebecca dragged me into a cook shop; she was doing an evening class in cake decorating and had some wonderful ideas of what she wanted to do. Little marzipan designs maybe, like little red bows, or Christmas trees, or Father Christmas's, and the gingerbread could have other things to make it seasonal as well as traditional, rum soaked fruit, proper glacé fruit...

I stopped... Ruthie hadn't said anything and I realised I'd been waffling on... I truly am an idiot.

There was silence, had she hung up on me? My face glowed with embarrassment, what a fool I was.

"Hello?" I said cautiously.

"Just a minute," and then silence. "What did you say about what to put in the gingerbread?" she asked in quite an abrupt way. "Rum, did you say?"

"Er... rum soaked fruit, you know like muscatel raisins, or proper glacé fruit... marrons glacés..."

I could hear her murmuring something and suddenly I could picture her, scribbling fiercely on her little pad.

"So how would you present them?" she asked in the same cool way.

"Well, I suppose you could have Christmas ribbon round the side with a bow, like a present, I don't mean cake trim..." I knew all about cake trim, I'd had a whole afternoon trying to help Rebecca decide what to put round our last year's cake. "Or you could have like a little crate, like a tiny wooden slatted crate, like you get tangerines in, but tiny... we had one with garlic in, it was smoked garlic..."

Ruthie was laughing now. "Thomas you really are a star! Give up being a solicitor and come and work with me!"

Paul took the phone; I was confused and embarrassed... why do I do this, why do I just go on about stuff, make a fool of myself?

He, however was laughing too, and said I was a genius... then he asked me about the family tree, and I gave him the rough outline, without going into detail about the workhouse, or Thomas's mystery marriage to Thirza and then Lamy. I told him John had given me some information about the family, Uncle Jim and so on, and I was going to have a look at it later, so going from now backwards, hoping to make a direct line to Thomas.

I asked him if he could do the same and he said he couldn't remember much, but he'd do his best. He asked if I was going to look at the Magick family, but no... I was going to concentrate on the Radwinters... maybe another time. He agreed, one thing at once; then he suggested I got in touch with Marcus and go over to see if he had anything like photos, or birth certificates, anything like that.

I didn't fancy that... I still get very nervous when I'm with Marcus... but on the other hand, Paul was different with me now, so maybe it was me who was different, and if I went to see Marcus, maybe I'd find that we could be closer too.

"See if you can find any Quillens, I'd love to know where my middle name came from!" Paul said as we finished the call, and I said I would.

Monday, October 28th 2013

The office was very quiet, which made me uneasy. Gerald was out but there was a mysterious veil drawn over where he was which was quite unusual; normally we're very open, whether it's some sort of appointment, or one of the people with kids having to go to school about something, or when Martin drove his twin daughters up to Leeds where they were going to Uni... or even if someone was popping out for a few minutes, to the shops, to the chemist, to the bank... Vicky for her prenatal appointments...it was all quite open and laid back, and no-one took advantage; if anything we worked over our hours, coming in early if there was something important, working lunch, staying late...

So it was strange that Gerald was out, and even stranger that Sandra had gone with him, yet no-one said where they were going. Everyone seemed subdued, Vicky and Kylie had their earphones in and were working on their computers, heads down; Martin and Gordon who usually chatted in a quite irritating way about football and Bruce Springsteen were working quietly... it was odd.

Suddenly Kylie stood up, rammed in her wheelie chair noisily, said "Fag!" and gave me a ferocious stare and walked out. I sat back and looked down the office; it's a long open plan room, divided up into work areas, with Gerald's office at the end, and the waiting room and the small rooms to interview clients out of the main area by the stairs and lifts.

Nobody took the slightest notice of me as I got up and left and went down the stairs.

I found Kylie by the exit to the cinema.

"You should have put your coat on," I said.

The wind was freezing and she looked pinched with cold, her nose was red and I was reminded of how Jessica looked some mornings, struggling with morning sickness. It seemed impertinent to ask Kylie if she was pregnant. She was standing arms folded, so they were hugging her, one hand stuck out with her cigarette. She was wearing a short sleeved blouse and a very short black skirt.

She said nothing, just stared balefully, and dragged on the cigarette. I took my jacket off and put it round her; it was miles too big and looked ludicrous.

"Now you'll be cold," she said, which I suppose was her way of saying thanks.

"Too fat," I said, but I was very cold. "How are you?"

"Really worried. I've been looking for another job."

I asked if she'd had any luck, but she shook her head and dropped her cigarette on the floor.

"I don't suppose you know anyone who needs a clerical officer?" she spoke resentfully, as if she hated having to ask.

I thought and shook my head... jobs weren't easy anywhere now... and I didn't know of anything anyway.

"They're over with Lyon Abrams today, that's where Gerald and Sandra have gone."

"How do you know?" I asked, wondering if she'd hacked into Gerald's dairy. One thing Kylie is brilliant at is computers... well, she's brilliant at lots of things, apart from being pleasant.

"I'm doing a degree and if I don't have a job I won't be able to pay for it... and it's not cheap," she looked away from me and I wondered if the rapid blinking meant she was trying not to cry. "You're supposed to say something like, 'fuck Kylie, *you* doing a degree? Are you clever enough?'"

"Why should I say that? I think that's brilliant, it must be really hard, working and studying."

"Anyway, just thought I'd tell you they're over at Castair today."

She slipped my jacket off, thrust it at me and marched back to work, leaving me wondering what else she knew… was she warning me? Was my position not secure? I'd have to look at my contract…

I made my way back, wondering who I knew who might have a job for Kylie.

John had written out a list of the family, us and our cousins. He'd done it in a sensible way, Dad, then us, starting with Marcus, then he'd gone to Uncle James – Uncle Jim as we called him, and his family, then Aunty Angela who I don't know at all, and actually don't remember having met.

There was a short note about my mum; two sisters, both unmarried, and *'no known children'* John wrote. There was also a little note to me in brackets beside this, 'Thomas if you do have time to find out anything about the Magicks I'd be interested since it's my middle name, but don't worry if you can't…'

1.
- Edward Marcus Radwinter m Sylvia May Magick
- James Charles Radwinter m Maureen Taylor
- Angela Sophia Radwinter m Maurice McIlhinney

2. Edward Radwinter
- Marcus Edward Radwinter
- Paul Quillen Radwinter

- John Magick Radwinter
- Thomas Marcus Radwinter

2. James Radwinter m Maureen Taylor

- Samantha Jane Radwinter
- Maxwell Samuel Radwinter
- Anthony James Radwinter

2. Angela Radwinter m Maurice McIlhinney

- Geoffrey McIlhinney
- Brian McIlhinney
- Susan McIlhinney

3. Marcus Radwinter m Jill Edwards

- Sarah Radwinter
- Paula Radwinter

3. Paul Radwinter m Susan Jones

- David Django Radwinter
- Luke Dylan Radwinter
- Samuel Otis Radwinter
- Tom Bowie Radwinter

3. John Radwinter m (1) Eleanor Marple (2) Fiona Richards

3. Thomas Radwinter m Rebecca Smith

Uncle Jim, he reminded me, died two years ago in 2011, and he'd added in brackets that he thought that my unknown cousin, Geoffrey McIlhinney had moved to Canada, and possibly had two sons who probably had children of their own. Brian had moved to Australia and had three possibly four daughters, who no doubt also had children, and Susan McIlhinney was living in Scotland where Angela and Maurice had retired, although both were dead now, and that she had a son who lived near Dumfries and had several children.

On a second sheet of paper, he'd gone back a generation... to my father's parents, my grandparents and it was clear that John had been struggling to remember the names, and had jotted down some notes about things that he half-remembered but wasn't sure of... *check with Marcus and Paul,* he wrote.

Our grandparents... *Charles Henry Radwinter (d 1986?) Helen Radwinter (d 1980?)*

Charles Henry had some brothers... Maybe Michael, and I'm pretty sure there was a David, and the name Horace rings a bell, I don't know. His mother (Ellen? Or am I muddling that up with Grandma? I think she was Irish... or maybe her family was...) I think there was some Manchester connection somewhere... and I keep thinking Cambridge.... But why I have no idea so you should probably ignore that. There was also someone called Sailor Billy, or Captain Billy, but whether that was Grandpa or whether he was just a family friend, or maybe just a character Grandpa knew, I really have no idea.

You really need to ask Marcus, he's sure to remember, being so ancient! He was well into his twenties when Grandpa and Grandma died... also he will remember Dad and Mum best and might remember more than I do...

I'm guessing you've asked Paul and been baffled by his amnesia... he claims he doesn't remember much about his childhood (which is why I think it's strange he's the one who's asked you to do this... BTW I'm glad he didn't ask me, I'm interested in what you find out, but have no interest in playing the detective!)

Good luck, Thomas, I'll be interested to see what you come up with, I'll help if I can, but I'm really not into looking at old docs – I like my fiction set in the future!

I used John's notes to make another family tree, with Charles Henry's unknown father at the top. What did strike me was the possible Irish connection, and Quillen, Paul's middle name, I'd found out was Irish... I jotted a note on that, but didn't for the moment put this possible great-grandma into the tree.

Out of nowhere came a vision of carrot cake... my mind was perpetually on food, I'd even taking to reading Rebecca's cookery magazines in bed! I texted Ruthie: *I know you'll be fed up with me, it's Thomas by the way, but after doing Christmas stuff with gingerbread and shortbread, why don't you do Easter stuff with carrot cake? That could be in squares and made pretty with Easter colour icing and bunnies. You could do summer shortbread with strawberries.*

I went back to John's notes and clicked onto MyTimeMachine... it would be so easy to go into births and look up all the names of the people he'd given me, check on the dates of their marriages, look at the census for 1911 and see which Radwinters it threw up...

Somehow this more recent history made me anxious... I couldn't explain it... but I was putting off coming up to date... it seemed safer to be back in the 1840's and 50's even to being in the workhouse with Lamy and the little children. I went back onto the workhouse site and read up about them.

There'd been places for the poor going right back to the beginning of the seventeenth century... I already knew there had been a workhouse in Blechingley in the 1700's; the character of the places changed over time, but I got the idea that these were local charitable institutions which homed those who'd fallen on hard times as well as what they called 'vagrants'; sometimes 'poor relief' was given out, like people might get grants today, I suppose. However, it seems that in the 1830's things changed... I vaguely remembered doing The Poor Law Act of 1834 in history for A-level.

The establishing of the Godstone Poor Law Union in 1835, and its building four years later was as a direct result of the Act... along with fifteen thousand or so other parishes which formed into Unions and built new workhouses.

I read on with a sense of gloom; what cold and forbidding, unpleasant places they were... punishing people like Lamy and her little children, hardly more than babies, for being poor. In a time when James Chapman, aged nine could be a servant, and Lamy herself aged thirteen in service with the Newell family, to sink to needing to enter the workhouse must have been so degrading...

Apparently, through Poor Law Act, the threat of the Workhouse was supposed to deter able-bodied people from depending on it and there was a 'workhouse test'. Poor Relief would only be given, begrudgingly, to those poverty-stricken people who were so desperate that they would want to go into a workhouse; they were dreadful, uncharitable, cold places, punishing the poor for being poor, condemning the destitute for their desperation. And then I read something which chilled me; if an able-bodied man did apply to go into the workhouse, then his whole family had to go in with him.

Interesting... I wondered if that had a bearing on Thomas's disappearance? Was he able-bodied, but abandoned Lamy so he could find work somewhere else? Had he abandoned her anyway? I couldn't bear the thought of either of those scenarios, I didn't like to think of Thomas being cruel... but maybe they were cruel times.

To distract myself I went back to the 1851 census and began to enter the information on my spreadsheet... probably a useless waste of time... but it interested me in itself, to see the size of the families, the different occupations, the names... maybe I'd have a little peep at Radwinter in the 1851 census and see how it compared to ten years before... but no, I had to concentrate on what I was doing.

I worked solidly... it stopped me thinking about work and worrying about Kylie. I went and made a cup of tea and wondered if I would be any good at making biscuits and if I should try as a surprise for Rebecca when she got in. She would have eaten at work, but she liked a drink and a biscuit or a little something. But she probably wouldn't be pleased if she came home and there was a mess because I wouldn't have time to clear up.

I went back to the computer and texted both Paul and John: do *you know of any clerical jobs anywhere, a friend of mine is looking.*

Kylie, a friend of mine, well, I suppose she was.

On to Brewer Street in Blechingley... Elizabeth Newberry and her two sons and daughter, John Simmons another bricklayer... they were doing a lot of bricklaying in Blechingley in 1851, his wife and three children. Mary Duncan, a gardener's wife (where was Mr Duncan the gardener?) and their two sons and two daughters; Elizabeth Collister... another widow, Mr Collister had been a blacksmith, she was now a pauper... did that mean she got Poor Law Relief? No doubt she relied on her thirty year-old son Edmund, another agricultural labourer, and her three daughters Mary and Ellen, one was a servant in place and one a servant out of place… did that mean they were in and out of work? No idea, and little Sarah Collister, only eleven, probably a scholar although it didn't say so.

- Elizabeth also had a lodger, no doubt paying his way… I stopped and stared, and stared. I zoomed in on the entry for the lodger.
- Thomas Radwinsky, married, lodger, aged thirty-five, agricultural labourer… where born… Foreign…

I sat back and thought about it. Radwinsky, Radwinter, Radwinsky, Radwinter…

Back to the 1841 census, and there was another Radwinski, this time with an 'I' at the end not a 'y'… Tolik… aged twenty…

This was a different document from the other censuses. At the top of the page it said 'Name of the Institution' and beside it was written in a very neat hand 'Polish Refugee Hospital'. The information was in four columns:

- NAMES of each Person who abode therein on the Night of Sunday, June 6th,
- AGE – subdivided into of males and of Females
- OCCUPATION, if any
- WHERE BORN – subdivided into, Whether born in same County, and Whether born in Scotland, Ireland, or Foreign Parts

I had a good look at the entry for Tolik Radwinski; he was aged 20, he was a drummer – and from looking up to the top of the columns with the first man on the list, Casper

Wozniak, it was apparent that all the men on the schedule were 'in the late Polish Army'.

I was in a sort of trance as I looked through the list, soldiers, sergeants, bombardiers, another three drummers. I went to the first page of the schedule:

ENGLAND AND WALES SCHEDULE FOR PUBLIC INSTITIUTIONS

- County of *Southampton* (Parliamentary Division) *Southern*
- Hundred, Wapentake, Soke or Liberty of *Portsdown*
- Parish of *Portsea*
- City, or Borough or Town, or County Corporate of Portsea
- Within the Limits of the parliamentary Boundary of the City or Borough of *Portsmouth*
- Superintendent registrar's District *Portsea Island*
- Name of Institution &c: *Polish Refugee Hospital, Parish of Portsea*

The Polish Refugee Hospital, Parish of Portsea...

I took out a big sheet of paper, similar to the one I'd written our family on, took a medium rollerball pen and wrote the following:

- Anon Radwinsky father of Thomas Radwinter/Radwinsky born 1815, and Tolik Radwinski born 1821
- Thomas m (1) Thirza Downham b 1826 m (2) Lamy Coote b 1828
- Thomas and Thirza - parents of Tolik b 1845
- Thomas and Lamy - parents of Robert b1848, Thirza b 1850

I was convinced without proof that Thomas and Tolik were brothers; they had somehow ended up in England, probably from Poland, although whether Poland was the same shape in the 1840's as it is now I wasn't sure… Borders had changed so much and so often over the last nearly two hundred years, they could be Russian, they could be Austro-Hungarian, they could be Ukrainian for all I knew… or one of the new countries which I still wasn't really sure of.

Somehow Thomas ended up in Essex, and his little brother was hundreds of miles away in Portsmouth. Thomas had married Thirza, he'd left her and she remained as housekeeper in Essex. He ended up in Surrey with their child Tolik and two other children probably by Lamy Coote… who I don't think ever married him.

What happened next… where did he go? Can I find any trace of him or Tolik after this? Tolik doesn't appear in the 1851 census, did he too change his name? Did he go back to Poland…?

I need a whisky.

Wednesday, October 30th 2013, morning

Jessica wasn't on the bus and I worried that something might be wrong… perhaps she was just poorly, perhaps it was morning sickness. I felt very sombre; I was making progress, even if most of it was based on gut feelings, but I realised that I'd probably never find out more about Thomas and Tolik, it was tricky enough going into the past in England… trying to find something about a place which might be Poland… and just because they were in the army, or might have been in the army didn't mean they were necessarily Polish...

I played with my phone and Googled Polish Refugee Hospital Portsmouth and played around with the not very helpful results, until I came to a Wikipedia entry which mentioned Poles in Portsmouth under a heading of *'Immigration into Hampshire'*.

It explained that in 1834 a group of Polish soldiers arrived at the Portsmouth docks after fleeing Prussia where they'd been staying. This sounds intriguing, I need a map! They'd been in involved in a war (which war?) and had been ordered to return to Poland and many of them had been killed as they resisted being deported. They were subjected to forced labour along with common criminals and somehow or another (it's not clear) the Polish soldiers were given a choice of returning to Poland or going to America which is what they chose to do... *I wonder why!!*

They boarded three ships, but had to pull into different ports because of bad weather... hmmm, bad weather, it's a pretty grim autumn here! *The Elizabeth* docked at Le Havre, *The Union* went on to Harwich and *The Marianne* arrived in Portsmouth. When *The Marianne* got ready to sail, the Polish soldiers refused to get back on board the ship again, wanting to stay this side of the Atlantic, nearer to their homeland, I guess.

That explained it... so Tolik probably (but not definitely) arrived in Portsmouth on *The Marianne*; it didn't say when the ship had arrived, but it would have been sometime after 1834... Tolik would just have been a kid, about the same age as Otis or Luke...

I wondered if a similar thing had happened when *The Elizabeth* got to Le Havre and *The Union* arrived in Harwich; had the Polish soldiers refused to go further, had they stayed as close as they could to their homeland?

I sat bolt upright, joggling the elbow of the man next to me who was reading a newspaper; I apologised, and he smiled and asked if I'd nodded off. I glanced out of the window, I hadn't nodded off but I'd missed my stop! It didn't matter, I'd go into the bus station which would mean a longer walk, but never mind.

Harwich! The ship carrying a second contingent of Polish soldiers, *The Union*, had stopped at Harwich… I was sure Harwich was in Essex… There'd been a school trip to Holland, and we'd gone by coach to Harwich and then caught a ferry, and for some reason it had stuck in my head, probably because we were fourteen and were being stupid about somewhere with the word '*sex*' in its name.

How far was it from Harwich to Radwinter? If Thomas had been on that ship, maybe he'd not wanted to go to America either and managed to get off… and somehow ended up in Radwinter… had he seen the beginning of the name *Radwin*… so like his own name?

My mind was buzzing as I got off the bus… maybe he'd arrived in Radwinter, maybe it had taken him a while to get there, maybe he'd picked up odd bits of casual work on the way to get food and shelter… He would have been twentyish, early twenties, he would have been a strong lad if he'd been a soldier, farmers might have liked an Ag Lab who would work for a meal and a place to sleep.

He probably didn't speak English... was he literate? Was Polish written like English, or was it Cyrillic? I'd done a year of Russian as my contrasting studies unit for A-level.

"Ignoring me?!"

I jumped as someone shoved me. It was Kylie and she slipped her arm through mine; I wanted to shake her off, someone might see...

"Have you ever been to Essex?" I asked.

"Do they sell shortbread there?" she asked.

"You seem cheerful!" I said, she was back to her annoying self.

"Shall we go back to your place and have sex?" she grinned at me.

I was horrified and she laughed as if it was the most hilarious thing.

"God you are so easy to wind up!"

I couldn't think of anything to say, which she seemed to find even funnier. Once I'd calmed down I told her that I'd texted my brothers about a job.

"You're fucking ace, Thomas!" she screeched but there was just a flash of something in her eyes, almost gratitude, but then she jumped and kissed me on the cheek and I gave a falsetto scream of mock alarm and she laughed. She settled down then and we walked normally to work, and she didn't say anything else outrageous but told me she'd never been to Essex, and nor did she want to.

I wished she's take her arm from mine, I was nervous in case someone saw us, but we arrived at the office and she said she was going to have a fag before she went up. I resisted making a comment and went in to see what news there was, if any, about anything.

Wednesday, October 30th 2013, evening

Rebecca had turned out her bedside light and was drifting into sleep and I was propped up reading one of her cookery magazines. I've always liked food, and been interested in it. It is one of the things that Rebecca and I have in common.

We actually don't go out that much to eat, Rebecca is a great cook, and I like cooking too. I don't actually cook that often… strangely, although we have the same tastes in food, and although I like what she cooks and enjoy it, I always think that I would have cooked it differently. Also, when I'm cooking for her, I sometimes feel that I'm cooking the way she would cook things, rather than the way I would cook things, so she will like it. That obviously is the way it should be… but I sometimes feel that I'd like to just let things rip, and cook as I want to cook.

Someone told Rebecca she should go in for Masterchef… I actually think that is a great idea… but I also think I'd like to go in for it, if I was brave enough, to really be able to cook my own food, my way.

Something caught my attention and I read it carefully, then sat thinking about it.

"Did you turn out the light in the kitchen?" she suddenly asked because it's something I sometimes forget if I'm last to bed which I generally am.

"Are you awake?" I asked stupidly. "I know you like surprises for Christmas, but I've just seen something and it is the sort of thing I need to ask you if you'd like…"

She opened her eyes and looked up from the pillow; it's kind of cute because she is so short-sighted that without her glasses she can't see anything, and without her glasses her eyes are sort of unfocussed… which obviously they are… I do say some stupid things.

"You'd have a proper surprise present on Christmas Day, but I wondered if you might like this as well… it can't be a surprise really because I have to book it and I have to make sure with you first…"

She found her glasses and I passed the magazine and pointed out the advertisement.

The Olive Shed

Join Althea and Pat for a day of fine cooking and fine dining; cookery demonstration, then join us to enjoy the results. We cook, we show, you learn, you eat! Menus include fish, main, dessert and how to dress a cheese board; all recipes included. Accommodation available, bed and breakfast, dinner by arrangement.

I think it was the same place that Sandra from work had gone with her sister; she said it had been fabulous. They'd arrived for coffee and a variety of cakes, biscuits, then they'd gone into the kitchen where the woman had demonstrated cooking a meal… I think there'd been a choice of two dishes for each course; then they'd gone into a magnificent dining room and eaten the results. They were given the recipes as part of the day, and there were things they could buy such as jams and preserves, biscuits, that sort of thing…

Rebecca listened in silence, gazing at the advert as I told her what I remembered from Sandra's day; if it wasn't the same place then it was somewhere pretty similar. The Olive Shed was at Westopeness which I think is a village just near Westope, where I think an old aunty had lived... an old aunty? Which old aunty? I'd been very small when I visited her and I'd been put in front of her old TV while Mum went into the kitchen for a cup of tea... so a Magick aunt?

"The wife of Smithy went to one of these things, she thought it was amazing," she said slowly. Smithy was the other manager, slightly junior to her, but older.

"So would that be a nice Christmas present... as an extra I mean?" Rebecca did adore presents.

"I'm not sure I want to go on my own though..." did she mean she wanted me to come?

"Well, I could come too, but if you want it more of a girlie thing then why not ask your sisters, or see if one of your friends wants to go."

She seemed pleased and took her glasses off and we snuggled down but didn't go to sleep for a little while.

Monday, November 4th 2013

The Lebanese place had a different feel at lunch time and there were different things on the menu, snacky things which were a little cheaper, so again we had the mixed mezze, John and me. There were lots of Greek and Turkish things, and I noticed the lunch-time menu said 'Middle Eastern Mezze'. We were both going back to work, but he had a glass of wine and I had sparkling water. We chatted about things, work things, family things; the book trade was slow but the bookshop owner Alex Elgard was moving into on-line selling, and was developing a local network… John went on about it for a while.

I didn't say much about work, what could I say? To me, there seemed to be a lot of phone calls coming in which were taken privately by Sandra and Gordon, and a lot of quiet conversations in which I was not included.

I was the junior in the practice, but it had never seemed to matter before; now I definitely got the feeling that there was Gerald, Gordon and Sandra on one side, Martin sort of in their orbit, the clerical split between Julie and Vicky who were pulled into the office for whatever reason and Kylie who was just left to get on with her work, and me, sitting at my desk at the opposite end from Gerald's office. I'd never thought of it before, now it seemed I was out on a limb, socially as well as actually, and I felt miserable and unsettled. Would I have noticed if Kylie had never told me? Was I imagining things now? I don't know… so I didn't have a lot to say to John about work.

He was seeing another girl, but he still liked Laura, liked her a little too much, he told me ruefully which I guess meant he loved her.

"Were you surprised when Rebecca and I got married?" I asked, thinking of the conversation between Amelia and Andrea I'd overheard.

"I thought you got married too young; I wasn't surprised, I suppose… Rebecca's lovely but… well, I always hoped you'd meet someone with a bit more… before you got married I mean…"

I didn't really know what he meant.

"You always had this little spark, you were always so funny, and a bit… wacky I guess and Rebecca was very… well, she's lovely… but you seem quiet now… and sometimes," he looked at me with his piercing Radwinter eyes. "And sometimes, Tommy, you look sort of sad."

I could have burst into tears right then… I could have boo-hooed and bawled like a baby. Instead I put on a grin and protested that I was fine, I wasn't sad.

John looked at me in his kind way. "That's great then! Have another spanakopita and tell me about the family!"

He changed the subject and I attacked the flaky filo and cheese and spinach and nutmeg… was it nutmeg? Or was it some Lebanese spice…it didn't quite taste like nutmeg, unless it was nutmeg and something else…

"Mace!" I said, then seeing his surprise explained I thought the spice was mace in the spanakopita… He had a phone call which was from the shop so he had to answer, he apologised, but I quickly texted Ruthie 'spanakopita, falafel, kibbe, tiropita, kreatopita'.

I asked John if he wanted his notes back, but no, he was fine for me to keep them, which was useful because it helped me keep track of my sources. I would email him stuff if he wanted, but really he just wanted the headline news so to speak.

I told him that as yet, I didn't have proof of what I thought, and I might be researching a completely different Radwinter family, and I hinted at why I didn't want to work backwards from us… we were the goal… twenty-first century us was where the nineteenth century research should be leading…

In brief, I told him, I thought that there were two brothers Thomas and Tolik Radwinski who maybe were in the Polish Army in the 1830's, Tolik the younger one pretty definitely was; due to the persecution and generally dire, war-torn, annexed and ravished state of Poland which no longer existed at that time, they and many fellow soldiers had headed out from Prussia, bound for America. Tolik was on a ship called *The Marianne* which stopped in Portsmouth because of bad weather where Tolik and his fellow soldiers disembarked and then refused to embark back again. Tolik was still in Portsmouth in 1841, but had disappeared ten years later.

Thomas had been on another ship, *The Union* which stopped in Harwich and he too got off and made his way, somehow, to a little Essex village called Radwinter.

John looked astonished, excited almost. Thomas stayed in Radwinter and in 1845, calling himself Thomas Radwinter, he married Thirza Downham who was nineteen, and the same year they had a baby who they called Tolik. Something happened then because six years later, Thirza was still in Radwinter as a housekeeper to a local farmer; Thomas was in Surrey, now back to Thomas Radwinsky, working as an agricultural labourer, his little son Tolik Radwinter was lodged with another family in the same village. In the local workhouse was a woman called Lamy Radwinter with her two children, Robert, three, and Thirza, one year old. There'd been a woman called Lamy in Radwinter when Thomas was living there…

"And that's as far as I've got," I told John.

"Wow, bro, that's amazing! I can't wait for the next exciting instalment! How did you find all this out?"

It was time to get back to work so after paying, as we headed away from the harbour, I told him about my searches and trawls of the censuses... and I also confessed that I was a little nervous of my task, which was possibly why I spent such a long time looking at other stuff and making spread sheets.

John suggested we met again next week for lunch, he'd really enjoyed it, but this time he would choose a place to eat. We stood at the bottom of the High Street, flurries of snow in the bitter wind which whistled around us, checking our diaries.

"John, you know we were talking earlier... what did you mean about me and Rebecca... you said I was wacky and she was so... so something... What did you mean?"

He shrugged slightly; he didn't seem embarrassed, more as if he was judging what to say.

"I guess I just thought you would have ended up with someone else who was wacky... someone with a bit of personality," he stopped. "Not that Rebecca *hasn't* got personality, I just meant different..." He grinned suddenly. "That sounds rude... sorry!"

He gave me a hug and we said goodbye and he trudged up into the wind towards the shop, and I hurried back to the office.

Tuesday, November 5th 2013

Talking things through with John had fired me up to continue; maybe I wouldn't be able to get back to Poland, but maybe I could find out a little more about the Polish soldiers. I tried various combinations of searches and then thought of the ships Thomas and Tolik had arrived on.

I typed in *'1830's ship Marianne'* and up came a lot of entries including *'The Polish Memorial - Memorials and Monuments – In Portsmouth'* at the top of the list! This sounded like gold, but maybe it was about World War II, I knew there'd been a lot of Polish servicemen in Britain during the war, there was a lad in my class Andrew Luczak, whose grandfather was Polish from then.

I clicked on the link and went to the page. It was a site dedicated to memorials in Portsmouth and this Polish one was among them. The title of the page was *'Kingston Cemetery – The Polish Memorial'*. Down the left side of the page were some photos of the memorial, including the four plaques attached to it.

The memorial, I could see from the photo, was made of brick, with a central short wide block sloping inwards, and a wing on either side. The plaque on the left wing was an elongated regular pentagon; in the centre was a stylised crucifix above a rectangle, which I guess contained the names of the soldiers. On the right wing was a longer rectangular plaque. The memorial was set on a lawn with trees behind. There was a paved area in front of it with wreaths and flowers.

The photos below clearly showed what was on each plaque, and in the centre of the page was a transcription of what was written on them. The plaque on the left wing was a picture, if you can call something made of metal that; there was a central figure who seemed to be dressed in a soldier's uniform, with a tall, old fashioned hat, and carrying a flag over his shoulder. His head was on one side and he looked wounded or defeated. Behind him on the left was a wooden cross with what looked like a priest standing below it – but I could be wrong, I'm not very knowledgeable about costume. In the background was a city; on the right were marching soldiers, stepping out smartly with their guns over their shoulders, tail coats, breeches and the tall hats. There were shapes on the floor but I couldn't make out whether it was bones or stones... it made me feel a bit shivery.

The central plaque, as I'd guessed, was a list of names, but with much more detail of what ranks the soldiers had or in what capacity they served; it was all in Polish but when I switched to translate it came up as the ranks and sometimes where they'd come from.

The left plaque had another picture at the bottom, of men arriving in a small boat which had come from a masted ship further out on the sea. They'd come to a quay where people, men women and children, were stretching out their hands to them... the people of Portsmouth, no doubt. Above the picture was an inscription, a dedication really.

Down the centre of the page was a transcription of what was written on the monument; it was thanking the people of Portsmouth for their kindness and charity to the Polish soldiers who'd come to what it called 'Britain's premier naval port', in February 1834... Tolik would have been aged thirteen... a year older than Paul's boy Tom.

Then came a very interesting bit, which explained so much. The soldiers who arrived had, it said, taken part in an uprising against Tzarist Russia, Tzarist Russian oppression, to be exact, in Warsaw 1830-31.... 1830? When Tolik was *nine*? That couldn't be right; you might have a servant boy of nine but you wouldn't have a drummer boy of nine... would you? It then says that most of the soldiers were laid to rest there in a common grave... I don't quite understand that... I'll have to think about that later... I didn't like to think of Tolik being laid to rest in a common grave...

It then transcribes what's written on the central plaque, above the soldiers' names, that they'd come from Gdansk on the battleship Marianne in 1834. So the uprising happened in 1831, and they arrived in 1834... And Gdansk... is that in Poland? I think it is.

Then at the bottom of the transcriptions, before the list of names is a very interesting piece of information about what had happened before the soldiers had sailed from Gdansk. Apparently after the defeat at Warsaw, many of the soldiers escaped to Prussia, however this was already under the control of Russia and the Prussians had to get rid of the Polish troops. There was a choice, Siberia or America... no contest really, was there?

As I'd already found out, terrible weather forced *The Marianne* into Portsmouth and the soldiers disembarked but wouldn't re-embark, and thanks to the kindness of the people of Portsmouth they were able to stay, even though the government tried to send them to Algeria of all places to serve in the French Foreign Legion. So crackpot political solutions aren't just a modern thing.

The explanation finishes by saying what I'd guessed, that many of the men married local women, found jobs and trades, had families and remained in Britain.

Phew! I went and made a cup of tea and wondered when Rebecca would be home. Her shifts seemed to be very erratic at the moment; she was so conscientious that if there was a bit of a crisis she would stay on until it was sorted even if Smithy was on duty.

I returned and went back to Google and almost immediately had a hit with something which looked at first sight not very relevant, 'The Roman Catholic Church in the History of the Exiled Polish Community in Britain (1939-1950)' by Jozéf Guloz, which he'd submitted to the University of London, the School of Slavonic and Eastern European Studies, as part of his degree for a doctorate in philosophy. I skipped through it, not because it wasn't fascinating, but because I am too easily led astray by the fascinating and I had to stay focussed. I found the introduction and it was entitled 'Sent by a storm' and it was the background to how and why the Polish soldiers had eventually ended up in Portsmouth.

I skip read it, just checking there were no names anything like Radwinski, and although I've stored the link in my Time Keeper's Cabinet and I will go back and read it properly to try and understand what experiences Thomas and Tolik must have had, for the moment I want to try and track down Thomas on board *The Union*, docking at Harwich.

I was g weary now, and sat back with my tea and then remembered I'd not checked on the Portsmouth memorial that Tolik's name was there. I scanned down and there he was between Josef Raczkus who was an *artyleria piesza*, and Franciszek Rodak who was a1 p.strz.konnych, there he was, Telek Radwinski piesza lwóv … His name was spelt differently again but I was getting used to this.

Josef Raczkus was 'an artillery pedestrian' according to Google Translate… he was a foot soldier who used artillery, cannons did it mean? It didn't come up with anything for Franciszek Rodak's rank, but when I just Googled *p.strz.konnych* I found it, probably the 1st mounted rifle regiment... I'm not sure on that one, I wonder if Andy Luczak, the kid I was at school with knows any Polish?

So Telek/Tolik was a foot lwów... Google asked me if I meant a different spelling and when I pressed it the answer was 'walking the lions' which obviously wasn't so... I'm sure the Polish Army in 1830 didn't have lions... unless they were mascots. Was Tolik a lion keeper?

I was very tired now so for one last throw I typed lwów into ordinary Google. Up it came with Lviv... a city in the Ukraine... Lviv in Polish was Lwów... Was Tolik Ukrainian? Did the Ukraine even exist in 1830?

My head was spinning and I shut down the computer.

Rebecca was really late, there must be some real crisis at the Willows... Just as I was wondering whether to ring, her key turned in the lock.

Friday, November 8th, 2013

The weekend came upon me unexpectedly, I'd lost track of the days. Rebecca was working; I felt sorry for her, she was putting in such long hours but heading towards Christmas it was always busy at the Willows. There seemed to be an influx of people, and then other people wanted to take their old folks home for the festivities, and Rebecca always wanted the people who remained to have a proper Christmas, so there were lots of events organised.

Apparently Ruthie was doing Christmas cookery and there were activities like concerts and carol singing in the chapel, and parties, and Father Christmas always visited, and then there was a big traditional dinner a couple of days before Christmas Day for families which we went to.

We always went to Rebecca's parents for Christmas Day and another Christmas lunch but like all Rebecca's family, her mum Maggie is a brilliant cook … and at some point we would see my family. Marcus, being a vicar, was always busy, but he would come down in the slack period between Boxing Day and New Year. We always saw Paul too, usually when John went over with the current girlfriend or none.

Recently, John had gone away with friends for the actual Christmas period; I couldn't understand why someone as genuinely nice as John had two failed marriages, and no children… he would be a lovely dad. Of all of us he is the nicest and kindest, and he's such fun too… I wished I just knew someone… the only unattached person I could think of was Kylie, but the thought of them as a couple actually made me laugh.

The night Rebecca had come home so late, she'd been very upset because Molly, the oldest resident, who'd been there since she first started, had died. I made her a hot drink and she went to bed, and then had to be in work early because of making arrangements about Molly; Rebecca had started at the Willows when she was eighteen, so she'd known the old lady a long time. I'd got a lift to work which was nice because there was snow everywhere now and it was mighty cold.

The office seemed back to normal somehow; no more quiet gossiping, no more secret phone calls, no more meetings in which I wasn't included. We were busy, lots of clients coming in, lots of reports to write up and I worked through my lunch hour, munching my sandwiches as I worked. Kylie had regularly brought me coffee and papers to work on, but didn't engage me in any sort of strange conversation apart from calling me a twat and a tart which I took as being friendly. I'd suggested to Rebecca we went out for a meal as it was Friday night; sometimes she was too tired, but I tried to give her a little treat if I could. She suggested her favourite Italian place, Nonna Ysabel, which was alright by me.

I like Italian, and this place was owned by a family with a real love of traditional Italian food, and the mother of the family ran the kitchen… she actually was probably a grandmamma, and probably she was Ysabel.

The food was always wonderful and sometimes I saw her son Leo who'd been in my A-level group at school. He was there tonight, so we had a bit of a chat; he has three children two girls and a boy and I asked after them, ignoring the suspicious look Rebecca was giving me.

Leo had once told me he came from the East coast of Italy, but I wasn't sure where and I'd never really thought about it much before but this evening I noticed the big map on the wall was of part of Italy, the part which would be the calf of the leg of the boot shape, opposite Croatia.

Rebecca had what she usually had, Crespelli in Brodo… little crepes served in a chicken broth, and I had Taglierini alla Chitarra which is a special sort of pasta in a tomato sauce with bacon bits and basil, then Rebecca had the same as ever, basically Italian roast chicken, Pollo Arrosto, and I had lamb… which seems to me quite unusual for Italy… maybe I should ask Leo about it, Agnello al Cardi… Rebecca calls it sheep in a cardigan which was quite amusing the first time she said it…

I was driving so I only had a glass of wine, but it was nice that Rebecca had a couple and she had her favourite chocolate and chestnut dessert with cream. I hadn't mentioned family again, and I'd decided not to mention moving house either, she's so busy at the moment. After Christmas I'd make a suggestion and see what she thinks. I was tempted to start looking in estate agents, but wisely, I think, I decided to wait.

I'd told her about Tolik and Thomas, and my thoughts that they were probably Polish but might be Ukrainian. She wasn't really very interested, but did say that one of her staff was Ukrainian, and if I wanted to know anything, maybe she could ask her. That was kind.

Saturday, November 9th 2013

So Saturday... and Rebecca was in work, again, poor girl. I decided to do some paid work, and put aside thoughts of Thomas and Tolik and the Polish Army

The phone rang and to my surprise it was Leo from the restaurant, I had a moment's panic that maybe I'd not paid the bill, or not paid enough or... However, he was asking if I was doing anything tonight, and if I wasn't did I want to be on his quiz team, the Dolphins? It was at his local pub in Easthope, and it was on a Saturday to try and get more punters in rather than them going into town for a night out; Saturday was a strangely slack night, so the landlord was doing a one off pre-Christmas quiz and did I fancy coming? The pub quiz was usually on a Tuesday and the rest of his team apart from one were going into town.

It seemed a great idea... I don't have many friends and I do sometimes feel a little lonely. I said I'd check with Rebecca and Leo asked if she wanted to be in the team too, he only had one other person so far. I rang Rebecca, prepared to text her instead if she was busy as she often is, but she answered. She didn't want to go, but I was really pleased because she almost insisted that I went, she said it would do me good to be out with my friends instead of on the computer all night.

How considerate she is, how kind… I had a sudden inspiration and rang John; he was up for it, so I rang Leo back and we had it, a team of four! I was quite excited!

I went into town and met John at the bus station, and we got on the Easthope bus together; he lives in a flat in Strand, not far from the bookshop. He asked me about the Polish connection, and I told him there might even be a Ukrainian connection, but I was beginning to get to the end of my limits. I would see what I could find about Ukrainian history in the 1820's and 1830's but it was getting to be a bit testing, and my single year of Russian wasn't up to much.

We spoke about the family, and he suggested again that I spoke to Marcus; he would remember our grandparents… it wasn't beyond possibility that he might even have been born when our great grandparents were alive. I squirmed a bit; Marcus and Jill had virtually brought me up, and I'd lived with them while I was at Uni until I married Rebecca. Had that hastened my decision to do so, I suddenly wondered? Was marrying Rebecca a way of escaping my big brother? I loved him, of course I did, but he had very high standards. He'd worked so hard himself to achieve what he had, in many ways sacrificed a lot too, and without supportive parents; he'd taken me on and expected much of me.

Would I be like that with my children? I thought not; I would expect a lot but whatever they achieved I would be proud. I missed what John was saying and he had to nudge me.

"I was just asking about children," he said. I wondered if I'd blurted something out as I do when I'm thinking, without realising I've spoken. "I just wondered if you'd had any further conversations with Rebecca?"

I confided in him about how much I wanted to have a family, asking him not to mention it to anyone, especially not Rebecca. She would be a wonderful mother, I knew from seeing how good she was with the old folk, and how hard she worked, at the Willows and at home. For some reason she seemed not to want a family at the moment; I know her job is so important to her, but having a family is important too.

"I'm beginning to think by the time I meet the right person I'll be too old," John said; he spoke with a grin but he sounded sad too.

"You'd make a great dad, John," I said genuinely. If ever a man was designed to be a dad, he was.

The bus stopped in Easthope and we got off and went into the pub, the Lark, and found Leo and his friend Damian at a table with the picture round already there in front of them. Half of the twenty pictures were flags of the world, the other half were various celebrities. John insisted on getting me a drink so I looked down the flags and impressed Leo and Damian by knowing all the rest of the ones they hadn't got, including Azerbaijan, Belarus and Estonia. That got us off to a good start although I was hopeless on celebrities.

John came back with the drinks, and the landlord, once he'd sorted out he PA system, began round one of ten questions. Between us we reckoned we'd got them all right, and we went on to the next round which was history and geography, and again we were pretty secure in our answers. I suddenly realised that I was really enjoying myself; in between questions we chatted and made jokes, and I went and got us another beer.

We came a little unstuck on TV and film; I don't watch much, John hasn't got a TV and neither Leo nor Damian was much better. The last round before the break was 'in the news', and several of the questions were about current soap storylines which I didn't really think counted as news, but it didn't matter we were here for the fun of it!

At half time when the smokers including Damian rushed out for a cigarette I quickly texted Rebecca to make sure she was alright, although why she shouldn't be when she was intending to watch some romantic film and attack the box of Lily O'Brien chocolates I'd bought her, I don't know, but I texted her all the same.

The landlord wanted to hurry the quiz along, before people started drifting away into town so the next rounds went through at quite a pace, but somehow not having too much time to think seemed to get the answers snapping out. I had chatted a little to Leo at the break, as usual the topic coming back to food.

Leo worked in the restaurant, doing a lot of the cooking as his Mum got older, but working out front as well. He told me he really wanted to have his own place, to have a different sort of Italian food... he was fed up with the usual run of the mill stuff. His family came from the Abruzzo region, their village was near L'Aquila, he told me and he'd like to do some typical food from there... he felt Strand was ready for something a bit more exciting and different in Italian cuisine.

I was really interested but then the quiz restarted and Damian came scooting back in with a couple of answers he'd picked up from the other smokers. There was a music round which I was hopeless at, but between them, the other three had most of the answers and then it was time for the papers to be swapped between the teams and the answers were called out and we marked an opponent's paper.

I was charged with keeping a score of what we thought we'd got right, and out of nowhere I remember Paul having said I had a memory like an elephant.

The papers were collected in and we sat back, waiting for the results.

"Cor, look at that!" said Damian suddenly.

I looked up and Kylie was stalking towards me; she had gold sparkly legging and extremely high heeled black patent ankle boots, a low top that went down to... well, down but barely covered her... well, her...

Her mouth was painted almost luminous pink and she had wild and scary eye-makeup and had frizzed her hair out in an Afro so it looked like a flaming halo.

I squeaked something as she advanced on me and suddenly she sat on my knee, straddling me, grabbed my face and kissed me full on the mouth... I tasted smoke and rum and coconut and her tongue was hot as if she'd been eating chilli or fire.

"Hello, Thomas! Having a good time?" then she stood, grabbed me again, and kissed my forehead and then stalked off and out of the pub.

I thought I was going to faint; everyone was laughing, the whole pub was laughing. I thought John was going to fall off his chair, almost crying with the hilarity of it. Then everyone was applauding and then the landlord was shouting for quiet as he was going to read out the results.

"Who was she?" asked John, wiping his eyes.

"Friend of yours?" Leo was also red-faced with glee.

I took a big drink of beer, and managed to say that I worked with her.

"She was certainly working with you!" exclaimed Leo, but Damian shushed him, because it seemed as if we'd won the quiz.

The landlord came over with an envelope for us.

"I think you've had your prize already!" he announced so all the pub could hear.

I didn't know if I was embarrassed or angry or upset, but I grinned weakly and tried to think of something to say but just bleated pathetically.

I had to put up with a lot of banter, but eventually the subject changed and we discussed the answers we'd got wrong and reflected on the lucky guesses we'd got right.

We piled into a taxi to go back to Strand, and I was quite drunk really, and probably got a little bit loud... but I couldn't get rid of the taste of smoke and rum and coconut and chilli.

Sunday, November 10th 2013

It was Sunday and I thought I would make Rebecca breakfast in bed; I'd thought I might be hung over, but I felt surprisingly well, in fact I felt great. I put the kettle on and thought back to the quiz; I liked Leo, and thought

Damian seemed a nice guy too... I think he said he was a teacher, but some aspects of the evening were a little blurry. Our prize had been cash, plus a ticket for a free pint next time we went in the Lark, plus free entry as a team on the next quiz night. I thought that was generous; we'd used the cash for the taxi into Strand and a kebab, and then I'd got a taxi home and stumbled in at goodness knows what time.

I pottered about, put the kettle on and got everything ready; Rebecca only likes a light breakfast so I found some yoghurt and defrosted some blueberries and found some croissants.

I went to the bathroom and glanced in the mirror, and then glanced back. I thought at first I had a big wound on my forehead, then with a ghastly flash it all came back... Kylie, the sparkly leggings, the high heeled boots, her vivid pink lips... the kiss... oh my God, the kiss... then she'd kissed me on the forehead. I could see now right in the middle of my forehead was a great big pink kiss!

I hastily found some of Rebecca's make-up wipes and scrubbed it off, but there still seemed to be a pink shadow on my skin...

I texted John furiously, why hadn't he told me I had a great big lipstick kiss on my forehead? But then I deleted it... I decided I wasn't going to think about Kylie, I wasn't going to think about being kissed by Kylie...

As usual, we were going to Rebecca's parents for Sunday lunch; we always have a nice meal there, her mum, Maggie is a good cook which is where Rebecca obviously got it from, and there is always plenty to eat, they are very generous. They are such nice people, but I still feel as if I'm a visitor rather than a member of the family, I just don't feel very relaxed.

Her father Phil is mad about sport and always talks to me about football, or rugby, or whatever is topical and I always flounder around and try and be interested when I don't really know what he's talking about. When I remember to, I read the sports pages before we go so I can make some sort of response. One or other and sometimes both of Rebecca's sisters are there with their families and even Rebecca struggles with that. The children are, to my mind, really badly behaved and seem to spend a lot of time running around screaming, and squashed round the table with them is always trying because they seem to have no concept of table manners. Rebecca remarks on it, her sister, whichever one, Lauren or Georgia, then makes a comment back and Maggie tries to be a peacemaker... I think both of us are glad when we get home...

I wonder if this is why Amelia and Andrea describe us as middle-aged... Is that how we seem, frumpy and old-fashioned? And what sort of word is frumpy? I bet no-one else my age uses it.

Rebecca went on her game in the study and I messed about trying to find where Tolik went between 1841 and 1851. I ended up looking at pictures of Portsmouth, I've never been there... the Mary Rose is there, and the Victory.

I made us a cup of tea and went back to the computer and then for some reason typed Plymouth instead of Portsmouth. But that looks an interesting place too... perhaps we could go there for the weekend when it's our anniversary. I was looking at photos and there were some of some plaques mounted on a wall by the harbour and I guess I looked at them because I'd been looking at plaques on the Polish memorial in Portsmouth.

Three caught my eye:

PLYMOUTH MEN WHO HELPED FOUND MODERN AUSTRALIA...

These were the captains of ships who had sailed to Australia, Furneaux, MacArthur, Arthur, Lockyer and Captain Bligh later of the Bounty...

From Plymouth on 13th March 1787 sailed the transport ships 'Friendship' and 'Charlotte' carrying men and women convicts bound for Australia;

From near this spot thousands of Cornish people sailed for South Australia during the nineteenth century...

I wondered just how primitive the conditions had been for those poor souls who were transported, not much better for the soldiers and guards who supervised them.

I sat back and drank my tea.... Had Tolik committed some crime and been transported? Was this why he wasn't on the census? Why should I think he might have been? But that was the way my mind worked, and I remembered ages ago finding the report of the man who'd been whipped and the other man who'd been hanged.

I found a lot of Australian genealogical sites with lists of convicts and suppressed my interest and concentrated on searching for Radwinski or something similar. Interesting though the results were, there was nothing of any help. I typed in '1840'2s Portsmouth to Australia' and came up with Migrant Ships Arriving in South Australia 1836-60.

On the left side was a little picture of a sailing ship, on the right it said 'Passenger ships arriving in Australian Ports';

below the picture there were links to other areas of Australia, but the page I'd ended up on was South Australian shipping (I felt a little daunted, there was so much information, (NSW (1837-1899) QLD (1840-1915) SA (1836-1860) VIC (1837-1899) WA (1829-1889) NZ (1839-1905) and also Convict Transports 1788-1868) I think I might have trawled the convict lists... but what a lot of data...

There was nothing for it but to go through the stuff, taking 1841 as a start date and going through to 1851, because he might have sailed before the census was taken. There were lists and lists and lists of ships arriving into Porte Adelaide on the first page from places as far afield as Mauritius, Boston, Bremen and Liverpool and with a sinking heart I realised that even if Tolik had gone to Australia, he might have sailed from anywhere...

The comments beside the details of vessel, were dates of arrival and departure, name of captain... whaler, voyage of 127 days, small brig which put in for repairs, from London via Plymouth and Swan River...

I ignored the dispiriting thought and ploughed onto the next set. 1836-1860; more interesting comments

I trawled though the details of ships and ports, looking for Portsmouth, but only came across one or two and usually it was where a ship had stopped off en route to Australia but although I checked the names there were no Radwinski's, or Rad- anything, or even any Polish sounding names that I saw.

I've entered the names of the Polish soldiers on another spread sheet... just in case I need to go back and check something, it's easier having it here on paper beside me, rather than doing an internet trawl again.

I look at the information for *The Trafalgar*, which arrived in Port Adelaide on the 2nd Jul, 1847 with two hundred and seventy eight people (no cabin passengers). No cabin passengers, did that mean they just slept in the hold, or were there big rooms they all slept in together? Two hundred and seventy eight of them? There were families with children, John Burlery and wife (nameless) and four children; Edward Lahor and wife and four children; Nicholas McNamee, wife and five children, and saddest of all, Barney Doolan and wife and child (Jane Doolan, aged 16 died on the voyage) There were no Radwinskis or anything like it. Many of the people on the Trafalgar sounded of Irish origin, Cassidy, Corrigan, Kennedy, Leonard, Lynch...O'Brien, Ryan and Kavanagh...

The Samuel Boddington left London on the 27th September 1848, and left Plymouth on October 10th with Captain Hurst to arrive in Port Adelaide on the 12th January. There is an interesting note attached to this:

"One of the passengers wrote 'that The Samuel Boddington, whilst having a pilot aboard, heeled on her anchor below the bar. The water casks were all started aft, and all the passengers ordered forward to lighten the vessel astern, and by those means she was got off. The captain said the event would have involved an expense of £1000.' (This was reported in the October 10, 1849 issue of the South Australian REGISTER)"

Things sounded pretty dire on board *The Samuel Boddington*, and when I looked down the passenger list in search of Tolik, I was shocked to see how many people had died en route: the Whiteman's infant son; Frederick Cheeseman aged twenty-five and buried at sea; the infant daughter of John and Elizabeth Hender; the Hoopers' infant daughter; Ann Lee another infant; not only the wife of Richard Salt, but the baby son born to her as well; the wife of John Martin – Jane Martin; and yet another little baby, born and died at sea, tiny JohnTrewar...

I felt quite melancholy. I kept thinking of Richard Salt, who having lost his wife Eliza and baby son, had arrived in Australia, widowed, bereaved and with a little one year old daughter, Ann, to look after

I looked at *The Candahar* from Plymouth, which sailed under Captain Fraser to Port Adelaide and arrived on the 10th February, 1849. On board, among others was Mr. Foster (surgeon-superintendent, and lady) Julius Haast (later Sir Julius von Haast) poor Mrs Bird who died, and not only were Mr and Mrs. Stapley and their five children on board, and Mr and Mrs Giles and their six children, but also Mr. and Mrs. Pascoe and their eight children. Eight children, Good heavens! ...and we didn't even have one child...

I searched through the names of the passengers who had travelled on *The Madawaska* in 1849. The ship was built in 1847 in Quebec for Fieldon & Co. Of Liverpool; she was a three-mast rig (561 tons) under Captain John McKinnel; she left London and Plymouth on March 26th 1849 and arrived on July17th, with the mutual co-operation of the passengers, whatever that meant... Four months, they were at sea for nearly four months! I expect they must have stopped off at places for supplies, but four months!

A cup of coffee then back to the ships registers; it was a hopeless task... there were literally thousands of ships which had gone to Australia... and why should Tolik have been on any of them? He might have emigrated to Canada, he might have gone to any of the colonies to seek his fortune, he might have changed his name and be lost to me for ever...

There was a bip of a text; John saying how much he'd enjoyed the quiz, and since we had free entry to the next one, and a free beer waiting for us, why didn't we go on Tuesday, and if Leo and Damian had their usual team all there, then we could be a team of two until we found someone else to join us. It sounded a great idea; Tuesdays were when there was a team meeting at the Willows. Quite often they went on for a pizza somewhere, so I was sure Rebecca wouldn't mind if I went out.

I would look at *The Prince Regent*, 528 tons, and then I'd give up; it was an old ship, built in 1811 by Frinsbury for Buckle & Co. of London. The information rather chillingly added that it had been used as a ship to transport convicts in 1820, 1824, 1827, and 1830. However, on April 8th 1849, under Captain William Jago, it – or should I say she, left Plymouth and arrived on July 29th 1849 in Adelaide. There were three cabin passengers, and again I wondered where the others all were; the marvellously named Sinclair Blue, a surgeon superintendent, Mr Cleaver, and Mr and Mrs Foales and their two children.

Sinclair Blue? Is that really a name? I have to deviate and do a quick MyTimeMachine check, and yes... he was married in 1839... Back to work, I mustn't deviate...

I begin to look down the long list, and there is more information, the ages of the passengers and a little note about some of them; from Somerset, from Cornwall, from Hertfordshire, Gloucester and... Westmeath? Isn't that in Ireland?

Strange names... the Beaglehole family from Cornwall, the Bloodworths from Gloucester, the Brutins, the Carbis family with their six children... and the four-year-old is named Pascoe... that's a nice name... Pascoe Radwinter... That is a nice name...

I pause a moment and think about Lillah and Pascoe Radwinter... *Yes, and these are my children, Lillah and Pascoe, and baby Isabella...*

... Anne Culleeny form Count Clare, an agricultural servant aged twenty-six; Mary Fidock aged fourteen, the Gauleys, the Guppy's, Frederick Haggett and Thomas Halpin, The Jewells, the Odgers...

"Cup of tea?" I nearly jumped out of my skin. Rebecca was right behind me, looking over my shoulder at the passenger list on the screen. "What are you looking at?" she asked, almost suspiciously... I hadn't heard that tone of voice for quite a while; I thought maybe she'd got over being jealous of some imagined female interest.

I began to tell her what I was doing, and the unusual names, the Shuggs and the Torpy's and the Varcoes.

She didn't seem interested though. "I just wondered what you were smiling at," she said in what I thought was quite a cool way.

I think I'd been smiling at our imaginary children.

"There are loads of Irish people who went to Australia from Plymouth, lots of people from Westmeath, look, the Travers family, someone here from Galway, and look at this name, Rosa New Holland from Armagh!"

She looked at me as if I was mad, said she'd make a cup of tea and went rather briskly into the kitchen. I was a little troubled... I wondered if the outline of the lipstick kiss was still visible... but her mother would have commented, or Lauren, her sister, she was always ready to make comments too, but not nice and kind like Maggie.

I followed her into the kitchen.

"Are you alright, Becca?" I asked. Perhaps she was cross with me for coming in late last night, but she'd been asleep and I'd been very quiet... and she'd been fine this morning... in fact she'd been lovely this morning... so pleased at breakfast in bed that... well, anyway, she'd been fine. She replied that she was alright. "Is everything ok at work?" I asked.

"Yes! Why shouldn't it be?" she replied rather sharply.

I mumbled something and returned to the computer. There was nothing of any relevance on *The Prince Regent*, lots of interest, but nothing of...

I stared in disbelief; between Benedict Quick a twenty-eight year old carpenter from Cornwall, and the Richards family, also from Cornwall, Mrs Loveday Richards aged fifty-two and a housekeeper, and her children, Ann, Jonathan, Elizabeth and Enoch... between Quick and Richards was Radwinski...

I got up and wandered round and then went into the kitchen; Rebecca was staring at the calendar almost absent-mindedly and I went and put my arms round her waist.

"Are *you* alright, Thomas?" she asked in a strange way.

My feelings of anxiety, never far away, came galloping back; I'd felt for a while something was wrong, maybe Rebecca felt the same, maybe she wanted to talk about it... whatever 'it' was. I was worried about work, and I was worried about my marriage... I wanted children, more and more I wanted children, and although it was a forbidden subject, I knew that Rebecca just didn't... she didn't want children now, and maybe she didn't want children in the future.

"I'm OK, Becca, just work getting me down... I expect after Christmas everything will be fine."

"I expect so... I'll pour the tea," and she moved out of my arms, and I wondered if I should have asked... should have said...

I went back to the passenger list, took refuge in the nineteenth century...The passenger list was divided into two; on the left side was the entry of surname and a brief note of the passengers:

- Radwinski, T, and wife and three children.

On the right side was an expanded entry:

- Radwinski, Tolik, 27 (musician, bootmaker)
- Radwinski, Julia, 22 (wife of Tolik)
- Radwinski, Taras 3
- Radwinski, Julia 2
- Radwinski, Casimir 1

So... so Tolik had a family... a wife and three children, and he took them round the world, and none of them died on the voyage...

What happened to him when he was there, musician and bootmaker? Did he have more children? Did they become successful and more than that, were they healthy and happy? Would I ever know?

Probably not... I should concentrate on the Radwinters; the Radwinskis would have to stay in Adelaide until I return at some time, and discover where they went... if I can.

So back to England, and back to Thomas Radwinter, but I was tired from all the trawling though shipping lists. I saved everything in my Time Keeper's Cabinet, updated my MyTimeMachine page and went and sat beside Rebecca and watched some programme she likes...

Monday, 11th November 2013

Kylie was late in which was unusual for her but it was better for me. I'd had to use my inhaler twice already, once as I got off the bus, thinking I might bump into her as I walked to the office; I sometimes had in the past but usually she hurried ahead to snatch a quick cigarette. I had to use it again in the lift, but she wasn't at her desk and I hurried to mine, switched on my computer, got out my files and got my head down to work.

Everything was calm and everyone was quietly working; Mondays sometimes seem like that, as if everyone wants to get stuck into the week.

"Post!" Kylie dumped my mail on my keyboard and made me jump. "How are you, Thomas? Had a good weekend?"

And she turned and marched away without waiting for me to reply. She'd managed to hit some keys and I'd lost the page I was working on. My phone rang and made me jump; it was Gerald asking if I could come into his office. I was unexpectedly nervous and it wasn't helped by Kylie giving a low wolf whistle as I went past her desk.

"Ah, Thomas, come in, sit down! Coffee?" and without waiting for me to answer he poured me one anyway. "So how are things, Thomas, how's Rebecca? She does a splendid job at the Willows, runs a very tight ship! Good manager, damned fine manager! Organised!"

I'd noticed before that Gerald tends to talk in exclamations sometimes... He usually talks quite normally, like when I was asking him about the family tree, but sometimes he goes all hale and hearty.

I couldn't imagine that someone like him, Captain of the Yacht Club and a Free Mason would be nervous, especially not talking to the most junior member of the team. Someone once told him he looked like Michael Caine... well, he was once blond and has a squarish sort of face, but I can't see it. I was dreading he was going to lapse into a mock Michael Caine accent... no, Gerald, just no...

I answered that I was fine, Rebecca was fine, and thanked him for his kind words about her. He deviated off and talked about the Willows for a while; his wife's uncle was there, and I'd actually met him a few times when I went in to social events.

Gerald asked me what I was working on, which he must have known, or could easily have found out. He asked me how I enjoyed working here, and obviously I answered that I really enjoyed it and found the challenge exciting etc.

"Gerald, is this my review... I thought it wasn't until next February?"

"No, good heavens, no, Thomas! No I just felt I hadn't had the chance to chat with you recently, just wanted to see how things were going!"

He asked me about a contract I'd done, but again it was something he could have found out without all this conversation.

"So. Thomas... How do you see things panning out for you in the next few years? Someone with your abilities has the world at your feet, and with Rebecca at your side, well you must be thinking about what's coming next?"

This was very strange... was he sounding me out to see if I wanted promotion? Did he wonder if I was thinking of leaving? Did he *hope* I was leaving? I really didn't know what to say. If I were to be honest with him I might say I was becoming bored, I might say I wanted a new challenge, not necessarily a promotion or more responsibility, but who would say no to that... I mumbled something meaningless again about challenges and teamwork... trite aphorisms.

"I hope I'm not being indelicate, and tell me to mind my own business, but I expect you and Rebecca will be thinking about the patter of tiny feet before too long?"

That was definitely out of line, and it stung, but again I blandly remarked that coming from a big family it was something that most people want at some point and who knows what the future will bring.

"Indeed... who knows what the future will bring...." He seemed to muse on this and was saved from continuing this mysterious interview by Vicky ringing and saying that the phone call he was expecting was on line one.

"Well, thank you, Gerald, kind of you to take an interest, thank you very much, much appreciated," I burbled and he looked the tiniest, tiniest bit guilty.

I didn't think I was going to be getting a promotion any time soon... a really fabulous reference, but no promotion...Perhaps Kylie was right, perhaps things were going to happen. I left Gerald and as I slowly closed the door I heard him say "Fraser, good to hear you!"

The only Fraser I'd ever come across was Fraser Abram, great nephew of the original Isaac Abram who had founded Lyon Abrams with his brother in-law, Nathan Lyon.

Unusually Rebecca texted me at work; could I ring her, no panic, but could I give her a ring. Well, of course I did panic. There was nothing to panic about, she was right; Ruthie had been in to see her about doing a demonstration with some of the residents. Rebecca had mentioned the cookery day I'd wanted to give her as a Christmas present... she hadn't actually said whether she'd like it or not, and Ruthie said it sounded a wonderful idea. Rebecca suggested I talk to Paul and see if he would buy the day for Ruthie as well and then they could go together.

This really cheered me up for lots of reasons; it had been such a strange weekend...I was still keeping my head bent over the computer so Kylie wouldn't catch my eye... and then Rebecca herself had been so odd yesterday evening in a way I couldn't really define. I'd tried to tell her about Tolik and his family but she wasn't really interested, such a distant connection, if it even was a connection.

I finished the call, turning away to face the window to say 'I love you,' and when I turned back I inadvertently looked at Kylie. She stuck her tongue out at me in a very rude way and I was annoyed to find myself blushing. I went back to my computer and pounded away, writing absolute nonsense. Then luckily a really boring client rang who reminded me of Rebecca's great-uncle Herbert so I was able to lose myself in trying to explain the patently obvious to the old fool in a kind and caring and professional way.

I almost felt as if I was taking refuge in the past. I plunged straight in and looked up Thomas in 1861; I jumped out of my chair and almost danced around! I couldn't believe it!! I looked back at the census form in front of me and then I actually did a little dance. If Rebecca had been here I would have given her a big kiss.

The phone rang and I snatched it up. It was Paul. I was so excited he could hardly make out what I was saying. *It wasn't certain, it wasn't absolutely certain... but it could be that Thomas is the one!*

"What are you talking about?" he interrupted my jabber. "Are you drunk? What are you on about? Why could you be the one?"

"Not me, Paul, the other Thomas Radwinter, the first Radwinter," I tried to calm myself down. I explained that I'd found Thomas originally in the village of Radwinter in Essex, I'd followed him to Surrey, and now... now he was in Easthope in 1861!! What was even better, and I felt quite emotional, Lamy and the three children were with him.

Paul laughed, and congratulated me and then asked me about the Olive Shed. It seemed a brilliant idea for Ruthie and Rebecca to go together; either he or I could drive them as wine was served with the meal at the end of the demonstration when the guests sampled what had been cooked. Then if the girls wanted, we could go out for a drink together in the evening... he and I could find a bite to eat somewhere or he could cook something...

It sounded perfect. As soon as Rebecca and Ruthie could find a date, we could check it was available and book it. I wasn't sure there would be any before Christmas, but that didn't matter.

In 1861 Thomas Radwinter was in Easthope; he was in a pub called the India Inn, and not only was he in the pub, he was the publican! I can't tell you how thrilled I was. He was no longer an agricultural labourer, which in the middle of the nineteenth century must have been a dreadfully hard life, he no longer had one child in lodgings with another family, however nice, kind and loving they were, they really were only paid to look after him, and best of all his wife, or partner as we would say, and his two babies were no longer in the workhouse.

Here he was, in Easthope, not even twenty miles from where I was sitting right now.

I calmed down and looked at the census form.

- 27 Mill Lane, the India Inn, Thomas Radwinter, married, aged 47, publican, foreign.

The India Inn! I couldn't think of a pub called that; I'm not very familiar with Easthope, or its pubs, but I thought I might remember somewhere called that.

- Lamy ditto, married, 32, wife, Radwinter
- Tolik ditto, son, aged 16, general, Radwinter
- Thirza ditto, daughter, aged 12, general, Epping
- Robert ditto, son, aged 10, scholar, Lambeth
- ... I gazed at the page feeling quite emotional emotion:
- Osman ditto, son, aged 9, scholar, Godstone
- Benjamin ditto, son, aged 8, scholar, Portsea
- Susannah ditto, daughter, aged 8 scholar, Portsea

- Taras ditto, son, aged 3, Easthope

So Thomas was the father of seven children, five boys and two girls... I looked back at my notes on Tolik Radwinski, he too had a son called Taras... these linked names must mean something, I just knew they were brothers. After they left Gdansk on two separate ships, did they ever see each other again? Imagine if I never saw my brothers again? Imagine if something terrible happened and we had to flee from our homes and get on any ship we could, if we didn't have telephones and the internet, however would we find each other again?

I felt closer to Paul and John than I ever had; somehow we were now friends as well as brothers, I felt equal to them... well almost. And Marcus?

I picked up my phone and on an impulse rang him. His wife Jill answered in her slightly reserved way, giving the name of the vicarage. I asked how she was and my nieces, Sarah and Paula, all well, and the grandchildren; she gave me various bits of news about them and for once I was interested... So Paris had learned to crawl... wonderful... Was that very young to be crawling? And Boston was going to Tiny Tumblers... what was that? A gym club for two-year-olds? Good heavens... and Phyllis and Joan were starting nursery...

"You sound very well, Thomas, you and Rebecca fine?" Jill sounded a little warmer, a little more interested. "So what's your news?"

Was she wondering whether Rebecca was pregnant, had my interest in the grandchildren been a little too keen? No news, really, I said, I was in a quiz team with John; Paul and his fiancée were coming round to dinner some time... work was OK...

She sounded a little disappointed and asked if I would like to speak to Marcus; while I waited for him to come to the phone I wondered what he thought of his grandchildren's modern names, Paris, Boston, Phyllis and Joan... opposite ends of the naming spectrum... and none of them Radwinters.

"Hello, Thomas, how are you?" he sounded dutiful. I could imagine his thin face, the piercing eyes, below straight, bushy brows, a straight nose, straight tight-lipped mouth, greying beard, wild hair.

I relayed my thin spread of the latest about us; he asked me about my work and he sounded like Gerald, except he sounded as if he'd expected great things and received a disappointment. He was obviously wondering why I'd rung, as Jill had, and I suddenly felt a little nervous...

"I'm doing some research about the family tree," I said, trying not to sound like a schoolboy who'd taken up stamp-collecting. "Finding out where we came from."

"You're doing what?" he interrupted. "You're digging into the past? Whatever gave you that idea? I'm not happy about that at all, Thomas!"

I was astonished, I'd hoped for interest, had expected disinterest, but not a sharp reprimand. I tried to explain that I wondered where the family had come from, I'd never heard the name before apart from our cousins and I just wondered...

"I don't think is a good idea at all! You don't know what you're going to find!"

I felt a bit defensive, and to my surprise I actually answered Marcus back. "Well, I think we came from the Ukraine or Poland in 1834! I think we changed our name to Radwinter from the village in Essex! What's wrong with that?"

There was silence for a second as if I'd surprised him.

"You mean you're going right back?"

"Yes, I wanted to find out how we came to be here... and I think we came to Easthope in the 1850's, Thomas Radwinter had a pub called the India Inn and he had seven children!" I spoke a little sharply, I'd thought Marcus might be interested, or at least impressed... it was the child in me wanting my big brother's approval, a big brother who never would be pleased, proud or impressed by my efforts.

"I see," again the silence as if he was thinking. "So you're not going to be poking about into... anything more recent?"

Was he thinking of Dad and Mum, I guess so... which was understandable, he probably knew much more about all that than any of us.

"Well, there's no point is there? We know when Mum and Dad were born, and Uncle Jim and Auntie Angela... No, it's where we came from, that's what I'm interested in."

"I see," I could imagine him frowning now, as he used to when he read my school reports, or when he saw that I'd got one 'B' among all the 'A's for my mock GCSEs... at least I'd managed to get all A*'s for the real thing, and for my A-levels... "Because I really would not be at all happy at you poking about..."

I interrupted him for the first time in my life. "I am not 'poking about' I am researching, and if you're not happy with it, well..." and then I couldn't think well what... I'd never spoken to him like that before, had never 'answered back'... I guess I'd never really stood up for myself.

"I didn't mean that, Thomas, I'm sorry. Let me know how you get on," he sent his regards to Rebecca and finished the call as formally as ever.

I'd hoped to ask him if he had any photos or maybe certificates, birth certificates and so on... I could order copies through MyTimeMachine but it wouldn't be the same thing as having the originals.

I wandered about the flat; I didn't know how I felt. I'd never spoken to Marcus like that before, and it was unsettling... what was more unsettling was that he hadn't told off for being rude or answering back...

Rebecca had left a Thai curry for me and when I took the lid off the container there was a delicious smell of lemon grass and curry leaves and coconut... Coconut... Kylie's mouth and tongue had tasted of coconut... and rum... and smoke...

Friday, November 15th 2013

There was such a panic before Ruthie and Paul came for dinner; we seemed to go through every cookery book and cookery magazine there was in the flat and Rebecca cooked enough practice dishes to fill the freezer. She nearly snapped my head off when I suggested she cooked one of her usual recipes, and as for me suggesting I cook something... so I just kept quiet and drove us to the shops several times, and even went out to the twenty-four hour store at midnight to get some more saffron.

I'd gone to the quiz with John, and Leo's other mates had brought a couple of friends too, so we made two teams. We didn't win, but we did quite well; I didn't drink more than a couple of pints, and I made sure I sat with my back to the wall and the table square in front of me, but there was no sign of Kylie, although the others teased me about it. If a thirty-something solicitor can have street-cred, then I think Kylie had polished mine... it made me anxious all the same.

I'd also met John for lunch again, this time at a Portuguese restaurant where we had petiscos portugueses, sort of Portuguese version of tapas; we stuffed ourselves with peixinhos da horta and ovos verdes, which the menu comically translated as garden minnows and green eggs, *garden minnows and green eggs*! - salteada de luinguiça which was some sort of sausage, camarões com amêndoas which were big fat prawns with almonds and lemon, and a sort of salad with tomatoes and chourico and quinoa, but we resisted whelk salad... that somehow didn't appeal! We didn't resist the Rioja though... but only had one glass.

I didn't have much time to do any research, but I quickly printed off various census returns, my spread sheets so far, and other things which I put in a real folder, not a virtual one. I also made a list of things I had to check so when I did have time to come back to it, I'd remember where I was up to... for some reason on MyTimeMachine this was called 'cogs, springs and pinions' rather than 'to-do list'.

In the event after all the nightmare and tension of preparation, with Rebecca in tears more than once, and me retiring to the bathroom to get to grips with myself, with a last minute trip to buy a new tablecloth and napkins with matching tablemates, the evening was wonderful. Paul and Ruthie were such pleasant and easy company, genuinely complimentary to Rebecca for the fabulous meal she'd prepared, that with a few glasses of the lovely wine Paul had brought, we were soon completely relaxed.

Rebecca had decided to go with a traditional English menu 'with a twist' she said, as the cooks in Masterchef so often do. She used only seasonal vegetables and game and put together one of the best meals I'd ever eaten. I was so proud of her... she wouldn't want to, but if she went on Masterchef, I'm sure she would win.

Rebecca loves cookery books, we have more of them than anything in the flat; a lot of my books once I've read them have to go to the charity shop, there is a LEPRA shop in town, near where John works, which has a good book section so they're always taken there... it's a little annoying sometimes when books I'd like to reread vanish, but Rebecca's right, we do only have a small flat... maybe we ought to start looking for another place... she did mention it... maybe once we've found somewhere with more bedrooms and a garden and a bigger kitchen...

A book Rebecca actually bought from the LEPRA shop is called *'English With a Difference'* by Steven Wheeler, and even though it was published nearly thirty years ago it is a favourite of hers and she's cooked lots of lovely recipes from it. I like it too, there are good illustrations and nice photographs, and the food is always interesting, 'With a Difference' as it says.

I thought her menu was too ambitious but she was really trying to impress, and I can understand that. She'd made a lot of little nibbles to start with, including tiny cheese twists with paprika. She made duck consommé with port; we'd had to have duck a couple of times leading up to this so she had the carcases to make the broth. Then we had a trio of little starters... she'd seen these small and oval dishes in a store in town and bought them before deciding what to put in them. They were in three segments, so she made potted salmon and toasted walnuts, microscopic cheese and courgette soufflés and an aubergine dip...

She presented it all beautifully, you could tell Paul and Ruthie were really impressed. For the main course we had beef in red wine with pigeon - the gravy was heavenly! - with red cabbage and apple, cauliflower cheese and roast potatoes.

Pudding had been such a dilemma for her... we'd had plenty of tears and sharp words and slammed doors over that! In the end she'd made what Steven Wheeler calls Plum and Almond Shuttle, which is like a plum and frangipane turn-over. I had to be quite firm about her not making her own puff pastry...

She actually trusted me to get the cheese; I'd forbidden her (well, told her not to) make biscuits for the cheese and bought the most expensive hand-crafted, locally made from locally milled organic flour, selection, and local butter for good measure.

It was a wonderful, wonderful, never to be forgotten meal, but I just hoped it wasn't repeated too soon... I didn't think I could stand the agony and anxiety.

As they waited for their taxi, Ruthie thanked Rebecca again.

"I know we'll have a wonderful day at the Olive Shed, Rebecca, but I doubt we'll get a meal as good as this... I mean it!" and she did.

Paul rang me later to thank me and Rebecca... I'd done nothing really, and he also asked about the other Thomas Radwinter who we hadn't mentioned during the evening. I told Paul about the surprising reaction I'd had from Marcus; he said who could ever tell how Marcus would react to anything. My two oldest brothers are such different, Marcus dry chalk and Paul rich cheese.

I called up the birth certificates of Thomas's children, the four younger ones; the actual records were handwritten, in what must have been the way everyone wrote, what looked to me the most beautiful copperplate hand.

- Osman Radwinter, 1852, male, England, Surrey, Godstone
- Benjamin Radwinter, 1853, male England, Hampshire, Portsea Island
- Susannah Radwinter, 1853, female, England, Hampshire, Portsea Island

And lastly Taras Radwinter, born here in Easthope in 1858. In those days there was no requirement to include the mother's maiden name, which was a little frustrating, but I couldn't imagine there were many people called Lamy. I just tried to imagine the household; Thomas and Lamy; Tolik was a similar age to Luke, Paul's boy, and was, I believed, the son of Thirza and Thomas, and Lamy's stepson. His occupation was general, so I guessed maybe that meant working in the pub, the same as his sister Thirza.

Then there were the four children who went to school, Robert, Osman, and the twins, Benjamin and Susannah, and at home being looked after by Lamy and possibly Thirza, little Taras.

I wasn't sure where Portsea Island was… And I found it was in Portsmouth… where the Polish Refugee Hospital was… Had Thomas brought his family across southern England in the hope of finding his brother? And he'd arrived four years too late…

In April 1849, Tolik had sailed away to South Australia with his wife and children… I checked back and looked up the dates of birth for the children, all born in Portsea, Taras 1845, Julia 1847, Casimir 1848. So the cousins Taras and Tolik would be the same age…

I imagined a family get together at the India Inn in 1861, just after the census… supposing Tolik had brought his family back… there would be the two brothers Thomas and Tolik, and the two cousins Taras and Tolik, aged 16, Julia 14, Casimir and Robert 13, Osman 9, Benjamin and Susannah 8, and little Taras 3…

I Googled the India Inn in Easthope, it didn't exist now but I came across it on a web-site devoted to defunct pubs. It is an amazing website… I didn't realise there had been so many pubs in Easthope, The Bleeding Heart, The Durham Ox, The Grasshopper, and The India Inn. I clicked on it but the information was merely that it had closed in 1962.

It was in Mill Lane, which I knew, but can't remember having been down and couldn't think of a building which might have been the pub. Perhaps John and I could go to the quiz early next week and wander round and have a look for it… It would be dark but we might be able to find it. I felt quite excited.

Now having somewhere I knew the family had lived gave me a real chance of finding out a little more about them. There were new buildings in Easthope, obviously there were, but the main pattern of the streets remained the same. I could walk where Thomas had walked, go down to the sea and look across to Farholm Island as he might have done... Maybe find the school where Osman, Benjamin and Susannah went...

Their names rang a bell and I looked back at the various spread sheets I had and with a jolt saw the connection. Lamy had been a servant to the Newells, Benjamin the father and his possibly second wife Susanna and one of their children was Osman... he was the baby of the family in 1841, only a year old, Lamy would probably have had to help look after him. Nearly twenty years later she'd called her own child Osman.

I looked down at the list of children at the imagined reunion party in the pub... something struck me... a puzzle I didn't think I would ever be able to resolve... but I just wondered... just wondered if maybe Thomas had originally been Taras... Taras Radwinski and he'd arrived in Radwinter and become Thomas Radwinter. Taras... Thomas, Taras... Thomas... He'd reverted to Radwinski (Radwinsky) when he and Lamy were in Blechingley, in order for her to be housed in the Godstone Union... Dreadful, terrible, but at least the little children would be fed and have clothes to wear and somewhere to sleep...

Was he Taras? He and his brother had each named their first born with a Ukrainian name... he'd named his own youngest child Taras...

Monday, 18th November, 2013

Having had such a good weekend, and since for once, we hadn't gone to Sunday lunch with Maggie and Phil, but had gone to meet Smithy and his wife for drinks at a pub down the coast, I felt a little more confident going into work on Monday. Smithy wasn't someone I liked very much, but he and Rebecca were great friends – must make working easy if you like your colleagues! Smithy's wife spent most of the time texting, even though I tried to chat to her… I gave up in the end…

I didn't know what the strange conversation with Gerald had been about, but I had to accept that worrying about it didn't help. I was feeling different in some way… maybe because of things with the family, not least answering Marcus back, even if it was in the most meek and mild way, and finding that Thomas had come to Easthope… or maybe after the meal with Paul and Ruthie things were better with Rebecca… maybe we could have a kid-free life and be happy, I told myself.

It seemed that everyone who could email me, had emailed me and I waded through the mail which was all important and had to be dealt with conscientiously. I printed some stuff off but when I went to the printer it had run out of paper. Reluctantly I looked round for Kylie, she attended to that sort of thing; she was nowhere to be seen and I realised I hadn't seen her this morning.

I asked Vicky if Kylie was away, but no, she was here, just not in the office. Vicky looked wonderful, almost glowing and I asked her how she was, and told her how marvellous she looked. She has very black hair, like Rebecca, but I think she might put some extra colour on it; in fact she does look a little like a smaller version of Rebecca, and I wondered for a moment if this is what my wife would look like if she ever... Vicky was pleased at the compliment and called me 'sweet', which she never has before.

I went to get some paper; the stationary cupboard for some reason is on the floor below, by the offices of a small publishing company. They didn't actually publish the books here, that was all done in Hong Kong or somewhere, but their offices were here.

I keyed in the code and then the door wouldn't open; I guess I'd put the wrong code in or pressed the wrong buttons. I concentrated and pressed again and turned the knob but the door didn't give so I gave it a shove with my shoulder and it was a replay of the time I'd ended up in the cupboard in Paul's house. The door opened suddenly and I fell in and it shut behind me.

This time I wasn't in the dark and I wasn't alone. Kylie glared at me as I crouched on the floor on hands and knees.

"What on earth's the matter?" I asked in genuine concern; her face was red and smeared where she'd been crying, she'd rubbed tears and make-up all across her cheeks.

"Fuck off and leave me alone!" she hissed and a choking sob escaped.

I got up and spontaneously and probably surprising myself as much as her, I put my arms around her and hugged her. There was no point in asking anything, she wasn't likely to tell me, but she was so upset and sobbed in my arms as I patted her shoulder and murmured that it would be alright, whatever it was.

I found a handkerchief; I really don't like tissues and always have proper cotton handkerchiefs which makes buying Christmas presents for me easy.

She wiped her face and turned away from me; she was like a cat you've just rescued, angry and a little embarrassed… not that I've ever rescued a cat…

"I just need some copy paper," and I grabbed a couple of reams and left the little room.

As I was going upstairs it struck me what a strange thing had happened… I'd probably never know what the problem was… I couldn't even imagine… unless she'd found out something about her job… she'd worried about losing it… maybe that was it.

I got on with my work but was aware all the time of Kylie's empty desk. Julie came and asked me where she was, I said I'd been looking for copy paper which didn't really answer the question.

"She's been away from her desk for half an hour," said Julie.

"Maybe she's poorly," I suggested. Julie shrugged and went back to her computer and a few minutes later Kylie came in, her face like thunder, her make-up perfect. She sat down and even from where I was I could hear her pounding her keyboard. She had her head phones on and kept her eyes focussed on the screen.

Even though Julie had just asked where she'd been, and even though I'd suggested she might be poorly, Julie stayed in her place, and so did Vicky, the pair of them frowning across at Kylie. Perhaps being pregnant made you grumpy, but Jessica my bus-buddy seemed radiant and cheerful, when she wasn't feeling queasy and nauseous.

Jessica seemed amused at my interest in her pregnancy until I confided in her, as I had to no-one else, that I thought Rebecca didn't want a family. Jessica tried to be encouraging and was definitely sympathetic, but as she didn't know Rebecca, and had never met her, she couldn't really understand why I was so sure that Rebecca wouldn't change her mind.

We'd had a few conversations about names, and the difficulty of choosing them... easy for me, Tolik, Lillah and Isabella. Jessica had patted my hand, I must have sounded sadder than I meant to.

I must have drifted off into some other thoughts because I missed the start of it; Julie and Kylie were standing a few yards from each other having quite an argument. Martin had his head down behind his computer, Gordon wasn't in the office and Vicky was just sitting staring. This was most unprofessional, a client could come in at any time.

I got up and strode over.

"Stop this!" I said firmly. "What on earth do you think you're doing? This is not the way to carry on!"

"She should not be going on a cigarette break! She's already been out of the office for half an hour without permission!" Julie was very angry.

"*She? She?* I do have a name you know!"

"If there is a problem then you should talk to Martin," I said, as Martin seemed to be burrowing in a cupboard beneath his desk.

"I'm the office senior!" Julie said, and I thought she was rather rude to me.

"Are you? Is that official? I didn't know that," I replied quite forcefully.

"Oh forget it!" Kylie said. "I was only going for a pee anyway. I'll just sit down and wait till I have permission to go to the bloody toilet!" She gave Julie a venomous glare and sat down, snapped her headphones back on and began typing furiously.

"Well, thank you for your support, Thomas!" Julie was furious. "I shall tell Gordon how you handled this!"

"Excellent, I shall be pleased to discuss it with him."

I went back to my desk and picked up the phone and dialled a random number. The random number, to my surprise was Ruthie's and she was pleased to hear from me and we had a little chat and I explained what I'd meant by the mysterious text from the Lebanese restaurant… She could do high class mezze snacks, I could see them in little boxes with dividers so each thing was separate. Rebecca had received some soap as a gift and it was in such a pretty box that I'd kept it on my desk and put paperclips and staples and picture cards from my camera in it… I apologised, Ruthie didn't want to know about paperclips… but she was laughing at me, and I'd come to realise that when she laughed at me, it was in a fond nice way, that made me smile too.

"Coffee," Kylie put a cup down beside me with less force than usual, and there was no coffee slopped over the edge but when I lifted the cup there was a big lipstick kiss drawn in the middle of the saucer. I put it down hastily, but no-one was looking at me, everyone working, including Kylie.

Wednesday, 20th November, 2013

This was the beginning of not exactly war but certainly unrest between Julie and Kylie. Vicky was on Julie's side, but didn't say anything, it was just the way she looked at Kylie, and the way she and Julie talked in low voices to each other, glancing across at her. Since I had spoken sharply to Julie she was very cool with me, and Vicky followed her lead; Martin just seemed generally embarrassed and didn't want to be drawn into anything, although he too was a little distant with me, as if I shouldn't have tried to involve him in the original tiff. At least Sandra and Gordon seemed as usual, indifferent.

The office had always been quite a pleasant place to work; obviously people had little squabbles from time to time, but this seemed different. Kylie was always what I'd heard Gordon call 'a character'; she was off quite a rough estate, had gone to a pretty dreadful school, and yet had somehow risen up to take A-levels and now, she'd told me she was studying for a degree.

Gordon and Martin had both gone to Ardales, a very posh and expensive independent school halfway between Easthope and Castair. They hadn't been there at the same time, Martin was a little older, and they'd been in separate houses, which apparently meant they were virtual strangers. Martin was less senior than Gordon, and rather than being resentful, seemed always to be sucking up to him... he was like a fair haired, washed-out version of Gordon, he even styled his thinning hair in the same way.

Gerald had gone to a boarding school somewhere so I was a little bit out on a limb having just gone to Strand High School, even though it was such a good school... in fact people moved to Strand just to be able to send their children there.

Sandra came from Northampton so I don't know what school she went to and Julie went to school somewhere in Scotland where her family had lived for a while, even though they originally came from round here. We all knew this and it had never seemed to matter but now there seemed to be a sort of elitism creeping in, little snide remarks and comments, apparently directed at no-one in particular but it was pretty obvious who the target was. It was a very subtle sort of bullying and more unpleasant because of it… and I didn't know what to do.

Kylie had said she'd given up caffeine and sugar so she wouldn't be putting money into the coffee jar any more, she'd just drink water, and I wondered if she couldn't afford to do it. It was only a couple of quid a week, nothing to me, but maybe it was too much for her. When she had mentioned it, Julie had said if she was on such a health-kick she ought to give up smoking, and Kylie had venomously replied that she already had.

Kylie seemed to be avoiding me and I was sorry because I wanted to say something… goodness knows what, to show I was on her side… because actually I was on her side.

I'd had a good time at the quiz again; we didn't win but came second and received a token for a free pint each next quiz night and again I sat with my back to the wall but this time I rather hoped Kylie would come in… not for a repeat performance, but because I wanted to talk to her… I didn't know what I wanted to say, but I was worried about her.

It was absolutely pouring down with rain when John and I met as before at the bus station and caught the bus to Easthope, so when we arrived I didn't suggest we went and looked for where the India Inn might be... in fact I didn't mention it to him.

John spent most of the journey talking about Laura... he was quite depressed although to anyone else he would have looked smiley. I realised I didn't know much about my brother, I didn't know who his friends were... I seem to remember someone called Dave and someone called Ray... He'd been friendly with the brother of his first wife, but that had gone by the wayside. John had kept in touch with Laura, just texting, and they'd met for coffee and he'd tried really hard to maintain a 'just good friends' front, but he thought she guessed how he felt. He wanted to ask if she was seeing someone else but hadn't in case it seemed as if he was either prying, or jealous... and he admitted it would have been both.

I tried to think of things to say, and did witter on as I usually do, but it seemed like meaningless platitudes. John was cheerful enough in the pub, and drank more than I did so he was quite merry when we all took the taxi back into town. It was still raining so we didn't bother with a kebab but all went our separate ways and I caught another taxi back home.

I'd enjoyed the quiz, I really had... I felt sort of... normal... as if this was what people normally did... and I was smiling as I got undressed in the bathroom because Rebecca was already asleep and I didn't want to wake her.

My phone bipped twice... a message from John... *'Thanks bro ... appreciate your wise words'*... really? The second was from Ruthie... did I fancy meeting her sometime for another food-chat session? Lunch would be nice... Lunch with Ruthie would be very nice.

The India Inn... No doubt there would be local information I could trawl, maybe old newspapers, maybe directories, maybe even Easthope Museum, a tiny but interesting place, but instead I went to the 1871 census to see how things were progressing with my family. Were they still in Easthope at the India Inn? Had they moved somewhere else, maybe not even with a pub anymore? Had they got more children? The younger children would no longer be 'scholars' and surely they couldn't all work in the pub...

"Oh no!"

"What's the matter?" Rebecca asked... she was in a grumpy mood again, for no reason that I could think of so it was probably work getting her down... she loved it but she worked so hard, was so committed, it must get her fed up sometimes. I tried to be extra considerate and loving, but somehow that irritated her, so I just tried to be quiet and not say silly or annoying things.

Jessica had mentioned that she felt very emotional at times, and sometimes snapped at David... I wondered, without much hope it might be so, if Rebecca might be pregnant, and that her protestations against having a family were because she felt a little panicky and not ready for it... I very wisely said nothing but kept my mental fingers crossed.

"I can't find Thomas!" I searched again, just general search for Radwinter and up came a group of names, Tolik, Osman, Susannah and the other children and a few others but no Thomas and no Lamy. They were all in

Easthope except for Robert and Osman; the two brothers were in a village near Castair.

"Well, perhaps he's dead!" she sounded almost brutal but I was shocked. I counted from 1815, Thomas would be in his fifties... young to die now, but in those days... what was the average age for dying...? And no Lamy either...

I had a quick search for what would be the average age to die in Britain in the 1860's but came up with nothing concrete... and anyway it didn't matter... they were gone... I wondered if they might be buried in Easthope. There was the new cemetery on the Strand Road, but the old cemetery was in Backtown, an area which had been the back of the town when Easthope had been a busy little harbour and fishing village.

I returned to the census feeling a little sad... but obviously Thomas had to die at some time... I pencilled in an approximate date of death, c1815 – c1860's on my wall chart and went back to see what was happening with the children.

The family, most of them were still at the India Inn

- Tolik Radwinter, head, married, 26, publican, Radwinter
- Emma Radwinter, wife, married, 22, publican's wife, Easthope
- Thomas Radwinter, son, unmarried, 4, infant, Easthope
- Emma Radwinter, daughter, unmarried, 1, infant, Easthope

So Tolik had taken over his family pub, and how wonderful, he had a wife Emma, and two children, another little Thomas, and an Emma. I quickly called up their birth certificates, his wife Emma born 1849, little Thomas 1867 and little Emma 1870.

Also in the pub

- Thirza Radwinter, sister, aged 22, umbrella maker assistant, Epping
- Benjamin Radwinter, brother, aged 18, instructor, Portsea
- Susannah Radwinter, sister, aged 18 teacher of music, Portsea
- Taras Radwinter, brother, aged 13, scholar, Easthope
- Albert Radwinter, brother, aged 10, scholar, Easthope
- Georgiana Radwinter, sister, aged 9, scholar Easthope
- Cazimir Radwinter, brother, aged 8, scholar, Easthope

Cazimir… that rang a bell and looking back I found the details of Tolik Radwinski who went with his family to Australia… they too had a son, he and Julia, a son Casimir… this pattern of names was too coincidental… could Thomas and Tolik be naming their sons after another or older brother, their father, an uncle? This wasn't tangible proof, but it was proof to me that Tolik and Thomas really were brothers… I went to the family tree and wrote Casimir as the father of Thomas Radwinter and Tolik Radwinski with a big question mark.

The Radwinters didn't seem to have easy lives… Tolik Radwinter, younger than I am, was here in Easthope running a pub with his wife and two children, plus seven brothers and sisters… even though the older ones were working and must be contributing to the household, it would be very hard to have that many people living in a small pub... and I knew the buildings in Mill Street were very small, I remembered that.

I called up and printed the remaining birth certificates for the children, Albert 1861, Georgiana 1862 and Cazimir 1863... so Lamy and the first Thomas must have died between 1863-1871... I looked for a death certificate for Lamy, putting off looking for Thomas. It took a little finding because she was Lamy Coote again, 1863, birth year 1828, age 35... Thirty-five... nine children in fifteen years... and then she died...

My mum had died at fifty-two, when I was eighteen, she'd had four children...

Feeling very sombre I put Thomas's name into the search with dates 1862-1871... and came up with nothing. I tried Ths, Thos, T Radwinter, I even tried Taras Radwinter, Taras/Thomas Radwinsky/Radwinski, but still nothing. I tried Radwinter and Radwinski/Radwinsky without any name... nothing... no Radwinters had died, not even poor Lamy who had finally reverted to Coote... which seemed cruel somehow...

So where was Thomas... once again he'd vanished.

It was a nearly a month until Christmas, and by some fluke because there had been a cancellation or something, Ruthie and Rebecca were going to the Olive Shed on Thursday. Because Paul was more flexible with his work... as the boss he could delegate, he would act as taxi; he had some business to do in Overstaunton and he would pick them up afterwards. I would drive over to his house after work. It all sounded very satisfactory.

I kept watching Rebecca secretly for any other signs she might be pregnant… but she didn't seem ill in the mornings, she hadn't gone off or onto any particular food, she was pleased she was losing weight on the 5:2 diet… but she still seemed bad tempered with me. She even snapped at me because I was looking at her in a funny way, when I replied it was because I liked looking at her, she was lovely, she gave me what I thought was a strange look, so I'd gone back to my work… actual work, not Radwinter research.

Monday, November 25th 2013

I was walking towards work on Monday when someone jumped on my back as if for a piggy-back, nearly giving me heart failure. It was Kylie, of course. It was snowy and slippery and when she jumped down and linked arms with me, I complained that I could have fallen over. She laughed and called me a twat. I didn't mind, it was nice to see her cheerful again, even though she was rather alarming. She had very pink lipstick on and had done her eye make-up differently.

"What are you staring at?" she asked as we went past a baker's shop which was sending delicious steamy smells out into the gloomy morning.

"I was just thinking how nice you look," I said and could have bitten my tongue; I'd answered her as I would answer Rebecca.

"Don't be an idiot," she said but she looked a little taken aback.

"OK, I was thinking how horrid you look," I replied feebly trying to make a joke.

I suddenly couldn't resist the smell of the bakery and turned round and we went back to the shop. They'd just brought a tray of croissants through and I just couldn't help it... they looked too delicious.

"What do you want?" I asked Kylie; I couldn't help thinking how upset she'd been... catching her in the stock cupboard like that had somehow got me over feeling awkward about her kissing me... she'd obviously been drunk and had just been playing a trick.

"Nothing, I don't eat in the mornings," she replied but she was staring at some sausage rolls in a tray beside the croissants.

Suddenly I knew she was really hungry and I thought she looked thinner. She is a slim girl anyway, but I thought she looked a little gaunt... I don't know anything about her personal circumstances, but I'd heard Julie making some sneering remark about Primark and I knew it was a cheap place because Rebecca had mentioned it.

I don't know what Kylie earned, but if she was paying for a degree, well, that wasn't cheap. I bought two large sausage rolls and two croissants.

We walked on to the office and she seemed to be drooping as if she was tired and she didn't say anything rude or silly to me. We got to the doorway and I thrust the bag of sausage rolls into her hand.

"Your breakfast," I said and before she could say or do anything I moved quickly inside and hurried over to the lift.

I went straight to my desk, suddenly thinking how stupid I was. Knowing Kylie she would come in and dump the sausage rolls on my keyboard with some obscene remark about them…

"Thomas!" Julie came over to me, and she was smiling which made a change from how she'd been recently. "Somehow we've forgotten to organize the Christmas 'do'… we made a booking for Honor's in Easthope, if you remember but then we had to cancel because it clashed with that big conference Monty and Gerald are going to in Manchester… so we've managed to get a table at the Oriel… there are a couple of evenings available, I just wanted to check which is best for you, and whether you would prefer us to be with or without partners."

I mumbled something about dates and got out my phone to check whether there was anything Rebecca had organised. I didn't mind either way about partners; Rebecca had been keen to come to every social event at the firm at one time, now she wasn't bothered, so she said, but I don't think she likes Gordon. He'd made some joking remark once which had offended her; he was good at being offensive in his sly, slimy way. He had a dry skin and very narrow lips; he reminded me of a rather nasty lizard, and I'd cheered Rebecca up by telling her that. She'd been at school with Martin's fiancée and they didn't like each other… oh what fun we always had on our work 'do'… not.

"Isn't it rather expensive there?" I asked as I replied that either date would be fine… but I would double check with Rebecca.

"Oh we can afford to splash out once a year, can't we? I've emailed the menu to you, so let me know a definite date."

I could afford to splash out, sure, but could Kylie? She'd slipped into the office without me noticing and was at her computer already working, no sign of the brown slightly greasy paper bag which had held the sausage rolls.

I had to meet a client to discuss updating his will, nothing very exciting or difficult but he was an elderly bore who was determined to make mountains out of the tiniest molehills and also tell me all about his life in the rubber extrusion industry; he was very wealthy, gave the office a lot of business, was distantly related to Monty's wife and for some reason he likes me... so I had to spend an hour and a half *(... an hour and a half!)* with him, going over the microscopic alterations he wanted to make to his will.

When I got back into the office there was that sort of lull there is sometimes when everyone seems to be between jobs.

"OK everyone," Julie called. "It's booked, no partners, table for nine at the Oriel on the 18th of December! I've sent you all the details, it's all booked and I'll need a deposit of fifteen pounds, as soon as possible."

Oh joy. This would be one tortuous evening... Rebecca didn't like these events any more, and I certainly didn't. Everyone gets very drunk... not that I mind getting drunk, and then we go onto a club which I really don't mind, and somehow I always make a fool of myself and then seem to spend the time till Easter hoping that everyone will forget It. Last year we'd been to a new curry house which was very good but I'd eaten too much and drank too much and lost my wallet and had to walk home without my coat because I'd left it in the restaurant when we'd gone on to some club.

The year before had been a Chinese place with a similar pattern, except thankfully, Rebecca had been with me so I'd managed to restrain myself. We'd had good meals in nice surroundings, and reasonably priced… the Oriel was completely different… I looked at the menu with dismay, not for myself but for Kylie, how could she afford £35 before drinks?

"That OK for everyone? OK Thomas? OK Kylie? We want everyone there, no excuses!"

And I thought, *what a cow you are Julie, what a real cow.*

As I did sometimes, I hung back from pressing on with the family, and deviated back to Blechingley, or Bletchingley as it is now. I also thought I should find out about Portsea Island, it's in Portsmouth which is somewhere I don't know but looks nice from my brief investigation… but one thing at once, so Bletchingley.

There's a village web-site which tells me how charming the village is, which I already knew from doing my Google search and trying to find the workhouse. It's a medieval village, dating back to Saxon times, and near the M25… which would be handy if I ever go to visit, which I would love to do. Apparently it has a historic centre, which again I saw on Google, lots of really old looking houses, some dating back to the 1500's, good heavens! There is a farm on Brewer Street which dates back to the 1400's, it's a Grade I listed building… Brewer Street… Brewer Street where Thomas Radwinsky lodged with the widow Collister and her family, while his little son was with the Charlwoods, and his wife and two other children were in the workhouse…

Bletchingley is really picturesque. I stopped for a moment and thought that maybe I could do a family trail, maybe John would come with me if Rebecca wouldn't... we could start in Harwich, and go to Radwinter (how desperately I want to go there!) we could look at the other places mentioned like Saffron Walden, then we could go through Epping to Lambeth and then to Portsmouth.

Back to Bletchingley where the High Street is very wide because there used to be a market there. It sounds a good place for me and John to go, five pubs within walking distance and an Indian restaurant! If by some chance Rebecca wanted to come with me there are antiques shops (shops, plural) and a coffee shop.

Like Radwinter, the village church in Bletchingley is St Mary's and it's over nine hundred years old, and part of the building dates from 1090... that's only twenty-four years after the Norman Conquest! I read on; there was a spire but it was destroyed by lightning and there is a village pond which never dries out and was mentioned in the Doomsday Book... Radwinter was mentioned in the Doomsday Book too. Nearby is a Tudor mansion where Anne of Cleeves lived...

I came across another site which told me just a little about Bletchingley castle: it was built by a Norman knight, on the site of an Iron Age hill fort. One of the reasons it's famous is that the knights who murdered that turbulent priest (you see, I do remember some history from school) stopped at Bletchingley Castle on the way to murder Thomas á Becket in Canterbury.

... this could be a real history trail as well as a family history trail!

Tuesday, November 26th 2013, evening

It was quiz night, and it was also a fine, pleasant day drifting into a fine pleasant evening; I texted John and told him I was going to stay in town then go to Easthope early to have a look at some Radwinter stuff if he wanted to come with me, otherwise I'd meet him at the Lark. I'd eat in town - I'd wondered about going to Leo's restaurant, Nonna Ysabel, but wondered if it might seem I wanted a cheap or free meal as we were becoming friends now.

John messaged me back and said he was intrigued and would love to come on a Radwinter hunt, did I want to eat first; there was a sushi bar just opened, did I fancy it? Sounded a great idea so we met and I brought him up to date with the latest I'd found out about the family, and showed him the family tree I'd made on MyTimeMachine.

I told him about the mystery of Thomas's lack of death certificate, and wondered if he'd gone back to Poland or the Ukraine… I didn't know what the political situation was in 1860's-1870's Eastern Europe…

"Perhaps he's gone to Australia in search of his brother? Perhaps his wife dies and he suddenly thinks about the fragility of life etc… you said he was in Portsmouth for a bit, maybe he found out his brother had gone to Oz, so now he's settled and his children are earning and the oldest one's married, maybe he tries to find his brother."

John was a genius! It made perfect sense… I might be disappointed, but it was worth looking for him… but maybe Thomas had disappeared from England as mysteriously as he'd arrived and I would never find him… but at least this gave me an idea of where to look.

It also occurred to me that Thomas moved around quite a bit, to England and Radwinter, to Epping, to Lambeth, to Blechingley, to Portsea and finally to Easthope... and that is only what I know; he might have been in other places too!

I was pondering on this when John said one of the nicest things anyone has ever sent.

"Well if my little brother had gone missing, I'd search the world to find you," he gave me the Radwinter look, the piercing blue eyes, and I felt my own eyes prick with tears.

I just smiled at him, he grinned and we decided to count our little bowls and pay up. We caught the bus and arrived in Easthope at about quarter to eight. The quiz kicked off at nine so we were in plenty of time and it was pleasant to wander for a little.

John wanted to check out the display in the other bookshop owned by the Elgards, the original one in Easthope; there was a certain amount of rivalry between the two shops, the woman who was managing this branch seemed to think there was a competition and she'd caused a little unpleasantness with John... I understood about having unpleasantness at work, and I told John a bit about it.

He laughed at the memory of Kylie, it still made me uneasy and I felt a little squirmy at the thought.

"Just enjoy the memory, bro, she's gorgeous! Pity she's too young for me, I wouldn't mind some action there... count yourself lucky!"

I stuttered and protested and tried to change the subject... the memory of Kylie kissing me, her mouth...

"Here's Mill Lane!" I exclaimed rather too loudly. I realised I should have checked the number of the India Inn on the census, it had a number, and even if it had changed in the hundred and fifty odd years, it would have given me some idea.

Easthope is a funny little town; it's a seaside town but rather off the beaten track and seems almost in a time warp. Quite a few of the older houses have been bought and tarted up as holiday homes because people from elsewhere think it's quaint. There are more shops selling craft items than there are shops selling fruit and vegetables, and since there have been a couple of supermarkets opening on the outskirts, several of the smaller places have closed.

There are still little pockets of older houses, probably owned by landlords and rented to local people and not holiday makers, which are run down and in need of renovation. The problem is, anyone wanting to buy them would be taking away more reasonably priced accommodation for ordinary people.

I know this because several of the crappy houses we'd lived in when I was a kid had been bought, done up, then sold for extraordinary amounts.

"This reminds me of Fletcher Street," said John, reading my thoughts; Fletcher Street was where he'd last lived with us before he followed Paul and left home. Then there'd been me and Mum… not a happy time… and then we'd moved somewhere worse than Fletcher Street…

It was a narrow street, one side was the lower part of the remains of a back wall of some building, maybe an old warehouse had stood here since we were so near where the wharf had been. The row of terraced houses in actual fact weren't too bad, or wouldn't have been if they'd been properly maintained. They were solid looking brick built, with yellow Castair bricks... or in the best condition they were yellow.

Among the row of maybe a dozen houses there was the occasional one which looked as if it was cared for, but too many of them looked lived in but neglected as if they were rented, maybe by students, maybe by others who didn't care or couldn't afford to care about their property.

"This is a bit sad," said John in a low voice. I was glad he was with me, I wouldn't have wanted to come down here at this time on my own... but maybe I'm just cowardly and easily intimidated, or maybe I've been beaten up by bullies too often...

As we walked past a couple of the houses on the narrow badly paved and rubbish strewn path, dogs barked from within, huge, deep voiced dogs by the sound of it. Potholes in the road were big mucky puddles which we had to pick our way round in places where there kerb was broken, treading carefully in the dark.

There were a few cars parked, but no sign of anyone; curtains and blinds were drawn, one window we passed seemed to have a sheet stuck to the window with Sellotape... altogether it was tatty and rather sad because the houses themselves were decent, and could have been nice.

There was no sign of a pub or any house which could have been a pub. At the end of the terrace was a little alley which no doubt ran down to another which was along the backs. We were quite near the River Hope, I could smell it, the tide must be coming in.

On the other side of the alley were some bigger buildings, a similar age to the terrace, but looking more as if they had been businesses; their rendered walls must have once been white. We walked past and the very last of them, on the corner of a track leading down towards the wharf, undoubtedly had been a pub.

"I think this might have been the India Inn," I exclaimed. I would have to come back when it was light and take some photos, if I dared. Maybe during the day the place wouldn't be as threatening. "Well, this certainly was a pub, whether it was the India Inn, I don't know... do you think there were more buildings further down?"

Beyond where we stood was an open area which suggested other buildings might have been pulled down; now it had lorries parked there and a few trailers. There was no security to speak of, or none visible, and I thought that I wouldn't like to leave my lorry here, if I had one, which obviously I haven't.

"I don't think so; the river runs along there, and this must have been like another quay or wharf... Maybe there were more warehouses, like back there?" John had pulled a beany hat on and I thought he looked almost goblin like with his sharp features and little beard making his chin seem longer in the yellowy light from the street lamp on the other side of the road.

It was the only light on Mill Lane... I hadn't noticed any others as I passed, but maybe they were here and broken, or maybe there were none. I turned back to the old pub; the main door was on the corner, welcoming in its day regulars from the own, or from whatever had been there before. It would have been just right for anyone finishing work loading or unloading the ships which used to come up the river to here, and the ships' crew, just right for them to drop in for a pint or two.

There was a large window round the corner, next to the entrance, all boarded up and had graffiti tags sprayed all over it; and there was another smaller boarded window on the Mill Lane side. I looked at the upper floor and counted the windows... how would the Radwinters have managed with all those children? No wonder Robert and Osman had left home by the time Tolik had the pub in 1871; with him and his wife and two little children... they probably didn't have a bathroom, they probably didn't have hot water, but they had love and the family... I hoped they had love...

"What are you thinking about?" John asked, his shoulders hunched and I realised there was a mist in the air, rolling off the river probably. "Sometimes you go somewhere and I've no idea what you're thinking."

"In 1871 Thomas had disappeared, his wife had died, his oldest son had the pub and was living here with his wife and two children. Thomas's next two sons had left home," I needed to find out where they were and what they were doing. "His four other sons and his three daughters were all living here... how did they all live in this one place? How did they manage?"

"I think we should go to the Easthope Museum some time, they may not be able to tell us about this place, but they might be able to show us something about life in the 1870's or whenever you said... there's a big exhibition, or there used to be, about Easthope the port... we could go and have a look, couldn't we?"

Couldn't we... I grinned, then shivered, it was almost raining and the Lark was not far away, an open pub, with a log fire and good beer and a quiz which we might win this week… and friends.

"I just want to go and look at the front door…"

There was a worn step and the wide door which looked as if it might even be original, had a white notice in a plastic bag stuck to it; it looked like a planning notice, or something official, but there was no way of reading it in the dark with it splattered with drops of rain. There were decorative columns on either side, stuck with flyers of some sort.

There was a big round door knob and I reached out and touched it. I nearly had a heart attack as it was flung open and to my astonishment, and to hers, Kylie stood there. I don't know who was more shocked. John exclaimed something, he was startled as well.

"*What the fuck are you doing here*?" she shrieked and looked as if she was going to attack me.

"I-I-I-I - " I was stuck in a stammer and literally couldn't speak.

She leapt past me, shouldering me out of the way and slamming the door behind her; she shoved John so he fell backwards, tripped over something and ended up sitting on the wet road, and then she almost literally flew down the street as if pursued. I know I've said 'literally' twice…

Stunned I helped John up.

"Your friend from the pub!" he exclaimed as he got to his feet. "Didn't you say you work with her?"

The pub was boarded up, surely no-one lived here, surely Kylie didn't live here? It was a mystery, and, pondering on it, and a little shaken, we wandered back to the Lark to have a beer before the quiz started... and this time I sat on a stool, not with my back to the wall.

Wednesday, November 27th 2013

Jessica was so excited; she'd had a scan and showed me the photos of her little child growing within her. I was thrilled for her and gazed enviously at the grainy picture, the tiny but clearly defined head, the little arms, one miniature hand appearing to be doing a thumbs up. She and David were calling the baby Riley for the moment, because the person who'd done the scan had exclaimed 'blimey, Riley!' at the little fist with its thumb up.

Their surname is Sampson and I said I thought Riley Sampson sounded nice... and although they were only calling the bump Riley, Jessica agreed with me... and said maybe her child would actually be Riley Sampson, although they were dithering over Frances or Ian at the moment. We walked up to where she turned off and then stood chatting for a little. It was sunny again, the miserable winter weather had disappeared for a moment, and we had a brilliant sky and sun making the few remaining golden and red leaves on the ornamental trees shine like jewels.

"Do you know that girl?" Jessica asked. Kylie was on the opposite side of the road, scowling at me. My heart sank.

"Yes, we work together," I replied. The traffic was speeding by, and not even Kylie could cross.

Jessica said goodbye and headed off to work and I stood and waited for Kylie; my heart was thumping, and I gripped my inhaler. The traffic slowed enough for Kylie to dodge between the cars.

"What were you doing last night?" she demanded. I'd half expected her to come into the pub, and the anxiety had put a dullness on my enjoyment of the evening, even though we once again won.

I didn't know what I would have said if she had come in… but in the event we didn't see her, although John had asked me about her… he was quite interested I think.

Now, in the cold of morning with specks of snow whipping about us, Kylie looked ready to hit me; she was so angry.

"I was looking for my family's pub," I wondered whether to take her arm and begin to walk her towards work.

"There isn't a pub down there, don't lie!!

"That house… the house where you were, that used to be a pub and it was called the India Inn and my ancestor Thomas Radwinter was there with his wife and ten children, and then she died and I think he went to Australia but I'm not really sure, I haven't checked the shipping lists because John only told me last night, but I'm guessing he might have gone there to look for Tolik – that's Tolik his brother, not Tolik his son, because Tolik his son was left with his own wife, not his step-mother who died but his wife and their two children, so how they all managed I don't know because although Robert and Osman had left - "

"For God's sake! I wish I hadn't asked!" she was calming down a little.

I tried to tell her again a little more clearly but she still didn't know what I was talking about, just stood staring fiercely at me, her nose red as it had been when I'd caught her crying; her golden skin looked sallow in the cold and there were shadows beneath her eyes.

"Who was that guy with you, and don't tell me a story, just tell me who he was!"

She was shivering and when I looked more carefully at what she was wearing, I saw that her jacket which she was hugging round her was just a thin fashionable thing, and although she had leggings she didn't have any socks on, just those funny little flat shoes which I don't know how they stay on people's feet... Rebecca had some but gave up wearing them because they kept slipping off.

I took Kylie's arm quite firmly.

"I'm going to buy you a coffee and then I'll tell you what I was doing so you understand that it was just a coincidence and I wasn't spying on you or whatever you think I was doing there."

"I don't want any fucking coffee!" but she let me pull her a little way up the High Street where there was a tiny little coffee bar with a single table by the counter but all the other seats downstairs.

"Well. I'll buy you a fucking hot chocolate!" I replied, feeling unexpectedly in control. If she liked John, and he liked her... I wasn't sure how old she was, probably older than she seemed, maybe twenty-four, twenty-five; from the little things she said I knew she'd had to take an extra year to do her A-levels, then worked in a couple of offices before she got the job with us which was two years ago.

She didn't really resist but went down into the little seating area where I knew there was a heater because sometimes it gets too hot. I got a double espresso for me and a hot chocolate with cream and sprinkles and marshmallows and a flake. I was tempted to buy her a cake or a pastry or a sandwich but I didn't think she'd accept that.

She looked a little warmer but still combative.

"I haven't got any change," she said as I put the chocolate in front of her.

"That's alright, you can pay next time, and I'll have a double carrot cake."

I began to tell her again about the pub but in a more controlled way, and that it was a coincidence that we'd been there.

"Why were you trying to open the door?"

"I wasn't… I just thought that maybe if it was the original door then maybe it was the original doorknob, and maybe Thomas had opened it… but obviously it can't be, you couldn't have a hundred and fifty year old door knob."

She smiled a little and I thought she was going to call me a knob. I finished my coffee and told her I'd better get to work, I had a call to make first thing to the old buffer whose will I was rewriting. I told her in quite a bossy way to stay where she was and finish her chocolate and then to pick me up a Financial Times from the newsagent near the office. I put some change on the table then rushed off, anxious that she would do something stupid if we went in to work together.

I looked up umbrella makers and in nineteenth century Easthope there was an umbrella-maker called James Dean, yes really, James Dean & Sons. I'd never ever thought about umbrellas, they've always been there, everyone knows what they are and I'm sure there aren't many people who ever actually think about them or how they are made, or their history.

Maybe if I'd had to answer a question in the quiz about umbrellas I might have guessed they started as sort of sunshades, parasol sort of things, and obviously parasol is a word which means against the sun, protecting against the sun. And I think I might have guessed they came from China or Egypt... and I might even have guessed that umbrella was somehow linked to umbra or shadow... but that was as far as my knowledge of umbrellas went. Thirza worked for an umbrella maker... was it James Dean she was working for?

I found a really interesting site about umbrellas from which I found out that waterproof versions of the parasol had started in the early 1700s and that a French purse maker had first developed a way of making a folding umbrella. Whalebone was used to make the ribs, and then when steel was invented that was used instead...

I came across another site which told me about an umbrella manufacturer which still makes umbrellas today, founded in 1809, James Ince & Sons of Spitalfields, and the sixth generation, Richard is still busy making beautiful umbrellas.

I spent a long time looking at this site, wondering which of the jobs Thirza might have been doing, and wondering how well-paid her job had been. I would guess that maybe she'd been doing cutting and sewing of the fabric... but I can't find any information about James Dean & Sons at the moment, so I will just have to imagine her working.

I looked up schools in Easthope but I couldn't find where Benjamin might have been an instructor, nor where Susannah might have been a teacher of music. Tolik, their uncle had been a drummer with the Polish Army... I ought to look up passenger lists for Thomas... but once again a sort of reluctance came over me in case I didn't find him... or in case I found he'd gone to America and started a new life, abandoning his children... I couldn't believe this, somehow.

So I went back to the census and tried to find where Robert and Osman might be. They were not that far away... they were living in the village of Baster, now part of Castair... but when Robert and Osman were there it was a village... and they worked as brick maker's assistants, and the brick maker, I discovered was a Mr John Smith. I was reminded of the number of bricklayers there'd been in Blechingley in 1851, some living in the same street as Thomas when he'd lodged there under the name of Radwinsky.

I sat back and wondered what to do next... check passenger lists, go to 1881, maybe look at newspapers archives as someone had suggested when I was telling them about what I was doing. I was almost tempted to click 'search all records' but as a beginner I wanted to do things methodically and to do them in my way... it was becoming an emotional journey as well as just academic.

I looked up Robert in 1881; the page looked very much the same as previous censuses, still handwritten, but it interested or maybe should have appalled me that the last column had, after the *'Where born'*, a final column entitled *'If (i) Deaf-and-dumb, (ii) Blind, (iii) Imbecile or idiot, and (iv) Lunatic'*.

Perhaps at Robert's age of thirty-three it wasn't surprising that he'd married Fanny Collins, and had four little girls, and a boy; he was still brick making. I deviated slightly to look at the history of brick making… obviously it's an occupation that's thousands of years old, and was pretty much the same until the middle of the nineteenth century… which tied in with my family.

As with many industries, over the centuries brick making had been small scale, just a couple of men, digging the clay, forming it into bricks, usually by forcing it into moulds of some sort, letting it dry, baking it in a kiln. There was a site I found which simply describes the process and how things changed, including the different kilns which were developed to be more efficient, hotter, safer. Apparently, as well as there being brick works as we would understand them, settled in one place, there were smaller works set up where there was a lot of building going on. Castair had been a bit of a boom town in the nineteenth century… I wondered why Blechingley had so many workers connected to bricks.

There was an interesting piece of information which linked the improvement in sanitation and the clearance of many of the city slums, to the huge surge in brick-making. It boomed through the 1880's and into the twentieth century. Clay was vital to the industry, and the sophisticated railway system and improved roads aided the efficient delivery of the raw materials in, and the finished bricks out.

Robert, Thomas's second son, had moved and was living on the far side of Castair in Bunstead, which was now a 'new town' with masses of new housing… all made of bricks… Robert would have been busy if he'd still been here.

He was still married to Fanny (now there is a name which has dropped totally out of fashion and I cannot imagine it ever reviving) and his daughters were Mary, Jane, Annie and Susan, his son was William … I 'cheated' in my way of following the story and looked at Robert in 1891, a different address, and another daughter, Grace… he was still in the brick making industry but he was now manager… and in 1901, with all five daughters and son living at home, but Fanny was missing, possibly married.

The 1911 census was very different; *'This Schedule must be filled up and signed by, or on behalf of, the Head of the Family, or other person in occupation, or in charge, of the dwelling (house, tenement or apartment)',* and the actual form was very detailed. This was the last census available; Robert was at another address, now in Castair, and his two eldest daughters were still living at home, Mary and Jane, and staying with him were two small boys, Sidney and Arthur Radwinter, described as grandsons. Also in the house were two women described as 'servants'… it sounded as if Robert was happy and prosperous and had family…

I didn't like to do this, but I checked Robert's death record; he'd died in 1931 at the age of eighty three, in Castair… this didn't depress me… he'd had a difficult beginning to his life, from being in the workhouse in Blechingley, and then down to Portsea before arriving in Easthope. He and his brother had left the family home and gone into brick making, no doubt being just labourers to their master, and he'd worked his way up to living in a large house in Castair with servants, children and grandchildren. To be sure his wife had died, but he must have looked back on his life and decided that on the whole it had been good… well, I hope he did.

I followed Osman now; he too married but he moved away and by 1891 he was in Birmingham with his wife, Estelle, and his four children, George, Henry, Maud and Harriet; he'd become a builder and by 1911 his children had all left home and he and Estelle had three servants and was still described as 'manager building', so no doubt was still working. Estelle died in 1920, and Osman died three years later. So maybe there were Radwinters in Birmingham... and again they would not be too distantly related... I have yet to find a direct connection to our family from any of Thomas's sons... but I am becoming more and more convinced there will be one.

I looked at the remaining brothers, Tolik, Albert, Benjamin, Taras, Cazimir... which one of them was my grand-parent, however many greats ago? I was excited but determined not to hurry in my quest... I wanted to do it properly, I wanted to be sure...

Thursday, 28th November 2013

Rebecca and Ruthie had a wonderful day at the Olive Shed; in fact it was so good that Rebecca even texted me halfway through to say how wonderful it was, and how much she was enjoying herself. I don't mind that she doesn't text me about things, that's just her way, although she does use her phone a lot and is always texting her friends, but she uses it just to let me know things or ask me things, or remind me of things, and that's fine... I don't mind. But... but I was thrilled to get her text.

It cheered me up because although I couldn't put my finger on what was wrong, something was; sometimes she seemed to be looking at me and I couldn't read her expression, and when I asked she made some remark such as she was just thinking about something, or just thinking about nothing in particular. She would play her game in the spare room but often the door would be shut; I always knocked, obviously I did, but I always got the feeling she'd closed the screen or changed it to the game, as if she was looking at something else. I didn't mind, of course I didn't... maybe with Christmas coming up it was to do with presents and decorations... it seemed that every year we had to have new decorations for the flat and the tree, even though we didn't get many visitors. I didn't mind... it was her way ... well, I mean it's *our* way of doing Christmas!

I know she Skyped her friends from her game a lot, but most evenings now I could hear her murmuring in a low voice as she played her game; maybe it was coming to a crucial part in the buying and selling of goods.

She also seemed quiet... not that she's ever noisy, she's not one to be chatting all the time, or singing or humming or anything like that... but she seemed quiet in a different way.

I could write a whole book about occupations in the nineteenth century if I deviated and followed every trail that caught my interest... But I had to stay focused... Later when I'd found the direct link to us... Then if I wanted... And maybe now I did want to... I couldn't imagine not wanting to find out everything I could about Thomas and his family.

I'd followed Robert and Osman, now I looked at Thirza in 1881... And she was not to be found. However, I wasn't too disheartened because, just as her three brothers had got married, so might she have done... And her name would have changed to that of her husband.

I went to marriages and typed in her name and it bobbed up straight away... She'd married a James Dean, no doubt of the umbrella making family. He might not be the owner of the business as on the census when I traced him he was the same age as Thirza, and there they were with a child, a little boy called James. I found another James Dean in Easthope who was aged fifty-nine... And a third James aged eighty-five. The middle one was an umbrella maker, the older one was living on his own means with his wife, another Fanny, like Thirza's little niece.

I would follow Thirza's life another time, Benjamin too was married and now living in Cambridge... I used to have this notion that people in the past didn't travel but stayed in their own village or town for the most part, maybe going to the nearest big city or town once in a blue moon, or maybe going to market or a fair or a family event, a wedding maybe or a funeral, but my family seemed to be going all over the place. Susanne could not be found; there was no record of her having married or died so for the moment she would be another mystery but somehow now I had confidence that these mysteries would be solved, one way or another.

The phone rang and Rebecca answered it, so quickly that I wondered if she was expecting a call from someone, but in fact it was Marcus for me. He greeted me in his cool way, asked how I was, asked how work was going and then asked when we would be able to get together. Leading up to Christmas is very busy time, and Marcus is a good vicar and works hard, especially for older people and lonely people, and I knew he does a lot of work with people with addiction and alcohol issues... Surprising, or maybe not surprising, thinking about Mum.

He suggested a date but when I asked Rebecca, who is similarly very busy at the old folks' home at this time of year, she wasn't free, nor any other dates Marcus suggested. I was getting anxious, feeling as if we were being awkward with him, but he was completely understanding. Rebecca suggested I went to see him and Jill on my own on the original date... I didn't really want to do that but she was so insistent that we settled it, and Marcus asked if I would stay overnight. He might be a vicar but he likes a drink like any ordinary bloke would, which definitely *is* surprising when you think about Mum.

He asked me how I was getting on with my search and I gave him a rough outline; I would tell him more and show him the family tree when I went to visit. He seemed a little more laid back about it, but did just mention again that he didn't think it would be a good idea to look at the immediate family. I reassured him...what was the point when we knew it already, and, I didn't add, no doubt he was thinking that the recent past, our own lives, hadn't a been the happiest so why would we want to even think about that?

Rebecca said she'd get the presents for Marcus's family sorted out and I could take them with me, she just needed to wrap them. I left all that to her... I can't remembered which of John's wives it was but one of them always went mad on wrapping and did the most beautiful presents you could imagine...she could have opened a business wrapping presents for people... It was lovely except it then became a sort of competition between her and Rebecca as to who could produce the most stylish, tasteful and elegant gifts for the family... I got a bit fed up with it I can tell you. Now John is single again but the mad present wrapping activity continues...

Saturday, November 30th 2013

It was Saturday and I was in town with Rebecca, continuing the Christmas shopping; usually she drags me round asking my opinion and then disagrees with everything I say. That makes her sound argumentative, she isn't really, she just wants me to agree with her, and I always think I'm hopeless at buying presents because I always seem to have bought the wrong thing. However, today, she suggested we went off in different directions and meet up later.

I wandered round to John's book shop but he wasn't working today; it didn't matter, it's always pleasant in there and I spent a while looking at some history books, wondering if any would help me with learning more about life in the nineteenth century.

There was a local history section, but it was full of newly published books for the Christmas shopper, lovely, interesting, but not what I wanted. I was looking for things about pubs or bricks or umbrella makers... maybe I was looking in the wrong way, and I kept getting distracted by books about other things. I bought Rebecca a book on Italian regional cookery which I hope she will like as it has the recipe for the chocolate and chestnut dessert.

I left the shop and was just rambling along, killing time really, when I passed the LEPRA charity shop and remembered that it always had quite a good selection of books, unusual books; it was where Rebecca had bought her favourite,' *English With a Difference'*. I glanced in the window, with its Christmas display and then turned in to the doorway and bumped straight into someone coming out.

I apologised and then realised it was Kylie. She looked shocked to see me.

"Cookery book!" I said, surprised to see her. "Or maybe a history book…" something about this girl made me stupid and I always said completely ludicrous things.

"What the fuck are you talking about?"

"Have you found a bargain?" I asked, back to feeling foolish, imagining I could smell coconut.

"Came to drop some stuff off… fucking forgot to give it to them!" she thrust the bag at me and barged past me and rushed away. She never seemed to walk slowly… except in my dreams when she stalked across an impossibly long bar towards me in her glittery tights and high heeled black shoes…

I stared after her for a moment and then turned to go into the shop with the bag in my arms. I stood for a moment; the bag was a LEPRA charity bag… I dithered, not knowing what to do, then went into the shop.

Just as I pushed the door open there was a tremendous scream which made me jump. A woman with wild purple hair was wrestling with one of the elderly ladies who worked there. The old lady gave her a shove and the purple haired woman crashed into a rack of clothes which fell over.

Another of the elderly shop workers was yelling for someone to call the police but the other shoppers and I just stood there as purple hair jumped up and started throwing things at random. A book whizzed towards me and I ducked and then it all went mad as other people started throwing things and shouting.

There was nothing else I could do but escape and I hurried away from the mayhem, wondering what on earth was going on.

I stopped and found my inhaler; violence always makes me anxious... I'm sure it does to everyone but I'm no good at fighting, or standing up for myself as Marcus used to say, and it always seemed so easy for other kids to pick on me, the little ginger fatty. My hair has become brown now although my beard is still a bit reddish, and I'm still fat... I don't seem to have an off switch when I start eating. Rebecca once called me greedy, and I was so upset that she's never said it again but is always trying to put me on a diet. The 5:2 Diet seems to have gone by the way... I guess we're both so busy and she works such long hours it's difficult for her to supervise me.

I was standing by a Polish shop and I stared in the window at all the foods on display, some of which I knew but some I had no idea and couldn't read the labels either. I wandered in... there wouldn't have been any Polish or Ukrainian food in England when the brothers arrived... did they ask their wives to make some of the dishes they remembered from their childhood?

I wandered in and a lady behind the counter called something to me.

"Dzień dobry!" which I guess was good morning as it sounded a little like добрый день, which I remembered from doing Russian and I made a try at an answer, which was silly because she then launched into a whole lot more Polish.

"Извините… I'm sorry, I don't speak Polish!" I said and could feel my face burning with embarrassment.

"I thought you must be Polish… you have the look," she said with a grim smile which I couldn't tell if it was friendly or not.

"I think very distantly my ancestors were… or from near Poland," I said.

"Perhaps you should learn to speak Polish then… you know a little Russian."

I took another drag on my inhaler.

"Would you like a cup of tea… you look not well," and she called something into the back of the shop behind her.

"I just get a little breathless, when I'm anxious," I said. "You have such interesting things in the window, I was just looking… I don't know what they are… in fact I don't really know what Polish food is like."

A young woman came from the back of the shop; she was tall and pretty with dark chestnut hair pulled loosely back from her face. She gave me a glass in a silver holder with pale tea and a slice of lemon.

I thanked her but she just smiled and I guessed she didn't understand me. So I tried a little Russian.

"Спасибо!"

"That's Russian, you need to say 'dziękuję'," the lady told me. She still looked quite fierce but I was beginning to guess that was just her expression.

I had a go at saying it and the pretty young woman smiled at me and said something back pleasantly.

I drank the tea and it had sugar in it but it made me feel better, and I asked the lady about the food in the shop and asked if there was something nice I could get my wife as a little present, not a Christmas present, just a little treat. She showed me a bag of Mieszanka Krakowska which looked like fruit pieces covered in chocolate; underneath it said 'galaretki czekoladki'.

"Chocolate jellies," the lady said.

The young lady said something and laughed and indicated they were very nice. She was lovely looking and I wondered if John would like her; he was older than me but somehow I was beginning to feel that the years were disappearing and I felt almost protective towards him... He was so sad without Laura, even though he was pretending to be cheerful, and I could just tell by the way he looked at women, and the things he said about me and Rebecca that he wished he had a wife or a partner. He would love a family, I realised, as much as I would... but at least I have a wife.

I settled on the chocolate jellies and some sesame snaps, sezamki waniliowe, flavoured with vanilla.

"Have you any Ukrainian food in your shop?" I asked the lady who'd told me her name was Dorata, and her niece was Justyna.

They found me some borscht in a tin, and some yushka fish soup which to be honest I didn't fancy, but I bought it because they were so friendly and I bought some little dumpling things, pyrogys. They didn't ask why I was interested in Ukrainian food and I paid, and with my purchases stowed in a nice carrier bag with a Polish flag on it, I left them.

I looked at my phone, checking I hadn't missed Rebecca calling me to meet; I was a little surprised because it was getting near lunchtime and I thought we were either going home or having a snack in town.

"Hey, bro!" it was John, looking pleased to see me. "You've been shopping, I see!" and he indicated my bags, from the bookshop, from the Polish shop and the LEPRA bag which I'd forgotten about... I'd have to go back to the charity shop and return it, no doubt the purple-haired lady had left by now.

I was a little troubled by it, because although I hadn't looked inside, I was sure it would contain things Kylie had just *bought*, not *brought* to donate. I gave John a brief summary of the charity bag and we walked back towards the shop.

"Hey, she's nice, another friend of yours?" John indicated, and Justyna was coming towards us with her lovely smile, waving at me.

I'd forgotten the Юшка, yushka soup... honestly, it was a genuine error.

"Это мой брат, John," I said, forgetting of course that I couldn't speak Polish and what I was speaking was Russian, this is my brother, I was trying to say. "John this is Justyna, she's from the Polish shop."

This couldn't be more perfect; I'd thought John might like her, and had never imagined that within five minutes I would be introducing them.

Justyna seemed to understand me and said *'czesc'*, which later I found meant *'hello'*, and she and John shook hands and to me, not an expert I know, but to me, there seemed a little something flash between them. She was a little taller than him, but had the same chestnut coloured hair but without the grey threads, and the same tanned look to her skin but her eyes were a greeny brown, not blue like his.

My phone rang and it was Rebecca; she'd met up with someone and would I mind if I did my own thing for lunch… or I could go home and pick her up later. That was fine so I suggested lunch to John.

Justyna was heading back to the shop having given us a little wave. I wanted to call her back or say something, but apart from shouting *'oy!'* like Kylie, I hadn't the Russian let alone Polish. We deviated by the LEPRA shop, and we had to go past the Polish shop which was convenient so now John knew where it was… he probably did anyway as the bookshop was just a little further on. The LEPRA shop was shut, so I was stuck with the bag of things… which meant I could genuinely give them back to Kylie.

Sunday, 1st December 2013

I needed an old map of Easthope; I wanted to see where the umbrella factory was, and find out where Thirza was living in relation to the pub; also if the other children moved away and married. I wanted to see where they were living, and find out if the roads were still there. In many ways Easthope seemed to have changed little, but obviously there was great changes by the river as it was no longer a port and with only a few fishing boats down by the harbour. The family had been living in the pub for over ten years, but would they remain there? Might they move to Strand?

It occurred to me that I'd automatically thought that we, us four brothers would be descended from Tolik as he was the oldest… but maybe our forefather had been one of the Birmingham Radwinters who'd returned to the family. It is an exciting thought; I don't want to hurry, I'm enjoying what I'm doing so I'm not going to race through to try and find the answer… where did we, my three brothers and me, where did we come from?

I returned to Robert's family and began to check through the marriages of the children, and obviously as the only son, William Radwinter bears our name, I paid particular attention to him. William was born in 1880, and he married in 1905, when he was twenty-five. He married a young woman called Helen Grosvenor who, I discovered was born in Coventry in 1886. In 1911, according to the census they were living in Coventry; how had he come to meet a girl from there?

Coventry was in the Midlands and I did a quick check and saw that it wasn't that far from Birmingham where William's uncle, Osman lived with his family… maybe William had come to visit or to find work and met Helen. I wondered if Helen and William lived near her family, and pondered on how big Coventry was in 1911? They had two children by then, Sidney and Arthur, and from checking the birth records I found they had another child, Howard in 1913… this was getting very close to a terrible event in 1914, and my heart began to fill with dread.

I jumped straight to the death records, looking for William, looking for him without success… he couldn't still be alive, one hundred and thirty odd years after he was born… I checked 'all records' on MyTimeMachine… and then I found him…

William died at Ypres in 1914 … I'd studied the war poetry of World War 1 and unbidden, Owen's poems came to mind.

This shook me… and I didn't want at the moment to find out more… I didn't have a picture of William in my head as I did with some of the others. I somehow imagined the original Thomas looking a little like me, but a beefed up version, taller, slimmer, much, much more muscly and maybe with my brothers' blue eyes. I imagined Thirza Downham looking a little like Justyna, tall, strong with calm eyes. I imagined his brother Tolik to be slim, maybe not as tall, maybe John's build, and for some reason with dark hair as Paul had when he was younger and he too had the steely Radwinter eyes.

Lamy I saw as a wispy thing, pale and faithful but with not much personality, nothing except her love for Thomas and the children for whom she would have worked so hard, maybe even working herself to death… I shivered at this, at poor Lamy, born Coote, died Coote.

Thomas and Thirza's son Tolik I imagined like a thin version of his uncle, maybe a quiet but strong man. He'd been taken from his mother in Radwinter, and trailed across the countryside with another woman and his father, more children arriving, put into lodgings with strangers when he was only four, his step-mother and the little ones somewhere else, a forbidding, hated building, and his Dad living in another house with other people…

Then on to Portsea Island, more children, then at last to the India Inn which became a settled home for him… so yes, I imagine him as a quiet, strong young man, with a steely core. His step-mother had died, his father had disappeared and when he was much younger than I am now he'd taken on the family pub, and a wife, and two children, and his brothers and sisters… A strong man…

William… I had no picture of him, and I felt I needed to before I investigated more of his life, and more of his death. I shivered.

"You're not getting a cold are you?" Rebecca asked a little peevishly.

She seemed cross with me most of the time… not that she said anything, but it just seemed I did nothing right at the moment. I wondered again if she might be pregnant, she seemed very moody. I was a little worried about Jessica, I'd not seen her for a few days and if she'd been going on holiday or even just taking a few days off she would have told me. I'd been catching the bus every day recently because of Rebecca's shifts; I didn't mind, it was quite nice to sit listening to my music and just thinking, or looking at my notes, or trying to keep up with the news for the 'In the news' round at the quiz.

"No, I'm fine, I've just found that someone died at Ypres, in the First World War," I told her, pointing to the screen.

"Millions of people died, that's why we have Poppy Day!" she replied sharply although she must have known what I meant.

I went back to my research and got out the family tree sheet, to see where I was up to. It was now spread over several sheets of A2 paper which I'd got from work; I'd asked Gordon and Julie if it was alright if I took some, and they both looked at me as if I was mad for asking. I was now down to the fourth generation of Radwinters and was beginning to wonder how I was going to manage it all.

I had a copy on MyTimeMachine, obviously, but when I'd tried to print it out on A4 sheets they were all separate, though numbered, and I'd found it difficult to put them together in the right order; I'd wondered about Sellotaping them together to make a giant sheet, but I'm not very good with Sellotape which is why Rebecca always wraps the presents... although I do wrap hers, obviously.

I found that I was acquiring a lot less peripheral information... in the 1841 census I'd made a spread sheet with everyone in the village, and also with Blechingley in 1851... I'd not bothered with Portsea Island at all, because although the Radwinters were there in the 1850's they were in Easthope by 1861 and I'd only really glanced through the 1861 census, concentrating on the India Inn.

I sat back and thought about William... I would spend a proper amount of time on him to pay tribute to his sacrifice, but I would follow his boys to see if there are still Radwinters in Coventry. How could I do that without census information? I could check to see if they married. I typed Sidney's name into the marriage search but came back with nothing; I typed Arthur's name and had the same result and then with Howard, the youngest. Surely they didn't live as three old bachelors together?

I thought about their ages, so young when their father had died in the first war... but supposing they had died in the second world conflict? They would have been in their thirties when the war started, they would have joined up or been called up... how sad for their mother... With a heavy heart I typed in their names one by one into the 'war deaths' search but the result was zero... had they changed their names for some reason? Or had the family moved abroad as others had?

I had a sudden inspiration and typed Helen Radwinter into the marriage search... and there she was; she had married Walter Brunty in 1916, and in 1917 she had twin daughters, Ruby and Elizabeth.

I typed in Sidney Brunty, and there he was married in Coventry in 1932; I tried and found Arthur Brunty and he too had married, also in Coventry in 1938, and lastly their brother Howard in 1946, in Manchester. I wouldn't try yet to trace their descendants... they were Radwinter by birth but not by name... that could come much later but one thing for sure, we boys hadn't come back to the Easthope area via Coventry. I did just check to see if they were still alive, but no, all had died, and their sisters too.

They had families... there were distant cousins... but would any of them have a memory of the story of a grandfather who'd died nearly a hundred years ago?

Rebecca called me for dinner and I felt quite sombre as I sat down to the nice meal she had made us, salmon steak with lemon and butter, roast vegetables and crusty bread... it obviously wasn't a fast day today.

Tuesday, December 3rd 2013

Jessica wasn't on the bus again; I knew she was on Facebook; I wasn't but I could start and find her that way... but then what? Message her and say 'Are you alright?' and then it might be awful if she wasn't and so much worse if the baby wasn't. I'd never met her husband and I couldn't imagine ringing him and saying that I was a friend of hers and worried about her. I knew where she worked but again, I couldn't just wander in and ask after her, they wouldn't tell me anyway.

I was worried about Kylie too; she hadn't been in the office and when I asked Sandra she just said she was ill. I couldn't ask anything else, it would have seemed odd. I didn't know Kylie's number either... nor if she was on Facebook. The office seemed curiously tense, although I couldn't explain why; everyone seemed irritable and Julie was pestering everyone for the money for the meal. I'd paid and was tempted to pay for Kylie and sort it out with her later, but again, it would have seemed odd.

John rang me, ostensibly about the quiz tonight, but he just mentioned he'd been in the Polish shop but Justyna hadn't been there. I said I'd not been back in, and Rebecca hadn't like the chocolate jellies, but she'd taken them and the tin of fish soup to work because there was an old man on respite who was Polish, so maybe he'd like them.

Ruthie rang me; she apologised for letting me down, as she put it, with the family tree; she'd been so busy she hadn't been able to help me at all. I reassured her that I was getting on just fine... and in fact I was working on it in such a back to front sort of way that probably she would have been quite annoyed with me.

"Thomas, whoever could be annoyed with you? That's not possible!" she said, laughing. She went on to apologise for Paul not having been in touch either; he was really busy too, this time of year was always manic, and he'd been coming on some of her demonstrations, talking about the wine he would serve with each course, adding a little extra interest to the demos.

I told her I'd love to come sometime, and asked if she'd given any more thoughts to doing something similar to what they did at the Olive Shed. She had, she said, and she wished Rebecca was interested because she was such a very good cook. I couldn't imagine Rebecca demonstrating something like that; she was very confident and efficient in her work, but she wasn't the sort of person to stand up in front of people… she was quite shy in a way.

"Have *you* any thoughts on my plans?" she asked. "How I could make it different? I don't want to just be copying what the Olive Shed does, I don't want to pinch their business either. They are well established and I don't want just to seem an imitation of them… and anyway, I'm not them… I'm different… I suppose I'm a bit younger too."

It was my lunch hour, so I was perfectly free to sit at my desk and eat my sandwich and talk to Ruthie on my phone.

"Well…" I hadn't really been thinking about it, too busy thinking about the family… but a little corner of my mind had been playing about with some ideas. It hadn't been enough to just suggest different snacky things whether they were fancy shortbread, gilded gingerbread or a new take on Middle Eastern snacks. "When I looked on the Olive Shed site I saw that they only have their courses running every other day, but they are also doing a lot of other things like bed and breakfast and evening meals and lunch parties and so on… if you were just doing demonstrations then you need to be doing them every day… but that would probably become tiring and maybe even boring, and also would you have a big enough market, since the Olive Shed is already doing it in the area, and I guess other people might be too. And also you have your other things, like your shortbread and stuff, and the other demos you give at schools and colleges… which are maybe only things to keep you going."

I stopped; Ruthie was a great one for listening in silence which was good in a way, but also made me nervous and wonder if I was babbling on.

"You would have to have a place... I'm guessing you've thought of that... a house or place big enough to accommodate an audience; if you're going to follow a similar pattern to the Olive Shed where the audience eat the dinner, then you need some sort of smallish big place... But anyway, John and I have been eating out a lot recently, and we've been to lots of different restaurants and cafés, you know, sushi, Portuguese, Italian, and well my friend Leo, his mum has the Nonna Ysabel, I don't know if you've been there, well, it's Rebecca's favourite place but John hadn't been and Leo is in the quiz team with us and so I took John..."

"Stop, stop, stop!" she said laughing and I realised I'd gone into one of my flows.

"What I mean is... you could you have sort of like a franchise, where different cooks can come and do a day's cooking... so Leo could do dinner from Abruzzo, and someone from the Lebanese place could do lunch from the Lebanon... do you see what I mean? And then there is a Polish shop not far from here, and there are lots of Polish people so you could do something different like that. Then while they are doing their stuff, you could be doing your other stuff. You might need someone to manage the whole thing and keep it together... and do the washing up!"

I finished but there was utter silence... had she hung up... had I become irritating? Then she laughed, said I was brilliant, said she had to go, said she wanted to meet me to talk it over, and said goodbye.

Brilliant. Really?

Tuesday, December 3rd 2013, evening

It was raining, so John and I ate at an Arab place in Strand and then caught the bus to Easthope and went straight to the Lark. To be honest, although The Luxor, as it was called, was fine, clean, nice, good service, reasonable priced, we were a little disappointed in the actual food... it was just a little dull. John had beans in a sauce which was... nice. I had a kufte type of thing which again was... nice. The rice was properly cooked, the salad which came with it and the dips were fresh and OK, but it didn't thrill us, and I wasn't sure I would go again... not when there were so many other interesting places to explore.

We didn't go and look at the India Inn again, I wanted to do it in daylight and maybe take some photos, but on the other hand I didn't want Kylie suddenly springing out and attacking me... maybe I should try and find out more about the place and I made a note on my phone, adding it to the list of other things to look up, including where the umbrella makers' was.

John asked about Kylie as we sat waiting; I didn't tell him much, because to be honest, I didn't know much. I didn't tell him that I thought she was struggling for money, I didn't tell him about the LEPRA charity shop bag which was still in my rucksack that I took to work with my work files. There was something sparkly in it I'd glimpsed accidently.

I told him about the Birmingham and Coventry Radwinters... and how I couldn't quite face finding out about how William had died. John looked grave, and said that maybe there would be more; how many sons were there born after 1880? Any of them and some born before could have joined up or been called up.

"Ciao, amici!" it was Leo and his cheery face broke our serious thoughts. He sat down with a beer and we exchanged news.

He was feeling a bit fed up; we all had days like that, said John, and I agreed, although sitting here in good company, with people who liked me and liked being here with me, always raised my spirits. He told us that he'd had a bit of a row with his mum; not really a row, but a disagreement, and she was very fiery so it was always exhausting to have *'an exchange of views'* with her. I feel like that with Rebecca sometimes, and certainly John's first wife had been very temperamental.

It was all about the same old thing… the menu. Mama was convinced that the menu was what brought the customers in; they liked the regional food she gave them, they loved the recipes she was using that she remembered from her nonna's kitchen, her grandma's kitchen. They didn't want different things and new recipes.

Well, it was true that Rebecca liked going there because it was always the same. John and I sat and nodded and commented as Leo talked about his ideas, his thoughts on food, how to make it exciting and modern and yet to retain the distinct Abruzzo flavours and style. When they went back to see the family, the restaurants in L'Aquila and Pescara were modern and current and interesting; when they visited his cousins their home cooking was not in the old style and yet they still used the vegetables they grew on their land, and the other food stuffs from the local markets…

I suddenly had an absolute epiphany! I thought of the conversation I'd had with Ruthie... Leo was a prime candidate to showcase his food in the way that Ruthie was beginning to imagine... or the way I hoped she was beginning to imagine.

Before I could say anything, and probably thankfully before I blurted anything out, Damian came and sat with us.

"Your friend's at the bar," he said as he joined us. I thought he was talking to Leo but he was talking to me and looking over I saw Kylie leaning against the bar, her face like thunder... which I guessed meant she was very unhappy. Damian began to tell a funny story about teaching, I hadn't realised he taught at my old school.

There was about ten minutes until the quiz started; trying not to think about what I was doing I went over to Kylie. I'm sure she must have known I was in the pub, she couldn't have missed seeing me, and I sort of wondered whether she'd come in because she knew I would be here. I didn't know why she'd been away from work, no-one had said and when I'd made a casual, I hope, comment on her absence, Vicky had just raised her eyebrows and tutted. Kylie had never been away as far as I could remember; she was always on time, and apart from when she used to go out for a cigarette which she no longer does, and lunchtimes, she was at her desk.

"You know I have a brother called Paul," I said without greeting her, which was not what I meant to say at all... why do I say such stupid things? When I'm at work I'm pretty professional, I don't go wandering off into ridiculous nonsense like I do when I talk to real people. Kylie looked surprised as she might.

"That him over there?" she snapped with a bob of her head. She had a hair band in so her hair was pulled back from her face and then sort of fluffed out in a big fuzz... I expect there is a proper name for it, but with the light coming through it looked like a golden halo and it was momentarily distracting.

"Um, no, that's my brother John, but my other brother Paul has a fiancée called Ruthie and she had this idea, well you know like when people do cookery in their own homes?"

"What the fuck are you talking about? I cook in my own home!"

"No, I mean people go to someone's home, like my wife and Ruthie did they went to somewhere called the Olive Shed and someone cooked and showed them how to cook like a really fancy meal, it was my Christmas present to my wife, and Paul did the same to Ruthie, and anyway they went there and this woman cooked a meal and it was very good but the woman was a bit old fashioned, and anyway Ruthie had this idea she could do something similar," the woman behind the bar who I'd waved at came over and I ordered a pint for me and John and a Malibu for Kylie.

Kylie was looking less thunderous.

"Thomas, you are an absolute twat," she said, with something like her usual way of speaking to me.

"Yes, I know, you've told me before, but if you could just listen and tell me if it's a good idea... you see Ruthie is amazing, and if she did a cookery thing, a demonstration, then it would be brilliant and different, but I had this idea so she didn't have to do it all the time and could do other things, then maybe she could have another chef in, like someone else who would take over the day and do their food, not Ruthie's…"

"You mean like a celebrity chef?" I was amazed that Kylie had followed something of what I'd said. I was just talking at random really, just so I wouldn't have to ask her if she was alright which I could see she wasn't.

"Well sort of, but you see the guy over there with the smiley face and curly hair, not the one with glasses and not my other brother?"

"John?" so she'd noticed him and noticed his name… he'd been interested in her…

"John, yes, no, the one with chubby cheeks and the pale blue and white football top, that's his home team in Italy, I think it's Pescara Dolphins or something like that, I'm not very interested in football, but that's why our quiz team is the Dolphins."

"Get to the point, Thomas before I have to hit you," she was definitely feeling better.

The landlord was beginning to make feedback noises over the mic as he got ready to start the quiz. I took Kylie's wrist and pulled her with me, and surprisingly she didn't resist.

"I'll tell you the rest later," I said.

"I can't wait,"

"Don't say anything, don't tell Leo."

"Who's Leo?" but we'd reached our table and I introduced Kylie and to my surprise and relief she sat next to John and I quickly went back to the bar to get my pint.

I realise I've not actually thought about the day Ruthie and Rebecca had at the Olive Shed; they both enjoyed it, in fact Rebecca loved it and said she'd like to go back again at another time of year when there was a different menu. They repeated the same menu over the period they were doing the demonstrations, so Ruthie and Rebecca had the Christmas and winter menu, which lasted six weeks from halfway through November to December; the previous session had been called Autumn's Bounty and Fireworks, and also ran for six weeks from halfway through September.

There was a spring one too, but that was it, so unless you wanted to eat the same thing twice you only had three options through the year… and I could tell, as Ruthie spoke about it when we met back at Paul's place, that she thought, even then that there was an opportunity to do more… it was only when I spoke to her on the phone in my lunch hour that the idea had properly popped into my head about having guest chefs in to vary the programme.

Rebecca was still in a wonderful mood when eventually I drove us both home that night and I'd opened a bottle of wine, as I hadn't drunk at Paul's and we'd enjoyed that and went to bed early…

I tuned in back to the quiz…

"Come on, where was Sennacherib king of?" Leo nudged me. I'd lost track of the questions and was thinking of food again.

"Assyria," I whispered, goodness knows where that came from.

It was the end of the round and halfway through when the smokers rushed outside and everyone else rushed for the bar. Kylie poked my knee and leant across.

"Lend me a tenner so I can buy a drink," she hissed in my ear, then sat back. "What do you want, John, my round?"

"I'll help you carry," I said and headed for the bar.

"I'll give it you back," she said.

"I know you will," I replied. "But there's no hurry," and I looked at her straight in the face.

Kylie glared at me, then called to the lad behind the bar by name and we soon got served.

"You've not asked why I've not been in work," she said.

"I guessed you've been poorly," I replied.

"Poorly, what sort of word is that!" but she didn't tell me why she hadn't been in work.

I'd surreptitiously slipped her twenty pounds, she didn't want the others knowing she was borrowing money. I quickly went back with John's beer before she could give me the change and then went to the Gents.

I hurried back because the second half was starting and John and Kylie were deep in conversation, their heads bent close together. I think I must be a bit paranoid because I thought they were talking about me as they broke off what they were saying when I came, but then the music round started and I didn't think anything more of it.

We didn't win but we did well and I was just wondering what would happen next as we usually got a taxi into Strand and I didn't know where Kylie lived... I couldn't really believe she lived in a boarded up old pub... when she suddenly stood up said she was going and rushed out.

"I thought she was you girlfriend, mate!" said Damian.

"I'm married!" I was offended; did he really think I'd carry on with someone behind Rebecca's back? Then I was shocked that he thought I might, and then I was embarrassed because he was probably joking. "No we just work together," I added hastily and wished I could say something funny and bloke-ish.

"She's a looker alright, if I wasn't gay... but there we are," Damian winked.

I was surprised I hadn't realised he was gay, but why should I have? He and Leo were talking about Kylie, John was strangely silent and all I could say was that she was very clever and I'd known her for a couple of years but didn't really know anything about her. Stunning was the way Leo described her, and they teased me a bit, probably because I'd seemed outraged at the notion of that sort of connection between me and her, and because I was blushing and stuttering.

The thought of Kylie as a girlfriend, even if I wasn't married, was utterly terrifying... John would handle her better... and I blushed again at that thought.

Wednesday, 4th December 2013

Kylie was back at work, but Jessica was still not on the bus; I'd rung Paul, hoping for a chat even though I knew he was busy, but Otis had answered and although he was cheerful and friendly he was going out somewhere. The bookshop was getting busy and John couldn't meet me for lunch either; I felt a little lonely. I plunged into the family story, plenty of other Radwinters to keep me company.

I peered at the information on the screen and exclaimed something out loud. Above William's name, below that of Radnall, H., Private, Royal Scots Fusiliers, were three more names which jumped off the page. I'd been so focussed on finding William, trawling up the page of the National Roll of the Great War from Ragan, L., Ragan, J., and Rae, J. that I hadn't realised that there were three other Radwinters... *three!* Our tiny clan had given four of its sons to serve the King and die for their country...

Thomas Radwinski had served with his brother in the Polish Army, he wouldn't be alive to see the awful horror that engulfed western Europe, and would not know that his own grandsons and maybe great-grandsons had died... because although the roll of honour included the names of those who had survived, I was horrified to see that all four Radwinters were dead.

I sat with my head in my hands; I felt like weeping. Rebecca put her hand on my shoulder.

"I'm sorry I was rude to you, Becca," I said in a low voice. We'd had words over something and nothing, I'd wanted to leave the cheese out of the fridge...

"That's alright," she said and moved away. "I'll make us a coffee," and she went into the kitchen.

I wanted her to hug me, I wanted her to ask me what the matter was, to be sorry I was sad, to try and make me feel better.

I took out my phone and scrolled through the numbers but couldn't think of anyone to ring. I printed off the page from the National Roll of the Great War, and saved the link into my Time Keeper's Cabinet, and then went to find some biscuits in the kitchen.

RADWINTER, W.R., Pte. 1st Royal Warwickshire Regt.

Volunteering in September 1914, he proceeded to the Western Front. Whilst in the theatre of war, he took part in many engagements, including the Battles of La Bassé, Ypres, Neuve Chapelle and Hill 60 where he was killed in action May 1915. He was entitled to the 1914 Star, and the General Service and Victory Medals.

227 Sherbourne Street, Coventry

So; there he was, poor William; Thomas and Lamy's grandson, son of Fanny, née Collins, and Robert Radwinter, husband of Helen née Grosvenor and father of three little boys. I sat feeling very low; he was unknown to me, I didn't even know what he looked like, but I knew enough about the 1st World War, had seen enough programmes and films about it to imagine what he must have been through.

Rebecca made some comment about me being moody, and I'm afraid that I snapped at her; she was taken aback at my sharp words and went into the other room and shut the door very firmly. I should have gone to apologise straight away but I felt quite down... and not just because of William Radwinter. I just felt low, and as Christmas came nearer I just felt worse.

Friday, December 6th 2013, morning

Jessica was not on the bus again, and now I was seriously worried about her. It was sleeting a nasty cold miserable wet horrible fucking bloody awful cold…

Someone pounced on me; it was Kylie. At least she was back to pouncing, maybe things had improved for her… I just wish they would improve for me but I couldn't even say what was wrong that needed improving.

"What's wrong with you, then?" she asked slipping her arm through mine. I was shocked to see she was just wearing a little thin jacket again; it was semi-waterproof, but it clung to her where the wind blew the sleet against us. She was grinning at me, but she still looked so thin. "Family tree getting you down? Had a fight with your brother?"

I stopped; I just didn't know what to say, I was just so… so…

"Cheer up Thomas!" she said, and I could see she was a little disconcerted by my misery. "Is it cos you've left your furry hat at home?"

I shrugged. I was cold standing here, my fringe plastered to my forehead, Kylie must be frozen but I just felt rooted to the spot.

"Buy me a chocolate; we've got time before work!" and she tugged me and I walked with her to the little café we went to before and this time I bought two hot chocolates, with marshmallows, whipped cream, chocolate sprinkles, and Christmas sprinkles of tiny edible gold stars. Rebecca always tells me not have hot chocolate because it gets in my moustache and it makes her cross. She really wants me to shave, but I would look so silly, I'd look about fourteen.

Downstairs we drank our chocolate in silence and gradually I felt as if the cold bit inside me was melting.

I began to talk to Kylie, and in a general way told her things weren't right with Rebecca because of me for some reason; I told her I wasn't looking forward to Christmas, and wasn't looking forward to visiting Marcus; I told her that the sight of William's death, nearly a hundred years ago had upset me, which was ridiculous, and I felt depressed because I was upset. I was worried about Jessica, I wished John would find a nice woman he could settle with (and I didn't mean anything by saying that to Kylie) and I was worried about her.

She was so startled by my last comment that she blew into her hot chocolate and ended up with speckles of whipped cream and gold stars all across her nose... which made her look kind of cute.

"You're worried about me?" she exclaimed.

"Yes, and you've got cream on your nose and I've got to go," and I snatched up the remains of my drink, grabbed my bag and ran upstairs. I was halfway to work before I realised I still had my mug in my hand.

When Kylie arrived in work about five minutes after me she had my scarf round her neck which I must have left in the café.

I'd barely sat down when Gerald called me into his office and we went through the coffee routine again even though I didn't really want any as I was full of hot chocolate. We then went through the general chitchat routine again, asking after Rebecca, saying how wonderful she was and then I got a little inkling of where this might be going.

"Marvellous, manager, marvellous, with her qualities and skills she could get a job anywhere, anywhere in the country, be an asset to any organization… and I wouldn't mind betting before too long she'll wanting a place of her own… care-homes, they're the business to be in, aging population and so on, " and he went on to tell me about someone, it might have been a brother-in-law's cousin or some such distant relative, who had a string of care-homes across the north-west; she was so wealthy now she only worked because she chose to.

"I think Rebecca is quite happy where she is," I ventured to remark.

Of course she was, he boomed… he has a boomy voice when he's not totally confident in what he's saying, or a little uncomfortable… I almost wished he'd revert to his crappy Michael Caine impression.

"But it won't be too long before she gets that twinkle in her eye…" he gave me what I think he thinks is an avuncular smile, as if he's about to give me a fiver for Christmas.

"Twinkle?" I repeated, dreading what I knew he was going to say. I'd tried my hardest not to think about babies and children, had tried to lose myself in all the offspring my ancestors were having as I looked further into their lives. I tried not to think of my own little Tolik and his little sisters Lillah and Isabella. I think they will just remain in my thoughts, I think I'll grow old and just have them as might-have-beens.

"Christmas is such a special time for families, children absolutely make it, don't they?"

You crass idiot, I thought; *for all you know Rebecca and I might have been trying for years to have a child.*

Something must have shown on my face because he changed the subject.

"So, Thomas, thought any more since our last chat?"

"Thought?"

"At your age you should be thinking about broadening your horizons, looking at that big wide world out there and seeing what opportunities are there for the taking. You're a bright chap, Thomas, very bright, and you have done some sterling work for us. Any time you want any advice, or even a reference you know we'll do our utmost for you. Monty and I might seem like old stick in the muds, but we have been in this business for long enough to have some good contacts all over the place. Anytime you need it, I'm sure we could have a word in the right ear, if you get my meaning."

I didn't know what to say to this... the subtext was pretty clear though. I thanked him half-heartedly and then fortunately for him there was once again a phone call... I'm sure it had been pre-arranged with Vicky.

"Looking forward to the Oriel, we'll have a splendid night, won't we! Make sure you take a taxi, no drinking and driving, unless Rebecca will come and fetch you!"

I thanked him again and left the office; the way Gordon and Martin looked at me as I passed between their desks, Gordon with his reptilian eyes... I'm sure he has one of those extra eyelids. They knew what my meeting with Gerald had been about. Julie had her head down, but she knew too, Sandra was on the phone, but she glanced at me. Vicky was typing something, headphones in as she listened to the dictation and Kylie was working away at her computer. I sat down and picked up my phone and dialled at random and this time it was The Willows; I didn't know the woman who answered the phone fortunately so I just apologised and said it was a wrong number.

So… I was being invited to apply for a position somewhere else, anywhere else, and I wasn't sure whether they were being kind and considerate doing it like this, or whether I would prefer them to just say straight out that there was some sort of deal going on with Lyon Abrams in which I wasn't included.

Should I actually start looking round for something else? Should I talk it over with Rebecca, openly or obliquely? Should I talk to Paul or John? I was going to stay with Marcus on Friday, should I discuss it with him? Marcus no doubt would say I was ready for promotion and look on this as a golden opportunity; if I was clever enough I could put sufficient leverage on Gerald and Monty to get a good deal… but if I stayed and didn't jump but waited till I was pushed, would I get some sort of pay off. I would have to look at my contract… but did I have the heart to?

Kylie came over and slapped some papers on my keyboard making me jump as usual and the curser started flicking about all over the screen and the page itself started shivering. How annoying she was, why couldn't she just give me the papers?

The top page had her writing scrawled across it. *'Text me'* and it had her number. I folded the page and slipped it under my keyboard and began to look through the pile of correspondence which I had to deal with.

I began to feel a little annoyed… which actually made me feel a little better. I was annoyed with Gerald at his lack of honesty. Why couldn't he just tell me what was going on?

Why couldn't he just tell me that soon there wouldn't be a job for me here?

I texted Kylie, '*thanks*'. I glanced across at her and she winked at me and then we both went back to our work.

Friday, December 6th 2013, evening

As I drove up to see Marcus I had the usual feeling of unpleasant anticipation which was ridiculous; Marcus was kind, loving, and devoted to the family, and had just about brought me up. Before I was with Rebecca his home was my home, he'd had a parish in Strand then. His daughters, my nieces were younger than me but in a way they were almost like sisters… I say that, but actually we weren't very close.

Sarah the oldest was very religious, even more so than her parents, and started going to another church where she met the man who became her husband. She married when she was twenty and now has the two little girls, Phyllis and Joan. She had Marcus's cool restraint, but he is a very affectionate man behind that control, whereas I never got the feeling she was. I don't really know what she thinks of me, but she certainly doesn't like Rebecca and the feeling is mutual. She has a slightly superior air, although why I have no idea, because neither Marcus or Jill is like that.

Her sister Paula is pleasant enough, but I always get the feeling she's a bit dopey, in a pleasant enough way, but she left school at sixteen and trained as a nursery nurse for several years, then she too got married quite young, to someone from the school where she worked. She has two quite little children, Paris and Boston… I bet there weren't many children called those names in the nineteenth century.

I pulled onto the drive of the vicarage, which is just an ordinary modern detached house on the edge of a newish estate, near the church. It is a large house, five bedrooms, but that's because Marcus has to accommodate various people to do with the church for time to time. I was surprised that it was OK for me to take the car; usually when I come up here Rebecca has the car for work, and I catch the train and Marcus or Jill meet me at the station, but Rebecca very kindly said it was fine for me have it, which was a lot more convenient.

The door opened even before I pulled on the brake and Marcus came out and opened the door for me, smiling in his rather serious way, but undoubtedly pleased to see me. Like all my brothers he is a handsome man, and like all of us he has a beard. My beard, which Rebecca doesn't like, is sort of a ginger and just sort of round my face, whereas Paul and John have a definite style, John's is black and Paul's is silvery black but very suave and they both have theirs properly shaped… I sometimes wonder if I should go to a barber and ask them to do mine like that, style it I mean… but I think I would just look silly.

Marcus has a sort of straggly beard, as if he doesn't bother too much with it and it's all down his throat…now Rebecca just would not tolerate that, I have to shave every day because of that. He has quite a high forehead, his hair isn't receding, he just has a very high forehead and then he has very bristly eyebrows, Rebecca would not let me get away with it!

My brothers all have the Radwinter eyes but Marcus could bore a hole right through you with his look. When he smiles a full smile he looks so like Paul, but too often it's just the corners of his mouth which go up as if he isn't wholeheartedly happy. He gave me a full-on smile now; we are all lucky to have good teeth and anyone seeing Marcus smile as he did just then would think what a very handsome man he is.

I got out of the car and he gave me a big hug, and I hugged him back and for a moment almost clung to him. I can never remember a time without Marcus being there. We greeted each other cheerily and I suddenly felt light-hearted, the anxiety which had almost given me heartburn vanished as Marcus welcomed me, and helped me with my bags, an overnight case for me and the bag of Christmas presents for his family.

Jill was on the doorstep and she too gave me a hug and a kiss, and there was a lot of muddled conversation as I came in and the door was firmly shut on the cold and my coat was taken and drinks were offered. There was a delicious spicy smell; Jill had made a hot punch for me, and we sat in the sitting room by a roaring open fire, catching up on each other's news and drinking the toddy.

As I'd driven up over the moors, I'd wondered gloomily why my relationship with Marcus was always the same, and wondered if it could ever change as my relationship with Paul and John seemed to have changed. They had both become friends somehow... now the way Marcus spoke to me seemed different too, more as an adult talking to an adult, rather than a disapproving but loving father-figure talking to a recalcitrant and rather useless boy.

Jill seemed impressed I'd remembered about the baby gym classes, and the crawling and the two girls in nursery, and I could tell by the new radar I seemed to have developed that she wanted to ask about me and Rebecca and children.

I think I surprised myself more than them when I confided my worries that maybe Rebecca 'wasn't ready' as I put it, for a family.

"You would make a great dad, Tom," said Jill. She was the only person who called me that. Paul sometimes called me Tommy, but no-one else called me Tom.

"I'd love to be a dad," I said, and tried not to sound too mournful. "But Rebecca and I are happy with each other, perfectly content as we are, so what will be, will be," Jill seemed satisfied with the cliché but Marcus gave me a thoughtful look from under his wiry brows.

"Come through for supper both of you," said Jill.

She is a tall willowy woman; I could imagine her being very sporty when she was at school and probably school captain… or head girl or whatever they are. She had blond hair which these days was a rather strange colour so I guess she must put some colour on it. People often ask if Rebecca dyes her hair because it is so very glossy and black, beautiful, but no… that's just her natural colour.

"How's work then," Marcus asked as we went through into the kitchen where we were going to eat.

"I'd like to talk to you about it later, Marcus, if that's alright… I'm a bit worried about it, actually," I was surprised when I said that… I'd imagined him quizzing me and in a bit of a panic I'd blurt it out and it would all come out muddled and wrong and make me seem stupid, and I'd resolved to try and avoid talking about it directly, so I was quite shocked when I said that to him. What surprised me more was that I almost felt a sense of relief sharing it with someone. "I haven't told Rebecca anything... you'll understand when I tell you why I don't want to make her anxious."

Marcus said nothing but put his hand on my shoulder and gave me a squeeze.

We had toad in the hole for dinner... which was lovely, with mashed potatoes, peas and carrots and really nice gravy. Then Jill had made a fruit crumble from blackberries she'd picked in the summer and apples from their garden, and we had a big jug of custard... Wonderful!

After dinner, Jill had gone round to a neighbour; I'd thought it must be a pastoral visit but it was her book club and I was a little surprised to see her taking a bottle of wine with her, surprised because I thought book clubs must be rather serious affairs, and I didn't think that Jill was someone who enjoyed wine, particularly. She and Marcus had always seemed rather austere... but maybe with two girls and a brother to look after and see through university, and college and nursery nurse training, then they had to be.

Marcus asked me about my research, and again I detected a slight anxiety on his part... which disconcerted me. Marcus was always so sure, so certain; his faith apart from anything else gave him a sort of courage to face anything. What could I possibly find which might cause him to feel... unsure? I was a little puzzled but the moment passed as I showed the tree I had.

I showed him Tolik and Thomas, and told him I had a feeling their father might have been Casimir. I showed him the different trees of their children, the evidence of

Tolik's voyage to Australia, Thomas in the village of Radwinter, his marriage to Thirza, the move to Surrey with Lamy via Epping and Lambeth, to Portsea Island and to Easthope. His name change from Radwinski to Radwinter, the birth of more children, his disappearance, the arrival of the grandchildren, and lastly my sad discovery of his grandson William's death in 1915, and the other Radwinters who appeared on the Roll of Honour. I must have been talking for some time, carried away with enthusiasm, passing him papers, and certificates, and copies of census returns.

"I am most impressed, very impressed, Thomas," he looked through the different things I'd given him, working out where everyone fitted. "Where are we?"

"Well, I'm not sure yet; we could come from Tolik junior's children, not Robert's because their names changed to Brunty, and I have a feeling that unless Osman and Benjamin's families moved back to Easthope, we wouldn't be descended from them."

"Osman, what a strange name... it sounds like a Muslim name to me," he smiled across the hearth rug at me, and I was struck that I'd rarely seen him looking at me with such an open expression. Once again I wondered why and how things had changed with my brothers... or maybe I had changed.

I explained about baby Osman Newell who Lamy had cared for and suggested the name came from him; I didn't know if the Newells had any other Osmans in their family... I maybe would investigate. Without seeming rude, I mentioned the names of Marcus's grandchildren, and suggested that maybe in the nineteenth century, just as today, parents wanted unusual or different names for their children.

I hadn't got as far as Taras, Albert or Cazimir's Radwinters families, if they had them.

"Tolik was eighteen when Cazimir was born," I remarked.

"Well, I was twenty-one when you were born," Marcus spoke gently, as if reminiscing, and I could see that he didn't just love me as a brother or parent might, he was fond of me and liked me too. I felt quite emotional and took another sip of wine.

My phone bipped and Marcus said he was going to get us another drink. I thought it would be Rebecca but it was Kylie. This was the first time she'd texted me. *'You OK?'* it said. *'Yes, with my brother in Lebanon,'* I replied. *'John or Paul?'* *'Neither, Marcus, my big brother.'* I waited but nothing came back. *'Are you OK?'* I texted her. Marcus returned with another bottle of wine, one of Paul's and a very nice one too.

He asked me about what I would do when I got as far as granddad, Charles; well, nothing I replied, we know the rest, but if I could find any cousins I might ask them what they knew about our ancestors… I meant new distant cousins, not the cousins we already know.

"I know we are descended from Thomas Radwinski, but I just need to prove the link… then I don't know what I'll do, go to Australia to find his brother Tolik I guess!"

I slept in a small guest room but it had an ensuite… A bit different from the draughty vicarage with cold corridors where Marcus had first been vicar. Lying in the comfortable single bed, I thought about the unexpectedly pleasant evening I'd had and wished Rebecca had been with me to see this different side of Marcus and Jill; I'd had too many glasses of Paul's lovely wine that Marcus shared with me, but I was just pleasantly drunk and I lay in the dark wondering what the evening would have been like if she had been here... and I was thinking the melancholy thought that maybe the evening would have been different, Marcus may have been different, if she'd been here.

I'd texted her *'goodnight xxx'* but she was probably already in bed because I heard nothing from her. I didn't realise until the morning that I'd also texted Kylie *'goodnight'* and she'd texted back *'sleep tight'*.

Saturday, December 7th 2013

Marcus asked if I would like to come to the church Christmas bazar; it was just a friendly invitation but there was just a hint in the way he spoke that he would really like me to come. Usually I was eager to leave; much as I loved him I always found it a little stressful being with him... but this time it was different.

"I'd love to Marcus, will there be mince-pies?" he laughed but was obviously delighted and Jill told me there was an annual mince-pie competition, and she seemed pleased too as she poured me more coffee.

He had to lend me some boots to walk through the snow to the church hall and he introduced me to people as we joined the other villagers making their way to the Christmas bazar; I actually had a really good time. He made me guest judge for the children's mince-pie competition, and I bought lots of silly things and won some nice bath oils in the tombola which I gave to Rebecca when I got home.

I set to, following the family links... to trace the children of Thomas's sons; I'd eventually trace all the descendants I could, but I was concentrating on the Radwinter name for the moment. In 1880 Benjamin, now a school master, was living in Cambridge with his wife Mary Ann; by 1891 they had two sons, Horace and George; I wonder if Benjamin knew his brother also had a son called George? In 1901, Benjamin and Mary Ann had another son Anthony, aged five, the first time this name had appeared in the family.

It rang a bell and I looked at the National Roll of the Great War; Radwinter, A., Pte., he'd enlisted in December 1914 when he was only eighteen years old, and he'd died the following year, like his cousin William... So young... the same age as Django, Paul's boy...

I left my computer for the moment and went into the kitchen where Rebecca was cooking; we were having her parents round for Sunday lunch tomorrow. This was definitely much better than going to their house and having Rebecca's sisters and families join us.

This morning after a nice lie-in I'd joined Jill for breakfast in the kitchen; Marcus was out visiting someone but he returned, bringing a freezing gust of wind in with him. It had snowed in the night and he said it was bitterly cold so he was very glad of the porridge Jill put in front of him. They had an Aga, Rebecca was quite envious of it but we could never have one in the flat... maybe another reason to move? I had kept my eye on properties for sale in the paper, but everything was very slow because it was so near Christmas, and nothing new had come up for a few weeks.

She was in one of her quiet moods and I asked her if she'd been lonely on her own last night but she said she was fine. She was making a goulash for dinner and I asked if I could help but of course I couldn't so I made a pot of tea and told her about how nice and friendly Marcus and Jill had been; I'd been very touched as we said goodbye, me with the presents he'd given for me to take home, that he said Rebecca and I would be welcome to spend Christmas with his family if I wanted although he guessed we had other arrangements. I thought it might be quite nice, but we would be going to Rebecca's parents as usual. I thanked him and said we couldn't this year, but maybe next year.

"What design is our Christmas cake going to be this year?" I asked, thinking of the lovely display of cakes at the bazar; they would all be going to local care homes or elderly people on their own.

"Can you find the sour cream, it's somewhere in the fridge," she said, and obediently I burrowed to find it. "And we need a clean table cloth, if you wouldn't mind."

After I'd laid the table and put the other cloth which looked perfectly clean into the laundry basket I went back into the kitchen to pour the tea and asked again about the cake. Rebecca always made a traditional cake, although sometimes she tweaked the recipe a little to give it a Caribbean twist, or a citrus flavour, and one year she'd used dried apples and pears which had been lovely, and I'd really liked the ginger one she did a couple of years ago…

"We're not having one this year," she said, stirring the pan busily. "We've both been trying so hard to lose weight, I thought it was better not to have one."

"No cake?" I exclaimed, disappointed. "We've got to have a cake!"

"Well, it's too late to make one now… and I won't have time to decorate it anyway, it's mad at work, as you know!"

"Oh, but…" I was really disappointed. No doubt her mother would have made a cake, so at least I would have some… we usually had our own little Christmas celebration on the Boxing Day, with a small turkey crown, or duck, or something as a bit of a treat. "We have got a Christmas pudding, haven't we?"

"It's not good for us, all that sugar and fat! Don't worry, we'll have something nice, you won't starve… I haven't had time anyway, I've been so busy."

She had been busy I know… but I could have had a go at making a cake, I did food studies at school and I knew how to make a fruit cake… It wouldn't be as good as Rebecca's, obviously… She was a little snappish so I didn't pursue it, but maybe I'd make a cake as a nice surprise for her… I'd ask Ruthie if she had a recipe that would be good without having the usual maturing time.

I poured the tea and took my cup back to my computer and began to find dates and census information for Benjamin and his family. Anthony had died so young, and I couldn't help but wonder what effect it had on the family; Mary Ann died in 1919 and I wondered if the loss of her son had anything to do with it, but also remembered there'd been a terrible influenza epidemic.

I looked it up and there was a terrible pandemic, known as the Spanish Flu, killing almost forty million people across the world between 1918 and 1920. Apparently more people died in one year from flu than died in the four years the Black Death was in England… but how it compares in percentage of population I'm not sure. There were three times the deaths from flu as from the World War… so maybe Mary Ann Radwinter died from flu, or maybe something else, or maybe a broken heart.

Benjamin remarried at the age of sixty-seven, Ethel Diamond, a widow, and he died, in Cambridge in 1938… the Radwinters seemed to be long-livers. Benjamin's other two sons, Horace and George survived the war; they didn't appear on the National Roll so maybe they were in reserved occupations, or maybe they weren't fit enough. Horace married in 1912 but he had no children, George married in 1914, in Saffron Walden, which was near Radwinter… I wonder if he ever visited the place? I wonder if he thought his family might have come from there, or that maybe he'd been told that his grandmother Lamy had come from there? George and his wife Elizabeth had two daughters, Winifred and Marjorie, and I filled in all their details, on my database, on my spread sheet, on my tree, and on my big piece of paper.

"I'm sorry we haven't got a cake, Thomas," Rebecca broke into my thoughts. "It's just that I've been so busy, and as there's only two of us, and we have been on the diet, I didn't think you would be upset about it!" she seemed a little defensive; she had no need to be.

"You're right, Becca, it's just silly; sorry if I sounded upset, I was surprised that's all. I was looking forward to seeing what lovely decoration you were going to do this year, and what your special 'twist' would be," I was trying to sound understanding, instead it sounded as if I was trying to make a point.

"Well, I'll make a cake if you really want one," she was a little flushed, I expect it was stirring the goulash.

"No really, sweetheart, I mean it... you've done so well on the diet, it would be a shame - "

That was wrong too and she turned and without a word went into the other room and shut the door. All the pleasant happy feelings vanished; the lovely glow I'd felt driving over the snowy moors after such a pleasant time with Marcus, the positive energy I'd had when I arrived home, disappeared. I felt as I had last week, gloomy and pessimistic... gloomy and pessimistic about everything... home, work, Jessica...

But at least my eighteen year old son hadn't been killed in a dreadful war, far from home...

RADWINTER, A.J., Gunner R.F.A. and Sapper, R.E.

He volunteered in August 1914 and shortly afterwards proceeded to France, and was in action in the Retreat from Mons, and at the Battles of the Marne, the Aisne, Ypres (1) and was twice wounded and gassed in 1915. He was unfortunately killed in action and gave his life for King and Country at Loos on September 25th, 1915, and was entitled to the 1914-15 Star, and the General Service and Victory Medals.

"Thinking that remembrance, though unspoken, may reach him where he sleeps."

217 Metcalf Street, Cambridge

I went and got a DVD and put it on the TV and sat and watched 'Hot Fuzz' until I got caught up in the events in Sandford and the adventures of Nicholas and Danny, and forgot about other stuff.

Monday, December 9th 2013

Rebecca gave me a lift to work on Monday; we were both very quiet. After our row that wasn't a row on Saturday evening she'd been on her game in the spare room and I could hear her talking so she was obviously Skyping someone who was also playing. I heard her laugh a couple of times, and was pleased she was being cheered up as I was with 'Hot Fuzz'.

Lunch with her parents had been pleasant enough, until as I was washing up in the kitchen and Maggie was drying the glasses that Rebecca doesn't like to put in the dish washer, she asked me in a whisper if Rebecca was alright.

I answered quietly that she was fine, just very tired from working so hard, and that I was a little worried because she did put in such long hours. I added for good measure how proud I was of her, which is true.

Phil brought in the cups and saucers we'd had coffee in, and as soon as he was out of the kitchen Maggie was close beside me again.

"Thomas, I've been wondering, I shouldn't ask, but I am her mum," my heart sank. "I won't say a word I promise, but are you and Rebecca expecting?"

I concentrated on the washing up.

"Is Rebecca pregnant?" Maggie whispered.

I went bright red, I could feel the flush starting on my cheeks and spreading out all over my face so even my ears were hot.

"No, Maggie… well, she hasn't told me… maybe… but no I don't think so," and I remembered we'd had to deviate to Saversplus to buy some Tampax last week.

"It's just she seems a little moody, and then sometimes emotional, and then sometimes she's on top of the world… I just wondered… Lauren was just like that when she was expecting," Maggie was standing with her back to the draining board now, so she could look at me, and also see if either Phil or Rebecca came in. "There isn't a problem is there? Have you been trying for a baby?"

"No, no, not yet, that's not our plan just yet, Maggie."

For God's sake woman, look at my face, see that I don't want to be having this conversation.

"You do plan to have children don't you? At some point? Because really, despite there being so many older mums about, really it is better to have children when you're younger."

What the fuck could I say? I mumbled something about how happy we were as we are, and that our careers were important to us.

Maggie went on… and on… and on… The glass I was washing must be wearing thin with the amount of rubbing I was giving it. I stood trying to answer her without answering her, praying that Phil or Rebecca would come and rescue me… unless he was having the same conversation with her, as her mother was with me.

My phone rang and I quickly dried my hands, excused myself and answered. It was John, just checking if I was OK for the quiz, and could I make lunch tomorrow as he had a sudden free spot and he'd found an Armenian café not far away. It sounded great, it would really cheer me up to be with him… he hadn't had a great success with his marriages, but maybe he would have some perspective on mine.

I kept him talking, telling him about my stay over with Marcus, and I wandered into the lounge on the pretext of asking if anyone wanted more tea or coffee, but really to check out the conversation. Phil was reading the paper and Rebecca was watching TV.

The parents-in-law left late afternoon and eventually after a rather strange evening of not talking to each other, but not in a 'not speaking' way, we went to bed rather earlier than usual... but Rebecca watched something on her iPad, I read a cookery magazine until I felt sleepy enough to turn out my light.

So our journey into work which seemed longer than usual, despite the fact we'd left earlier than usual, was in a polite silence from us, and Radio Strand Cool giving us music local news and traffic updates. It had snowed here as well but the roads were clear and the traffic was moving well so we made good time and Rebecca dropped me off by the bus station which was the best place to stop in all the traffic. I gave her a kiss on the cheek as usual but she didn't turn her face towards me to blow a reciprocal kiss in my direction as she usually does...

I got out and big blobs of snow began to drop out of the sky. I love snow, even though I was the boy who everyone threw snowballs at, I just love it. It had been wonderful up in Lebanon with Marcus, clumping through it all ankle-deep and so brilliantly white, wearing Marcus's boots and everyone greeting us, pleased to see him, and pleased to be introduced to me. '*My brother,*' he'd said, not '*my little brother*' or '*my baby brother*', but '*my brother*'. I could tell he was well-liked and he seemed more open and cheerful than he used to; when we were in Strand, when I was living with him and Jill and the girls, he'd been rather strict and serious, and almost patriarchal with his fierce blue eyes and piercing stare.

I wonder what his services would be like in the little village church; I used to have to go with him and the family, and then I was in the choir, and his sermons had been rather severe and I have to confess, a little on the boring side. He was – he is so fervent in his faith, and cared so much for his parishioners, and their souls, that there never seemed much levity in the service.

Next time I went to see him I would try to go so I could attend his service; I'm not a Christian, but I guess I try and live decently and honestly... and for the first time in my life I felt pleased at the prospect of seeing Marcus again.

It was too early to go to work; the office would be open and the friendly cleaners, Pyotr and Irina would be there, but I just didn't really want to go in yet, although it was cold hanging around in the bus station. I'd go to the little café and if I saw Kylie on the way I would buy her a chocolate too. I was thinking of her, her unsuitable clothes, how thin she seemed, the fact that the last time I'd seen her in the pub she'd been drinking what looked like orange squash before I bought her a drink, that she'd come out of the LEPRA shop with a LEPRA charity bag... which I still had in my rucksack, slung over my shoulder... I hadn't quite found the moment or the way to ask her what I should do with it.

I was wandering around the bus station, faffing about really; sometimes John came in by bus... Then the 207 came in, the Easthope bus, the one we caught to go for the quiz, and people bundled off, but no-one I knew. There was a figure walking towards the bus station, impossible not to recognize the long stride, but the shoulders were droopy and the head was down. I was going to wait for her but then I had second thoughts and turned and wandered again. I glanced over and Kylie emerged from behind the 207. She had a hat in her hand and was shaking the snow from it, and stamping more snow from her feet as she walked.

I walked round behind the newspaper kiosk so I came round to meet her.

"Yo, Thomas, hey man!" she said.

"Hiya… I got in early and I'm bored now… hot chocolate?"

"You're bored? I know a good way to change that!" I just smiled, I was getting used to her silliness. "Aww, Thomas, you don't even blush any more, you look so cute when you blush!"

"My heart is hardened against your charms," I replied as she slipped her arm through mine.

"I've got another good way to soften your heart and - "

I cut her off before she could say anything really rude and began to tell her about the Christmas bazar, and she asked me about Marcus and shrieked in a really stupid way when I said he was a vicar. She asked me which church I went to, and I said I wasn't a Christian and asked her which church she went to. She didn't answer directly but told me she'd take me with her any time I wanted to go.

I wondered if it was some sort of gospel church with wonderful singing, I could somehow imagine her singing in a choir. My mind was wandering to imagine her in a choir with a sort of surplice, when I realised she was telling me about the bus, telling me she'd come in on the bus... coming in from Easthope on the 207.

"Do you live in Easthope?" I asked... she hadn't come in on the bus. I'd seen the bus arrive, and I'd seen her walking in to the bus station.

"You know I do!" she exclaimed.

The wind had picked up and was driving the snow into our faces, it was almost a blizzard, and I kept tight hold of her, afraid she might slip, although she was wearing some sort of boot things. Rebecca has Uggs, proper ones that I bought her last Christmas, they were really expensive and I think they look awful and ugly, but apparently they are wonderful, and really warm, and they were the third pair I'd bought her.

"I didn't know you lived there!" I replied, we were bent into the wind now, it was fiercely, bitterly cold and snow was actually settling on us. Kylie had pulled her hat back on and her face was screwed up.

"Yes, you do!"

We arrived at the coffee shop and almost fell in; I told her to go downstairs and get warm, she was wearing a sort of cardigan thing which was black with wet... she must be soaked through. The lady behind the counter was beginning to know me, and laughed when I gave her back the mug I'd inadvertently walked off with; she had cardboard cups for takeaways, she said. She asked if I wanted two hot chocolates with all the trimmings, as she expressed it. I jolly well did, and I asked for toasted teacakes too, a double serving, they would be warm and nice and I wasn't sure that Kylie would have eaten anything.

As I stood waiting, I thought about Kylie. I had no idea what she earned, but whatever it was she was certainly very hard up; it was obvious to me that she must have walked from Easthope which was probably about five miles, if not more... I had no idea of her personal circumstances... did she live with her parents, did she live with a boyfriend... she might even be married for all I knew... but whatever, she was struggling for money, and although she always looked fashionable, it was all cheap stuff, and she had no proper winter clothes... And walking in from Easthope... did she do it every day? Could she not afford a bus?

The first time I'd seen her in the pub she'd been drinking Malibu... the next time she'd been on orange squash... what had changed? She was worried she was going to lose her job... anyone might be... in fact I was... but were her personal circumstances so dire that losing her job would be a disaster?

The lady said she would bring our teacakes so I went down the stairs, hoping my expression was the same as normal and didn't reflect my thoughts. Kylie had chosen a seat right next to the radiator and her hat was laid along it. She'd opened the cardigan thing, the woollen coat and I could see that she was wearing a scarf... and I recognized it as mine... well I didn't mind her hanging on to it, no doubt I would receive a new one for Christmas, I generally did... people seemed to like buying me scarves... or maybe they couldn't think of anything else to get me.

"So how many brothers do you have, every time you tell me about them you've got one more!" She looked what Jill would have called 'peaky'.

"Just the three... and you?"

But she didn't tell me... so I told her about the Christmas bazar and although she kept rolling her eyes and sighing, I could tell she was interested... I guess my boring life is very different from hers.

The lady brought down the teacakes and I pretended to be texting so I didn't have to watch Kylie trying not to scoff them all.

"Any news on Lyon Abrams?" I asked pulling half a teacake in half again as if I wasn't bothered with it.

"It's all going swimmingly for them... I'm going to be out of a job in the New Year, Thomas," she used her spoon to find the last scrapes of cream and sprinkles.

"I think I might be too," I confided as I had to no-one else. She looked startled. "I know you won't tell anyone, and it's not been said directly, but I've had a couple of odd conversations with Gerald," and I told her about them.

"It'll be easy enough for you to get another job, you're so clever anyone would want you... I want you!" she gave a rakish wink, looking more like her old self.

"Don't be ridiculous... but to be honest... I'm sort of bored... You know what I was telling you the other day about Rebecca... well, everything seems boring... and... please don't tell anyone, please, no-one else knows," so why was I telling this kid? I don't know what I would have confided but at that moment a voice interrupted us.

"Well, this is very cosy!" it was Julie.

"I'm just going!" and Kylie was up and out of the little lounge like a whirlwind.

"I've nearly finished too, Julie, but come and sit with me," I said in an unusually friendly way. "Rebecca dropped me off early and I came here for a hot chocolate, it was so cold, and here was Kylie! Have you got any of their syrups in your drink, they look a bit sickly to me, but I did quite like the look of the salted caramel, but then I thought there would be loads of calories, but there are loads of calories in hot chocolate anyway, and Rebecca keeps putting me on a diet… Do you know the 5:2 Diet, Julie?"

Sometimes my nervous burble was useful, and Julie wasn't really sure whether I was insulting her or not by mentioning the diet. She sat down and sipped her cappuccino while I wittered on about the diet, and Rebecca, and what to get her for Christmas until I was able to glance at my watch and say I had to go, and was she ready because we could walk to the office together.

"I didn't know you and Kylie were friends," Julie said, hastily drinking the rest of her coffee.

"I wouldn't say friends, colleagues, I guess, like you and me," which wasn't exactly true, on either counts… I think Kylie might be becoming a friend… and I hadn't many actual friends, whereas Julie really was merely a colleague, and I had no desire to change that in any way.

It was still snowing and I pulled on the hat Kylie had left on the radiator, it was a woollen knitted thing, sort of like a bobble hat without a bobble. I'd seen Paul's boys wearing them; there'd been a stage when Django just wore it all the time and I think there'd been some trouble at school over it and he said he was a Rasta and it was part of his religion… but that all went by the way when he discovered Dubstep and got in a band Knife II Two… I know this because Rebecca and I went to a gig in a pub in town… she lasted about ten minutes and then we had to leave… I did text Paul later to say how good I thought it was…

Kylie's hat was warm and dry now and I pulled it down right over my ears. Julie looked at me in amazement but didn't say anything, and I knew I must look a bit stupid, but at least my head was warm and so were my ears.

Monday, December 9th 2013, evening

Portsea Island... I thought it must be an actual island, and I'd imagined the family getting there by boat and had wondered what sort of boat a ferry might be in those days, in the 1850's when they were there. I wondered how I could find out where they might be living, and what they might be doing. Somehow Thomas had changed from being a farm labourer to running a pub, and I wondered if any experience he'd had on Portsea Island might have allowed that transition.

Wikipedia tells me that Portsea Island is a small, flat and low lying island off the south coast of England and that it's completely within Portsmouth, and also has a large proportion of the city's population. I looked at a Google map and can see what Wikipedia means. There is Fareham Lake to the west of it, and Langstone Channel to the east. I look back at Wikipedia and find that Portsea Island has the third-largest population of any island in the British Isles, after the mainland of Britain and Ireland. It is an island, for sure, there is a small channel which separates it from the mainland, called the Portsbridge Creek, and I can see there are lots of bridges going across it.

It looks a nice place, an interesting place, with lots of history; I wonder if Rebecca would like to go for a weekend... maybe getting away from Strand, and the family, and work would be good for us... and I would try to be extra willing to do what she wanted, shopping, or the cinema or whatever, and not go on too much about the family. I'd just wander around with her and soak up the atmosphere of the place... the Isle of Wight wasn't far away, maybe we could go on a day trip...

I think I was fooling myself; she was out this evening with a friend from work so I was on my own. The day at work had been curiously tense. Julie had announced that she had to have the deposit for the Oriel by the end of the day. I'd met John for lunch, and we agreed that the tiny Armenian café was an absolute gem... replacing the Lebanese in our top ten... not that we'd been to ten... but on the way back slipping and sliding on the slushy pavement I saw Kylie.

She was coming out of a little shop on the corner of a street; she came out quickly, her head down as if she didn't want to see anyone, and she almost scurried away. As we passed the shop I noticed with a sinking heart that it was a pawn-broker's...

I got back to work and went up in the lift with Martin who made what seemed awkward conversation with me about football; he obviously knew something about my situation that I didn't... but to be honest, I didn't really care... I was back to being downhearted again.

We went into the office and Kylie followed us; she pinched my bottom which made me jump and when Martin asked if was I alright and I said I had hiccups, she guffawed loudly. Martin tutted at her and gave her what Rebecca would call 'a look'.

"Here you are, Julie, here's my deposit!" Kylie gave it to her and Julie tried to smile pleasantly, but there was no mistaking the fact that she didn't like her. Julie caught me looking at her and was a little embarrassed but then made a big fuss about reminding everyone that we had to pay the rest of the money by next Monday.

Kylie sat down and snapped on her earphones, Martin went to Gordon, bending over his desk to talk in a low voice, and I was about to go to my desk when Gerald popped out of his office and summoned me... but it was merely to tell me about a position he'd seen advertised in Cambridge which he thought offered a wonderful opportunity for me... and he was sure there would be plenty of care homes in the Cambridgeshire area...

"Thank you so much Gerald, I have distant relatives in Cambridge, wonderful," and I took the paper from him and later fed it through the shredder without even looking at it.

So... Portsea Island... I found a website about Portsmouth and its people and it gives an idea of what it must have been like to live there. I'm sure Thomas and Lamy and the children were only able to live in the cheapest accommodation, probably all in one room, maybe even sharing their living space with another family.

Portsmouth is a naval city, I know that already, and it was well-fortified against attack from Europe over the centuries, so there was a lot of military/naval building as I understood it. There would have been people from every corner of the world, I would guess... I wonder if Thomas found any Polish or Ukrainian people he could have talked to in the language of his youth? Would he have managed to find some of his old comrades who'd escaped from *The Marianne*? I felt sure he must have... I imagined him as a combination of my brothers, strong, determined, resourceful... where did he go in the 1860's?

I went back to looking at Portsmouth, and tried to trawl for parish records of baptisms of the two Radwinter babies born there... but with no luck. I knew Portsmouth had been bombed in the war, was that why there were no records I could find? Or was I just unlucky? Or was I just looking in the wrong place? There was a TimeTraveller notice board, where people posted queries, or made friendly comments to each other or looked for lost relatives... Should I post there? Ask for help?

Ask for help... I felt as if I needed to ask for help about everything.

Albert Radwinter, Thomas and Lamy's fourth son (Thomas's fifth) was still living in Easthope with his brother Tolik in 1881, but by 1891 he was living in lodgings, with his sister Georgiana; he was a gardener, she was a milliner. Their landlady was a Mrs Martha Gray, aged sixty-two, and her daughter Edith Gray also lived in the house. It was on Taylor Street... I wasn't sure where that was but a quick check showed that it was still there, and number 27 was one of a little row of terraced houses. They were all still in the same house in 1901, Albert was still a gardener, Georgiana and Edith were both shop assistants (haberdasher's) and in 1911, the last census I could access, there they still were, old Mrs Gray now eighty-two, Albert was fifty, Georgiana forty nine, and Edith Gray was forty-eight. Old Martha Gray died aged a hundred and two, what an achievement for those days! Albert died in 1945, and Georgiana in 1947... did my father know them? He would have been in his teens when they died. Edith Gray died in 1952...

I was tired and fidgety; I wanted to trace Taras, and Cazimir to see if they had children, and I wanted to go back to Tolik who I'd left in the India Inn in 1871 with his wife and two babies... how long did he stay there? Did he stay in Easthope... is he my great-however-many-times grandfather? Or are we descended from Taras or Cazimir?

I called up the map of the Ukraine again, and went to Lviv... I was sure this was where the two brothers had come from originally, although I couldn't imagine how they'd ended up in the Polish army.

I looked up the Ukraine and began to make some notes... after all, my blood might be Ukrainian! Apparently it's a very fertile place, and the Carpathian Mountains are in the south west of the country. The Crimean Mountains are down in the south. It borders the Black Sea, and has a lot of neighbours, Russia, Moldova, Romania, Hungary, Slovakia, and Poland. It is a constitutional republic and its currency is the Hryvnia, Гривня ... and I have no idea how to pronounce that.

The history was a little depressing, invasion, tyranny, absorption... and that was before the dreadful events of the 1930's... In one of the history modules I'd done at school we looked at the famine of 1932-3... genocide our teacher called it, we'd been talking about the genocide in Rwanda in one of our other lessons, and our teacher linked the two...

I picked out the headlines of Ukrainian history... It had been called Kievan Rus, which gave its name to Russia, it was an important political and cultural centre and became orthodox Christian in the tenth century; it was powerful until the Mongols swept though, then it fell under the power of Poland, until the country asked for Russian protection from Poland... and that was the end of an independent Ukraine as Russia absorbed it, the end of independence until 1918... which lasted until it became a

Soviet republic two years later. It threw off the Soviet yoke in the 1990's...

I was bored. I rang Paul but he and Ruthie were out, Django told me; I asked how his music was going... he was in a new band, and I promised to come to their gig in January at a pub in Easthope... a pub in Easthope.

I rang John; he didn't answer but then texted me that he was watching a film with Bella... not Justyna then.

I rang Marcus; he was pleased to hear from me and asked me how the tree was going and I told him that I'd been looking at the Ukrainian connection, and how I was narrowing down our link back to Thomas, lack of boy children and in the case of Albert, no children.

He told me how successful the bazar had been, and how grateful he was to me for judging the children's mince-pie competition, and how good I'd been with the contestants, and how funny I was. Really? I'd said silly things to the children and clowned about a bit when I was eating the mince-pies, but I didn't think I'd been funny.

Then he told me something which I found quite exciting. He said it in a funny sort of way, so I didn't really know what he was leading up to... but he said he and Jill were coming down to Strand to see Paul and his family, and to meet Ruthie, and he would bring some photos for me... photos? Old photos of the family... I was very excited and stuttered my thanks... he laughed and said he hoped they would be useful.

Afterwards I couldn't really properly remember what he said after that, except once again he was checking that I wasn't going to be looking at our family, our present family... but just the oldies, as he said... I'd reassured him, but as I treated myself to a Staropramen, I did just wonder why he kept going on about it... probably something to do with Dad... Well, Marcus rest assured there... he is one member of the family I have no interest in!

Tuesday, December 10th 2013

It was Tuesday... I looked forward to Tuesdays, quiz night. I was getting to know some of the other people in the pub, some off the other quiz teams, particularly our rivals the Long John Silvers. When John and I walked in we were greeted by people and whoever was behind the bar knew what we wanted to drink, two pints of Otter... I'd never been in a situation like this, I'd always seemed a bit on the outside, now I was on the inside... and it felt really good, easy and comfortable.

I'd caught the early bus to work then hung around the bus station to see if Kylie was walking in as she had yesterday. It had snowed a little more and where it had thawed during the day yesterday it had frozen overnight, so there were big ruts and icy lumps and it was tricky to walk on.

The 207 came in and everybody got off, but no Kylie. I wandered about a bit more and went to the kiosk to get a paper; I didn't always bother but it was something to do.

"We can't go on meeting like this... they're already beginning to gossip," she grinned at me. "Here!" She held out a crumpled five pound note. "I'll give you the rest soon."

"I don't want that tatty thing... I want a crisp new twenty!" I pushed it back at her; she stuck her tongue out at me and pulled a silly face; if it had been anyone but Kylie I would have thought she was near tears. "I haven't had any breakfast," I lied. "And I need you to show me how I can get on Facebook."

I took her to the Armenian café I'd been to yesterday with John; I could just imagine Julie deliberately going to the coffee shop to try and spy on us. I bought us breakfast of eggs and Armenian bread and coffee and then some pastry things; I need to go back there because I can't remember what they were all called, the bread was matnakash I think.

I kept ordering more, pretending I was hungry, when really I was struggling, but I wanted Kylie to eat. I could see how thin she was; she seemed to have lost weight in the last few weeks. I remembered her saying something about an eating disorder… did she have one? She was eating all right now.

I gave her my phone and told her to get me on Facebook, and I explained about Jessica. Kylie asked me if she was my girlfriend, and I told her not to be ludicrous, pretending to be offended, but she saw through it. Her cheeks were pinker now, she looked better. I wished I could buy her a coat or something warm but she would never accept it. I remembered the LEPRA bag still in my rucksack.

"God, I am an idiot!!" I exclaimed. "I've been carting that charity shop bag around…" and I told her about the purple haired woman and the Polish shop and Justyna but just stopped before I mentioned John, just in case Kylie did like him. I offered to take the bag back, unless she was going that way… She didn't look at me but concentrated on my phone and told me to give it to her later.

She looked up. "You can *give it* to me later alright," she said rudely, leering, and I blushed like an idiot and told her not to be silly, which made her even more cheerful. "You're going to use your real name?" she asked.

"Yes – um, no – um not..." Rebecca was on Facebook... "No... I don't think so... Thomas Radwinski, put Thomas Radwinski."

She looked at me as if I was mad and I told her about Thomas; she vaguely remembered because I'd bored her with it before.

She showed me how to use Facebook... I did sort of already know, I'd looked at it before, but I let her tell me and she looked for Jessica's name... but there were loads of Jessica Sampsons... Then it occurred to me that she might be using her maiden name on Facebook and I had no idea what that was.

"Here!" said Kylie. "This woman is Sampson-Ison and she lives in Westope, is this her?"

I looked at the little picture, and Jessica grinned at me from under a silly hat. I asked Kylie what I should do, explaining my dilemma about not wanting to enquire in case anything was wrong.

"Well, to be brutal, if she's lost the baby, she'd be back on the bus by now, if she hasn't then she maybe having to rest at home and not be in work, or she might even have to be in hospital with it until its born," she was going to say something else but stopped abruptly and gave me my phone. "Just say hello it's Thomas or something stupid like you would say."

I dithered and she decided I should have a photo so I submitted to her taking photos of me, and was a bit silly to make her laugh, because actually, Kylie is very pretty when she laughs.

We decided on a picture which she said was nice, and assured me she meant it, even though I thought it made me look even fatter than I am and I wondered if she wanted me to look ridiculous. *But, no, man, I'm not as bad as that*, she protested and stuck it on my page. She kept all my details simple, and set it to 'friends only' and then we composed a brief message to Jessica, 'Hi Jessica, all ok? From Thomas your bus-buddy.'

I noticed the time; we would have to hurry to work now.

It was snowing again, and as we prepared to leave the little café Kylie said "You don't have to keep paying for me, you know," very brusquely, and a little while ago I would have thought she was being rude.

"I know I don't but I feel guilty eating alone, you're just an excuse so don't give yourself airs!"

She punched me playfully but quite hard and said *'give myself airs'* a couple of times.

We went outside and the wind tugged the newspaper from my gloved hand and I retrieved it and pretended to pick up something else.

"Is this yours?" the wind was blowing the snow into my face, and I handed Kylie the bus pass I'd bought at the kiosk. It was for twenty journeys on any of the region's buses at any time. "It was on the floor," I lied.

She took it then handed it back. "Not mine," she said honestly but regretfully.

I looked round, there was no-one else near us.

"What should I do with it? I don't need it, I've got one," I looked round again. "Have you got a one? Do you need it? Or do you know anyone who does? It's no use to me! Come on, I'm turning into a snowman here!"

She took it and slipped it onto the pocket of the little thin waterproof thing she was wearing again today, and put her arm through mine and we slithered our way to the office.

Tuesday, December 10th 2013, lunchtime

I stayed in the office all day, I didn't want to go out at lunchtime, and I was on my own, eating my sandwich and messing abut with some work.

"Do you mind if I join you, it's lonely up at the other end on my own?" it was Julie who'd come in from Gerald's office.

I tried to sound as if I thought it was lovely, in fact I might even have said lovely. Julie had a plastic box full of rice and vegetables.

She asked me how Rebecca was, they'd met a couple of times at social things and strangely they seemed to quite like each other; maybe Rebecca thought she was no threat... I think I've mentioned that Rebecca gets oddly jealous when she has absolutely no reason to be. She's my wife and I would never be unfaithful to her, and also who would ever want to have a romance with me? Rebecca was my first proper girl-friend and apart from Kylie being silly, no-one else has ever shown any interest in me. I'm not complaining, I'm just saying...

Julie asked me what we were doing for Christmas, same as always, going to Rebecca's parents, and then we would have our own little Christmas and I would go to Paul's at some point. As I said that I thought to myself that I couldn't remember when I'd gone to Paul's at Christmas and Rebecca had come with me... not that she doesn't like Paul, I think maybe she finds all the boys and all the noise a bit overwhelming. I had a happy little thought that maybe she would come with me this year as she and Ruthie seemed to get on so well together.

There was a phone call which Julie went to answer, leaving her lunch on my desk. I texted Ruthie as I'd not been in touch for a while. It was just a little 'hello, how are you' friendly text, and I added I hoped to see her and Paul again soon. I would take the presents over before Christmas as usual, and again I thought about how Rebecca usually didn't come and I would go on my own. Maybe we could find time to go together, when she wasn't doing a late shift.

Julie came back and brought coffee for us both, which was kind but sort of strange; she wasn't usually this friendly.

I tried to rally my enthusiasm and asked about her Christmas; she had divorced her husband last year, I wasn't sure why and I didn't really care. For a while she seemed very flirtatious with Martin, but he's a bit of a wet blanket and things seemed to have cooled between them. He is divorced and has a fiancée but they've been together for years and years and there never seems any sign of them getting married… I'm not sure if they even live together.

I tried to listen as Julie told me about various relations and her parents and her grandparents and then she suddenly said something which came right out of the blue.

"So do you and Kylie see a lot of each other? I've seen you coming into work together a few times, I didn't realise she lived over your way, I thought she lived in Easthope?"

I wanted to protest and be outraged but then that might look as if I had something to hide.

"Yes, just recently I've had to catch the bus in because Rebecca has been working such long hours, and I've bumped into Kylie a few times at the bus station."

The office phone rang again and with an exaggerated sigh, Julie got up to answer.

I texted Kylie. 'Help! Rescue me! Julie's torturing me! Help!'

Julie hurried back, eager to plunge into the conversation again. I actually didn't really care… if they thought there was something going on between me and Kylie, well so what… it seemed as if we would both be out of a job before long. Vicky had brought me another advertisement from the Times, love from Gerald, a job in Leeds this time.

"I know this might sound a bit rude, Julie, but have you been doing your hair differently? I was sitting here the other day, and I just happened to be looking at you, and thought how nice you looked," I gave a nervous titter. "Sorry, that does sound very rude, you always look very nice, lovely, but I just… oh dear… I'm sorry… oh…" I faltered to a stop, but she was smiling and looking at me in an almost smug way.

"I didn't think anyone had noticed, I've gone a honey colour," she touched her hair. She had it in what I think is a bob; Rebecca has long hair, wavy and dark and lovely, much nicer than Julie's which is sort of browny-blond, but Rebecca was wondering whether to change her style last summer and she asked me about whether a long bob would suit her; she wasn't very satisfied with my answer because I said I thought she would look lovely however she had her hair.

"Yes, it's sort of warm, and sort of autumny," I waved my hand as if I might like to touch it but didn't quite dare.

I don't know how this dreadful conversation would have proceeded with me pretending to flirt with her, and surprisingly seeming almost successfully, but the door to the office burst open and Kylie leapt in as if she'd been fired from a siege weapon.

"It's bloody freezing out there! Fucking Baltic!"

"Kylie!" Julie jumped up. "Please! That is not the language to use here," and she went off into one of her periodic attempts to metaphorically slap Kylie into shape.

Kylie didn't care and in fact seemed almost pleased at the response, but I was sorry to see she really did look cold. She had my scarf wrapped round her neck, but I still had her hat although I had given her the charity bag, which she stored inside another carrier from Saversplus.

Martin and Gordon came in then and everyone settled down; we had several clients come in and we were all busy all afternoon.

It was getting towards the time we all started for home, but I was going to stay on for a little while and meet John at a curry-house for an early meal before we went to Easthope. My phone bipped and it was a text from Leo; Damian couldn't make it, could I ask Kylie if she wanted to make up the team as she'd been really good on TV, films and music.

I texted her; I didn't want to keep Julie's gossip-mongering fuelled…not that it mattered to me, but it was important that if Kylie was going to lose her job, that she get as good a reference as possible.

She texted back that she'd try; after a moment I sent a message asking if she wanted to come for a cheap curry with me and John and then go into Easthope on the bus together. Can't, she replied, wrapped my scarf round her neck and rushed out of the office.

As usual when I wasn't going to see Rebecca, I texted her to ask how her day had been; sometimes she was too busy to reply, and when that happened I felt so sorry for her working so hard. I thought I'd try and make Christmas really special for her; I'd seen in one of the food magazines that there were cooking courses in other countries like Spain and Italy, combining a nice holiday in beautiful surroundings with classes from a proper chef. It was quite expensive, but I thought it would be a lovely break for us, and she would enjoy the course; she loved foreign holidays, loved the sun but because her skin is quite fair despite her black hair, she usually stayed in the shade until the afternoon.

I finished all I had to do, closed everything down and headed out to meet John, looking forward to a curry, and hoping I might find a way to talk to him about all the things which were worrying me…

It was a good lamb curry, and I had chapattis instead of rice and John had kufte and naan; I like naan but it always fills me up… considering my size I don't really eat that much, I guess I eat the wrong things and snack a lot… and I do have a sweet tooth.

I asked John about Bella, nice enough but he wasn't going to see her again… and anyway she wasn't that interested in him either. I asked about Justyna; he'd been into the Polish shop but she hadn't been in, a man had been working there. I asked tentatively about Laura… he gave an enigmatic John smile and said that was definitely over, unfortunately...

We talked about Christmas; he was going away with some friends. I imagine it must be painful for him being with people with happy marriages like me and Rebecca and happy families like Paul and Marcus. He was going to Italy with some mates, they'd got a house in Sienna which sounded beautiful... I wondered if they did any cookery courses there.

He asked me about work and I confided in him that I thought I might not have a job there for much longer; I'd checked into my position, and if things did go awry then I would be entitled to a pay-off... not a vast amount as I'd not been there that long... I wondered how much Kylie would be entitled to, she'd been with us about two years. I remembered she'd started on Guy Fawkes Day and there had been jokes about fireworks when she was introduced to us. Fireworks... that summed her up.

"What are you smiling at?" John asked and I was going to tell him but I thought it might give him the wrong idea so I told him about the cookery courses I'd seen.

"Rebecca is very lucky," he said with an affectionate smile as we buttoned our coats and headed out of the restaurant, sucking our complimentary mints.

"No, John, I'm very lucky, very, very lucky!"

The wind had blown up and there were spits of cold wet stuff in the air as if it was deciding whether to snow or not. As we hurried to the bus which had just come in I told John that Damian couldn't come but Kylie might be able to, and when we were in the bus he asked me about her, just in a general way, but I really could tell him nothing. I didn't know if she lived at home with her parents, I'd somehow got the idea that her dad was in Tobago, and I now knew she lived in Easthope although I couldn't imagine she lived in the boarded up pub... unless she was squatting there...

It was a thought which hadn't occurred to me before, but she was obviously desperate for money, and seemingly more desperate recently, but I had no idea why her circumstances might have changed. I couldn't remember now whether she'd said she was doing a University course, or hoping to... but they certainly weren't cheap, and despite her A-levels, she had a fairly lowly position at work.

So maybe she was squatting in the India Inn... poor girl... I would have to try and think of some way to help her... if she fell for John and he for her, she could move into his flat, he would be a kind and caring partner to her...

I suddenly had a most peculiar feeling which for a moment I couldn't identify and then with a shock I realised. The thought of her living with John made me feel... made me feel a little *jealous!*

How ridiculous! I shook it away and acknowledged I was becoming fond of her as I was fond of Jessica or Ruthie, that was all...

Leo was pleased to see us, but told us he might not be able to come for the next weeks leading up to Christmas; it was going to be really busy, which was great, but it was the same old thing. He was becoming more and more dissatisfied with the menu, and the 'new' Christmas menu wasn't new at all but last year's, which was the year before's and the year before that's and so on… it all seemed boring and dull and he felt as if he wanted more… more out of life as well as more out of work.

I sympathised, I was beginning to feel like that too! Luckily perhaps or perhaps not, I might be forced to start on a new path if I had to leave… supposing they did offer me a place in Castair at the new office which I still didn't officially know about? Would I take it? I almost began to feel that I wouldn't.

I hadn't talked to Ruthie again about my thoughts about day cookery courses… and without mentioning her, but just talking about what Rebecca had told me, I talked to Leo about the idea of having an Olive Shed style format but with different chefs doing different things.

He was really interested, extremely interested, and quizzed me about it, and I set off onto one of my babbles, letting my imagination run away with me.

"Hey, man, you've really thought about this, haven't you?" exclaimed John. "And I thought our lunches were all about brother bonding and really you've just been using me to research your future menus!"

I was about to protest but saw he was joking and we all laughed and then all began to talk, fantasizing in a more and more extravagant way as we drank our beer waiting for the quiz to start.

A pair of icy hands clamped over my eyes and then a freezing mouth whispered something in my ear. Kylie slipped her arms round my neck and greeted John and Leo but I couldn't hear what she said because she was hugging my head. Whatever it was they laughed even more and John got up, kissed her cheek and gave her his chair next to me then went to buy drinks.

Leo kissed her too and I wondered if I should but I didn't like to. She unwrapped my scarf but I could see she was shivering. She was wearing the woollen thing again and the Ugg-type boots but her hair was sprinkled with snow which sparkled in the light.

"What you staring at Thomas?"

"I was wondering if-" I clamped my mouth shut. This habit of blurting things out was dreadful, embarrassing, and I was bright red now even though I hadn't finished my sentence... *'if I should kiss you'*... because being silly she would think I meant something quite different... which I didn't... well, maybe... my head was spinning with the ludicrous thoughts... I'd only had one Bangla beer with my curry, and only a pint of Otter now, but I felt drunk.

"Have you heard from Jessica?" she asked abruptly, and I was so grateful she didn't make any further comment about me.

I'd quite forgotten Jessica and I passed Kylie my phone to have a look on Facebook. John returned as the quiz began and we passed Kylie the sheet with the photos on for the picture round which were all of people wearing Christmas outfits, celebrities, sports people, even some politicians.

In the few minutes between the first and second round when the landlord was checking that everyone had heard the questions, Kylie showed me a message from Jessica. She was thrilled to hear from me; she was OK, the baby was OK – thank goodness! – but she was in hospital and would probably have to stay there for quite a while. She thanked me for getting in touch, and hoped I was alright, and asked me to write back with my news... and she said she would love to see me if I could find a little time to visit her in Strand Royal.

I was so relieved, I could have burst into tears with relief… having seen the picture of little Riley with his or her tiny thumb stuck up so confidently I couldn't bear the thought that something might have happened.

John who was now sitting opposite me squeezed my knee, the next round was on food he said. I passed my phone back to Kylie so she could see the message and with a happier heart I answered every single question without a second thought… I think we were going to be on a winning streak!

Tuesday, December 10th 2013, night

I was right… even though we had to go to a tie-breaker with the Long John Silvers. The last round in the quiz is a particularly difficult one set by the landlord each week and called 'Up With The Lark'. There is a roll-over cash prize and we've never won it, never been close, but tonight… tonight amazingly we did… there was huge applause and even though we'd probably drunk more than normal we had another round and the landlord gave Leo the envelope… £120… that was thirty pounds each! It was great for any of us, but the expression on Kylie's face almost melted my heart… thirty pounds was little enough for me, but for her…

I didn't say anything or make a fuss as I gave her the money. She looked at it and then tried to give me a twenty back.

"It's not crisp and new," she said.

"No, it's not… keep it until you have a crisp new one," I said. She kissed Leo and John on the cheek, kissed me hard on the mouth which caused much hilarity from my brother and friend and then she was gone and we stood around chatting, laughing and waiting for the taxi.

There was a blast of a car horn and we stumbled out of the pub, into the freezing night to find our transport to take us home.

Out of the whirling blizzard a figure jumped at me; it was Kylie, grabbing my arm and pulling at me, shouting that I had to help. I tried to ask her what the matter was as the taxi driver honked his horn, Leo and John were already inside.

"Please Thomas, I'm begging you!" she shouted. "There's an old man, I can't help him!"

I waved at the taxi to drive on but John bobbed out asking if I was OK. I told him to go, I'd get another taxi, and they zoomed off into the night as Kylie pulled me along.

She was saying something about a tramp and as we turned off the High Street and went over the bridge towards Mill Lane she shouted above the wind that there was an old tramp, collapsed in the snow. I would have gone straight past him; he was huddled against the curving wall of the bridge where it went down to the River Hope. He was just a snow-covered lump; I squatted down beside him and was enveloped in the stink of urine, cheap booze and old clothes, and considering how cold he was, he must be powerfully filthy.

"Hey, old chap, what are you doing here?" I asked, shining the light from my phone on him.

Kylie crouched beside him and wiped his face with her bare hand and that simple gesture made me suddenly feel a huge lurch of affection for her. She had so little herself and yet she had so much compassion.

"Are you ill? Do you feel alright?"

He opened an eye and squinted at me from under his snow encrusted brows. He mumbled that he was going home but just needed a little rest.

"Where are you going?" I asked. He couldn't stay here. "Come on, old man, tell us where you live and we'll get you home."

He began to sing *'I was born under a wandering star'*, in a quavery drunken voice.

"Let's get you onto your feet and we'll see what we can do," I took his arm and Kylie took the other and we managed, with much slipping and nearly falling over, to get him upright. He was a little fellow and must be wearing a bundle of clothes because although he was very stout he didn't weigh much.

He lurched against me and despite the reek of him I held on to keep him upright. He was very cold and was shaking but he began to sing again. I tried to ask him where he lived or where he was going, but he was obviously just a tramp or street person. Kylie was clutching the other side of him to keep him from falling over and for once she had nothing to say.

"Ring the police," I told her and gave her my phone; we couldn't stay here and however charitable Kylie was making me feel I wasn't going to take this old fellow home with me. "I'm going to take him over there," and I indicated the doorway of the empty shop on the corner of the street, one more little business which had folded.

I tried to get him to move, but his legs kept buckling so in the end I had to wrap his stinking arm round me neck, put an arm round his back and virtually carry him over to the doorway where I let him subside into a heap.

"Got a couple o' coppers for an old man?" he wheezed and then started coughing. With any luck a couple of coppers would arrive in a police van and take him off to a nice comfy police cell for the night.

Kylie hurried over to us; her face a pale blob. The police weren't interested if he wasn't doing any harm to anyone; they'd said their cells were full, that if we thought he was ill or hurt, we should ring an ambulance and get him taken to hospital but otherwise there was a night shelter in Strand for rough sleepers.

"What are we going to do, Thomas?" she asked, not sounding like herself at all.

"You go home and get yourself warm; I'll ring this shelter place and see if they can take him, and if they can't I guess I'll have to get him to hospital... I can't think of anything else."

But she took my phone and she rang the night shelter, and I thought thank goodness for modern technology. I was beginning to get cold now, Kylie must be freezing in the stupid woollen thing which was not even waterproof. I took off my coat; she thought I was going to drape it over the old tramp but I put it round her shoulders. She said nothing just looked at me.

I rang the taxi firm because there was a place for the old man at the shelter but we would have to get him there.

"A taxi isn't going to take him," Kylie said, as if in despair.

"They will if I pay them enough," I replied. "Now you go home and make sure you get yourself warm and dry before you go to bed, and have a hot drink or something."

But she stayed with me, huddled into the doorway. The old man was singing again; he had rather a nice voice considering he was a rough old fellow.

The taxi drew up, welcome indeed in the foul night.

"Hey, Thomas man! I thought it might be you!" It was Shohib. "I didn't think there were many people called Radwinter! Get in, mate!"

I hurried over to him and explained, the words rushing out in a muddle. "I know he stinks, Shohib but I'll pay however much it'll cost to get your car valeted, he just has to go to the night shelter."

"Don't worry about that, mate, let's get the poor old guy into the car, I'll stick the heating on high so you'll have to put up with the smell of him but I don't want him dying in my cab!"

The charity of other people astounded me… and I wondered what I would have done if I'd walked past the man as Kylie had done, or had been the taxi driver arriving with my nice clean cab…

I tried to make Kylie go home but she got into the front of the cab beside Shohib and I got in the back with the old man. In the light I could see his face was filthy, with that sort of grey-green patina of a street person. He had a sack round his shoulders and his filthy old coat was tied with a bit of rope, and I was nearly gagging at the smell of him as I pulled his seat belt on. He had an enormous pair of white converses which must have been several sizes too big.

As we set off he began to sing *'Jingle Bells'*. The warmth from the heater was wonderful, but Shohib was right about the smell. I thanked him again.

"I'm a good Muslim me," he said. "You can buy me a pint next time we're together."

The journey to the shelter in Strand seemed endless and I was feeling almost sick by the time we got there; the beer, the smell, the snowflakes wheeling against the headlights. It was a nondescript house, an old Victorian one by the looks of things and I jumped out and went to the door and rang the bell.

The car had been warm and I started shivering in just my suit, my coat still round Kylie. She had remained silent during the journey although Shohib and I had chatted, which seemed very strange. Occasionally the old man would join in or start singing, then he seemed to be slipping into a doze, but when I touched his hand his bony fingers were nice and warm.

Shohib's gran had died, he told me and he'd been back to Bangladesh for the funeral which was why he hadn't been in touch with me. I felt a little guilty because although I had his number, I hadn't tried to get in touch with him either.

The door opened and a smiley but very tiny woman looked up at me and I explained that I'd rung from Easthope.

She grabbed what looked like a blanket and whisked it round her and over her head and came down to the taxi where Shohib and Kylie were trying to get the old tramp out.

"Hello, Bear!" exclaimed the tiny woman. "You're lucky to have been found by these good Samaritans!"

I took over from Kylie and between us, Shohib and I got him out of the car.

"Can you take Kylie back to Easthope, Shohib, and I'll get another cab; let me pay you now." I'd got the money ready in my hand before we'd got to the shelter; I knew Kylie would refuse or try and pay or something and even though now she had £30 thanks to our win, she needed that.

He didn't need any persuading, only too ready to get back into the warm of his taxi, and he shot away as I helped the little lady manhandle the old man up the steps. She asked me if I wanted to come in while I waited for a taxi but for some reason I just didn't so with her thanks and the old man's feeble shouts that he wanted to buy me a beer, I dashed back out into the snow.

I turned the collar of my jacket up and thought how perishing Kylie must be most of the time. I hadn't realised where we were, but once I got to the end of the road I saw I was very near the bus station, so thankfully I headed for shelter there, as I phoned for another taxi…

It was way past one, I was very cold and very tired, but somehow I wasn't unhappy… it had seemed like a bit of an adventure in my dull life.

Wednesday, 11th December 2013

I didn't hear the alarm and woke with Rebecca hitting my shoulder quite hard and shouting at me. She'd been in bed when I got home but had roused slightly, murmured something about me being very late and she didn't know where I'd been, but then fell asleep again as I was trying to whisper what had happened.

"Where the hell were you, last night?" she shouted now. It was very unusual for Rebecca to shout, but when she did it was very loud.

"Pub quiz with John," I mumbled trying to wake up. I had been so tired last night but had found it difficult to sleep, and now I was still tired and finding it difficult to wake up.

"Till two in the morning?" she wasn't shouting, but she was very angry, absolutely furious. I struggled to sit up still a little confused.

"There was this old man," I began to say but she was launching into a tirade about my clothes and my shoes and the smell and where had I been and who with and was I hung over.

I should have showered before I got into bed but I'd been so weary, and I confess I'd just left my clothes on the floor in the bathroom, so I could understand her being annoyed with me. I tried to apologise and explain but there was no stopping her.

"So where were you until two in the morning?" she demanded yet again and when I tried to explain. "Oh don't give me that! Why would you have anything to do with a tramp!"

"You could have rung me," I said, stung at her disbelief.

"Why should I ring? You should have been the one to ring me, unless you were too busy getting drunk with some little tramp... and I don't mean an old man with holes in his shoes!"

"He didn't have holes in his shoes, they were white Converses," I got out of bed. "I'll go and put my things in the laundry bin. I'm really sorry Becca."

She was in a terrible mood though, and followed me into the bathroom and told me my suit would have to go to the cleaners and my shoes were ruined and the rest of my clothes had to go in the wash right now and then the bathroom floor needed washing because of the stink, and had I pissed myself... she actually said 'pissed' so I could tell she really was absolutely steaming. It doesn't often happen, but when it does I find myself becoming more and more grovelling... and then she tells me to stand up for myself... although she wouldn't like it if I did...

And all the time I have this real rage building up inside me as if I am going to burst with it and I just want to yell at her to shut the fuck up, to shut her fucking fucking mouth... but I don't... I retreat somewhere, usually the bathroom and sit shaking and sweating until my anger passes and then I feel weak and sick and I want to cry... but I hold that in too...

She took me to work and I think she did it so she could continue with the verbal rampage; I had to wear the scarlet ski-jacket she'd bought me even though we don't go skiing, because of course, my coat was somewhere, maybe with Kylie or maybe in Shohib's taxi.

I texted him to say thanks again for his help last night and Rebecca demanded to know who I was texting; she sometimes seems to go into this fantasy that I have a girlfriend or I'm having an affair. I daren't even say the only girls I know are Jessica and Kylie because she would begin to imagine things about them.

We'd stopped in a queue of traffic and I showed her what I'd texted, and then as she was looking, it bipped and a message pinged back from Shohib saying he'd been glad to help and he hoped the old man was OK and he looked forward to seeing me again... and if I needed a cab ask for him when I rang the company.

I half expected Rebecca not to believe this and think it was some devious coded message... but she thrust it back at me without saying anything and I said I thought I must have left my coat in his taxi... She tutted but said nothing more and when she pulled up by the office, she turned her face away so I couldn't kiss her. I got out and resisted slamming the door, but tapped on the window and mouthed 'I love you' at her. She looked indifferent and drove away.

I'd been so happy last night...

Gerald called me into the office again and asked me how I was getting on with the applications for the jobs he'd passed to me. I muttered something; perhaps I should have asked him straight out why he was encouraging me to go, whether there was any truth in the rumours in the office... although to be fair the only rumour had come from Kylie. Perhaps I should have asked him, but I didn't. I felt in a way as if I had an advantage that he didn't know I knew.

He said if I wanted him to look over what I'd done on the application, or read through my covering letter, or practice my interview techniques – because he was sure I would get an interview...

I thanked him in a mumbly way and left the office without waiting for Vicky to ring with a pretend phone call for him.

I picked up a file from my desk at random and went over to Kylie and pulled up a chair beside her and opened the details of a property sale I was dealing with.

She looked at me suspiciously and pulled off her headphones. In a low voice, not looking at her but looking at the document, I asked how she was.

"You were brilliant last night, Thomas," she said taking an arbitrary sheet of paper and peering at it.

"Not me, you. I'd never have bothered with him, I'd have just asked if he was ok then walked on," I tuned the page over.

"You look very tired," she said not looking at me but beginning to type at random. "What did your wife say when you got home?"

"She was in bed," and how I wished I'd just taken the trouble to stick my stuff in the laundry bin and have a shower. Even before I'd snatched some breakfast, I'd put my yesterday's clothes which could be washed in the washing machine with the bedding; Rebecca had made me strip the bed, even taking off the undersheet and the underslips from the pillow, and I'd washed the bathroom floor.

"She didn't look too happy this morning," Kylie said, and pounded furiously on the keyboard.

"Oh... you saw her drop me off," I couldn't keep the dismay from my voice; I must have looked like a real loser.

"Face like a slapped arse. Ditch her and come to bed with me."

"Now you're being ridiculous!"

"Problem Thomas?" it was Julie, looking across at us from her desk. I must have spoken louder than I intended.

"No, just a little dispute over a semi-colon," and I picked up the file, gathered the random sheets we'd pretended to look at, and went back to my desk.

Kylie waited until everyone was in the office before she went over to Julie to give her the rest of the money for the Oriel... I was so glad she was able to do that because I know she would have refused if I'd offered to lend her the money, but I'd been so shocked seeing her scurrying out of the pawn shop... Kylie doesn't scurry... I couldn't bear the thought of her having to go there again.... and I wondered what had gone wrong in her life that she was suddenly so desperate for money... and I couldn't ask her...

I texted Rebecca for the second time and I thought she'd texted back but it was John asking what had happened. I took my phone and jacket and left the office so I could ring him; usually I would have gone outside but although it wasn't snowing, the sky looked a ghastly colour and it was cold and miserable. I stood on the stairwell and as I spoke to him, telling him the strange tale of the poor old man, and how wonderful Kylie had been, so caring and compassionate, I noticed the tinsel curled round the bannister rail and realised we'd not put up our decorations at home. Was that one more thing I'd forgotten to do? Was this why Rebecca was so cool at the moment, was she waiting for me to suggest we got the Christmas box out?

I was back to feeling down... I felt as if things were my fault... it was cold standing by the window looking out across the snowy alley behind our building and although I'd finished my call to John I didn't want to go back to the office... what could they do if I was away from my desk, sack me?

The door above opened and someone came into the stairwell. I stood still but their conversation continued.

"So go on then," someone said.

I would have gone back up the stairs but I heard my name mentioned and I sat down again.

"I was talking to Thomas the other day, he's kind of cute isn't he?" it was Julie! I could hardly believe my ears! Was she being sarcastic?

There was a murmur and I couldn't tell who she was talking to.

"I thought he and Kylie might have something going on, I've seen them together a couple of times," she laughed as the other person said something. "I know! But I think he's just being kind to her, feels sorry for her most like... he was very sweet when we had lunch together the other day."

Lunch together?! She sat at my desk with her box of salad, that wasn't having lunch together!

"So is there a date? There will be a hell of a lot to do beforehand... and we can't even start yet!"

Was she talking about the merger... she must be...

"After Christmas? Getting ready to rock from January? Great... at least I can enjoy myself and not have to think about it all... I must say I'm quite excited... It's going to be quite a shock for some people, isn't it?" and she laughed.

Her phone, or the other person's phone rang and the door went and I was left on my own, sitting on the stairs and looking at the decorations... hmm, Happy Christmas everyone...

Wednesday, December 11th, 2013, evening

I took refuge in the family tree... my family's history. I know I was going about things in a back to front way... but somehow that's how my mind works, so I left Tolik, in the pub, as far as I knew and continued to look at his brothers and sisters.

Robert, born 1848, had five daughters and one son, William; I would follow the daughters' lines one day, their children would be my distant relatives after all; Robert's only son William was killed in the first war, and his three sons had their names changed to Brunty.

Thirza, born in 1850, had married James Dean, and had at least one son, and I would return to the Dean family another time.

Osman had married Estelle, and had four children, two boys and two girls... how lovely that would be... I let my thoughts return to my children that I would never have, and I added another little boy... what should I call him? Taras, maybe because I really thought the original Thomas had been Taras before he became a Radwinter Tolik, Lillah, Isabella and Taras...

I made Rebecca and me a coffee... she was just about speaking to me... I'd bought her some special chocolates and some flowers to say sorry.

Osman Radwinter, born in 1852, married Estelle Chappell, from Coventry and they had George, Henry, Maud and Harriet. In 1891 the last column dealing with infirmities, still entitled 'If' had three categories: (i) Deaf and Dumb, (ii) Blind, (iii) Lunatic, Imbecile or Idiot, and I wondered where those poor folk were kept, and how they were kept. In 1901, they were still at the same address in Birmingham, and I noticed the census form had changed again; there was extra information given regarding the occupation in column 14, Employer, Owner, or Own account, and in column 15 it said 'If Working at Home'. The last column had reverted to four categories, (i) Deaf and Dumb, (ii) Blind, (iii) Lunatic, (iv) Imbecile, feeble minded.

In 1901 George Radwinter was a house carpenter, his brother Henry was a clerk in a tea merchant's, and Maud and Harriet were still at school. There was a change by 1911 for the family, because now all four of the children were married… and there were grandchildren! George had twins Ernest and John aged seven, Henry had a little girl Dorothy aged three and a baby Sidney aged one, Maud had two girls Florence and Gladys aged three and Harriet, who was only twenty-two herself, had a son called David. So Osman and Estelle had seven grandchildren at this point… how wonderful!

"What are you grinning at?" Rebecca asked. She'd come to collect my cup for the dish washer.

"Come and have a look at all the little Radwinters!" I said. "Look Ernest and John, they're twins, then Dorothy and Sidney, and Florence and Gladys and little David! Some of them must have had children… we must have got cousins in Birmingham!"

Rebecca stared at what I had on the screen.

"I think you're just wasting your time," she said.

Well, if she could play her game and buy imaginary houses then I could find my real relations... I nearly said that, but I held it in.

"We've not got any decorations up yet! I was just thinking about that today, shall I find the box and start?"

I didn't actually feel in a very Christmassy mood... I wanted to tell Rebecca about work, but what could I say, that there was a rumour? That I'd half heard a conversation, that Gerald kept giving me information about jobs hundreds of miles away?

"I'm fed up with all that old stuff, I'll get some new," she said... which she said most years.

"That's a good idea," I said trying to sound enthusiastic. "I think they've got late night opening at Castledown, should we go? We could eat in their restaurant?"

Castledown was a massive garden centre which always had big Christmas displays; in the past we've gone over there several times to get different things to decorate the flat.

After a moment she replied that she would go in before work one day when she was starting later. I hadn't really wanted to go trailing round looking at decorations but now I was disappointed.

"What's that face for?" she asked. "You don't like Christmas shopping, and you always moan about getting the dressings for the Christmas tree."

"We just never seem to do anything together; I just thought it would be nice to spend some time with you, do something together..."

"I can't help having to work late," she said defensively.

"I know Becca, I know, I'm so sorry that you do... couldn't you swap shifts with some of the others occasionally, we never seem to have any time together, and when we do you're tired," and as that sounded like another criticism I hastily said how sorry I felt for her, and how I wished I could do something to help... which was ridiculous because obviously I couldn't... except maybe to be more understanding and less selfish... to think of her more and not of me.

She gave a tight smile and took the cup into the kitchen; I followed her.

"Can we make a plan to go out together, it would be lovely to treat you to somewhere nice," I asked, and my mind did one of its funny things and skipped to wondering if anyone ever did anything nice for Kylie.

Rebecca took out her phone to check her diary; our calendar was hanging on the wall and I could see nothing was written in except for the Oriel on the 18th, a party at Paul's on the 20th. She used to put her work schedule up but it had got so erratic that she just kept it on her phone now.

"When is the Willows Christmas party?" I asked because I always had to go... had to, that makes it sound as if I didn't want to. There were always loads of activities there, carol concerts, a seasonal quiz night, a charity bazaar... There was usually a leaflet stuck upon our little kitchen notice board, I realised, but this year there was nothing.

"We could go out on the 18th if you really want," she said almost begrudgingly. I had a surge of anger, if *I really wanted*? If *I* did? I held down my anger... she couldn't help being good at her job.

"The 18th is when I'm going out with people from work," oh joy.

"The 20th?"

"We're going to Paul's," I reminded her. She nodded and put it into her phone then turned and finished putting things in the dish washer with nothing decided...

I left the kitchen and went back to my computer... something is really wrong with our marriage.

The 1891 census... Thomas Radwinter... but not the original Thomas, his grandson, now aged twenty-four, like his father, was the landlord of another pub in Easthope... the Lark! I burst out laughing and Rebecca came in from the kitchen to see what had amused me.

"But why is it funny?" she asked.

"Because that's where we go for the quiz, John and me! I can't believe it! How wonderful!"

"Why is it wonderful?"

"Well, Thomas might be our great-great-grandad, and there we are in his pub!" I went into the kitchen to get a beer to celebrate; Rebecca's phone was on the side and it rang her little text tune. I was going to take it to her, then I had a dreadful idea... that I should look at it... I don't know why I thought it and I resisted the thought straight away.

I carefully poured the Kozel lager, I would have drunk it from the bottle if I'd been alone. I returned to the sitting room and Rebecca was looking at my computer, she clicked something guiltily as she saw me.

"Very interesting," she said.

"It is," I replied as if I didn't realise she'd been checking out what else I'd been looking at. "Even when I'm not doing it I can't help thinking about it."

"Smithy is doing his tree too… on his mum's side, there are too many Smiths about to do his dad's," this was the first normal conversation, even though it was only a sentence long, that we'd had for a while. I wondered what Smithy's other name was, ever since Rebecca had worked there he'd always been Smithy… It had been a little joke between them because she'd been Smith before we married and that had been her nick-name at school.

"It depends what his dad's first name is, and where he comes from… if it's unusual or it's a small place where the family lived then it shouldn't be too bad," I tried to carry it on. "I'm sorry, Becca I didn't offer you a drink, would you like a lager, or a Kopparberg?"

She asked for a strawberry and lime Kopparberg and I went to get one; her phone sang again, and I was tempted just to look at it… but I didn't. I cut a slice of lime and found some ice cubes, and raided the strawberries she kept in the fridge for her breakfast. I hesitated behind the door and looked through the crack above the hinge… she was on my computer again…

I kicked the door as if by accident and said a not very naughty word, giving her time to get back on the right page and sit back, waiting for her drink.

People think I'm an idiot, people including my wife think I am. I'm not, not at all.

Thursday, December 12th 2013

I'd texted Kylie before I went to bed, just briefly, telling her I'd overheard Julie saying something interesting, but she didn't reply. I hung around the bus station and was relieved to see her getting off the 207.

The weather had cheered up a little it wasn't so cold but I suggested we went for coffee; she said she didn't want one, but I think she meant she couldn't afford one because she gave in when I pretended to be pathetic and said I didn't want to go on my own. She said again I didn't have to buy her a drink; I told her I was pleased to, it made me feel like a gentleman, and she laughed. She had my coat in the shopping bag she was carrying and I said thank goodness because I felt such an idiot in the red ski jacket. I said it was a pity it was too big for her, because I didn't want it.

"So you want me to look a real idiot?" she asked. We went straight downstairs in the coffee shop, the lady had called out *'your usual?'* and I'd called back *'yes please'*.

"If you know anyone who wants it take it, please," I said taking it off.

She was looking at it; it was very thick, very warm, and had been very expensive… but I hated it, and would take it to a charity shop…

She was quiet so I talked, went on about the family tree because it was safe; when it was time to go I put on my coat and stuffed the ghastly red ski jacket into a bag saying again that Kylie was welcome to it if she knew someone who could use it... and left it at that.

I was surprised that Rebecca texted me at lunch time; she never has texted me often, but she used to – to tell me what time she was finishing if she was leaving early or later than expected, or to ask me about dinner, or other usual wife to husband things. I can't now remember when she last texted me except in response to me texting her, so I was surprised and a little uneasy...

So it was nice when I read her text and she was saying that she was finishing early so if I wanted to go late night shopping tonight to look for decorations we could. I was really pleased and texted right back that I was happy to do so and if we wanted dinner, should I book at Nonna Ysabel?

Martin and Gordon were both out of the office and Sandra was in with Gerald as I got my lunchbox out; cheese sandwiches again, a sausage roll a bag of crisps and an apple. We never seemed to have very much of interest in the fridge these days. It was another reflection of how hard Rebecca was working, that she so often had to eat at the Willows and I'd make myself something simple; we usually had a Tesco's delivery each week but again that hadn't happened, or it would just be a couple of bags rather than a couple of crates.

We hadn't done any Christmas food shopping yet; usually we'd been trying different mince-pies for six weeks or so... I realised I hadn't had a single mince-pie at home this year... maybe Ruthie could do a range of mince-pies, just as she was for her shortbread... I felt a little sad that I hadn't seen Ruthie or even heard from her again... she was busy too.

I almost jumped as Julie dumped her salad box on my desk and went to get a chair. Kylie glanced across at me and pulled a silly face.

"Lunch time, Kylie, " I called, "Come and join us!" the moment I said it I realised that she either went out at lunch time or sat and worked through... she never ate anything... She used to bring something like we all did but I hadn't seen her eating at work since... since I'd realised that somehow she was very hard up.

Kylie didn't even look at me even though she heard me. The phone rang and Julie went to answer it. I opened my lunch box, took out the pack of sandwiches and went over to Kylie's desk while Julie had her back to us. I slipped the pack beside her keyboard.

"You can't abandon me to Julie, I think she fancies me!" I hissed and hurried back to my desk.

Julie went into Gerald's office and I wanted to say something to Kylie but didn't know what, so I went on Facebook and sent a private message to Jessica. We'd messaged each other a couple of times and she'd asked again for me to visit; Julie returned and launched into some trivial story about shopping for a Christmas present for her mother, referring to other people by name as if I should know who they were, sisters maybe or nieces...

I risked a look at Kylie, she glanced across and I looked pleadingly at her as Julie burrowed in her bag to find some photos and moments later Kylie stomped over.

"What's this then, lunch club?" she asked, slapping down my sandwiches and pulling up a chair.

"Thomas and I were just - "

Before Julie could say what she and I were just doing I interrupted.

"What have you got for lunch, today, Kylie? I've got a sausage roll," I raised my eyebrow slightly.

Kylie cackled and Julie tutted at her and I chomped my sausage roll, my emotional roller coaster chugging upwards again as Kylie ate my sandwiches and Julie tried to tell me all about her family. Julie was trying to eat slowly in the hope that Kylie would finish and go back to her desk, but I gave Kylie my apple telling her that fruit was bad for me and then, leaving them together, I went and made them coffee, then grabbed my coat and left the office.

I was working my way through the intricacies of a conveyancing procedure and had just passed the documents to Gordon when the phone rang and as Julie was working with Sandra I picked it up. A woman with a strong Easthope accent and a raspy voice asked to speak to Kylie.

I passed the phone to her and went back to my desk; I'd never known Kylie to receive a call at work... but it happened that any of us might from time to time.

I began to look at the next page when I was suddenly aware of Kylie standing beside me.

"I have to leave now, can I go, please can I go?" she blurted, looking sideways out of the window at the miserable day.

"Of course you can, is something wrong?" I had no authority to let her go but I didn't care. For her to ask me for anything was unusual, to ask for something like this was unique. She didn't answer but stared sideways, her jaw clenching. "It must be important so go, yes… go on."

I wanted to ask her if I could help, if she needed money, but something about her face made me resist. She grabbed the little blue coat, hoisted her bag on her shoulder and hurried out without even switching off her computer. I went to her desk and closed everything down and tidied everything away.

Julie and Sandra had turned away and I guessed they weren't working now but gossiping about something.

 "Something personal has cropped up for Kylie and I told her she could go," I said to Sandra.

"*You* told her she could go?" said Sandra.

"Yes, she so rarely has time off, and she's never had an issue like this before so I said it was fine," I wasn't going to apologise for my decision. "Is there a problem? Should I go and tell Gerald about it?"

I sounded rude, even to my own ears. I was fed up with the way I was being treated… I almost felt like saying '*oh, and by the way, would you like to tell me when exactly this merger that I know nothing about is going to take place?*' I didn't, I just stared at Sandra, waiting for her to say something.

"You should have referred it to me," she said; Julie was looking at me… and if I had to choose a word to describe her expression I would say 'coquettish'.

"Why? You were busy," I didn't smile, I wasn't feeling very smiley.

Sandra couldn't think of anything to say; she glanced across to Gordon obviously wondering whether to draw him into this. I went back to my desk at the other end of the office and carried on with conveyancing but minutes later Julie came over to ask if I would like a coffee. She'd never done this before and I had a terrible sinking feeling.

"You were great sticking up for Kylie like that," she whispered and then whisked away and made a drink, even though I'd said I didn't want one… oh dear…

Thursday, December 12th 2013, late afternoon

I met Rebecca under the clock in the mall and gave her a hug; I was so pleased that she'd decided to meet me. She seemed tired though, and I could tell I was irritating her, I was chatting because I was nervous… nervous with my own wife. I suggested we went for a drink first but she said she'd had a cup of tea before she'd left work and she wanted to get these decorations bought.

It was very busy, people pushing and shoving everywhere, it was a special night apparently when a lot of the shops were giving away prizes, and there were lots of stalls in the open area of the mall selling Christmassy foods like chestnuts and German gingerbread, the dry stuff which didn't taste very gingery. There was a school choir at one end singing carols, the Salvation Army band at the other and piped music from every shop in between. It was pretty chaotic and my pleasure at being out with my wife began to evaporate as we trudged from shop to shop, none of which had anything which pleased her.

There were loads of children about too because Santa was supposed to driving through the mall on his sleigh later; he would throw sweets at the crowd and the shoppers would give his elves money for some charity or other. There was a big Christmas tree and you could buy a star and write a wish on it and the money went to the Mayor's Christmas fund. Rebecca wanted to write a wish; I didn't ask what, I almost felt so apart from her now that I couldn't even guess what it might be.

As I stood waiting I noticed a little boy, a toddler really who seemed to be on his own. He was looking up at the tree, his eyes and mouth open with wonder.

"I wonder where his mummy is?" I asked Rebecca. At the same moment it seemed to occur to him that he was on his own. He was a little black kid with a red hat with ears, pushed to the back of his head and held by a strap under his chin.

"Stupid woman letting a child that age wander around on his own," Rebecca remarked.

No doubt his mum was anxiously looking for him right this minute, and I had a sudden flash of memory of me being lost in a crowd as a child and Marcus finding me and lifting me up safe in his strong arms.

The little boy was looking round anxiously now and although I couldn't hear him, I think he was shouting for his mummy. No-one seemed to be taking any notice of him.

"Come on Thomas, I want to go to Shapiro's, come on," Rebecca turned away from posting her star in a silver glittery box.

"We can't just leave him," I said and I bent down to talk to him. "Hello little man, where's your mummy?" I asked.

He looked at me and tears tumbled down his chubby cheeks; I don't know anything about children but I realised he was even younger than I'd thought.

"Where's mummy?" I asked again. He began to cry a jumble of infant prattle escaping from him. He was so little he ran the risk of being trodden on so I picked him up and stood looking round for a woman anxiously searching for her child.

"Oh for heaven's sake!" Rebecca was annoyed instead of being sympathetic... She is wonderful with old people, but she can't abide children and babies... *she can't abide them*... the thought was like ice... we would never have children, I saw that now.

"You go to Shapiro's I'll wait here until this little one's mummy arrives," I told her calmly so I didn't upset the child anymore; he was howling now and people were beginning to look at us.

Rebecca left me, and as I watched her pushing her way through the crowds, her dark hair pinned up on the back of her head, a brilliant turquoise scarf round her neck I had a dreadful feeling that she was leaving me in a different way too...

The little boy had grasped my beard in both his chubby hands and was saying something but I didn't understand him; I pulled a hankie from my pocket and wiped his little face... he was a cute little kid and I talked to him... nonsense no doubt...

"There we go, your facey is all wiped now, that's better isn't it! We'll have to go and look for your mummy soon, won't we, where do you think she is? Helping Father Christmas?"

"Kissmuss! Kissmuss!" he exclaimed and let go of my beard with one hand and grabbed the hanky; it was red with white spots and I think one of Paul's boys had given it to me last year knowing that I like proper handkerchiefs. "Mama! Mama!" he squealed, all tears gone, only excitement.

Kylie was pushing through the crowds towards us.

"Mama!" and the little one reached out to her.

I stood in utter astonishment, and then gave a grimace of pain as he tried to yank my beard off my face as he fell into her arms.

Safe in his mother's embrace, in Kylie's arms, he waved the hanky cheerfully at me, exclaiming 'Kissmuss! Kissmuss!' over and over.

Kylie stared at me expressionlessly then turned away and pushed back into the crowd.

I was shocked; I had never for one moment thought that Kylie might have children... It shows how little I really know about her, I didn't even know she had a boyfriend... or maybe she doesn't... I wondered whether to text her... but to say what? That I hoped the little boy was alright? That I hoped *she* was alright?

Was her poverty affecting the little boy? He looked healthy and clean and well, he'd been fine once his mama had appeared... in fact he'd been fine once he had possession of my red and white spotty handkerchief...

One more mystery about Kylie that I was never likely to know... I wouldn't ask her anything, it was none of my business, but I thought about how desperate she must be about her job, even more desperate than I'd realised.

I looked round at the people bustling past with their bags overflowing, buying more and more of what they probably didn't need. I thought of us buying more Christmas decorations that we definitely didn't need. A Salvation Army person walked past with a collecting box and I called to her and thrust a twenty pound note into the slot... it wasn't to make me feel better... and it *didn't* make me feel better... but maybe someone would get a bed for the night and a hot meal...

I rang Marcus that night; I felt so low. Rebecca was in the study and I could hear her talking and laughing with one of her on-line friends, someone in America or Australia or Timbuktu for all I knew. We'd had a proper meal together at home, not at Nonna Ysabel, but Rebecca had made a pasta and chorizo dish that I like... no doubt it was as nice as usual but it seemed tasteless to me and I opened a bottle of wine to see if that improved things.

We hadn't found any decorations but Rebecca had found some things she wanted for her sisters' ghastly children, they were the last things on her list apparently, everything else was done. There was a box of exotically wrapped presents for us to take to Paul, a bag with John's present, and a big bag of gifts for Rebecca's family, parents, sisters, brothers-in-law, aunties, uncles, cousins, grandparents... the pile along the wall of the study was enormous.

Marcus sounded cheerful and spoke warmly, telling me what had been happening in the parish, asking after Rebecca and her family, and work...

"What's wrong Tommy?" he asked suddenly, interrupting me. I don't remember him calling me 'Tommy' before. "Something's happened, what's wrong?"

Thank goodness he wasn't actually with me, because a tear rolled down my cheek.

"Nothing, Marcus, really... I'm alright."

"No you're not... do you want me to come to you?" the wind was howling outside, even through the double glazing I could hear the larches thrashing about. It would take nearly an hour for him to get here and goodness knows what the moors would be like... but he was ready to jump in his car and come to me.

"No, really, Marcus, I'm alright... just feeling a little low... I'm worried about work... and Rebecca..."

He asked if she was alright, but of course she was... well, I think she was.

I asked if maybe he was free at some point I could come up to see him, or maybe if he was down this way we could get together. He asked again if he should come now and I tried to buck myself up and sound a bit more in control... and that was it, I felt out of control... I'd felt strong and confident standing holding Kylie's little boy, I don't why but having his little fists clutched in my beard and wiping his tears I'd felt different.

"Perhaps I've got the winter blues or whatever it's called," I said trying to put a laugh into my voice.

"Do you miss Mum?" Marcus asked taking me by surprise. She was something which was never discussed, less so than Dad was never discussed, but it was as if the four of us never had parents somehow.

"I never think about her," I answered truthfully. Then I dared to ask, "Do you miss her, Marcus?"

"Yes, yes, I do, Tommy, especially at this time of year."

I didn't know what to say... I'd never realised... I tried to think how old he would have been when Mum died, older than I am now...

He finished the call by asking again if I was really ok and if I was sure he didn't want me to come down now, but I tried to reassure him, told him I loved him and we said goodnight.

I sat with my computer off, thinking about Marcus, thinking about Paul and John too and what their family life might have been like before I came along... none of us ever spoke of it. I lived with Marcus and Jill while Mum was ill and kept on living with them until Rebecca and I got married... and we'd never talked about anything... I thought I was keeping it back, holding it in, but maybe they were too... it had never struck me before. I began to understand why Marcus had been so reserved about my research... and I began to wonder why Paul had asked me in the first place.

My phone bipped and it was an unknown number. Suspiciously I opened the message. *"Kylie here, no phone. Thanks xxx."*

I was so deep in thought that I didn't hear the doorbell at first; to my surprise it was John. He was fed up he said so had come round to have a drink with me or take me out... going out seemed like a great idea... I told Rebecca, didn't ask but *told* her, I was going out with my brother, and it was only later he told me that Marcus had rung him because he was so worried about me.

Friday, December 13th 2013

As I was on the bus, missing my bus-buddy, and feeling a little hung-over, I texted Marcus to thank him for getting in touch with John and said I felt much better now and we'd had a good night. John had taken me to the Bolton Spanner where there was a band playing. I hadn't stayed out late but doing something different had lifted my spirits. I got home and Rebecca was already in bed so I carefully put away my clothes neatly and crept into bed as quietly as I could. She was awake however, and surprisingly had embraced me and we'd made love… the first time for quite a while I realised.

Now on the bus I remembered something which I'd forgotten when I'd got up this morning, groggy and with a head-ache nagging. I remembered that I'd drifted to sleep and woken and gone to the kitchen for a drink. The bathroom door was shut and I could hear Rebecca inside… sobbing. I'd tapped on the door and asked if she was alright, after a moment she replied she was fine and for me to go back to bed… I dithered for a moment but then did as she said. I'd meant to stay awake until she came back, but too much beer, love, and weariness overcame me.

I texted her now saying I loved her but not asking anything else… I would try and talk to her tonight… we had to clear the air of whatever the problem was between us… I couldn't say what it was… we seemed to be drifting, but drifting in opposite directions. I tried to persuade myself that the realisation I'd had yesterday that we would never have children was just me being silly… in the New Year we would look for a house…

To my surprise Kylie was standing at my bus stop when I got off.

"You're early," I said.

"Can't wait to hear the next exciting instalment of your bloody Poles or Ukrainians or whoever they are," she slipped her arm through mine and I decided I needed breakfast so we went to the Armenian café for eggs.

It was snowing like fury so we were both like snowmen when we arrived at the café; we hadn't been able to talk as we battled our way along and we spent a little time thawing with tea, not chocolate while the lady made our breakfast.

"I will pay you back," she said without looking at me. She was wearing the woollen thing again which was completely sodden. How she hadn't got pneumonia I couldn't imagine.

"I know you will... you wait until you see what interest I charge," I replied.

She gave a dirty laugh, gave me a look but didn't reply; there'd been tears in her eyes again. I was getting worn down by my piddling little problems, she must be almost crushed by hers. I wanted to ask so much... but I asked nothing... just told her more about what I'd found out, and how worried I was about what was happening in the Ukraine at the moment.

"Why should you worry? You don't know anyone living there," she tore off a bit of the warm fresh bread and dipped it into her eggs.

I had to confess it was rather silly, but watching the news, or catching up with it on line...

"You're just a very loving person, Thomas, and I think you should just be a little more loving with me!"

I laughed, blushed, made a facetious comment… then with a dawning horror, wondered if perhaps she was offering herself to me… to pay me back…

Suddenly my chest was tight and I was gasping for breath and fumbling in my pocket for my inhaler. I pushed my chair back and went outside into the blizzard, fighting to breathe. Kylie had rushed out with me, and it was the sight of her shivering beside me as she asked if I was alright that forced me to calm myself.

I apologised and we went back in to where the café lady was anxiously waiting with a cup of tea to help me breathe… I don't know what it was some sort of spiced concoction but what with that and my inhaler I was soon alright, but very hot and sweaty and feeling a little sick.

"Look what happens when you make me blush," I said to Kylie who was still looking at me fiercely, which I recognized meant she was anxious. "How's the little boy? I didn't frighten him did I?" I threw it into the stream of ordinary talk.

"He's fine," she looked at her eggs.

"So anyway, I'm getting a bit confused with all these later generations… I've got bits of paper all over the place with different families on," and I wittered boringly on about the Radwinters.

I went to Strand Royal after work to see Jessica; I had a feeling you weren't allowed to take flowers to hospital, I didn't know what the policy might be on fruit and thought other people would bring it anyway, and I wasn't sure how pregnant people felt about chocolate… One of Rebecca's sisters had suffered terribly from being sick when she was pregnant and so I thought perhaps chocolate wasn't a good idea.

I wondered about toiletries… but that seemed too personal, and a girlie sort of gift. I had to get a secret Santa present for work too; Gordon had asked me to organize it which meant me going round with a hat full of pieces of paper with everyone's name; I made sure I got Kylie's by the simple trick of not putting her name into the bag. I didn't want one of the others to buy something for her, I had the feeling they might do something as a joke which wasn't funny, but now I had the impossible task of getting something.

I decided on a book for Jessica and after gazing at the ranks of shiny new publications, ended up getting her the Man Booker prize winner, The Luminaries by Eleanor Catton. I knew Jessica loved reading, and I remember having a conversation about the Booker with her… if she had it already then I would give it to Rebecca. I also got her the latest Inspector Rebus novel… I know she's a fan and I thought if she's going to be spending a long time sitting around then maybe a good book would be just the things.

She was delighted to see me, and I was delighted to see her and to see her looking so well and so happy. She really was blooming, although she said she was being driven mad by being kept in hospital. I sat beside her and we gossiped and chatted and caught up with each other's news, not that I have much but I managed to pad it out. I thought how much I liked her, and I was amazed that we actually seem to have a real friendship, which had now extended beyond the bus.

Her husband David arrived and seemed as pleased to meet me as Jessica had been to see me; apparently she'd told him about me and he suggested that when Jess was home before or after Riley arrived, then Rebecca and I should get together with them. I said I had to go, no doubt they had things to talk about, and David shook my hand and I kissed Jessica and I went home feeling a little more happy than I had going home last night after the wretched shopping trip.

Friday, December 13th 2013, evening

In 1881 Taras was also working in the umbrella factory belonging to James Dean, but he was living with his brother Cazimir, a metal worker, on the High Street in Easthope. They were grown men now, and they couldn't be expected to be still living with Tolik... I was saving him till last because somehow I thought he might be our direct ancestor... I don't know why I did, maybe because I'd spent so much time at first pouring over the material from Radwinter and then my imagination had been caught by the mysterious way Thomas had left Thirza taking their son with him, accompanied by little Lamy Coote ... I somehow imagined her as a little wispy thing... but she must have been strong to bear all nine children and to move round so much.

Both brothers were missing from the 1891 census, but I couldn't find them recorded as having died and I wondered if maybe had moved away from Easthope, maybe left the country... I remembered checking the passenger lists for their uncle Tolik and finding him sailing to Adelaide... had the family ever thought about Tolik Radwinski, or even been in touch with him and decided to go to Australia too?

I realised how adept I'm becoming at searching for things, how quickly I can assess old documents or sources because I struck lucky within half an hour of searching.

The top of the page I found said SCHEDULE B, and beneath it, FORM OF PASSENGER LIST. Below that was a section for details of the voyage, six columns, *'Ship's Name, Master's Name, Tons of Register, Aggregate number of superficial feet in the several compartments set apart for Passengers, other than Cabin Passengers, Total number of Statute Adults, and Cabin Passengers which the Ship can legally carry, Where Bound'*.

The ship was *The Teutonic*, the Master was P.J. Irving, the tonnage was 4244, the Aggregate blah blah was 17616, the number of Statute Adults was 1012 and where bound... New York. So the brothers had gone to New York... I might have American cousins...

Beneath that the master, P.J. Irving had signed the declaration on 6th August 1890 (it actually had 188_ , but he'd added the '90') that he hereby Certified *'that the Provisions actually laden on board this Ship are sufficient, according to the requirements of the passengers Act, for 1014 Statute Adults, for a voyage of 32 days'*. The master had written in 1014 adults, rather than the 1012 which was legal... I don't quite understand that, but it doesn't actually matter.

Then there was a table for the details of the passengers entitled *'Names and Descriptions of Passengers. (N.B. – Cabin Passengers must also be included in this Schedule, after other Passengers. Sec 6 Of 26 and 27 Vict., Cap. 51)'* I have no idea what this last part means.

The table was divided into columns filled in by hand in blue ink, with quite a lot of crossing out; I guess these days it's easy to alter schedules and passenger manifests and so on, in those days it was a pen and ink job.

The first column was *'Port of Embarkation, LIVERPOOL, no. of ticket.'* Then came columns for name, whether Adults, Children or Infants, Profession, Occupation or Calling of Passengers, and then there were four columns for ENGLISH, SCOTCH, IRISH, FOREIGN, each subdivided into *'Age of each Adult of 12 years and upwards (Married or Single) Ages of Children between 1 and 12 years, and Infants'*. The very last column was *'Port at which Passengers have contracted to Land'* and there it was *'New York'*.

There were more than a dozen pages which followed listing the passengers, and there on page 15 (although the handwritten number was just a squiggle) below the family of Mr Lewis a housekeeper (I think), Maud aged 8, George aged 6, Isidor aged 4 and an infant, and above Mr W.A. Thompson a dressmaker (I think), were Mr T. Radwinter, umbrella maker, and Mr. C. Radwinter, plumber.

I sat back, staring at the screen, then continued looking through the passenger list to the end where there was a summary of steerage and cabin passengers. The numbers of passengers in each section had been added up, all done by mental arithmetic I guess, 41 married English men and 80 married women, 333 single men and 106 single women, 14 Scots adults and one each of Scottish children and infants, 92 Irish adults and 11 Irish children and infants, and an astonishing 260 foreigners with their 38 children and infants… I wonder if any of them were Polish or Ukrainian?

I sat wondering about the Radwinter children… their father Thomas must have spoken with an accent, he must have told them that he came from somewhere else… did they know where? Were they interested? Had they a smattering of Polish words?

I checked incoming passenger lists from the USA, but no Radwinters... I could buy an extra option on MyTimeMachine to be able to look at other records and maybe I would one day... but my next task was to go back to Tolik... He must be our ancestor...

Saturday, December 14th, 2013

There was a Christmas bazaar at the Willows on Saturday and as I walked in I wondered when I had last visited; I used to come fairly regularly to the different things put on for the elderly residents. I'd always been pleased to come with Rebecca, proud of how well thought of she was, and pleased at all the lovely things staff, residents and their families said about her.

I used to come to all the activities when I could, but somehow over the past year that had dropped off. I'd come to the Christmas party last year, and the carol concert, and the quiz night... but when I looked at the notice board I saw that I'd missed the concert and the quiz this year; I'd missed the local silver band coming in and the U3A choir, and the party, which was next week had not been mentioned.

There were a lot of new residents who I didn't know, but when I spoke to one old chap he said he'd been here since February; he told me that he'd come in on Valentine's Day and there had been a party and he'd thought this was the right place to come to. Events at the Willows aren't very exciting but I sort of feel it's my duty to come to support Rebecca; they're always quite jolly, and although many of the residents have memory problems, some of them are just old and are interesting to talk to. I tried to remember when I'd last come... to the summer fete, I think...

There were a lot of new staff, but I got chatting to Smithy and his wife. She seemed in a grumpy mood but he was amiable enough; I don't really like him that much, he's what Marcus would call a smoothy and always seems obsessed with his car. He talks to me about cars and I really have no interest in them at all except to get me from here to there.

Like us, they don't have any children... I thought about Jessica sitting in the chair beside her hospital bed looking lovely... radiant. Even though she was fed up with being there, she didn't really care as long as the baby was alright. Her husband David, although clearly desperate for her to come home, had seemed pleased that his wife and child were being so well cared for.

I thought of Lamy and her nine children... and for all I knew she may have had other children who died... for some reason I'd not checked births in general, just looked up the children who appeared on the census... I must remember to do that.

Smithy's wife was called Emily or Emma and I could never remember what it was even though I'd met her many times and we'd gone out for a couple of rather dull evenings together; I could never think of anything to talk about to them, or would blurt out silly things and Rebecca would look daggers at me.

I realised I'd glazed over while he was talking about something and now I had no clue what he was going on about. Luckily he then asked me what I was doing with myself these days and I was able to mention my family research, remembering that Rebecca said he was doing something similar. His wife, Emily or Emma pulled a bored face and walked away; she's very tall and had her blond hair tied back in a ponytail so it swung as she strode out of the day room.

Smithy has a way of talking which somehow irritates me; he makes remarks he thinks are funny which I don't or I just don't understand. Last time we went out with him and Emma or Emily he and Rebecca did a lot of laughing, sometimes I think at me, and Emma/Emily just looked bored and texted a lot.

Now he was asking what cars my brothers had, clearly thinking that ours was of little interest; John doesn't have a car, Marcus drives an old Zafira with plenty of room for parishioners and transporting things, and as for Paul… I actually don't know… I think it's red and it might be a BMW or it might be something else German… it didn't really matter because actually Smithy wasn't interested, just wanted an excuse to talk about motors, as he called them.

Smithy isn't chubby at all, in fact he's quite slim, but he has a roundish face; Rebecca thinks he looks a bit like a young Colin Firth… I've no idea, but I do always think his attitude to me, although superficially friendly, is rather superior and demeaning. He makes little comments about lawyers and leeches, and about people who've been to university whereas he's been to the *'University of Life'*.

He once tried to give me one of those handshakes where you bump fists and clasp the other's hand in a funny way but I didn't realise and just ended up grasping his thumb which was a bit embarrassing, especially as he and Rebecca found it hilarious and always tease me about it when we meet.

I was standing holding a plastic glass of supposedly wine supposedly mulled and a plate with a mince-pie and a sausage roll, trying to be interested in miles per gallon or whatever it was, when Rebecca came over. She was wearing a soft red woollen jumper with sparkly threads running through, and she looked gorgeous with her dark hair which she had loose for a change.

There'd been an accident with a tray of cheese straws, there were crumbs and biscuits all over the place, she told us, and I offered to go and find a dustpan and brush, anything to escape Smithy.

Rebecca beamed at me and I felt shivery and happy; I wanted to kiss her right there but I handed Smithy my plate and plastic glass and hurried away to do what Rebecca wanted.

I thought I knew where the cleaning cupboard was, I've done little jobs here before over the years involving, brushes, mops, buckets... the usual things you might expect in an old folks home. It showed I'd not been here for a while because where the cleaning cupboard used to be was a storeroom. I tried a few other doors, an office, what looked like a linen cupboard, a sluice, and then I opened a door and shut it straight away.

I hurried down the corridor, my face hot with embarrassment; I'd walked in on Emma/Emily locked in a passionate embrace. I was shocked, totally shocked, not because she was kissing a woman, but because she was kissing anyone other than Smithy in the very place he worked.

"Thomas, hello! Long time no see!" it was Milly who is head of secretarial/clerical. She is probably in her fifties and is absolutely lovely, she's one of the nicest people I know.

She hugged me and asked how I was and remarked that it was a long time since we'd seen each other. She took me to find a brush and pan, walking with me and chatting, catching up on my news... Well, I have none, so I asked about her family, she has two sons a bit younger than me. All the time I was thinking about Emma/Emily... was the kiss just a one-off, was she having an affair with the other woman whoever she was?

Going back into the day room where the bazaar was beginning to wind down I was pleased to go and sweep up the mess, and chat to the old lady who was upset because she'd knocked the plate over with her shaky hands; anything so I wouldn't have to speak to Smithy, feeling sure that something in my expression would look strange.

Milly was talking to Rebecca who had her coat on, time to go apparently, and no sign pf Smithy.

"Looking forward to the Christmas party, Thomas?" Milly asked.

"Oh he can't come, it's his quiz night, and nothing can come between him and his quiz team!" Rebecca exclaimed before I could answer.

"I can miss that, is it next week?" I asked, a little surprised at what Rebecca had said. The lights were reflecting on her glasses so I couldn't tell what her expression was.

"No, that's fine, Thomas, you like to go out with your brother and have a drink with your friends," she said firmly in a way I knew there was no point in disagreeing with. Then she went on to tell Milly about the old man I'd rescued... I'd forgotten about him. She seemed quite proud of me now, she'd been furious when it happened, she'd made comments about it for days afterwards.

Smithy came hurrying over, some family were leaving and wanted to say goodbye to Rebecca so she went off with him, heading through the big doorways towards the lifts and I was left with Milly.

"Is everything OK, Thomas?" Milly asked in a low voice.

"Yes, of course, why?" I was surprised.... Why would she think it wasn't?

She gave me a long look which reminded me of Marcus, the way he could look at me and see into my heart. Then she laughed and made some ordinary comment about ordinary stuff and I laughed too and pretended it was tears of laughter prickling my eyes.

Rebecca returned, buttoning her coat and tying her scarf. She hugged Milly then went round saying goodbye. As we got ready to leave, Milly hugged me too and gave me a little card.

"My phone number, Thomas... just in case... if ever you want to ring for a chat or anything... anyway there's my number!" and she hugged me again and wished me Happy Christmas and then Rebecca was taking my arm and it was time to go.

Monday, December 16th 2013

Rebecca dropped me in town early and I said I'd go and have a coffee as I didn't want to be too early in the office. It wasn't snowing but there was a bitter wind. I hadn't felt very well yesterday, no particular reason or symptom so I'd just stayed in bed all morning, reading the newspaper and messing about on my laptop. I remember a time when Rebecca and I would both stay in bed together like this on a cold winter's weekend morning…

She'd decided to clean the kitchen, and she never likes me helping as I put things back in the wrong place or don't clean things properly; she quite likes housework really, quite likes to be busy. I'd found the box of decorations and arranged some of them, I hope in the right place, and put up the artificial tree… it's only a small one and I would have like a real tree like Paul has, and Marcus has at the vicarage… he has an enormous one in the church…

We'd gone over for lunch with her parents and both ghastly sisters, and husbands and children were there. It was so awful that after lunch I joined Phil and my two brothers-in-law to watch Norwich vs Swansea on the TV… that was better than being in the kitchen with the women, or the sitting room with the dreadful children… I tried to think how awful the kids were to put me off the idea of a family, but my mind would drift back to Kylie's little boy, beaming at me and waving the red and white spotty hanky. I tried not to think about Smithy's wife, in that passionate embrace, her hand up the back of the other woman's jumper…

Now I trudged through the snow wishing I'd bought a hat… Maggie and Phil had given me one last Christmas, a furry thing with flaps which made me look ridiculous, but I would've liked it now. Someone jumped on my back and I almost fell over, but somehow I clutched hold of Kylie's legs and continued along, giving her a piggy-back.

"Should I buy a hat?" I asked over my shoulder. She was wearing thick knitted tights with reindeer on but she still had the Ugg type boots, already soaked from walking through the snow which still lay thickly over the ground. "I really look an idiot in a hat, but my ears are so cold."

"I can warm up your ears!" and she put her cold mouth over my right ear, her hot tongue...

I gave a silly shriek and hitched her up and began to run so she was bumped about on my back and then my bag began to slide down my shoulder and I had to stop because I was already out of breath and she slipped off, laughing and looking quite happy.

"You look as if you've had a nice weekend," I said as we continued at a more sedate trudge.

"I've had a fucking awful weekend," she replied.

"So why are you so happy if it's been so fucking awful?"

She punched me quite hard, it really hurt.

"You are a fucking idiot, Thomas!"

"Sorry," I was a bit upset. I don't like physical pain and I rubbed my arm, and I also don't like being told I'm an idiot.

We stood staring at each other, almost angrily.

"I am sorry, Kylie," I apologised. "I've had a fucking awful weekend too..."

She turned abruptly and began to walk away and I hurried after her.

"Please don't walk so quickly, I'll get an asthma attack again and then I'll fall over and die."

She stopped and waited and I put my arm round her without thinking and we went for hot chocolate.

When we were sitting downstairs in the nice warm, a huge chocolate in front of us (I'm sure the lady gives us extra cream and marshmallows and chocolate) I said "I won't tell you about my horrible weekend, if you won't tell me about yours, but shall I tell you about what I heard Julie say?"

And we gossiped about work and about how much we were dreading the Oriel on Wednesday and then I told her about Taras and Cazimir going to America, and then reluctantly we went to the office.

I had reasoned that there were lots of complicated negotiations going on between us and Lyon Abrams and that nothing could be said while the main players were delicately picking their way through everything; I guessed it was still at the talking stage and we, the lowly ones, would be told when it was a certainty, to give ourselves time to find new jobs...

I still haven't said anything to Rebecca, I dread it, and being a coward at heart I'll wait until I have no choice. She'll be furious! Furious that I'll effect be sacked, she'll see it as a real insult, but she'll also blame me for not being good enough to be taken with them. She'll think I've failed, even though I'm the junior in terms of being with the firm, I should have done more she'll say, done more to advance myself, or looked round for something better sooner...

Julie continued to share my desk for lunch, and it was too cold to go out at lunch times; it didn't stop her sending Kylie out with the post on Tuesday. The red ski jacket was still sitting in its bag so I asked her to take it to the charity shop... hoping she would take it to the pawnshop or one of those buy/sell/exchange shops and get herself something decent.

"That girl!" exclaimed Julie, as Kylie left the office with the post and the ski jacket. "You asked her to do one little thing and she looked as if she could have killed you,"... or kissed me.

It struck me that I was beginning to know Kylie well, despite the fact that I actually 'knew' nothing about her. I sat eating my sandwiches which tasted like sawdust... I couldn't keep giving them to her, she was too proud and I didn't want her misinterpreting why I was doing it... she would hate anyone feeling sorry for her or pitying her. Perhaps I should ask Marcus what to do...

I thought about this as Julie wittered on about nothing as if I was her best friend. She was so excited about going to the Oriel, she said... and I had a horrific image of being stuck between her and Gordon... a whole evening of enforced bonhomie... at least the food would be good... well, I hoped the food would be good...

I had a sudden inspiration, and told Julie that I was going out. She asked if I wanted her to come with me... no! I did not! But instead of saying what I felt I told her it was going to be a surprise. She simpered at me... *oh for heaven's sake! I'm married you stupid idiot!*

I pulled on my coat and hurried out of the office, out of the building and over to the supermarket where I bought a large panettone, a box of a dozen mince-pies and a huge stollen. None of it was very expensive, it was all the cheap range, but no doubt it would be fine.

As I came out of the shop I saw Kylie trudging up towards me, she was staring at the ground and just plodding along... but she was wearing a different coat, she was wearing an emerald green puffer jacket thing, and where the feeble sun caught it, her blond curly hair looked like a crown.

I waited for her and when she saw me she walked more quickly, swaggering a little... how brave she is.

"Do you think eating lots of sweet things gives you diabetes?" I asked as she came up to me. "I had to escape Julie and I suddenly thought I really wanted a mince-pie, I've hardly had any this year!"

"Being overweight gives you diabetes, Thomas... I know a really good way to use up calories," and she leered at me in almost her old way. She looked tired though, and not just physically tired.

"Can I ask you a favour... and no I don't want you to be rude..."

"But I'm so good at being rude!"

"Yes you are... you are the rudest person I know, I'll give you a prize for it if you like!" and before she could say anything else, I asked her if she would come with me to buy a hat because my head and ears really were suffering.

We could cut through Tesco's and out into the shopping mall; I did want a hat but there were other reasons I'd suggested it... and I don't want to think about all of those other reasons.

"So what are you buying your wife for Christmas, Thomas?" I noticed that in the busy shopping mall Kylie did not take my arm and walked a little away from me.

I told her about the cookery book, and about maybe getting perfume, and the cooking holiday I'd planned for her. Kylie made no comment but asked what I wanted for Christmas… I couldn't think of anything… except perhaps for things to be how things used to be… but at the same time, things had been boring, dull before… before what?

I thought of what I'd overheard my cousins' wives say about me and Rebecca, *'an odd couple, old-fashioned, like an old aunty and uncle, from a different generation…'* That had made such an impact on me… but I felt different now, maybe it was the changing relationships with my brothers, the family tree, the quiz night…

"Are you coming to the quiz tonight?" I asked, not answering the Christmas present thing. She didn't reply; we'd stopped by the Christmas tree and I gave some money to the woman dressed as an elf and got a couple of stars and handed one to Kylie. "Make a wish," I said and took a couple of pens.

I was stuck for a moment for something to write… it all seemed a bit silly, but it was raising money for charity and I wondered what Rebecca had written.

'I wish Kylie all the best', I wrote and stuck it in the silver box. She wrote something too and then we walked on and she decided Animal might be a place for a hat for me. I was used to passively waiting for Rebecca to decide what I should wear… *'old-fashioned'*… so trying to choose something was difficult… Kylie just laughed a lot at whatever I put on, and although I was pleased she'd cheered up, it was a bit annoying and embarrassing.

"Oh fuck it, I'll stay with cold ears," I flung down whatever it was; there was one, a trapper's hat or a trucker's hat I think, which I'd liked but it had so convulsed Kylie that I went hot and embarrassed and felt a bit wheezy. She declared I needed the Samoens Tibetan Bobble Beanie; I was a bit sulky though and told her to try on some hats so I could laugh at her... I was getting fed up with the whole hat thing, I can tell you.

She tried some on, clowning to make me laugh; I think she could see she'd upset me by finding me quite so ridiculous. She tried on a white aviator's hat with long tassels and white bobbles at the end and she looked... utterly adorable... I was shocked as I thought it... *I'm married! Things aren't right at the moment between me and Rebecca, but she's my wife...*

I glanced at my watch... We ought to get back to work... I didn't want Kylie in trouble for being late... I took the Tibetan bobble hat, and then as Kylie wandered to look at the children's clothes, I snatched up the aviator's hat as well.

"Are you in a bad mood now?" she sked as we hurried through the mall.

It was just the wretched depression sneaking up on me again...

I told Kylie I had a phone call to make and that I needed the loo, so that we didn't walk in together. I pulled on the Tibetan bobble hat and walked slowly up the stairs... feeling utterly miserable... I would spend a while with the family tree tonight... that would take my mind off things... but it was the quiz tonight... I was meeting John there as he was busy at work and hadn't time to meet me for a meal.

Julie thought my new hat was wonderful, and everyone appreciated the Christmas treats I'd bought and I made sure I shoved plenty on the plate I gave Kylie... I did notice that she surreptitiously wrapped most of it in some paper, so I went round again with my tray of offerings and even knocked on Gerald's door.

"Aah, Thomas!" he exclaimed but I whisked out having deposited a bit of everything in his paperclip tray before he could say anything or give me more details of another job. I put the rest of it on Kylie's desk and told her openly to take it if she wanted it because I was supposed to be on a diet and Rebecca would be cross if she knew I was eating mince-pies.

As I sat down I wondered when Rebecca would be making her mince-pies... her pastry is divine, so light and crisp and yet flavoursome... mmmm.... But no mince-pies yet. A week today would be Christmas Eve... I went on-line; there was a site called culturediscovery.com which seemed perfect for cookery holidays until I noticed how expensive it was... Much as I love Rebecca I couldn't afford that! I found some more affordable ideas on the Guardian holiday offers site, including a seven night cookery/photography course in Morocco... I couldn't afford for us both to go... but maybe she would like to have a break away from me... I know she gets irritated by me being so... whatever it is I am that irritates her.

However when I looked at the details, it was more photography than cookery... There was an Italian one which would really stretch my budget... but it was six nights and in Italy, and her favourite food is Italian... I printed off the page and cut out the picture and details. In my desk drawer I had the Christmas card I'd bought her, 'To my beloved wife...' and I stuck the picture inside it, opposite the soppy message.

I signed it, stuck it down and put it back in my desk and then it occurred to me what I'd written inside... 'To

Rebecca, from Thomas'... no 'darling Rebecca', no 'love from' or 'with all my love'...

I'd have to get another card.

Tuesday, December 17th, evening

I arrived early at the Lark and sat at the bar looking round; it must have changed enormously in the hundred and twenty odd years since Thomas Radwinter had been the landlord. It is a nice pub and it serves excellent beer, Otter from a brewery in Devon, which unsurprisingly, considering the name, is on the River Otter.

You come into the pub straight off the street and to the left is one room with bench seats along the wall beneath the window. The window has a stained glass panel with a bird swooping across a blue sky above some fields, the lark, no doubt. There are tables and chairs and stools and we usually sat along there, near the door looking down the other room which leads down to the back and the toilets and rear exit.

The bar is L shaped so wherever you sit it is easy to get to. There is a big fireplace on the end wall of our part, and another one on the wall opposite the long bar leading to the back. On the right side of the door as you come in is a little seating area, but it is a bit poked away and I think it might have been a separate room at one time.

I felt at home here; I'd never had a local pub and although I wasn't local to Easthope I was becoming familiar with this place... maybe we could find a house here and then this really would be my local.

"Usual, Tom?" the landlord called. I didn't realise he knew my name, and it was nice... yes, I would definitely look for houses in Easthope.

I hadn't mentioned it to Rebecca; maybe I should take her out for a lovely meal where we wouldn't be distracted by computers, and chores, and work, not Nonna Ysabel, but somewhere we didn't know and where no-one knew us. Then maybe we could talk, talk about what was wrong...

I would be understanding but I would ask why she had to work such long hours; for all I know, there might be things afoot at the Willows just as there were with my place, maybe her job too was under threat... I thought again about Smithy's wife kissing that woman...

I would tell Rebecca that I was worried and anxious about the future, trying to excuse any change in my behaviour because maybe she sensed I wasn't telling her something. I wouldn't ask about children, but I would ask in the most casual way I could, about whether she had any more thoughts about us moving, and would it be nice when we had time off over Christmas and New Year to drive around looking at property so we knew where we might want to live.

"Do you live round here, Tom?" the landlord broke into my thoughts with uncanny coincidence.

I told him I lived in Strand, but I liked Easthope very much... I wondered if it was a nice place to live?

"Great little place, Tom, loads going on and everything you need... you got kids? Been down to the beach? You got kids they'll spend all summer down there, plenty of swimming and surfing and then there's the yachtie's club!"

I wasn't sporty, I'd always been too fat and too timid, but little Tolik and Isabella might be, little Lillah might be a great little swimmer…

"No, we don't have any children yet," I paid for my beer. "I think an ancestor of mine might have had the license here… way back a hundred and more years ago… you don't have any old pictures or stuff about the pub in the nineteenth century do you?"

"Well funny you say that, Tom… just a minute!" and he disappeared into the back of the bar.

A couple of other people came in and greeted me by name… how nice that was. One of them asked me if I played pool, they were one short for the team since somebody or another had dropped out. I hadn't played since I was in the sixth form… thinking back I hadn't been too bad, but not good enough to play for a pub team.

"You don't have to be good, mate, you just have to be here!" a man with a very long fair beard called.

"We're all bloody crap, we're always last in the league… one more crap player will fit in fine!" his dark bearded friend replied.

I said that maybe after Christmas I'd have a game with them, and then we'd see… but I felt really cheered by their invitation, even if they would have asked anyone who was just sitting here.

The landlord reappeared with a great big wooden board; it looked like an old notice board, all dusty and grimy, and that was just what it was. It was a board with a list of license holders on it going from 1812 to 1964. I could just make out the gold lettering but it was too filthy to see any detail.

He laid it on one of the round tables and got a bar cloth and wiped over the face of it. It was about four foot long and about two and half foot wide and it was a little like the wooden memorials you see in churches... but this wasn't in memory of soldiers, but of landlords.

"What's this then?" Kylie slipped her arm round my shoulder.

"Look!" I was very excited. "Look!"

The dates were down the left side and against them were names, and there 1890: Thomas Radwinter!

"Is that someone then?" asked the landlord, grinning at my delight.

"That's his name, Bob," said Kylie. "He's Thomas Radwinter! Is he your granddad then?" she asked and she looked so happy, so free from worry, smiling at me, and I could have kissed her, I very nearly did but instead began to wheeze a little and took a drink of beer as Bob the landlord wiped the board better so all the names, from 1812: John Hanger, and Elijah Soar (and drover) 1827, to 1964: Stanley Goodyear, were plain to see.

"He can't be my grandfather, I'm sure... he was born in 1867 – this Thomas I mean, so he would have been twenty-three when he took it on... my dad was born in 1931... This Thomas would have been..." I tried to work it out.

"Sixty-four... not impossible," Kylie was quicker. "Take a picture on your phone!"

"True, it's not impossible... but more likely to be his granddad... that is if it's him and not the brother or cousin of my ancestor.... How amazing is this!" I took out my phone.

"Hey, bro!" It was John but I was so excited that I could barely explain; as soon as he saw the name on the board he understood.

"Fucking hell! Sorry Kylie!" He was almost as excited as I was, peering at the board, looking at the dates, trying to work it all out.

The landlord, Bob, was pretty excited too, and bought us all a drink. I told John again what I knew, that Thomas was Tolik's eldest son and born in 1867; he was the grandson of the original Thomas, and he had a sister Emma, named after his mother, and he had been brought up, certainly from 1861 in the India Inn, and now he had the Lark. He held the license from 1890 until 1917… when he was fifty.

"The India Inn?" asked Kylie. She had my phone and was taking pictures but stopped and looked at me.

"Yes, that place in Mill Lane…" I stopped. I heard John say 'oh' as he realised… and everything went sort of cool.

The door swung open behind us and I hear Leo's voice and John moved away and Bob the landlord took the board back behind the bar.

"That place in Mill Lane where I live," she said. She had green eyes, a pale cat green.

"I didn't realise you lived there," I said stupidly… how could she live there, it was all boarded up.

"You know I live there, you saw me." She looked angry… her usual expression. I stared at her stupidly.

She stared at me… so where was her little boy? Surely he wasn't back there now, in that shut up squat?

She grabbed my arm and dragged me down to the back of the pub, through the door that led to the toilets and out of another door into the back yard.

"What are you playing at?" she demanded.

"I'm not playing at anything! I don't know what you mean, Kylie."

"You never ask me anything!" she sounded angry.

"Anything like what? What do you mean?"

"Why don't you ask me about him?"

Because it was none of my business... "He's such a sweet little man... what's his name?"

Kenneil, she said, and her shoulders drooped. I'd never heard the name before; Kenneil Pemberton... tentatively I asked where he was now... with her sister, I didn't know she had a sister.

"Reneasha, she's called Reneasha."

"That's a pretty name... should we go inside now... you have snow in your hair."

She laughed at me, but she sounded near to tears and I didn't know what to do...really, I had absolutely no idea what to do... about so many things.

She nodded and turned to go back through the door with the leaded window. I caught her arm.

"Kylie... if you ever need anything, or want anything... for him... just ask me... or if I can do anything..." her back was to the light now and I couldn't properly see her expression. "I'm not being... it's not because... it's because... because..."

"Because you can't finish a sentence?" she asked.

I shrugged because I didn't really know what I meant and we went back into the pub.

As usual being in the crowded pub, squashed in among all the other teams, whispering and scratching our heads over the questions, and the picture round and puzzling over the music questions and struggling with Bob the landlord's difficult last round, it was easy to forget about other things, other worries.

We went to a tie break with our usual rivals, the Long John Silvers, and I almost felt sorry for them because we beat them again although we didn't win the bonus prize with Bob's round; as usual we put the £10 winnings into the pot to save for buying the quiz sheets next time. When the others and then Damian had left the team, the team pot had been shared out with them, but we had a new kitty going. Apparently when it reached a certain amount, if it did, then the team used to go out for a meal together... which sounds fun, although Kylie might prefer the money.

Kylie departed as abruptly as usual, kissing us all as she usually did... rather too long and lingering for comfort with me, full on the mouth although she'd kissed the others on the cheek. They teased me as usual and I blushed and stuttered and felt foolish and wished the taxi would hurry up and arrive.

Bob the landlord came over to us with a large buff envelope in his hand.

"Have a look at these, Tom, take any copies you want," he said, and when I peered inside I could see sepia photos and yellowing pages and some newspaper clippings. "It's stuff I inherited from the last landlord... let me have it back when you're done with it, but no hurry!"

I was thanking him when the taxi arrived and we hurried out into the night. It was cold and beginning to snow again but we were laughing and jolly. Leo bailed out on the edge of Strand, his wife and children were with her sister and he was joining them and sleeping over with the in-laws so John and I continued into Strand, and I was just so glad Rebecca never went to stay with her sisters.

"Tell me it's none of my business, bro... but is there something going on between you and Kylie?" John suddenly asked.

I was shocked, horrified to think he might think so, and yet, at the same time... and yet...

I told him firmly that she was a friend... a sort of friend, because really we knew nothing about each other at all and for all I knew she had a boyfriend waiting for her in the boarded up old pub... and I was married and my wife was waiting for me at home.

"Things aren't right between me and Becca at the moment... she's working so hard and such long hours, and things are a bit strained, John, but I love her and I'd never..." and I couldn't finish because I didn't know what I could never do. "And Kylie is very vulnerable; I know she seems as tough and wild as anything, but really she's not, so I'd never do anything which might hurt or harm her," and I spoke truthfully. "But honestly, John... Kylie would never feel that way about me... I mean look at me, look at her... so no, no for lots of reasons, there isn't anything going on, and there never will be."

"I know you wouldn't bro, I know you wouldn't, I never thought you might..." he lapsed into silence and we looked out of the window of the taxi. "Rebecca was your first girlfriend, wasn't she?" He knew she was… I felt a little uneasy at where this might be going… and I didn't want to hear what he might say so I began to talk about the envelope Bob had given me, and how desperate I was to look at the contents… and we got to the bus station and John got out and I continued in the taxi back to the flat.

Wednesday, December 18th 2013, morning

Marcus texted me; he was meeting Paul for a late lunch over at a place Paul has shares in further down the coast, but could I meet him for coffee this morning in Strand; he apologised it was short notice, he'd been due to conduct a wedding this morning, but the bride had been taken into hospital to have her appendix out and he was now free to come in earlier.

I was delighted, really, I was… and I can't say I would have felt like that a few months ago.

I told Gordon I was going out to meet my brother, told not asked, and left the office putting on my new hat when I got outside. There was a watery sun and it seemed a little less cold today, but I like having snuggly ears. Rebecca thought it looked ridiculous, but for once I didn't give in to her opinion; I liked it and I had a warm head.

I wished Marcus had rung me when I was still at home because I would have brought some of the photos Bob had given me; I'd looked at them briefly last night, old photos of the pub, outside from the street with a horse and cart stopped and a man in a bowler hat and long white apron like an old grocer standing in the road, and some from the inside… more recent ones of the interior with everything looking polished and new so maybe a refit in the twenties or thirties? There were more of the pub and of people, and there were newspaper articles and old receipts... fascinating stuff.

I'd tried to tell Rebecca this morning but she was a bit snappy and not interested... we would have to talk... this couldn't continue... I couldn't stand much more of feeling distanced from her without knowing why.

I'd suggested the coffee bar Kylie and I went to, and Marcus came up the street towards me as I reached the door. He had a very long navy coat and a long, obviously hand-knitted, red scarf round his neck. His greying hair was quite long and his beard was very bushy, he looked like a very thin, trainee Father Christmas. He was grinning broadly as he approached, an open smile, happy to see me, and again I wondered what had changed this man who I'd thought so grim and austere.

He gave me a big hug, bending because he was taller than me, and my heart soared and I just knew everything, somehow, would be alright; my family loved me and whatever happened they would make sure I was alright.

"Usual Thomas?" the café lady asked and I wondered how she knew my name, but it was nice that she did.

We went downstairs and she brought us my chocolate and his coffee with ginger syrup, ginger sprinkles and a baby gingerbread man in the saucer. I asked about Jill and my nieces and their families, and sort of brushed over reciprocal enquiries about Rebecca and told him my exciting news about the Lark.

"The Lark... that name rings a bell... I wonder if Granddad used to talk about it?"

"Granddad?" I knew I had a granddad obviously but I didn't know him... he'd died before I was born... or if he'd died after I don't remember... and I hadn't looked it up. "I don't know anything about Granddad, I don't even know his name... I know so much about his ancestors, and yet I don't know the name of granddad."

"He died when you were a baby...I'm sure he talked about the Lark... I wonder if Paul remembers?" he sipped his coffee, smiled at the flavour and he looked a little ridiculous in a nice way with cream on his moustache. I always wiped my mouth after every sip otherwise Kylie would start making ridiculous suggestions... and I felt a little warm at the sort of thing she would say.

Thinking of Kylie made me remember she'd taken photos on my phone and I pulled it out and showed Marcus the board with Thomas's name on it. Like John he was thrilled; the photo wasn't brilliant but clear enough to clearly see the name; he'd been the landlord until 1917, when he would have been fifty. I'd been slacking a little, I'd have to go back to Tolik and Emma and find out more about their family and how long they'd stayed in the India Inn.

Kylie had taken quite a few photos, of the board, of me and John bending over it, his arm round my shoulder, and then of the name, Thomas Radwinter in gold paint. Marcus was excited, and I wondered at his initial reluctance at me exploring our family... well, I had no interest in finding out anything about our dad, if that was what he was worried about.

Kylie had kept my phone and I'd forgotten or not realised she'd taken photos of us during the evening, lots of me and some of John and a couple of Leo. I guess she was hoping I would make a silly face without realising it so I'd be embarrassed when I looked at them. I looked quite normal, I was surprised to see… in fact I even thought I looked quite nice in some of them.

"What a great photo of you, Tommy!" Marcus showed one of me laughing, not in a stupid red faced way, but just in a happy way, and I could see I looked a little like Paul which surprised me. "And another of you and John!" I was saying something to John and he was looking surprised in a comical way. "You look really happy, I'm so glad!"

Last of all were some I do remember her taking, of the four of us squidged together in a selfie, all pulling silly faces, then one of just me and her. I'd turned my head to say something to her, she was looking at the camera and winking.

"So who's this nice young lady?" Marcus asked, and I explained that she worked with me and was in the quiz team. I almost mentioned where she lived, and had a sudden shiver at the thought of it… did she have any heating? Was she cold at night? Were their mice in the old place, rats even? She always looked clean and neat and her make-up was always impeccable in a wild sort of way…

I asked about granddad. His name was Charles and Marcus thought he'd been born just before the war, the first war… he gazed into his half empty coffee and then dipped his little gingerbread man head first in it, which I thought was rather cruel.

"Is Rebecca interested in what you're doing?" he asked suddenly.

I was taken aback… what made him say that?

"Not really... to be honest Marcus... she's not much interested in anything I do... she works so hard, such long hours, and I try and be helpful at home and do things... but somehow it's always wrong... " and I began to tell him how much I would love us to have a family, and how horrified she was at the idea, and how I thought maybe if we moved to somewhere larger with a garden she might see how good it would be.

I told him about my job, that I feared I would lose it in the New Year, that although Gerald had been pushing other jobs at me they were all far away and I didn't think Rebecca would want to move... but I hadn't even talked to her about it... she had no idea, and I didn't know how I was going to tell her. I told him how distant we were from each other... and how I was struggling to know what to do about it because I couldn't even talk about it to her...

I told Marcus about Kylie, how worried I was about her and her little boy who was living with her sister... I didn't tell him that she was the girl in the pictures from the quiz, but no doubt he guessed.

He sat listening, occasionally looking at me, but his gaze was gentle, not strict as it used to be.

"I don't know why I've told you all this... there's nothing you or anyone can do..." I finished lamely and drank my cold chocolate.

"Why not come up again and stay over then we can talk properly," he said.

"I'd like that, Marcus, very much...maybe after Christmas?" I tried to speak briskly, trying to shake of the annoying emotion which constantly seemed to be about to trip me up these days.

He needed to get going to meet up with Paul, and I told him to tell Paul that Rebecca and I were looking forward to his party on Friday night... well I was, anyway, but I didn't add that.

We wrapped up as we emerged from the café and I said I'd walk with him to the carpark, behind the bus station.

"Isn't that your friend?" he pointed, and Kylie was standing by a now closed card shop.

She saw me and hurried over with her purposeful walk, head slightly forward as if she was ready for anything.

"Thomas!" she said in a way which made me nervous. "What change have you got? Give me some change! Hello!" she said to Marcus then turned her fierce green-eyed gaze upon me as I rifled through my pockets and gave her a handful of coins. "Thanks!" and she strode back towards the closed shop.

I began to follow her and intrigued, Marcus came too. She was bending over someone in the shop doorway, talking to him and I think I'd half-guessed who it was before I properly saw him. It was the old tramp we'd rescued.

She turned back and saw us walking towards her and she came over.

"It's no good giving him lots of money, he'll just get boozed up; couple of quid and he can buy a hot drink," then she was gone, striding up the hill towards town.

I explained to Marcus about the tramp, about how Kylie had found him in the snow and how we'd taken him in a taxi to the refuge. It wasn't far from the bus station so I hoped he was still going there every night. I told Marcus about how thoughtless I'd been when I'd come in from that strange adventure and just left my clothes on the bathroom floor, all wet and smelly for poor Rebecca to find in the morning.

We passed by the old boy, sitting on a heap of cardboard, his hat pulled over his face. Marcus didn't comment about how inconsiderate I'd been but remarked on Kylie, what an extraordinary woman she was... extraordinary, he said, and he smiled at me.

"I know you're worried about her, but I think she can be a good friend to you Thomas," he said.

We stood by his car, wishing each other the best for Christmas and the New Year, and he said again he looked forward to me coming to stay, or just coming to see him any time. He'd correctly judged that I did not want any advice or suggestions... I would ask for help when I wanted it... for the moment I wanted to try and work things out myself...

Wednesday, December 18th 2013, evening

I was dreading the works 'do', really dreading it. I hate things like that at the best of times, and I could just imagine me getting drunk and blurting out a lot of angry things about the way we were being treated, or being rude to Julie who'd been flirting with me all day, much to Kylie's amusement.

We'd given out the secret Santa presents this afternoon; I'd received some handkerchiefs with snowmen on them which I was quite pleased with because I always use proper handkerchiefs not tissues. I've no idea who bought them for me, one of the women I guess. Kylie knew I'd bought her the white aviator's hat, I thought she was going to burst into tears when she saw it, but I think only I could tell that. She put it on and stalked round the office being silly and everyone laughed, but I didn't like the way Gordon and Martin were looking at her.

I decided to take the car to the Oriel, then I would have to stay sober and I could escape as soon as I was able. Rebecca had a series of 'do's' at her place, for the management, for everyone, for office, for nursing, others…. Smithy would be there… did he know about his wife? Anyway Rebecca was out tonight as well and was being picked up and brought home so it didn't inconvenience her at all.

It seemed strange getting ready to go out and be going out separately. I'd been to the barber's and he'd trimmed my beard and moustache and cut my hair, not changing the style, but just making it shorter and neater.

I decided to wear my grey suit and then couldn't decide what tie to wear… I was tempted to wear the black bow-tie with silvery spots on that one of Paul's boys had bought me for Christmas last year. I liked it and thought it was rather seasonal, but Rebecca thought I looked silly with a bow tie so I chose a maroon silk tie she'd bought me, even though I wasn't sure it looked alright with my red beard.

She was wearing a dress I hadn't seen before, a soft almost midnight blue which showed her lovely curvaceous figure and had little patches of silver on it. I just stared at her when she came into the sitting room. I wanted to make love to her so badly I couldn't resist and went to her with my arms outstretched.

"You look wonderful, Becca," I embraced her, but she stood rather stiffly and when I kissed her neck she moved a little.

"Careful, I've just done my hair and make-up," she said, and took a little step backwards.

"You can do it again, sweetheart, can't we just..." and I kissed her face, her mouth...

I thought for a moment she would respond, but she pushed me gently away... should I have persisted? Should I have? I didn't... I let my arms fall to my sides, and felt... pain, and hurt, and... defeated...

"Later, then," I said, trying to keep my voice light. "Later, when you come home... it's just you look so lovely, I love you so much..."

"Thank you, Thomas."

Her phone rang... her lift was here early and she snatched up her silver mock fur coat and her bag, gave a little wave of her fingers and was gone.

I was almost late by the time I got to the Oriel, but I was lucky because I was able to park not far from the entrance. I should have bought my coat but I'd left the flat in a miserable trance and in fact I couldn't really remember the drive to the hotel. It looked wonderful with all the lights shining, and small Christmas trees with white fairy lights in the windows. I crunched across the gravel thinking Rebecca would have struggled with her high-heels here, but at least the snow and ice had been cleared away.

I would eat my dinner, I would listen to the speeches that were bound to be made and then I would escape... there was a band in one of the other rooms which everyone was excited about, an all-purpose 80's rock tribute band... Since my memories of the 80's were rather blighted, it wasn't a time I remember much music.

The entrance was through a pair of etched glass doors up a wide semi-circular flight of low wide steps. I stepped into a spacious reception area with a place to leave coats, low sofas and seats round little tables, a small bar and the booking in desk. It was all beautifully and, I have to admit, tastefully decorated, but my heart sank at the thought of the night to come. I stood for a moment, wishing I had the courage to leave right now and text Gordon to say I was ill.

I turned and stared out into the night through the glass doors and I've no idea what I was thinking; and then... and then coming up the steps was Kylie. She was wearing what looked like a man's suit except it was in a silver Lurex material which clung to her. She was wearing a white shirt and had a black bow-tie with silver spot; she had her hair pulled back from her face and as she came through the doors I saw she had huge diamante earrings. Her make-up was wild, like a butterfly across half her face and I stood staring, open-mouthed.

"What's the matter with you?" she came right up to me standing so close I could smell the cold on her skin.

"You look stunning," I replied when I found my tongue. "You look sensational." She did; I had never seen a more beautiful woman in all my life.

I pulled my maroon tie undone and took it off.

"Stripping for action, Thomas?" she asked; she was so cold she was shivering.

I pulled my bowtie from my pocket and tied it... it's one of the things I can do, tie a bow tie.

"Is it straight?" I asked. It matched hers as if we'd bought it as a pair. She gave it a little tug and then I stepped back and held out my arm to escort her into the restaurant. As we turned to walk in all the people sitting around or standing at the bar were staring at us. For once I didn't give a fuck.

In retrospect it wasn't too bad; the food was very good... I'm not sure it was worth £35 but it was good. We started with what they called 'complimentary' smoked salmon with salmon eggs, quails' eggs stuffed with asparagus mousse and duck confit. Then we had starters and I chose pigeon, then we had a consommé, and melon and mint sorbet which I thought was rather unpleasant; for my main meal I had venison, and I had cheese missing out on dessert.

I was sitting between Julie and Sandra. When we'd walked in, Kylie and me, the last to arrive, there'd suddenly been a terrific fluster round the table of rearranging seats as the four other men all wanted to sit beside her. She had been cool and I could see she wasn't impressed by how they were treating her because she looked so different from 'the girl' who did the typing in the office.

She sat between Gordon and Gerald and I hated the way Gordon kept leering at her; I could imagine his long reptilian tongue snaking out and licking her... It wasn't my place to do anything, but if it had been Rebecca sitting there I would have said something, and sober as I was I would have pulled no punches. But Kylie was able to look after herself, I guess.

Julie kept putting her hand on my thigh which I ignored at first but then firmly moved, thinking that if she did it again I'd actually say something to her.

My mind was not really on the evening, I wondered where Rebecca was, who she was with, hoping and not hoping that she was enjoying herself. I couldn't remember which of the various do's she was on but guessed they must be somewhere equally as posh as the Oriel, and a couple of times I looked around in the hope of finding her sitting at another table nearby with her colleagues. I imagined her looking round too, our eyes meeting... and then she'd look away and laugh at something a colleague said...

I was overwhelmed with misery and I knew I was hiding a terrible suspicion from myself, a terrible, frightening doubt about the foundation of my present life...

A pair of warm hands covered my eyes.

"Truth or dare, Thomas!" and I heard everyone laughing round the table. "Come, on truth or dare... five, four..."

I tried to think of what to say as her fingers pressed my tears away.

"Three, two, one! You lose, it's truth *and* dare!"

She released her hold on me.

"OK, truth... Look round the table at all your co-workers..." they were all grinning and laughing. I would have been panicking normally, but Kylie's hand was on my neck, stroking me and I knew she wouldn't do anything too awful. "Now which one... which one of all these lovely people do you most want to... kiss!" they erupted with laughter but before I could say anything she bent her face so her ear was pressed against my mouth. "Ooooh," she said. "Thomas, really! Really? No!"

She stood up and pulled me to stand.

"You won't believe this," she said to all my 'co-workers'. "You won't believe this..." she took my hand and began to tow me round the table. "Monty, you are the lucky man! Now come along, Thomas, this is your dare, a peck on the cheek for Monty, and then we'll dance!"

Everyone was shouting things out and Julie and Sandra had their phones out taking photos; it was all so ludicrous and harmless and I kissed Monty on the cheek in a silly and exaggerated way and everyone applauded.

Kylie had looked across the table at me and seen my despair, and even though she didn't know I was thinking about Rebecca, she saw how miserable I was and she'd rescued me.

"Now dare, Thomas... let's see what you really dare do! Let's dance!"

Everyone except Monty pushed their chairs back and followed Kylie as she led me through to where the band were rocking out 'Red, Red Wine'... which I rather wish I'd drunk as I was feeling sober and awkward. It actually didn't matter because no-one could dance except the women so we all just milled around singing, and I felt a little better... a little... None of them could dance like Kylie, she was amazing and I could see that Julie and Sandra were looking a little resentful behind their fixed smiles.

I went back into the dining room; Monty was sitting there at our table, looking at his iPad, so I deviated and went to the bar and bought a sparkling water, wondering how long I would have to endure this.

I checked my phone, a *'hi, talk food sometime?'* message from Leo which sounded interesting. I texted Rebecca, hoping she was having a good time, saying I wished she was with me, that I missed her... I deleted the last bit and just put kisses and sent it. I finished my fizzy water and went back to our table and sat with Monty. He said *'Ah, young Thomas!'* but then went back to his iPad... which I guess says a lot about old people these days.

I sat at our table, wondering whether to go back to the ballroom where the band had moved on to Blondie. I took out my phone again and wondered whether to text John or Paul... but as I was seeing them on Friday it seemed a bit stupid.

Kylie sat down next to me.

"Wanna dance?" she asked. Her butterfly make-up was a little smudged but in a soft way which just seemed part of her look.

"I'm going in a minute... you look as if you're enjoying yourself, but I can give you a lift back to Easthope if you want?" I offered.

"Dance with me first then give me a lift." It sounds rude when I write it like that but she made one of her funny leering faces which actually cheered me up.

She took a random glass and drank the wine and then we went back to the dance floor where the band was murdering *'Sexual Healing'*; Julie was dancing with Gordon who I have to say is even worse at dancing than me, which is really saying something. Sandra was dancing between Martin and Gerald, and quite frankly, Gerald's dancing was so much worse than Gordon's it was almost embarrassing.

I just sort of stood still and swayed a bit, which is safer than making an utter idiot of yourself and Kylie toned down her dancing so that although everyone was watching her because she just looked so amazing, they weren't really staring. I gave up when another UB40 song came on, reggae was just beyond me, but I sat at one of the tables and watched the others, trying to smile, so I didn't seem a total killjoy.

Julie left Gordon and before I could do anything she'd pounced on me and dragged me up and then had her arms round my neck so I was forced to hold onto her... I was horrified, luckily she is shorter than me otherwise I think she would have tried to kiss me. I noticed Sandra and Vicky were sitting now, watching us and talking animatedly. Kylie was just standing near them and when I caught her eye she turned away but I could see she was laughing. *'Endless Love'*... I don't think I'll ever hear this song again without a shiver.

I disengaged myself and asked what Julie would like to drink, anything to escape; as the next song was *'9 to 5'* Julie let me go but then came with me to the bar, holding my arm as if we were together.

There were a few people at the bar now so we had to wait, and I took out my phone and quite pointedly told her that I was texting Rebecca.

"How are things with Rebecca?" Julie asked, her head on one side sympathetically.

"Fine, she's so busy at work, she's doing brilliantly, I'm so proud of her, but I'll be glad when the holiday comes and she can take some time off and then I can really spoil her!"

I was saved from further inquisition by Gordon who gave me a look which I interpreted as meaning that he was interested in Julie and I should clear off... how grateful I was to him! I hurried away thinking, *he's married, he has children, what he's thinking I cannot imagine*.

I was ready to go but if Kylie wanted to stay, if she was having a good time... I would wait for her, I couldn't imagine how else she would get home... in fact I dreaded to think.

Would I have enjoyed myself more if I'd had a drink? Probably not, and also I felt so on edge that I thought it would have been highly likely that I'd have said something unwise. I'd caught a couple of snatches of conversation between Gordon and Martin about *'this time next year'*, and Gerald and Monty had sat next to each other talking seriously...

But maybe Kylie was wrong... nothing had been said and surely someone would have told me something by now?

"I'm ready – are you ready to take me?" Kylie broke into my thoughts. She was swaying slightly, I was glad she'd had plenty to eat and drink, and although she had been discrete, I'd seen her slipping a couple of bread rolls into her bag and an apple.

I went round the table and said goodnight to everyone, and Sandra and Vicky both kissed me. Julie and Gordon seemed to have disappeared so I was relieved of the anxiety about her doing or saying something to me.

Kylie stood back and just waved, she knew what they thought about her, she didn't want the false embraces and cheery words.

I told her to wait inside while I brought the car nearer but she said she'd come with me, she didn't want me driving off and leaving her… I would never do that to anyone, she must know that, but maybe it had happened to her.

There was a break in the clouds and the moon looked almost full. We got in the car and she was uncharacteristically quiet as we left the hotel.

"Well, that could have been worse," I said.

"Julie's really got the hots for you!" Kylie sniggered.

I laughed. "Stupid cow!"

"Thomas! I've never heard you say anything nasty about anyone!"

"Well, she is stupid, and she is a cow… She's sly and she's unkind," I'd seen many spiteful little things that she'd done. Where my desk is, at the end of the office, I could see more than people realised.

"Sandra?"

"Dumb-ass!"

"Thomas!" she laughed at me; I was trying to cheer her up because under the brave and sassy exterior she was probably as unhappy as I was, and undoubtedly had more cause to be.

"Vicky?"

"Vapid."

"Gordon?"

"Smarmy and creepy, I nearly punched him tonight."

"Really? What did he do to upset you?"

We'd left Strand and were driving along the coast road and the car was buffeted by the wind straight off the sea.

"How would you have got home?" I asked, thinking that this must have been the way Kylie had walked before I had 'found' her a bus pass.

"So why did you want to punch him? Did you really want to punch him?"

"Slimeball... it was the way he was looking at you."

She said nothing for a long time until we were coming down from Castle Point.

"I'm used to it," she said.

I signalled and pulled over.

"The next time I see anything like that I won't just sit there," I was really angry, not at her, but at Gordon and the rest of them. "You are one of the most amazing people I know, and you're my friend, and I won't just sit there! It's not right!"

I put the car back in gear and we drove on down into Easthope. I asked if I should go to Mill Lane and she said yes. I drove down to the end and turned round on the open area. I stopped the car and turned to say something and suddenly she was kissing me... I was so shocked, so surprised that I didn't resist but then I was kissing her. She'd somehow released her seatbelt but I was pinned iby mine... I should push her away, I should turn away... I had never kissed anyone other than Rebecca since I'd first started going out with her...

No-one had kissed me like this before… no-one.

She pulled back, we were both panting.

"Come with me," she said, sitting back. "Come with me, Thomas."

I stared at her in the darkness… and couldn't think of anything to say… my mind was just a jumble, my heart was pounding… I don't know what thoughts were flying through my mind.

I could have wept; I could have burst into tears right then.

I undid my seat belt and pulled her to me and just held her in my arms. Was she asking this to say thank you for the lift home, was she *'paying me back'* for all the little kindnesses I'd shown her… or… or…

"I can't," I said at last.

And then I did something which I just can't believe; I lifted her chin and kissed her, *I* kissed her.

"I can't," I said again and kissed her again. I feel weak just thinking about it, I'm shaking just writing the words.

She pulled away and was out of the car and gone. After a long time I started the engine, turned, and drove away. And halfway home I stopped the car and sat crying.

Wednesday, December 18th 2013, night

Tolik and Emma had other children I discovered from the 1881 census; if I'd been remotely able to be amused I would have been because he had three sons, John, Paul and Mark… however my emotions were frozen at the moment, and I focussed my mind just on the census material, reminding myself of how I'd studied for my exams, cutting out everything else from the turmoil of my life.

My life as a child and teenager had been in chaos and maybe this was part of what had attracted me to Rebecca; she was so solid, so steady, so predictable. She liked everything ordered and organized; she was not demonstrative or emotional... I don't mean she wasn't loving, she was... and in our early days before she had to work so hard at the Willows...

But all through my teenage years I'd used study to insulate me from life with Mum, and when I lived with Marcus, it kept me independent and apart from his family... I allowed myself to wonder whether it had been my self-sufficiency which had made him seem cool towards me... maybe he'd respected the barrier I put up, maybe it was not he who'd changed recently but me...

John was born in 1873, Paul in 1876, and Mark in 1879; I wondered if one of these was my fore-father, and not their older brother Thomas who'd ended up in the Lark? My brothers would smile at this set of brothers... I didn't feel much like smiling.

I duly began to enter this latest information into my tree on MyTimeMachine when I noticed I had 'a postal delivery' as it describes email... Curious, I opened the post.

Hi, I'm trying to find my ancestors in the Radwinter family...

Oh my goodness!!

I am Dominick Radwinter and my ancestor is Mark Radwinter who came from England to South Africa to fight in the Boer War with his brother Paul; they either stayed on or returned here and married and had children. I live in Cape Town with my family; I'm struggling to find English connections and I have only just started this family-tree thing so this is just a shot in the dark really. I see you have put the name Radwinter in your 'interested' list... I know there is a place in England called that so I don't know if you're from there or if you have a Radwinter name in your family.

Kind regards
Dom Radwinter

Good heavens! I took a big swig of whisky... good heavens! I wrote back straight away.

Hello Dom, I am Thomas Radwinter, and I do have two brothers called Mark and Paul in my tree... in fact I have only just discovered them. Mark was born in Easthope in 1879, and Paul in 1876. Their parents were Tolik Radwinter and his wife Emma and they had two more brothers, Thomas born 1867 and John born 1873, and a sister Emma born 1870. I am not yet sure whether I am descended from Thomas or John... I'm not long into doing my tree either! Coincidentally I actually do have three brothers called Marcus, Paul and John!

I sent it and took another drink of whisky; I began to feel a little better, either the whisky or the email. I took out my phone, stared at it as if I could magic a message from Rebecca; I didn't want to text her again... I saw that I'd texted her four times this evening already. It was nearly one o'clock... I couldn't remember her being so late before after going out with the staff from the Willows; she liked them well enough, but she wasn't best friends with any of them. Her friends were people left over from school and college, and her cousin Hazel who now lives in London.

I texted John and told him about Dominick Radwinter, then I went to find more about Thomas Radwinter who'd the Lark in 1891. I'd promised myself I'd look at the photos and press cuttings more carefully on Saturday; as far as I knew we weren't doing anything, except probably last minute panicking over Christmas presents and what to take to Maggie and Phil's on Christmas Day. We weren't seeing them on Sunday, as we would be with them on Wednesday... I wondered whether to suggest to Rebecca that we started staying home on Sundays more often; going to her parents most Sundays for the last ten years was enough, I thought.

I poured some more whisky and thought moodily that Rebecca wouldn't like that suggestion; well, too bad, it was about time some things went my way in this marriage.

Thomas married Eleanor in 1891; they had three sons, Charles, Walter and Horace and in 1901 and 1911 they were still in the Lark, although by the time of this last census Sophia, wife of Charles was living with them. Someone had mentioned that our grandfather was Charles, was it Marcus? Charles was born in 1893... I did a quick calculation thinking how speedy Kylie was at mental maths... I thought about Kylie but quickly pushed the thought away... I could almost feel her in my arms, she was so slim, wrapping my arms around her had been like embracing a fairy or a sprite... I could almost feel her mouth against mine... I took a big gulp of whisky, it went down the wrong way and I coughed and choked for some time.

Charles would have been nearly fifty when my father was born... I was so maudlin, and quite drunk and I allowed myself a moment to think of Dad, and wonder when he'd died and where because I'd no doubt he was dead... I couldn't clearly remember him but there was a huge horrible ache and hurt associated with my earliest memories. Why on earth Marcus might think I would be interested in finding out about either of our parents...

I looked up Thomas and Eleanor's marriage... I'd been getting a bit lazy about following up all the marriage and birth certificates... I still was missing Tolik's wife Emma's surname. I found Thomas and Eleanor... Eleanor Quillen! I checked the census again and realised that I'd not looked at it carefully enough because it plainly said she was Irish! I was getting too drunk to be doing this properly, I ought to finish... go to bed without Rebecca...

I texted Paul and told him Eleanor Quillen was either our great or great-great-grandma...

A key turned in the door; Rebecca was home. I didn't move, just sat staring at the computer screen, wondering what either of us would say.

"Oh, I thought you'd be in bed!"

Thought, or hoped? I didn't say that but summoned up a cheerful response. "No, just sat down to do some of this and got a bit carried a way. Did you have a lovely time? Where did you go? I know you told me, but I've forgotten."

"Are you drunk? I thought you weren't going to be drinking?" she seemed a bit defensive, maybe she was worried that I'd had a drink then driven home... driven home via Easthope.

"I didn't; I had a whisky when I got in, I was a bit cold," *emotionally pretty frozen if you're the least bit interested, Becca.*

"What's that all over your face? You've got purple and blue all over your face?" she was definitely on the attack.

What I probably had all over my face was the purple and blue of Kylie's butterfly make-up. I rubbed my cheek and looked at my fingers.

"Someone was wearing face-paint," I took out my hankie and wiped my hands.

"So how come it's all over your face?" she staggered slightly; I was a bit drunk and so was she.

I shrugged. "I guess it was when everyone was kissing each other goodnight," I shut down my computer and stood up. "Shall we go to bed, Becca?" and I held out my arms as I had earlier.

"You need to get that muck off your face first, and I need to get changed," and she went into the bathroom.

I went through into the bedroom, got undressed and into bed without even cleaning my teeth. I was asleep before Rebecca joined me.

Thursday, December 19th 2013, morning

It was not the most sensible thing to do to try and talk to Rebecca on Thursday morning; I was a little head-achey, but not too bad. I'd woken with the bip of a text; it was from the same unknown number as I'd received before from Kylie using someone's phone. *'Sorry.'* I got out of bed and went into the kitchen to put the kettle on and I texted back *'I'm not'*, before I could think too much about it.

I made tea and then went back to the bathroom; I used some of Rebecca's make-up wipes to take the remains of the blue and purple off my face... I guess I would have to change the pillowslip; my skin was smeared with a smudged mess as if I was bruised... as if I was bruised...

It was a bit early but I foolishly wanted to talk to Rebecca before we went to work so I took her a cup of tea and gently woke her and then turned over my pillow so the messy side was hidden; I'd change it later.

I went back into the kitchen and found some almond croissants and heated one for her and put it on a plate she liked with kittens on it... maybe we should get a cat... instead of a child, a cat...

She'd pulled the covers over her head when I went back, and I gently said I'd brought her a croissant but would she like anything else? She mumbled something so I put it on her bedside table and went and showered and shaved. Perhaps I should get rid of my beard altogether...

I went back into the bedroom to find my clothes and Rebecca had eaten the croissant, but when I asked if she wanted anything else she was grouchy so I quietly got dressed and went into the kitchen. I couldn't fancy anything to eat...it had been a wonderful meal last night, I guess, although I'd not really been properly in the mood to enjoy it. I went into the bathroom to clean my teeth and when I went back into the kitchen Rebecca was up. She had my phone in her hand but put it down as I came in.

"I thought someone had messaged you," she said. She didn't look her best, her face is always a bit puffy when she first wakes up but her eyebrows were down crossly and I wondered if she was a little hung over.

I asked if anyone had messaged me, wondering what she would have made of it. She shrugged and switched the kettle on again.

"It's half-past six!" she exclaimed, glancing at the clock.

"I know it's early sweetheart, but I really want to talk to you before we go to work," I wanted to hug her but had the shocking realisation that I daren't, I daren't hug my own wife.

"It's half-past six!" she was very annoyed.

"I know but we just never have any time... sweetheart, I know I've done something wrong, but I don't know what it is... we have to talk about it... I can't go on like this."

"It's bloody half-past six!" she repeated. She never swears so for her to do it now showed how cross she was.

Like a fool I blundered on as I made a coffee I didn't really want. "You work so hard, it's wearing you out, and we never see each other... when was the last time we went out together that wasn't to your parents?"

"What's wrong with going to my parents?"

"Nothing, they're great people..."

"Great people? For God's sake, they're more than great people – they've been parents to you ever since you met them! Great people?"

I apologised immediately... why didn't I just retreat then, why did I keep going?

"I love them, adore them, but why do we have to see them every week? Why can't we spend Sundays together once in a while?"

This was going completely off track… and at the back of my mind I realised that Rebecca did this in arguments, shifting away from the real problem and side-tracking into something trivial. Her response should have been anticipated, but I wasn't quite prepared for the vehemence… and afterwards I tried to forget what she said, especially about my own parents… My dad was a disaster and my mum was an alcoholic, but they were still my parents.

I somehow managed to bite back a response to this, except to apologise for inadvertently seeming to insult her parents, never mind that she'd insulted mine who she'd never met.

"But what is really the matter, Becca? You're so snappy with me." *Snappy?* Ooops. "You seem cross with me all the time, and I just don't know why, I don't know what I've done."

This was met with a cooler but more hurtful reply; I was pathetic, I was feeble, I should stand up for myself, it was no wonder she got impatient when I allowed myself to be pushed around — look how they treated me at work. Shocked I demanded what she meant, using an angrier tone than I'd intended.

"They just think you're a joke! That fool Gordon is always sneering at you, Martin just does the same… Gerald is just a patronising arse, and as for the women, they just laugh at you… and not even behind your back!"

"That's not true!" except maybe it was.

"That Julie is a real sly bitch, and Sandra is always sucking up to Gerald, and Vicky is thick, and Kylie is just a common little tart!"

I slammed my mug down so hard on the counter it almost exploded, showering me in coffee.

"You idiot!" she screamed. "That was my mug!"

I realised that I had been drinking from a mug she thought of as hers and now it was smashed. I still had hold of the handle and I stared at it, noticing that my hand was shaking.

"I'm sorry, Becca," I felt faint and my chest was becoming tight.

"Sorry? *You're sorry?* That's all you ever say, that you're sorry! Well I'm sorry too! Sorry that I..." she stopped.

"Sorry what Rebecca? Sorry that you *what*?"

We stared at each other, then she turned and left the kitchen, slamming the door.

Something trickled down my cheek, I put my hand to my face and it was blood, one of the flying splinters of china had cut me.

I arrived in Strand at seven-thirty, an hour and a half before I was due at the office. I'd changed while Rebecca was in the bathroom, my jacket and trousers were splashed with coffee and there was blood on my shirt. I remembered that my other suit was still at the cleaners, I'd pick it up this afternoon... I put on my best suit, found another shirt and grabbed a tie at random, then I hurried from the house before I had to see Rebecca again and only as I was waiting at the bus-stop in the dark did I remember I hadn't cleared up the mess in the kitchen.

The bus station was cold but not as cold as it was outside, and not as cold as my heart. There was an old dosser sitting on one of the benches but he wasn't the old man we'd rescued. I went to the newspaper kiosk and picked up an Independent and bought a cup of coffee in a cardboard mug and a doughnut which I took and gave to the old man; he had an enormous red beard and an equally red face. It was too early for the Armenian café to be open or the other coffee shop so I sat down but was too restless to read, and wandered about. I wondered whether to go for a walk but when I got to the doors I could see it was snowing again in the dark morning, so I stood staring through the glass panel at nothing, thinking nothing.

"What are you looking at?"

"Someone called Dominick Radwinter wrote to me from South Africa. I think his ancestor was a brother of my ancestor, I don't know which one yet."

"What's the matter, Thomas?"

"I think my Radwinter was Tolik's son Thomas, he was the brother of Dominick's ancestor."

"Is it because of last night?"

"Thomas is the grandson of Thomas who came from Poland... or it might be the Ukraine... I think it was technically Russia at the time... I must check... I've sort of neglected that part of it..."

"Thomas, what's the matter, you're being strange... and your face is bleeding... what's happened?"

"I think Thomas, the first Thomas was really Taras, but he anglicised his name and became Thomas..."

Kylie tugged at my arm; I could see her reflection in the glass staring at me so I could see her profile.

"Do you want me to go away? Is this your way of ignoring me?"

I turned and looked at her. The exotic butterfly was gone and she was just wearing her usual make-up. She has quite a high forehead and perfectly eyebrows. Her green eyes are almond-shaped and she has incredibly long eye-lashes. She was wearing coppery coloured eye make-up and there was some sort of sparkle on her mascara. She has high cheek bones, a broad nose with elegant arching nostrils. She has a wide full mouth and I'd never noticed that she has a dimple in the middle of her fierce chin...

"Thomas, speak to me, just say something... are you ill?"

Her face became blurry as if there was a mist between us.

"Why are you crying? What's the matter?"

"I don't know... I don't know anything..."

She suddenly thrust her hand into my pocket and began to rummage through until she found a handkerchief. I took it and wiped my face and blew my nose and apologised.

"Buy me breakfast, I'm starving," she said.

I felt wrecked as she towed me through the bus station to the doors into the mall. The red-bearded tramp lurched towards us.

"Thanks, mate, you're a gent! Merry Christmas! Merry Christmas, pretty lady!"

Kylie was curious and I told her about the coffee and doughnut, and beginning to feel a little like a coffee and doughnut for myself.

I didn't want to tell her about Rebecca, it would sound too much like *'my wife doesn't understand me'*.

"Can I ask you about your family?" I said instead. "I just wondered if you have parents?"

"Yeah, my mum's not well at the moment, that's why Kenneil is with Reneasha… Mum can't look after him anymore. Reneasha works so he has to go to a nursery."

We went to Tesco's and their café was open so I bought her a fried breakfast and I had a doughnut and coffee.

"Why did you ask about parents, Thomas? Have you got problems with yours?"

How little we knew about each other.

"My mum died when I was eighteen so I lived with my brother Marcus, he was the person with me when you wanted some money for that other tramp."

"What the old geezer with the beard? I thought he was your dad."

I laughed and felt glad I could now. "No, but he was like a dad to me when I was growing up, but he's my brother… and we seem to be getting on really well, better than before," and I tried to explain about Marcus, how strict he'd been with me, but how much he'd cared for me, and what a responsibility it must have been. He had his own family but he'd taken me in and financed me until I was married and earning. Telling Kylie I began to really appreciate perhaps more than I ever had done before exactly what Marcus had done for me.

"So where's your dad?" she asked after a moment of thinking about what I'd said.

"Probably dead, perhaps he's a tramp too; he left mum when I was four. Marcus was already married then, and Paul had left home too so it was just me and John and then he went to live with Paul and his first wife when he was fourteen."

"My dad lives in Tobago; he's got another wife there now... and some kids."

"Why did you apologise?" I asked, indicating my phone.

I'd never seen Kylie blush before but she did so now, beautifully. She looked up from her empty plate with angry eyes and looked as if she might punch me.

"Please don't hit me!" I said in a squeaky voice, trying to make her laugh.

"I compromised you last night," she said.

"No, no you didn't," I replied firmly. "*I* should have said sorry, not you."

"Am I really your friend?"

"Yes, Kylie, you are my friend, and I hope I am yours."

She held her hand out and we shook and maybe I held her slim brown hand a little too long.

I got another coffee and then we spent our time enjoying a bitch about the others and how they had behaved last night.

Thursday, December 19th 2013, morning

The office was very quiet, everyone except me and Kylie suffering from the previous night; Vicky had overdone it and was not coming in today. For a pregnant person she'd done a lot of dancing. I actually didn't have a lot to do but I did a little housekeeping on my computer, organizing files, deleting old stuff, clearing it of anything that was no longer needed. I went through old emails, I tidied my desk drawers, I kept busy, my head down.

Julie came with a coffee for me and sat at my desk chattering about nothing; Kylie was grinning at her computer screen and did nothing to rescue me. However brightly Julie wittered on, her eyes kept straying to Gordon; she'd positioned her chair by my desk so she could see him at the other end of the room quite clearly.

I remembered my suit at the dry cleaners and was able to escape to go and get it. It had unexpectedly turned into a nice day; the fall of snow was still white and glistened in the sun and the sky was bright and cheerful.

I didn't go directly to the dry cleaners but walked down to the harbour and looked at the sea which was a brilliant blue and I even took a photo of it on my phone. There are some benches along the promenade and I sat and allowed myself to consider what had happened this morning.

I had a sort of conversation with myself.

Things aren't right... things have changed... I've changed... but so has Rebecca... or maybe she is just showing a side of herself she has concealed before.

So if things have changed, do you want them to change back to how they were?

No... I don't want things to be how they were, I don't want to be how I was.

So what do you want?

I want to be married to someone and have a family and live in a house with a garden, and I want my children to have a childhood different from mine; I want them to grow up to be like Paul's sons, or Marcus's daughters.

But Rebecca doesn't want that... She might want to move to a house, but she won't want a family.

I know that... I've known that for a while now... and maybe even if she did want children, she wouldn't be the sort of mother I would –

Stop! Rebecca is your wife!

Yes... I married her ten years ago... Ten years ago I was like a lost little boy who wanted someone to love and look after and be loved and looked after...

And now? Who are you now, Thomas? What are you now?

I don't know... I don't know anything...

I wandered back into town, I was in no hurry to go back to work, I hadn't much to do, and I was sure that sooner or later I would have no work to do at all, as however they wrapped it up in deals and packages, essentially I would be fired.

I drifted into the mall and stopped and stared at the Christmas tree, covered in stars. There was a new perfume shop which had opened, and although I had several things for Rebecca, including the cookery books and the promise of a holiday cookery course, I thought maybe I would buy her some perfume as well. She's very fond of perfume; at the moment her favourite is Marc Jacobs' Honey; there was an Eau de Parfum gift set which was £52 which seemed a bit much... There was a really pretty little spray called Oh Lola! which was in pink, her favourite colour, but that was even more expensive, I wasn't sure if she liked the smell anyway.

I put Oh Lola! back on the shelf, I'd give perfume a miss, maybe her parents would buy her some, sometimes they had in the past, when they'd been on holiday they would pick up some coming back through duty-free.

I wandered out of the shop but then stopped in the doorway. Opposite me standing by the Christmas tree was Kylie with another woman and without being able to hear I could plainly see they were having a full on row. The other woman looked a similar age, maybe a bit older, she was black and her hair was tied with a Rasta scarf. She was really having a go at Kylie, wagging her finger at her, but Kylie was standing, hands on hips, head thrust forward, no doubt giving as good as she was getting.

I dithered, not wanting to come out of the shop in case I was seen, but not wanting to stay staring either. My dilemma was solved by Kylie turning and marching away. The other woman shouted something after her and stood staring. I left the shop now and went to look at some scarves in Accessorize; Rebecca shops there sometimes and maybe I would see something which would catch my eye. I think I probably was just not in the mood because nothing seemed right. I ought to go back to work and I headed out.

The black woman who'd been arguing with Kylie was still by the Christmas tree but now she was with a tall white man with a shaven head and what I thought was a scar or birth-mark but was actually a tattoo under his left eye. The man had hold of her arm and was shouting into her face. There was no doubt that she was terrified by his aggression, and the shoppers and passers-by were scurrying round them, staring, fascinated. The man was taller than her and leaning down intimidatingly. He shook her and then to my horror he slapped her.

No-one did anything. I looked round for a security guard or someone to ask to help, but everyone was ignoring them, despite surreptitiously staring as they rushed by.

"Excuse me," I called hurrying over. "Excuse me!"

The man glanced up. "Fuck off!"

"Excuse me, I wonder if you could direct me to the promenade?"

He looked baffled and told me to fuck off again.

"You see, I want to go to the promenade and I wonder if you tell me which exit I should leave by? There is one over there to the bus station, would that be best do you think?"

"What you chattin', man?" he was genuinely baffled. He'd stopped leaning over the woman and I was mentally imploring her to just go.

"There's another exit over there," I waved my hand at random. "And then I could go out through Tesco's but I might be in the wrong place... what do you suggest?"

He was beginning to get angry with me, which was better than him getting angry at the woman or hitting her again. "You fuckin off your head mate!"

The woman wrenched her arm free from him and tried to get away; he lurched at her but I pushed her aside.

"The promenade? Where's the promenade?" I asked desperately, not looking at the woman.

His eyes were bulging with rage, he had a long lean face and shaved eyebrows and the weird tattoo under his eye.

"You taking the piss? You fuckin' takin' the piss?" he shouted. I was terrified.

He tried to grab at the woman again, who to my annoyance and concern was still there. I stepped between them and he punched me in the face.

I reeled backwards and tripped and sat down with a thump, knocking over a large model reindeer. I glanced around. The woman, thank God, had disappeared. The man was yelling at me now, waving his arms... he was either on something or mad, there were veins throbbing on his temples, froth at the corners of his mouth and if his eyes bulged any more they would start completely from his head.

He looked as if he could kill me and I scrambled to my feet with the aid of the reindeer.

The next thing is like a dream... I can't really believe it was happening because he *pulled out a gun*... this does not happen in real life, but a maniac, almost drooling with fury was pointing a gun at me.

I threw the reindeer at him and somehow the antlers caught his legs and the prancing back legs hit his face and he went over backwards into the Christmas tree and I just ran...

I almost fell through the door of the little café and collapsed onto the chair of the single table by the counter.

"Thomas, what on earth's the matter? Are you alright?" the café lady ran round to me, and bent over, dabbing my face with a cloth; I saw her name was Sue... I felt a little faint and concentrated on looking at her name badge.

I began to tell her what had happened... that I'd seen a man hit a woman and I went up and... it hardly seemed possible.

She made me a cup of tea and put sugar in it for me, and I began to calm down. She gave me the cloth to dab my face, the cuts from the broken mug this morning had opened up where I had been punched, just below my eye, thankfully not on the nose. Gradually the shaking subsided and I began to see the funny side of me throwing a model reindeer at a man who was attacking me.... But a gun... *a gun*... I didn't tell Sue about the gun.

She wanted to call the police, but I told her I'd ring them later and say I'd seen what had happened... I couldn't face all the complications of it right now. I thanked her for the tea and offered to pay but she refused, I'd been a hero, she said, which struck me as funny... but not as funny as the memory of me asking the madman for directions to the promenade!

Thursday, December 19th 2013, afternoon

I felt very shaky as I walked back to the office; I went up in the lift and went to the Gents. I looked at myself in the mirror and I seemed very pale apart from the big swollen red mark on my cheek. I had several cuts I could see, and one on my chin had bled into my beard. There were splashes of blood down my shirt... again; I'd have to get the Vanish liquid out when I got home. But what struck me more than anything was my eyes; I don't have the Radwinter eyes, that piecing, arresting blue, I can't say what colour my eyes are, but as I looked at myself they were cold and stone grey not hazel and I didn't look like Thomas Radwinter at all.

I got some toilet paper and wet it and dabbed the blood from my face and my beard, but it didn't change the man looking out of the mirror at me.

"Hello, Tommo!" Gordon came in. "Been in a fight?" he asked in his irritating way. I wanted to punch him in his lizard's face as I'd been punched in the face.

"Yes, I have been in a fight, and I walked away and left him on the floor."

I went past him and my shoulder caught his but I didn't apologise... I didn't mention the reindeer.

I sat at my desk and Googled the history of the Ukraine and read up about the country that might or might not be my homeland. Gordon came in and went straight over to Julie, and before long as I'd anticipated she came over to my desk. Kylie was frowning at me.

"Coffee, Thomas?" asked Julie and put one on my desk. "Are you alright?"

"I'm fine thank you, Julie," I said in a rather loud voice. "How are you?" I stared up at her and she blushed slightly. "Thanks for the coffee. Do you know anything about the Ukraine?"

"Um... the Ukraine?"

"I thought I might organize a trip there, it's a fascinating country, even though there are a few political difficulties at the moment. I thought maybe the firm could visit so we can see how the legal system works over there, what do you think?"

She didn't know what to say, and after a few flustered sentences about thinking it over, she left me and went back to her desk, where Gordon had pulled up a chair.

My email pinged and it was Kylie. '*What the fuck's the matter with you?*' I stared at the message, then mailed back. '*Fag?*' and I left my desk and walked out and went down and outside and stood in the doorway of the cinema exit.

Before long Kylie came out wearing her angry concerned expression.

"Look," I said as she came up to me, her arms folded against the cold. It was still a lovely day but freezing and the sun was just about to disappear. "Look, I know I sound as if I'm going mad, really I'm not."

"What was all that about the Ukraine, and what's happened to you? Someone's hit you," she put her fingers to my cheek.

"Yes... do you know I was never in fights when I was a kid. People bullied me and sometimes I got beaten up, but I was never in fights."

"I was always in fights," she said and some of the anger left her face.

I smiled... I felt normal talking to her. "I bet you were! You'd have defended me, wouldn't you?"

I told her the rough outline of what had happened... the woman arguing with the man, him hitting her and nobody doing anything. I told her about the ridiculous thing I'd said about the promenade and she laughed. She looked so lovely I wished I could make her laugh all the time. She laughed even more when I told her about the reindeer, and suddenly she hugged me and kissed my cheek, the other one not the hurt one.

"Wow, Thomas! ...and you didn't even know the woman!"

No, I thought, *but you do*. I told her about Sue the café lady and how kind she had been, and then I told her what I said to Gordon in the Gents and she shrieked and flicked her fingers so they cracked. There had been two black kids in my class whose parents were from the West Indies, I don't remember where, but we were quite friendly and I remember them trying to teach me to flick my fingers and I just couldn't and in the end they had decided my fingers were too fat... Vinroy and Fitzroy they were called...

"When Julie came over, Gordon had told her to, I just said some totally random thing to her!"

She laughed and hugged me again, glad I was alright. I was... and I very wisely held back from saying something I really would have regretted.

I was not surprised that Rebecca was working late again, but at least she texted me to say that there was an emergency, two old people had had falls and she had to go to hospital with them. I replied, thanking her for letting me know and apologising, again, for this morning. I got home and set to work with the Vanish and a damp sponge on my bloodied shirts and tried to get the coffee stains out of my suit. The kitchen was clean and tidy, so she'd not left it for me to do.

I was quite shaky again and had to use my inhaler... the incident in the mall kept repeating itself in my mind, and I felt a little sweaty at the thought that I might have been shot.

I was surprised to hear the doorbell; we so rarely get unannounced visitors. It was Phil with a bag of presents which apparently Maggie had forgotten to give Rebecca. I was a little surprised because since we would be with them on Christmas Day it seemed senseless us bringing our presents from them over with us.

Early on in our marriage we'd stayed over with them on Christmas Eve, and although they are lovely, thankfully we at least had that special night to ourselves now.

Phil accepted a coffee and we sat and chatted slightly awkwardly. For some reason he thinks I support Newcastle United, and he was congratulating me on their present form. They were playing Crystal Palace on Saturday apparently, and he chatted on about Alan Pardew, 'our' manager, and I tried to sound interested and knowledgeable. I did try to keep up with how Newcastle were doing, just so I could talk to Phil, but really I had no interest whatsoever... although I believe Newcastle is a wonderful city... Perhaps I could take Rebecca there for a weekend, really spoil her, the shops are supposed to be very good...

At last, coffee drunk, Newcastle's form discussed, Phil had to go, and then he said a very strange thing.

"We're really sorry you won't be with us on Christmas Day, looking forward to seeing you on Boxing Day though!

Maggie is thinking of getting a goose rather than eating left overs!"

I must have looked baffled because he went on.

"I just hope the directors of the Willows appreciate the pair of you! There can't be many managers and their husbands who would spend Christmas Day away from their families!"

I mumbled something about being proud of her, which I am, and tried to sound as if I knew all about it... Maybe she'd told me and I'd forgotten... But I knew she hadn't.

I said goodnight to him, and shook his hand, and then sat and waited for Rebecca to come home.

Inevitably, any discussion I attempted to have with Rebecca ended up in a row and she went into the study and I could hear her Skyping someone, the music of her game babbling in the background. I went into the kitchen and found some Bolognese sauce in the freezer and cooked some rice while it was defrosting. So, Christmas Day at the Willows, oh joy... but at least we wouldn't be with her ghastly sisters... and that did explain the absence of Christmas cake and mince-pies...

I tapped on the door of the study and called that dinner was ready. Rebecca replied she'd eaten already at the Willows. I left my dinner, pulled on my coat and Tibetan hat and went out.

Friday, 20th December 2013, morning

Rebecca and I didn't speak until the following morning which was pretty much a rerun of Thursday except I kept my hands off any coffee mugs, especially hers. I hadn't slept well, I kept waking from awful dreams, formless dreams, and now I was feeling irritable but I tried to keep it in check. As usual I started off by apologising which annoyed her, then I asked her about Christmas Day and she said well, I could go to Paul's or Marcus, since he'd invited me, but then she segued into her asking where I was last night and acting as if she didn't believe that I'd been out walking and thinking.

She was furious that I hadn't taken my phone… I hadn't even realised that I'd not taken it but left it in the kitchen and when I looked there was a couple of angry messages from her, and an even angrier voicemail.

"Perhaps we both need a holiday, why don't I book a week somewhere nice for after Christmas?"

She looked at me in such a strange way, a mixture of disbelief, suspicion, incomprehension… what was so unbelievable, suspicious or incomprehensible about a man suggesting he take his wife away on holiday?

"We could go away in January, you need a break from work, you do so much, work so hard… and I…" I might not even have a job in the New Year.

At least she didn't say no. In more restrained way she asked me what had happened to my face and I gave her the pared down version, not mentioning the reindeer or the gun. She said it had been a silly thing to do, I shouldn't have got involved, and when she asked what the woman had said to me and I told her that she'd just disappeared she was cross, but at least her anger was on my behalf.

I left the house not quite as early and not quite as upset as yesterday, and by the time I got into town the café was open. Sue was pleased to see me and said the incident had been on the local news last night and what had the police said. I'd forgotten completely about ringing them. She told me that the report had said there'd been an incident in the mall and a man had been arrested for possession of a weapon.

I glanced at the clock on the wall above the coffee machine and saw it was time for the 207 to come in so I went to see if I could find Kylie. I felt a subliminal worry about her all the time; worrying about where she was living, worrying about her little boy living with her sister, maybe her sister was the woman I'd saved from a violent man who'd pulled a gun on me… surely I'd imagined that… People didn't wave guns around in Strand shopping mall… I worried that Kylie would lose her job, I worried that she was cold at night, I worried there might be rats coming up from the river and into the old building…

She got off the bus with the aviator hat on and smiled at me, just a normal, happy, pleased to see me smile, and my heart turned over… I should not be thinking like this, I should not be feeling like this…

"Thank you for yesterday," I said as she came up to me looking utterly adorable. "I'm fine today! I shan't talk once about the Ukraine, I promise, unless you'd like to come with me to Lviv?"

She slipped her arm through mine and we walked back to the café and Sue made us our usual hot chocolate and brought it downstairs. I felt normal…

If the atmosphere in the office had been bad yesterday, it was even worse today but nothing I could explain except to say that tension almost crackled. Everyone seemed on edge and Sandra and Julie had a quiet row. Vicky wasn't in again and Sandra told us that she wouldn't be back until after the holiday, and may not even then.

The holiday... we were not coming in at all next week, so this was the last day until December the 30th... the last time I'd see Kylie for more than a week...

Julie, to be fair, tried to cheer us up by giving out silly hats at lunch time; she had a sort of fairy thing with tinsel, Sandra had a crown, Kylie had a pixy hat with ears, Martin had a sort of leprechaun's hat, Gordon was Robin Hood and I had some reindeer's antlers which were on springs so they bobbled and made everyone laugh; I made sure I went up and down the office a few times, to go to the printer, to get a coffee, to pretend to look at a file, but really it was because it made everyone laugh.

Monty had come in and brought in a selection of rolls filled with meat or cheese and I put an extra couple on Kylie's desk, knowing she would take them home. She was so thin, when I'd held her in the car she'd seemed tiny even though she's as tall as me... so thin...

Monty and Gerald retreated into their office and I went back to reading about the history of the Ukraine.

I vaguely noticed that Gordon was called into their office, but I didn't pay much attention; it was usual at this sort of time for various things to be reviewed by the partners. Then Martin went in and came out fairly quickly and sat hunched over his computer; as he came out he must have said something to Sandra because she followed him in. It was a bit like a game of tag or a relay, Sandra came out and Julie went in. Sandra sat with her back to the rest of us and I could see she was texting.

Julie came out and left the office and Kylie went in... they were leaving me till last and I mentally went over all the things I'd been working on, mentally checking everything had been done properly and completed and all the paperwork was properly up to date.

I side-tracked and became involved in the Partitions of Poland in the eighteenth century... how did anyone know where they were when sometimes they were Russia, sometimes Poland and sometimes the Ukraine?

"Thomas, Thomas! Gerald and Monty would like to see you," Sandra pulled me back to the present.

As I walked down the long office no-one looked at me and no-one laughed at my bobbing antlers; I wondered whether to take them off but then I thought, what the fuck.

"Ah, Thomas," Monty was staring at my antlers; Gerald who was sitting to one side was looking at a paper on the desk in front of him and Gordon who was halfway between being at the desk and not, was staring into the middle distance.

There was a chair in front of Monty's desk and I sat in it feeling as if I was on interview... in fact it had been very like this when I'd come for interview, although Gerald's father was still with us. I thought about Gerald's father; he would be well into his nineties now, he was over eighty when I joined the firm.

"I beg your pardon, what did you say?" I asked because Monty had been speaking.

He was telling me how much he appreciated me and the work I'd done over the years; I switched off and thought instead about the Ukraine in the seventeenth century. I knew what all this was building up to and I wondered at what point I would tell them to get fucked.

"So you appreciate the position, Thomas?" Monty said.

"I appreciate *my* position..." I said and looked at him straight in the eye, and I had the feeling it was the grey-eyed man who'd thrown a reindeer at a gun-toting maniac who was looking at Monty, not the Thomas they thought they knew.

They began to talk about packages and pension rights and good will gestures and references.

I stood up and wandered over to the window; there was a superb view across the rooftops and in the distance the sea sparkled; it was another lovely day.

They were telling me that Monty and Gerald would become partners at Lyon Abrams, effectively retire from active work...

"Thomas?"

"Do carry on, Monty, I'm all ears." There was a silence and someone whispered to someone else. After a few more murmurings, Gerald cleared his throat and he began to witter on.

I turned round and interrupted him. "Well, thank you for your impeccable timing, I hope you all have a simply splendid Christmas. Forward the relevant details to me," I looked at them expressionlessly, they were all embarrassed and awkward and hadn't a clue what to say.

Without another word I left.

As I opened the door into the main office, everyone looked at me… except Kylie. She had her head bowed and dabbed a tissue to her face.

I turned back to the three of them sitting round Monty's desk.

"So who will be lucky enough to be joining you in Castair? Gordon? Martin? Sandra? Julie? Vicky? Oh no, I forgot she conveniently got herself pregnant. And Kylie? Is Kylie transferring to Lyon Abrams?"

There was silence; it was so quiet that I heard the two-tone of an emergency vehicle pass by in the street below even through the double glazing. I could hear people in another office singing along to 'A Wombling Merry Christmas'.

"This has been the gossip of the office for the last couple of months, but no-one has had the decency or the balls to talk to me about it; it has been on the cards that I would be losing my job and Kylie would be losing hers, but no-one had enough common courtesy to tell us. I hope you realise how despicable and cowardly you are, I hope you realise how shabbily you have behaved."

Monty murmured something and the three foolish monkeys looked at the paper on his desk. I wanted to pull out the gun I didn't have and shoot their fucking heads off. I wanted to grab my model reindeer and throw it at them. I wanted to punch their stupid faces.

I walked the length of the room to my desk and then went past it to look out of my window across the town to the retail park on the outskirts. I picked up my coat and put it on and then picked up my computer and carefully put it on the floor. I pulled out each draw of my desk and emptied the contents, then tipped the desk over with a crash. It was stupid, childish and pathetic.

I picked up my backpack and without a word walked to the door, then I turned round, wished them all a merry Christmas!" then I left.

I waited in the shelter of the exit from the cinema and after a while Kylie came across. She had her green puffer jacket on and her bag with her. I put my arms round her and just held her.

"I don't know what I'm going to do, Thomas, I just don't know what I'm going to do."

"I'll help you however I can."

"But you're married to someone else..." she slipped from my embrace and ran across the snowy road.

Friday, December 20th 2013, afternoon

There was no point in trying to follow, I can't run, let alone across slippy ice and snow. I trudged towards the bus station wondering whether I should have a drink, or even have several, maybe get really, really drunk... but I went to Sue's café and had a cup of tea.

"I like your antlers, Thomas," she said as she brought the mug and a free mince-pie.

Had I really gone into the meeting with Gerald and Monty to be sacked, wearing bobbing antlers? Had I denounced their hypocrisy with them still on my head? With a sigh I took them off and put them in my backpack and sat with an empty head drinking tea. What one earth could I tell Rebecca, how on earth could I help Kylie? It was Paul's party tonight, how - really, *how*, could I cope with that?

There was a flurry of customers and I just sat drinking my tea… I wouldn't tell Rebecca tonight, we would go to Paul's party and maybe we would have a good time… she liked Ruthie and seemed easier in Paul's company now … and I wouldn't tell her when we get home tonight… and if we'd had too much to drink I wouldn't tell her in the morning until she was feeling ok… but I would tell her tomorrow, I had to tell her tomorrow.

"You've hit the headlines, Thomas!" Sue put the Strand Argos down in front of me.

'Mystery hero saves shoppers from gun horror!' *The lives of shoppers in Strand shopping mall were put at risk yesterday when a crazed gunman brandished a weapon, threatening to shoot innocent shoppers. He struck a woman in the face with his fist before an unknown passer-by intervened.*

"This guy was a hero," Sarah Johnson, 35, says. "He was just an ordinary guy with a red beard and he went right up to the gunman and tried to calm him." The bearded man was also struck in the face but then hit the gunman with a reindeer from the Christmas display. "I thought it was a TV show with this little guy knocking the gunman out with the plastic reindeer. It would have been funny if it hadn't been so terrifying," local shopkeeper Mark Sparks told our reporter. "He should get a medal," Mark, 42 says. "If he hadn't stepped up, there could have been a bloodbath." Steven McGurk is being held at Stand Police station and being questioned in connection with the incident. "This unknown man quietly left the scene as security officers from the mall apprehended the gunman and contained him until police arrived," Inspector Graham of

Strand Police told us. "We would very much like to talk to him as he may be able to provide us with valuable information concerning this incident."

I was horrified! Supposing people realised it was me? I read it though again and felt sick at the memory of what had happened. I should have rung the police, but now it had hit the news I didn't want to get my name all over the papers.

"What should I do?" I asked Sue. "I don't want a lot of publicity, it would just be so embarrassing… and things are difficult at the moment… I don't know what to do?"

"Well, it's up to you… but I think you should ring them… or maybe go into the police station and speak to them?"

"Perhaps I should ring them and then shave my beard off or dye it…"

Sue reminded me of Milly at the Willows, the same kindly, motherly person.

"I think you should… ring them, not shave your beard, it's a very nice beard!"

I took my phone out and rang the number given in the paper… it was no good thinking about it. To my surprise I was put straight through to Inspector Graham, and I apologised immediately for not getting in touch yesterday; I didn't give any reason why. I gave him the story, seeing the woman and man arguing, him hitting her… and the rest of it. Then I confessed that I had been very frightened and ran away through fear.

He said he was very pleased I'd been in touch and would I come in to make a statement; I explained that I was afraid of the publicity and wondered if perhaps I could meet him somewhere else and agreed with relief that he could come to the flat and interview me there.

I finished the call, and Sue said well done, she was proud of me, which was nice, and she gave me another cup of tea.

Friday, 20th December 2013, evening

I feared that maybe Rebecca would ring or text to say she was working late and wouldn't be able to come to Paul's but she arrived home at the time she'd said. A sergeant had come earlier and taken my statement and asked me a lot of other questions; I couldn't give a description of the woman, I hadn't seen her face properly, but she'd been wearing a black coat, and a Rasta hat. She was tall and slim, I thought, but I could say no more. I told a lie and said I'd never seen her before. I could give a better description of the man, he'd leaned over me with his mad bulging eyes.

The sergeant said I might have to go to court, and I said I was prepared for that, I would do my duty. He shook my hand, thanked me, and left.

I was desperate to tell Rebecca straight away about my job, or my lack of one, but I wisely held my tongue. I couldn't imagine how she would react... I could no longer imagine what she thought about anything... she'd become a stranger to me.

I did tell her the police had been and although she didn't say very much I could tell she wasn't pleased, and wished I hadn't been involved. As we were getting ready to go to Paul's she was sitting at her dressing table brushing her hair. She has such beautiful hair, thick and almost a blue-black and quite naturally so. I took the brush from her and began to do it for her, she used to like me doing that and now she let me do it again. I bent and kissed her neck and she turned and to my surprise kissed me and then she stood, and we embraced...

We were silent in the taxi; after we'd made loved she slipped from my arms and went to the bathroom and I fell into a sort of doze, and then had to hurry to shower and get ready and I thought she looked upset, but she said she was fine, just tired, and I didn't pursue it.

She was wearing a soft magenta dress I hadn't seen before which looked wonderful with her pale skin and dark hair. She had lipstick to match and I gazed at her as she sprayed perfume on her throat, Oh Lola!, I noticed.

"What are you looking at?" she asked.

"I nearly bought you a bottle of that perfume yesterday... just as well I didn't," she gave me such a strange look; I wondered if she thought I was being critical for spending so much. "I'm glad you treated yourself to something nice, you deserve it, you work so hard."

She looked at me speculatively as if she thought I was being sarcastic, seemed to decide I wasn't and just said 'thank you' quietly.

It seemed years since Tom had opened the door to me the first time I'd met Ruthie, and he opened it again now and was just as delighted to see me. He flung his arms around me and I swear he was taller. He greeted Rebecca and we came into the hall which was full of people, family and friends. Ruthie was there and exclaimed she was relieved to see Rebecca, and would she mind helping her in the kitchen, and my wife was towed away from me.

"Tommy!" it was Paul and I received a great hug. "Are you alright? You look different!"

"Do I? Is this better?" and I took out my bobbing antlers and put them on. I'd not told Rebecca I was bringing them she wouldn't have wanted me to… but I wanted them, they were my brave antlers… and I needed to be brave, I constantly felt on the edge of tears or the edge of anger.

Paul laughed and slapped me on the shoulder and told me to come and get a drink. I was intercepted by Andrea and Amelia, and I felt a little hot, remembering what I'd overheard them say about me, and certainly I now interpreted their friendly chat and hugs and kisses on the cheek differently… were they flirting with me? I bobbed my antlers at them and said stupid things and they shrieked with laughter, then each took one of my arms and took me through to find a drink.

I almost threw the hot punch down my throat, I had a desperate need to get drunk and blot out the muddle that was my life.

My cousin Max was in the kitchen and he too greeted me as if delighted… this was becoming surreal, since when had I been so popular? He asked me about the family tree, Paul had mentioned to him that I was doing it and it was a relief to retreat into something safe.

He called his brother Tony over; Tony was with a woman who looked vaguely familiar and then I realised she was his sister, my cousin Sammy. It was such a long time since I'd seen her, so we spent a little while catching up with our news, and it was only as I was saying everything was fine at work that I remembered it wasn't fine, it wasn't fine at all…

Rebecca was doing something by the stove with Ruthie so I didn't feel as if I was abandoning her; usually at do's like this we spend most of the time together and I was pleased to see that she was alright, it was nice to feel free to wander about and chat to my family and other people who were there.

I quite forgot the awful things which had happened today… except little flashes kept coming back… things I'd said to Monty, tipping my desk over, waiting in the cinema exit for Kylie… Kylie who I wouldn't see until… well, when would I see her? I couldn't remember what had been said about when I would finish working, but I was probably owed a lot of holiday so I'd go in and finish off anything I was dealing with and then never go back… or I might not even bother to do that.

"Sorry, Tony, what were you saying?"

He was asking whether there'd been anyone else in the family called Anthony; I was sad to tell him that yes, indeed there had been another Anthony, but he'd died in the Great War, like his cousin William; Tony was visibly moved when I said the other Anthony Radwinter was only nineteen when he died.

As I told him what I knew, and promised to email him more details, I noticed Ruthie and Rebecca leave the kitchen and was glad that my wife didn't want to be just stuck by me as if we always had to stay together.

There was a continual swirl of people, Paul and Ruthie were effortless hosts, moving round, chatting to everyone, topping up glasses and offering nibbles. They stopped by me and Ruthie mentioned that Rebecca was talking to a friend of theirs whose relative was in the Willows; as I turned back to Tony I just caught a glance between my brother and his fiancée. I pretended I hadn't noticed the exchange of looks, but I had no difficulty interpreting it. Ruthie and Paul between them were making sure Rebecca was alright... and I had no difficulty either in understanding, they were keeping us apart, liberating me.

Otis called to us that John had arrived, and we all laughed when he announced that my brother had come with *two* girlfriends!

Paul and I went through to greet him, and to my delight, there was Tom, being a gentleman and helping Justyna off with her coat. So John had managed to get together with her!

I called her name and went and said *'czesc!'* embraced her and introduced her to Paul. She was able to say a few things in English now and she looked so happy and so pretty... she's so nice, I just mentally wished that this would have a good outcome for both her and my brother.

I turned to John and my mouth must have dropped open, because standing shyly beside him was Kylie.

John grinned at me and then linked his arms through both women's. I kissed her decorously and told her I was so happy to see her.

"Are you really?" she asked sarcastically.

"He is, you can tell he is, if he smiles anymore it'll hurt," said John.

Now she smiled and pecked me on the cheek and I stood back so the three of them could go into the kitchen. My legs were shaking so badly I could hardly get up the stairs, but I left the cheerful racket below and went into Paul's room and collapsed on his bed, my mind in turmoil, my heart racing.

I came downstairs and went into the kitchen; it was probably very foolish to get drunk but that was what I intended to do.

Rebecca was there talking to two blond women, looking animated and cheerful. She introduced me smugly, which was at least how she has always used to introduce me. They were friends of Ruthie's and one of them was somehow connected to one of Rebecca's best friends.

"Have you seen who John's with?" Rebecca asked. "That tarty kid who works at your place."

"Vicky do you mean?" I asked, controlling myself.

"No, that Kylie, she's off the Hope Village estate," she said to the blond women. It obviously meant nothing to them I was glad to see. I'd never realised Rebecca was such a snob.

"I'll go and say hello to her," I said and walked away to find her.

I thought that maybe I hated my wife.

I wasn't exactly drunk when we went home, but I wasn't exactly sober either; I pretended to Rebecca to be more drunk than I was so I needn't have any sort of meaningful conversation with her.

I was pleased John had brought Kylie; he quietly told me that he'd seen her walk past the book shop looking so low and so lonely that he'd hurried out and called her in and made her a hot drink. I'd never mentioned anything to him about her financial state but no doubt he could tell. She'd been so miserable, not at all her usual self, as he put it, that he'd spontaneously invited her to Paul's. I don't know how he'd persuaded her, but John in his quiet way is as determined as Paul and Marcus are, and maybe as I secretly am too.

She was wearing the Lurex suit again, she just looked so…. I told her how lovely she looked.

"I can't tell you how pleased I am to see you," I murmured… there are many ears flapping at parties and I didn't want to be subject to any family gossip.

"Are you really, I thought you might get all grumpy and cross," she said it as if she didn't care.

"Do I need to ask what Monty and Gerald said, or can I guess?" I asked.

"Today was my last day. That's why I came here, so I could say goodbye to you," she was staring at Amelia and Andrea who were laughing with Tom and Luke, teasing them no doubt.

"Not goodbye… Definitely not," I said in a low voice.

"Well, whatever…"

Paul and Ruthie came over and we chatted, but Kylie was a little awkward so I moved away and found another drink.

"You look ridiculous with those antlers," Rebecca was beside me. "Take them off, you look an idiot."

"I am an idiot, so what does it matter," I replied snappishly.

"Are you drunk? I don't like you talking to me like that!"

"Yup, I'm drunk, that's what Christmas is about, isn't it?"

"Look at that girl, she looks awful in that suit!"

I gulped down the glass of wine which didn't deserve to be drunk like that but I think I might have done something I'd regret if I hadn't.

"Kylie? I think she looks stunning," I replied and poured some more wine.

"Don't you think you've had enough to drink?"

"No, not nearly enough!"

I actually felt very sober. I left Rebecca and went back to Andrea and Amelia who looked pleased to see me again and I was utterly ridiculous and when I felt more in control I wandered back to Kylie who was with John and Justyna.

Now Rebecca and I sat silently side by side in the taxi, each staring out of the window, me still with my antlers on. John had left at about ten with Justyna and Kylie; they hadn't stayed that long, but I'd mentioned to John to make sure Kylie got plenty to eat.

John was leaving for his Christmas holiday in Italy tomorrow, so we wouldn't see each other until after New Year, and I realised I'd miss him, even though he would only be away for ten days.

I'd said goodbye to Justyna, but I don't think she understood all I said, but she knew what I meant. I gave Kylie a big hug, wishing I could kiss her; she looked very fierce, but she was just emotional... I didn't know when or how I would see her again, but I would... She thrust something into my jacket pocket, a Christmas present she said... not much but it was all she could afford.

Sitting in the taxi I felt it, a book... I'd look at it later.

I began to sing... I sang about the platform of surrender... I sang that I was kind...

Rebecca poked my arm. "Stop it!" she said crossly.

"It's the Killers," I said, "it's called 'Human'.... Because we are, aren't we, human? Only human?"

"You're drunk!"

I started singing again... singing that I was nervous of an open door, I sang... I sang that I should shut my eyes, and empty my heart and cut the ties... the ties that bind...

"Shut up, Thomas!"

Luckily we arrived at the flat and she got out and slammed the door leaving me to pay the taxi-driver. I apologised for my singing, and he said he didn't mind, it was a favourite song of his and at least I had a decent voice. I thanked him and he wished me good luck... I'm not sure what he meant by that... but I rather thought I needed some good luck.

Maybe I should shut my eyes, and empty my heart and cut the ties...

Saturday, 21st December 2013, morning

Saturday morning... I'd guessed telling Rebecca I'd lost my job would be bad... I'd underestimated a hundred percent how bad it would be. We don't know our neighbours in the block although we occasionally hear them... they must have heard us, Rebecca screaming at me, me shouting back, doors slamming, more yelling, and maybe the sound of sobbing...

I was utterly exhausted by it and went to bed even though it was only the early afternoon; at one point she came in and accused me of sleeping off being drunk from the night before... I bit back my reply; telling her to 'fuck off' would not have been helpful.

In need of a cup of tea I got up; I hung up my clothes from last night and found the present Kylie had given me. It was a book wrapped in the sort of Christmas wrapping you might use for a child and I wondered if it was left over from wrapping something for Kenneil. Should I wait until Christmas Day, before we went to The Willows for our Christmas lunch, oh joy...

I sat on the bed in my shorts and tee shirt and socks and felt fat and wretched. I opened the wrapping paper carefully. 'Teach Yourself Ukrainian' by James Dingley and Olena Bekh. It was rather battered and when I turned it over it had a LEPRA sticker on it, and inside the front cover, if I tipped it to the light, I could see that there'd been a price written in pencil and rubbed out. £3.99. On the first page it said 'To you from me x'. Anyone could have written it, it was anonymous but I'd seen Kylie's writing often enough to know it was hers.

"What's that?" Rebecca had come in without me noticing.

I held it out to her.

"Why are you crying?" she asked, and really I couldn't answer.

She sat beside me and put her arms around me; she didn't actually say she was sorry but she was. Things were wrong between us, maybe terminally wrong, but Rebecca wasn't a horrible person, she wasn't really unkind.

"Why do you want to learn Ukrainian?" she asked.

I wiped my face without answering and then kissed her, and because we were both so miserable we made love, as we had last night, in silence.

We actually had a normal sort of conversation, lying in the late afternoon dusk, unable to see each other's face.

I could understand that she was anxious; if I didn't have a job then our income would be cut by more than half. I was sure I would find employment but I wasn't sure I wanted to go on doing what I'd been. The office had ended up as poisonous and I wasn't sure I could stand being in a situation like that again. I didn't say that to Rebecca though, but I assured her I would do all I could to get another job... I just didn't specify what, because truly I didn't know.

We were young enough to be able to renegotiate our mortgage; when we'd taken it on we'd decided think of the flat as an investment, not our forever home, as Rebecca put it. We would live there, comfortably, but try and pay it off quickly and then move on to something else. We only had about five more years to pay anyway...

"We could always sell here," she said, and my heart leapt. "We could move back home, back with Mum and Dad," my heart sunk... and then I had this horrible, horrible thought. If we sold the house, got rid of everything and then moved in with Phil and Maggie, it would be so much easier for me to leave her... because I suddenly saw, lying holding Rebecca, that our marriage wouldn't last. "How do you feel about that?" she asked when I didn't reply.

"I think it's a good idea... but not yet, let's keep that as an option, a good option, but let's just see how things go."

She sighed, with relief I thought.

I took a deep breath and then asked something which I just hope would not lead to another row, I just hate shouting and crying and doors slamming... too much of that in my childhood; maybe that was why I'd married Rebecca - placid to the point of boring, predictable, no threat, no emotion... just secure, dependable, safe... but real life shouldn't be like that, any more than it should be like the childhood I had. Real life was what Paul and his boys had, and Marcus and his girls.

"Rebecca, sweetheart, I don't want to argue about this, or for you to get upset or angry with me, I just want to know... just so I know... do you really, really not want children, do you really not want us to have a family? I'm not going to try to persuade you otherwise, or get cross or upset, I would just like to know..."

She didn't answer for a while, as if waiting for me to ask again... this was another tactic of hers which nearly always ended in a row. So I waited too. In the end, she said in a calm voice, a firm voice, "You know what my answer is; the same as it was last time we discussed it. I haven't changed my mind, OK?"

She got up, gathered her clothes and went to the bathroom, and I lay holding my Ukrainian book and thinking... OK...

Saturday, 21st December 2013, evening

Public House Riot.

A disturbance took place in The Lark, a public house in High Street, Easthope, at about 9 o'clock last night, and the police were called. Constables Robinson and O'Shea, arrived very shortly and found the floor of the place covered with glass, and a general uproar taking place among the men present. One of the men, Solomon Davis, who was recently imprisoned for a cowardly and cruel assault on a woman, attempted to strike O'Shea, but that officer took care of himself and Davis was soon in safe custody at Easthope police station, along with others who had caused the affray.

The landlord, Thomas Radwinter, was commended for his action in defending several of his customers, taking them into his private salon for their own safety. February 1892

BROKE PUBLIC-HOUSE DOOR.

Matthew Mudd and Matthew Matthews were found guilty of breaking a window of the Lark public-house and attempting to force an entrance. They were each fined 10/ and 11/6 costs. November 1893

Local History – Easthope – page 22

"Several other ale-houses were kept by Easthope brewers in the 18th century, including the Castle, near the site of Stope Castle, demolished in the Civil War. The Red Lion, established before 1750, was one of several half-timbered buildings on Hope Street; the Lark Inn, built on the site of the London sometime in the 1820's, remains open to the present; the India Inn serving the wharfmen on the Hope, was closed in 1962 and converted to a private residence. The Bull was converted in the 1920s into a Co-operative store, still open on the High Street. Easthope's friendly societies included branches of the Ancient Shipwrights, probably formed c. 1842, which had 37 members in 1892, and the Ancient and Honourable Order of the Old Foresters, with some 32 members in 1892, regularly *meeting at the Lark Inn, Easthope. Both were still active in the 1920s.In 1873 the Reverend James Purlieu started a working men's club with 50 members, providing a reading room and coffee house adjacent to the St James Church Hall, in association with the Church Temperance Society. In 1919, Mr Thomas Radwinter, formerly of the Lark Inn, in memory of those sons of Easthope killed in the Great War, and in thanks for the lives of his own sons, Charles, Walter and Horace, endowed the former reading room and coffee house for use by the Easthope Men's Club, which had over 100 members within a year and was still active in the 1980s."*

I looked through the photos, and it was tempting to think the slim, handsome prosperous looking man who featured in a couple of them might have been a Radwinter but there was no name on the back only 'The Lark' and dates in the 1890's. I would have to go to the local newspaper offices and see if I could look in their archives, because there was bound to be a report of Thomas Radwinter's endowment of the reading room and coffee house... and maybe other mentions of him as he seemed to be a stalwart of the town.

There were various bills of sale relating to the pub, with the name of Thomas upon them, but each signature was different so there was no telling who'd written it. One might be Thomas's but there was no way of knowing. In the bottom of the envelope there were a few torn pieces of old newspaper, but nothing of any significance. There was a strip of paper from along the top of a page with the tops of advertisements for various nineteenth century items... I turned it over.

'*RADWINTER TRAGEDY, LATEST ON DROWNI...*'

Tragedy? Drowning? Who? When? There was no date, no indication of when it might have been or what it was referring to… but nothing had so far suggested that anyone had drowned.

I was shocked out of my introspection and went and made a cup of tea, and Rebecca came out of the study to have hers and we made awkward conversation as I told her about the photos and news cuttings and the mysterious headline. She seemed semi-interested and suggested I Googled Radwinter, Easthope, drowning etc., and I said I would… we seemed like strangers… would things ever be right between us? Could things ever be right between us?

"I thought we'd leave about ten-ish tomorrow," she said as she prepared to return to the study.

"OK… where are we going?" I had it in my mind that Phil had said we wouldn't be with them for Sunday lunch tomorrow.

"I told you, we're having lunch with Georgia, Lauren's coming too as we won't see them on Christmas Day. I told you!" she was irritated, but she was also lying; there was no way I would have forgotten the ghastly prospect of spending a day with the two evil sisters-in-law… they weren't really evil… I just didn't like them. I said nothing. "Thomas? We're going to Georgia's."

"Right, fine."

I could have started another row about it, but what would be the point. The firestorm this morning when I told her I'd lost my job had exhausted me, I just hadn't the strength to argue about something over which I had no control.

"So we'll leave at ten," Rebecca repeated, and I knew she wanted me to make an issue about it.

"Fine, what shall I wear?"

Black cords she told me, and a nice shirt. She waited for a moment for me to comment but I just got my laptop and typed in Radwinter drowning.

I'd obviously disconcerted her because she came back half an hour later and asked if we should ring for a Domino's pizza; this is usually a no-no, she thinks it's bad for me, I quite like pizza but really, I'm not that bothered. I told her it was a good idea, and I'd have whatever sort she was having.

She sat beside me to ring Domino's and then sat messing with her phone. She suddenly said something but before I could ask her anything she got up and went through to her computer in the study. I guess she'd got a message on Facebook from someone, or a text to tell her to look at something.

I heard her shout out and I looked up; maybe she had won something on one of her games, or managed to buy something she was bidding for in her imaginary house, or maybe someone had outbid her... I had no interest.

"What the hell is this?" she was back and sticking something in my face, her phone.

Before I could properly see what she was showing me, she gave me a stinging slap across my face.

"What the fuck was that for?" I shouted, trying to get up but she hit me again, whacked me hard across the side of my head.

My laptop jerked from my lap and fell on the floor with an ominous cracking sound, but I managed to get to my feet and push her away from me, my head ringing.

"What the hell are you doing?" I shouted. The neighbours must be wondering what's going on in our life.

"What the hell am *I* doing? *What the hell am I doing?*" she screeched.

I have never seen her so mad and... and out of control. She was beside herself with rage, almost spitting with fury. She'd been angry this morning and said some poisonous things, but nothing like she was now. She was still shoving her phone at me but I couldn't make out what it was she was trying to show me.

She tried to hit me again and then shoved me so I fell back onto the sofa. She snatched up my laptop and holding it on one arm began to type something, then shoved it at me. It was a Facebook page and there was a photo of me... of me and Kylie walking into the dining room of the Oriel, arm in arm as if we owned the place. She looked as stunning as I remembered, and there was I, actually looking not bad with the bow tie which matched hers.

I stared at it as Rebecca stood over me panting, literally panting with emotion.

"What's the matter?" I asked aggrieved, although I knew perfectly well what the matter was.

"How do you explain that – you with that - that slut!"

"Don't call her that... there's nothing to explain, we went into the restaurant together... what the fuck is wrong with that, Rebecca?"

"Don't use language like that!"

"I can use what fucking language I fucking like… and if you ever hit me again I shall walk out."

"Walk out? How dare you! There are pictures of you and this… this… all over Facebook, and you have the cheek to say you'll walk out because I don't like it?"

"Show me these other pictures then!" Unless someone had been standing outside the car parked by the old wharf in Easthope, there would be no photos of anything… and indeed there weren't… They were Julie and Sandra's photos, who apparently are Rebecca's 'friends' on Facebook.

There were pictures of me sitting next to one or other of them, mostly looking glum and sober, there were pictures of Kylie between Gordon and Gerald looking bored. There was a couple of me kissing Monty on the cheek. There were pictures of me dancing with various people, and of Kylie… but nothing the least bit objectionable apart from the first one of us strolling in together. We both looked very cool, I have to say… it was a fabulous photo… but there was nothing wrong with it.

I put my laptop on the sofa and stood up.

"I meant what I said, Rebecca. If you ever hit me again, *ever,* I shall walk out, out of the flat and out of your life… get it?" I stared hard at her, then went into the kitchen, then had to go the bathroom to be sick.

Sunday, December 22nd 2013

She did actually apologise to me, although she didn't specify what exactly she was apologising for. Maybe we should go to marriage guidance or whatever it's called... maybe we need someone outside of the family to help us from this trench warfare we have somehow become engaged in. I was amazed I fell asleep, but I did immediately I turned out my light, and slept through in a leaden way until morning, waking to that curious colour of sky which says it's going to snow.

I was hungry but could only face eating toast, although I noticed that Rebecca had eaten some of the pizza. I got showered and dressed and tried to decide whether my face was bruised or whether it was just a shadow. The cuts had scabbed over, strange shield shaped marks on my cheek.

I put on my black cords and a pale blue shirt and a navy sweater... I didn't care how I looked. As we set off I asked Rebecca if it would be OK for me to drive up to see Marcus this afternoon; his village was only ten miles from where Georgia lived and I'd like to pop in to wish him Happy Christmas. Rebecca supposed it would be alright, and was that the only reason I was going to see him. When I asked her what she meant she just muttered something about Christmas which I didn't catch and couldn't be bothered to ask her to repeat.

To be fair the visit wasn't too bad; the older children had become involved in some game on their kids' tablets so they just played with them all the time, even during the meal which was a relief. One of the little ones was poorly so just slept in his mother's arms the whole time, and the other, with no-one to steal his toys or interfere with his little games, just played with his toy trucks.

Georgia, like her mother and Rebecca, was a great cook so we had a lovely meal; she'd done pulled pork with roasted rosemary potatoes and broccoli and cauliflower cheese. I had a bit of a head-ache, no surprise there, and I was driving so I didn't drink, but Rebecca did, Prosecco, rosé, Limoncello… I made my apologies and left once I'd helped clear the table.

I felt free and the tightness in my chest and pains in my neck disappeared as I drove up into the hills; I was following a snow-plough, so although it was slow there were no problems; the clouds had drifted away for a moment, the wind had died and it was beautiful. The driver of the snow-plough, kept looking back at me with an apologetic face, but I just grinned at him and gave him a thumbs' up… I didn't care that we were going slowly, we were going in the right direction.

I parked on the drive of the vicarage behind Marcus's battered old car and he came out to me as he had before, grinning his toothy smile which I now expected when he greeted me.

I struggled out of the car and almost fell into his embrace and then to my horror, I burst into tears. I felt utterly broken but Marcus wrapped his strong arms round me and held me so tightly that gradually the fears and the horrors seeped away and I was able to wipe my face and go with him into his warm welcoming house.

He took me straight into the sitting room, decked out for Christmas with a big tree in the window, and he built up the fire so it roared up the chimney, and Jill appeared and thrust a mug of tea into my hands and peeled my big coat off me and unwrapped my stripy scarf as if I was a giant toddler.

I sat on the settee with Marcus, and it sounds ridiculous but he held my hand as I stumbled out the story of my sacking... for however Monty and Gerald wrapped it up, that's what had happened; I told him about the disaster that was my marriage, because of something I'd done of which I was ignorant... that the photo of me and Kylie was just an excuse for Rebecca to... to attack me... that she didn't want children or a family and it was what I was beginning to want more than the love and romance of a marriage... that I was unfathomably miserable...

I told him about the terrifying incident in the mall when I'd been saved by a fibre-glass reindeer. Marcus exclaimed something, jumped up from the sofa and pulled a copy of the Castair Courier from a pile of magazines and newspapers. He pointed to the front page.

MYSTERY MAN SAVES SHOPPERS FROM BLOODBATH

"Oh my goodness, was that you?" he sat beside me as I read a version of what the Argos had published, describing me as a fat, red-bearded young man.

"Well, at least they say I'm young," I said feebly.

Marcus seemed genuinely lost for words, as was Jill who just popped in to ask about more tea. Jill asked who the woman was, I had no idea, I told her... and didn't mention I'd seen her and Kylie arguing.

"I can't tell you how proud I am of you," Marcus said after a moment.

"You always taught me to stand up for other people and respect women," I said. "It's the way you brought me up."

Now it was Marcus who looked emotional... so we had another cup of tea and I had several of Jill's delicious home-made mince-pies with home-made mincemeat, then I had to head back to Georgia's.

"What should I do about me and Rebecca," I asked as we stood by the car. The sun was low and it was very cold.

"You could always pray," he offered.

"I'm not religious... and when I try and think about things, it just goes round and round, and I can't see an end to it."

"Well, I'll pray for you."

I drove away feeling stronger but with no other idea how to get out of the mess that Rebecca and I were in.

Monday, December 23rd 2013, early morning

It was only when I was actually on the 7:30 bus into town that I remembered that I didn't have to go to work. I decided I would email Gerald and ask him if I needed to come in or if I could work from home to clear the small amount of outstanding business I had. If I had to go in I would get there at seven o'clock when the friendly cleaners went in, just so I didn't have to see anyone again.

So what could I do all day? John was away so I couldn't go and chat with him, I'd done all my Christmas shopping for Rebecca now... and I thought about the bottle of Oh Lola! sitting on her dressing table...

I didn't want to go back into the shopping mall... I wanted to go to Easthope.

I went back into the bus station and saw the tramp with the big red beard; he was staggering around singing Christmas carols, not really begging, but being a bit of a nuisance. I leant on a rail and watched him. If Kylie was with me she would have gone over and calmed him down or bought him a coffee or something.

I went over.

"Mate!" he cried when he saw me. "Mate!" I was surprised he recognized me.

"You want some breakfast? I'm all on my Todd, no-one to chat to, you want some breakfast?"

I think he thought it was some sort of trick but I took him round to the café and parked him on one of the chairs outside and went inside and saw Sue. She asked who my 'friend' was.

"Just some poor old bloke, he's harmless, but he's cold and hungry," I actually was quite cold and hungry too, I'd eaten nothing before I left the flat, but my cold and hunger was nothing like his.

I took him out a big mug of tea and a breakfast bap; I sat down with a coffee and a bacon sandwich but it was difficult to eat with the smell coming off him.

"Mate, you're a gent," he said, struggling to eat, because of his lack of teeth.

I told him I was Thomas and asked his name; Eddy, he told me, Eddy the Red, and he tugged at his beard and chuckled. He kept looking at me as he was eating, I think he was a bit suspicious of my motives.

I looked at my watch and pretended I had to go. Eddy thanked me again and held out his hand and I shook his filthy paw. He winked at me, I waved to Sue and then hurried off with nowhere to go.

Would this be my life for a while, wandering round with nowhere to go and nothing to do? It was sleeting now which was colder than snow and the wind was getting up but I found I was near the Polish shop and went in, hoping maybe to see Justyna.

The older lady, (Dora… Dora… Dorata!) was behind the counter; she nodded and may have smiled in her grim way when I called *'dzień dobry!'*. I picked up a basket and wandered around as if I knew what I was looking for. There were some chocolates which I think had marzipan in them, the label said 'czekoladki marcepanowe' and there was a little picture… I put a couple of bars in the basket, and some salami, and I got a cake called 'szarlotka' with a rosy apple on the label. I avoided the chocolate jellies and the fish soup though.

"Is Justyna here today?" I asked as Dorata scanned my shopping. As I paid I reflected that soon I would have to watch every penny… I'd got into the habit of buying things if I wanted them, or thought Rebecca might like them, without even thinking twice about the price.

"Holiday," came the stern reply. "Your friend, she is on holiday with your friend."

I was astonished; did she mean John? I'd thought he was going away for a lads' holiday… well, that must have been very last minute because he said nothing to me as he'd hugged me on Friday night. I told her he was my brother, as if that might somehow make a difference… because I got the feeling she didn't approve.

"He's a good man?" she asked.

"The best! I know he is my brother, but he is a kind person, a very kind person; he's a good friend to me as well as brother!!"

She nodded but didn't seem about to say anything else, so I took my plastic bag with the Polish flag on it and with a little wave and wishing her 'Happy Christmas', I left.

I went through the foul weather to the Armenian café and perhaps I shouldn't be surprised any more but I still was, to be greeted by name. I ordered a coffee I didn't really want, still full from breakfast with Eddy the Red but the man behind the counter who I think is called Vekan asked me if I would like a real Armenian coffee... he had to prepare it specially he said with a smile.

It was strong and spicy... cardamom I thought, and maybe... allspice? As I wondered about it and commented to Vekan how much I was enjoying it, I thought that it was a while since I'd thought very much about food... so much for me wittering on to Ruthie about cheesy shortbread...

If I had to pick a moment when whatever it was happened that had changed me and changed my life, I would have to say it was that moment in Paul's kitchen when I ate Ruthie's millionaire's shortbread and gingerbread...

I was different, and I couldn't go back to being how I was. The marriage I had with Rebecca which was so dull and safe was now just dull... and it didn't feel safe at all, it felt as if I would drown in the dreariness of it.

The job which I'd had for however many years was gone... and actually I was glad; I'd sat at the end of the office looking down along other peoples' desks as if I was in some Siberia cut off from the banter between Martin and Gordon, the gossip between the women... well, Julie, Sandra and Vicky. I had been just ticking over, nothing stretched me or engaged my mind, it was all just easy and boring and... and awful... and I was glad I'd escaped.

Drinking the strong Armenian coffee seemed like a little celebration, and I felt almost brave. It was quiet and Vekan came and sat at the table with me and we chatted about nothing very much at all, which was entirely pleasant and satisfactory. He was a very handsome man with very black hair and a beard and a rather hooked nose and very dark eyes; I could imagine him to be quite fierce, but with me he laughed and was generous and hospitable.

He asked if I would like 'a drink' since it was so cold, and he brought out a bottle of Armenian brandy, Ararat was the brand and the bottle he had was Ani… Oh well, it was nearly Christmas. It was just what I needed even at ten o'clock in the morning; it had an almost chocolaty taste and maybe some sort of hint of citrus, orange maybe… there was a nuttiness… Vekan seemed pleased at my comments and I asked him where I might be able to get a bottle, I thought it might be a nice gift for Paul. It was strong and warming and wonderful, and I felt ready to go out and face the dreadful weather raging outside.

As I left, Vekan told me next time he ordered some Ani he would get an extra bottle, and if I wanted it for my brother I could have it, but if I didn't then he would sell it anyway.

I wished him Happy Christmas and went out into a snowstorm.

The wind was incredible; I'm quite heavy but it was just about all I could do to stay on my feet. I took a short cut round the back of the mall to go in the car park entrance which was nearest. There was a huge skip full of rubbish and as I got to the door a man was struggling towards me with more stuff to go in it, including a fibre-glass reindeer.

"Oh dear, what's he done?" I asked and hoped he didn't notice the unintentional pun.

"Broken foot – it got done when that bloke was attacked by that mad bastard with a gun."

I forbore to say that I was 'that bloke' but asked instead if I could have the reindeer.

"Got kids, have you mate? They'll love it! Yeah, help yourself, it's only going to the dump!"

Monday, December 23rd 2013, mid-morning

Back in the bus station, after considering various options, the reindeer and I got on a bus and went home. At home in the flat, although we are not on the top floor the building seemed to shake with the buffeting wind.

It was strange being home during the day, and Rebecca not being here. I sat and flipped through the TV channels but there was nothing I wanted to watch. And all the time, all the time, I was trying not to worry about Kylie. She no longer had a phone for me to be able to text her, and I didn't like to use the unknown number she'd given me.

I wondered how Jessica was, she hadn't been in touch for a couple of days, so I messaged an all-purpose cheery, nothingy message. A message came back almost immediately from a number I didn't know; it was from Jessica's husband, David. Little Riley had arrived early and was in the neonatal prem baby unit at Strand Royal.

Hope all's well, love to you both and little Riley, I texted back, and got the message back, *thanks, fingers crossed...*

I knew nothing about babies or having babies, I couldn't remember when the baby should have been born to know how old it was or what chance it stood of surviving or being healthy... one more thing to worry about, one more thing I couldn't do anything to solve.

I wandered round the flat restlessly... I had so much to do on the family tree... so many ends which needed tying and would take no time at all to do... the mysterious tragedy... was Charles our grandfather, or was there another Charles a generation between?

I was standing with my hand on the reindeer's neck when a key turned in the lock and Rebecca opened it. We were astonished to see each other; she closed the door again as she struggled to get the key out and then opened it and came in.

"Have you finished early?" I asked hopefully, maybe we needed time together... we *definitely* needed time together.

"No, I've just popped in to get... what's that?"

"It's my reindeer, he saved my life!" Am I having some sort of mental breakdown? Am I going mad? Why do I want to wear bobbing reindeer antlers, and why do I say stupid things?

"You didn't tell me it was in the paper – you didn't say he had a gun!" instead of being proud of me, she seemed angry. "You could have been killed! Why did you do such a stupid thing for a woman you didn't even know, so you say!"

I was about to apologise and then thought, why should I? Why should I apologise for trying to help someone who was being hurt?

She stood waiting for me to speak but since I wasn't going to say sorry I didn't know what to say.

She went past me into the bedroom and moments later she was back with the magenta dress she'd worn at Paul's party, telling me to get rid of that ridiculous creature right now! She said she was taking her dress to be dry-cleaned and had I anything that needed cleaning. I went and got my work suit; I usually have it cleaned regularly… I wouldn't need to bother now.

"Why don't you stay and have lunch here," I suggested. "I'm sure they can spare you for an hour."

"Why are you back here anyway?" she asked.

"I just had to pop into work for something, it only took a minute, and then I did a little Christmas shopping, met an Armenian friend…"

"Armenian? Who's that?"

"Vekan, he has a little café where John and I go for lunch sometimes; why don't we go there and have lunch now? You'd love it, really you would!"

But of course she made some excuse; I managed to kiss her then she was gone and I went to the window and looked down and saw her jump into a car and be driven away.

I got some Christmas ribbon and tied it round the reindeer's neck, then had a look at his foot. His back hoof had broken off; it was the prancing hoof, so it didn't matter and he was quite stable on three legs.

I tried ringing Paul, desperate for a kind voice, and for someone to be pleased to hear from me. I thought he might be busy but he answered quickly and warmly. I told him I hadn't rung him to disturb him, but I just had to fill him in on the family gossip, that John was away with Justyna.

"He hasn't taken Kylie as well, has he?" Paul joked and my heart froze.

I managed to make some casually reply, slumping back on the sofa.

"That was just a joke, she wasn't the least interested in him," Paul chuckled. "She only had eyes for one person," he was laughing now.

I struggled to think of who at the party might have caught Kylie's eye. All I could think of were some friends of Django's who'd got their guitars out later on... but that was when John had left...

"It's you, you numpty!" Paul said. "She fancies you rotten! Look, kiddo, I've got to go! Give us a ring on Christmas Day and come over soon, love you, bro!"

Monday, December 23rd 2013, afternoon

The thing is with my brother Paul, he's a great joker and says outrageous things, and mostly they're funny but sometimes, without meaning to, he says something which ends up being really painful. When he said that about Kylie it was as if I'd been punched in the face all over again, except this time I'd been punched in the heart.

He's put it in my mind that she might be with John... I could just imagine kind John taking her with him on holiday... I thought he was more interested in Justyna, and that's the impression Dorata had given, that he and Justyna were together... but...

The wind was beginning to howl round the flats now...

It was lunch time but I had no appetite; I watched the news with the forecast of dreadful storms, of gales and floods... it was pretty dreadful here, and I watched the local news and weather on Coast TV... and it didn't look good. I hope Rebecca wouldn't stay late tonight, I'd be worried about her driving home in what the weather girl was describing.

I opened my laptop, but somehow I hadn't the heart to do any work, I just did some basic checking of dates, births and marriages of people I already had on the tree, tracing back the parents of wives and husbands.

Tolik's wife Emma had been a Wyeth before she was married, and interestingly she'd been born in Lambeth, where Tolik's sister Thirza had been born. I traced Eleanor Quillen in the census, it seemed quite nice to have an Irish connection... perhaps we could go there, perhaps us four brothers could go to Ireland...

I looked on the BBC news page and checked on what was happening in the Ukraine, I looked at a few things on Amazon, I made tea, I put a note on my phone to buy another mug to replace the one I'd smashed...

Maybe I could make dinner for Rebecca so when she came home, no doubt cold and tired, a nice meal would be waiting for her... I looked through the cupboards and the fridge... maybe something light, pasta carbonara maybe, or something light but tasty like a Thai curry... or would she want something warming...

And what would Kylie be eating tonight? She would be at her sister's with her little boy; they might not be well off but there would be food and there would be warmth and love, they would laugh, and maybe Kylie might be hiding her worries about her job or lack of it, but maybe she would sleep on her sister's sofa and not in the boarded up pub by the River Hope... the river...

I went back to the BBC weather page and checked all the warnings... There was a severe flood warning on the River Hope... there was a severe weather warning for Easthope for high wind and snow...

I wandered around, quite agitated... but there was nothing I could do. I turned on the TV. 'The Bridge' was on Channel 4... I'd watched it before but it was good so I sat, trying to ignore the weather outside and watched Daniel Ferbe struggling with his task...

I woke and it was dark. I crawled out of whatever strange dreams I'd been having and staggered around, switching on lights and trying to get myself together. I drew the curtains on the foul night, checked my phone and then rang Rebecca.

She answered curtly; she must be busy, in the middle of something.

"I won't keep you long sweetheart, I just wondered when you might be home, and what you fancied for dinner tonight?"

"No idea," she murmured something to someone else. "Sorry, Thomas, that sounded rude... Don't worry about me, I'll eat something here, you have whatever you want."

"OK, sweetheart, but don't leave it too late to come home, the weather is vile here..." but she'd rung off.

I watched the news, and then the local news, I couldn't bear to watch Celebrity Mastermind, and I couldn't think clearly enough to do any more research... I watched the news channel... except I wasn't watching it.

I'm not sure when Rebecca texted me... *staying over here, weather closing in, don't worry, I'll be fine x*

I texted back for her to get a taxi... but no, she would stay over... it had happened before occasionally... but I couldn't remember how long ago it had been... we'd so rarely been apart, I honestly couldn't remember when.

There was such a strange noise that for a moment I didn't know what it was. It sounded like wolves howling... or how they sound on TV... but it was the wind.

I looked at the weather page again, a red warning for Easthope and the River Hope.

Monday, December 23rd 2013, evening

I rang for a taxi, pulled on my big coat and Tibetan hat, and went down to wait in the vestibule. The glass panels were shaking and making a twanging noise, and I wondered whether they would survive the night. The lights kept flickering, and at times it seemed as if the building itself was shaking. Headlights showed outside and I ran out and jumped into the taxi and asked him to take me to the bus station in Strand.

He wasn't very talkative which was just as well because I wasn't in the mood for chatting. The drive was uneventful, the wind was behind us and although it was still snowing we whizzed along and got to the bus station without any problems. I thanked the driver and jumped out and hurried over to the office, to check the buses were still running but as I crossed the deserted lanes, I saw the 207 and I waved to the driver and trotted over and got on.

"I'm not sure how far we'll get, the weather's closing in," he said, but he sounded pretty nonchalant so I said I'd keep my fingers crossed.

I sat on the front seat behind the luggage rack and stared into the darkness as we left the bus station. It was a double decker and was rocked by the wind and I heard a little scream behind me. Two elderly ladies were sitting further back.

"I'm sure we'll be fine!" I called to them.

"I hope we don't get stuck in a snowdrift," one of them replied.

"Or blown over the cliff," her friend added… thank you ladies for your cheerful thoughts.

The driver was whistling though, and although we were going slowly, and the bus rocked from time to time, he didn't seem concerned as we chugged along the coast road and then up to Castle Point. I had to use my inhaler a couple of times, I was struggling, so anxious about so many things and I wished I'd brought my reindeer.

"Are we nearly there, young man?" one of the old ladies called.

"Not far now!" I called back and then the bus skidded and slithered and the driver shouted 'oh fuck!' and the old ladies screamed, but then we were moving downhill slowly and steadily.

I got up and went back to the old girls who were clutching each other and clearly terrified. I sat down by them and turned sideways in my seat.

"Don't worry, we're nearly there, the driver will get us safely to Easthope," I told them.

I began to chat to them about Christmas and shopping, and presents, and they rallied and chatted back. They were sisters and good friends too; their husbands were at home and they'd gone shopping in Strand and had treated themselves to a fish supper. Now they were regretting having stayed so late. I told them that when they were safely home, sitting by their fires with a cup of tea, they'd think it a great adventure.

"Glass of wine, young man, glass of wine," one of them said and we were laughing as the bus drew up on the High Street.

We all thanked the driver, who seemed untroubled by the adventure. I asked the ladies how they were getting home but they said they only lived a little way away, down Byron Street. I didn't like the idea of them struggling through what was now a blizzard, so I insisted on them each taking my arm and I walked them slowly home, just hoping I didn't slip over and bring us all down in a heap.

We arrived safely, and I would have really liked to go into their warm and cosy home, invited in by a smiling chubby old man, the husband of one. I declined, kissed each on the cheek to much giggling from them, shook the chubby husband's hand and set off, back to the High Street.

I stood on the High Street, all the good cheer evaporating. I crossed over and went into the Lark; it was absolutely packed, but I didn't want a drink. I wandered through the bars, squeezing between the merry-makers, surprised by how many people seemed to know me. I'd come in covered in snow, now I began to steam slightly in the heat and I took off my hat.

Suddenly there was a noise like an explosion, everyone went silent for a second, then there were a few screams and shouts of *'what the fuck was that?'* It seemed that the wind had blown the back door open and it had smashed back against something and the leaded glass window had broken. No-one was hurt thankfully but that seemed the sign for people to begin to depart.

I went out onto the High Street and if anything the wind was even more ferocious. I struggled down the road and turned the corner and was in a more sheltered spot. I took another pull on my inhaler and then headed for Mill Lane. I crossed over the bridge and could actually see the River Hope rushing beneath, even though there were no street lights; it was frighteningly quick and horribly high.

Mill Lane was mostly in darkness as if the houses had been abandoned for Christmas, and I wondered what I was doing here. I'd come to make sure Kylie was safe but I didn't even know she was in the India Inn tonight.

I made my way along the broken street, tripping over stuff, slipping and sliding, thankful I'd put my boots on rather than my shoes, glad of my big coat and scarf and above all, my Tibetan hat.

The night has been unruly: where we lay... Macbeth I thought. I got to the pub and stared up at the windows. The ones on the top floor weren't boarded over but were black and empty. I went to the corner where the door was and tried to turn the door knob but it didn't move. I stepped back and almost tripped over something hidden by the blanket of snow. I looked up at the window on this side and there seemed to be a faint glimmer of light, but maybe it was just a reflection of the snow.

I went back to the door and banged on it with my fist but the sound seemed lost in the uproar of the wind. What should I do? I thought again about the red flood warning and the river rushing by not far away. The single street light was out and I wished I'd brought a torch, I only had the light from my phone but I crossed the open ground where the warehouses might once have been and went to look at the water level on this side of the wharf.

This area must be like a little harbour or cut for the ships… I don't know anything about shipping, but the water was lapping the edge of the dock. I didn't go near it… I can swim, but not in freezing black water.

I went back to the old pub, there was no glimmer of light now, I must have been mistaken, but I banged on it again until my fist hurt. I sat down on the doorstep, and leant against the pillar. I was tired, but it was an emotional tiredness… and I knew I wasn't rational… something had gone wrong inside me… sensible people don't go out in a storm to see if a friend is safe when they don't even know if the friend is there… Sensible people find some way to talk to their wives… to talk to the people who employ them…

When did I last eat anything? The bacon sandwich with Eddy the Red. Was I hungry? I was too heart-sick to be hungry.

Should I ring for a taxi and go home… home to the empty flat. Should I get a taxi and go to Paul's? But supposing the water overflowed the dock, supposing the river burst its bank? Supposing the wind blew the roof off or the windows in?

I got up and went back to the dock and the water was beginning to spill over, quite gently, really. I went back to the bridge and looked at the river but it looked no different, dark and dangerous. I stomped back down Mill Lane, the snow even thicker.

On the opposite side from the houses was a wall, and an area of open land at a higher level beyond it, as if there had been some sort of big building here. Every so often there was a break in the wall with stairs going up to the higher level, I know this because as I was feeling my way along, I fell into the gap... and then fell into the next gap. I bumped my head but luckily my Tibetan hat protected me so although it hurt it wasn't too bad... it wasn't too bad but it almost made me cry.

I felt so wretched... was this how Eddy and the other old man had come to live on the streets... had they wandered out one night and not come home? Had my dad wandered out one night and never returned? Was he lying in some empty shop doorway stinking of piss and covered in snow?

I went back to the pub, banged half-heartedly then sat on the step again. I must have dozed a little because I woke with a start and pins and needles because the step was too low for a fat bloke to sit comfortably... Sit comfortably outside on December 24th in the early hours of a freezing cold morning. The wind seemed to have dropped a little and it was no longer snowing; I went to the dock again and the edge had disappeared beneath the water. The river was tidal but I had no idea what time tides were... maybe this was just high tide and it would ebb away.

I went back to the doorway and rattled the knob but it wouldn't open... was it the same doorknob Tolik had put his hand on, and Thomas, the first Thomas Radwinter? I was coddled compared to their lives... that first census when I'd found Thomas, he'd appeared to be living in an abandoned building... how cold he must have been...

Maybe Kylie was safely with John in Italy... I think he'd gone to Italy, I couldn't really remember...

The wind picked up again and it must have swung round a little because it was blowing straight at me now. I went back to look at the river again; maybe it was a little higher, I wasn't sure. I returned to Mill Lane, taking care not to topple onto the steps in the wall... until I toppled into one I hadn't noticed opposite the pub.

I fell into a shelter from the wind. I could sit on these steps with walls on either side, in view of the pub, a looming white mass across the road, and my legs weren't cramped. I pulled my collar up, and my hat down, and drew my coat over my knees. I checked the time on my phone... I would go and look at the water on the dock in half an hour...

At some point, when I went to look at the water, it was receding... the tide was going out... and I went back to my steps and fell asleep and dreamt of Kylie. During the night the howling of the wind woke me and it was so strong I couldn't even stand up in it, and as I subsided into my little sheltered stairs I think I might have cried a little.

Tuesday, December 24th 2013, Christmas Eve, early morning

I dreamt of Kylie, she was bending over me, brushing my face, and I tried to say something but the words made no sense.

I opened my eyes and Kylie was bending over me.

"You're a dream," I said.

"What the fuck are you doing here?!" she shouted, and she was brushing snow my face and picking ice from my beard. I couldn't properly feel her fingers, my skin was frozen.

"*Our chimneys were blown down; and, as they say, lamentings heard in the air; strange screams of death, and prophesying with accents terrible of dire combustion and confused events...*"

"Are you ill? Are you drunk? Speak sense to me Thomas!"

There were tears on her cheeks but when I tried to move my hand, my arm just swung wildly.

"It's Shakespeare, Macbeth, *new hatched to the woeful time, the obscure bird clamoured the livelong night: some say, the earth was feverous and did shake...*"

"Will you just be normal, you're frightening me!"

I sat up... waking properly from the weird dreams.

"I'm sorry, I'm alright... I'm just a bit stiff..." I grasped the top of the wall and with her help heaved myself upright.

"What are you doing? Why are you here?"

I apologised, I hadn't intended her to find me; in my muddled brain I'd thought I would have sneaked away, found a bus or a taxi.

The day was bright and calm, the wind had died, and the snow had stopped. I had snow piled up on my shoulders, clinging to the front of my coat, and my feet were dead.

"I was worried about you, I saw there were flood warnings, and gales… I was afraid the river might burst its bank…" it sounded ludicrous now.

She stared at me as if she couldn't believe what she was hearing.

"When? When did you come?"

"Last night… It was the last bus from Strand… the 207…"

"You were here all night?" she looked at me with a sort of horror.

"I was so worried about you Kylie, I couldn't bear the thought of something awful happening, you being caught in a flood or the roof blowing off…"

She flung herself at me and I held her against my snowy chest, her head on my shoulder, as she sobbed and sobbed as if her heart would break. What had I done? How could I be so stupid? I felt like crying myself.

She pulled back and stared at me; what a sight I must look. Then she was laughing, then she was kissing me…

"Thomas, you are mad… Why didn't you knock?"

"I did… the storm was so loud I don't think you heard."

"And you were here all night because you were worried about me, you must have been frozen…" her face became grave. "You must be very cold now…"

"I am, and I'm very hungry… is there somewhere we can go to eat?"

We ate breakfast in Tansy's Tearooms; I was so tired I was barely functioning, but at least the heat from their wood-burning stove thawed me, although I dripped rather a lot onto their floor. Kylie was quiet and, I think, quite emotional but I wasn't sure I completely knew why... maybe I didn't want to think too much about how she was feeling, I didn't want to fool myself into imagining anything.

"I can't stay long," she said. "Will you be OK?"

I told her I was going to go home and go to bed and sleep, sleep, sleep. She'd asked about Rebecca and I told her what had happened last night; I'd gone to the loo in the tearooms, and texted Rebecca while I was there but received no reply.

She got up to go and I stood to say goodbye to her.

"Kylie, don't do anything drastic, let me... let me... let me..."

"Let you finish your sentence, Thomas? I'll let you," she kissed my cheek. "Happy Christmas Thomas, see you some time."

And she was gone.

Tuesday, December 24th 2013, Christmas Eve, morning

I nodded off to sleep on the 207; I was so tired I could barely think... my emotions were all over the place, I'd slammed the door on so many thoughts, shoved them into little boxes to look at another time that I wondered I could think about anything at all. I texted Rebecca again, still no reply ... and what was the drowning tragedy... would I ever find out?

I got off the bus and suddenly felt very stuffy, my chest was very tight and the bus station felt claustrophobic for some reason. I went out the back way, and leant against the wall, trying to clear my chest. There was some shouting from round the corner, and being curious I wandered to see what was going on. There were about four teenage lads and they were mucking about with something on the floor... no they weren't they were kicking the shit out of Eddy the Red!

"Oy!" I shouted, Kylie-style and ran towards them.

It was unfortunate really... I was so wound up and angry about the mess that was my life, that I laid into the nearest kid and thumped him twice in the face before I realised what I was doing.

"Fuck off you bastards!" I shouted.

They were only in their teens, stupid, pale, gormless faces, trackies and baseball caps and great big trainers.

The lad I hit fell over and another one who looked as if he might be Asian came towards me but I hit him too. I don't know where I found the strength or the aggression... thirty odd years of being picked on and bullied I guess.

"You want any more?" I shouted so loudly that the one nearest to me quailed back. "You fucking brave men, picking on an old guy – four to one – you pathetic cowards! Fuck off before I call the police!"

"I'll call the police!" yelled one, one who I hadn't yet hit. My knuckles were on fire, I'd never hit anyone before.

"Do that, come on, do that!" and I rushed towards him and thumped the back of his head as he turned away from me. He stumbled over, scrambled to his feet and legged it.

The one who I'd hit twice was bleeding badly but I advanced on him again. I was so angry, blind, red-mist fury and I think I might have killed one of them if they hadn't then taken off, shouting that they were going to call the police.

I went to old Red.

"Mate!" he whimpered.

"Come on Red, let's get you on your feet," I put my arms round him and heaved him up. He was rank, but so what; he was a better man than the scum who'd attacked him. "Have they hurt you?" his face was bloody and he was crying, poor old fellow.

I found a hankie and wiped his face, and he kept thanking me, poor old soul.

The only place I could think of taking him was the night shelter. Someone came hobbling towards me and I recognized him as the old tramp Kylie and I had rescued. He was upset at the site of Red's bloody face and took his other arm, but he staggered about so much that he was more of a hindrance than a help.

Somehow we made it round to the street of Victorian houses and the old tramp directed us to the right one and rang the bell. The door was opened by the same little lady I'd met last time. She seemed more surprised to see me than the two old fellows.

Red's legs gave way and I virtually carried him in and lowered him into a chair in the wide hallway.

"We ought to take him to hospital," I told the little lady, and then *my* legs gave way and I subsided on the floor beside Red, overtaken by the shakes. My fists were bloody and I wondered if I'd broken my knuckles, I'd never ever fought with anyone... to lay into those lads as I just had...

"We'll get him cleaned up first and see what the damage is," the little lady said.

She must have called for someone because two big men, one with a shaved head and piercings all over his face, and the other with very long hair arrived.

Red patted my head and thanked me again.

"I love you mate!" he said and then the big men took him away and the other old tramp sat down on the chair beside me.

"Do I know you?" asked the little old fellow, peering into my face... would I ever get used to the stink? The little lady seemed indifferent to it.

"We met on a cold and snowy night," I told him. I was very tired... maybe I'd call a taxi, I wasn't sure I could face a bus journey home.

"I got lost in the snow once," he said, and began to sing 'In the deep midwinter' and although his voice was quavery he sang it well.

The little lady came back and with difficulty and leaning on the chair I got to my feet. She asked what had happened to my hands and I tried to be casual as I mentioned how I'd seen off the boys attacking Red.

She looked at my knuckles and then pulled me into to a little office where she found a first aid kit and mopped and bandaged me; she told me it might be a good idea to go the hospital for an x-ray. I asked her how Red was, and she said she'd take him for a check-up once they'd cleaned him up, he was having a bath at the moment.

I asked if I could use her phone for a taxi, I was feeling quite faint now, quite ill... but I think that was more to do with my mental state. I found my wallet and pulled out a couple of twenties which I gave to her, and asked her to get something for Red and the old man... maybe a warm hat, or gloves or something...

"You deserve to have a lovely Christmas," she said briskly; she wasn't an emotional sort, I guess she couldn't be working here, but she was very kind, a good person.

"I'll try," I replied despondently... Christmas lunch at the Willows... oh joy. I would spend no time with Rebecca.

"If you're at a loose end you can always join us here!" she exclaimed. "We've got a silver band coming, and Santa, and we put on a really good lunch, turkey, sprouts, pud, the lot... you're welcome to join us, or come and help."

"Thank you... another year... my wife has organised something for us," I replied... Christmas with Red and the old boy sounded a better option, to be frank!

Tuesday, December 24th 2013, Christmas Eve, midday

I don't normally like having a bath, a shower is easier when you're fat, but sometimes only a bath will do, and I lay back in warm bubbly water and just relaxed and dozed, and let my mind wander, trying to keep my bandaged hands dry. I let my mind wander to the past, to the distant past of Radwinter, and Bletchingley and Portsea, to names and dates, and marriages and children, to umbrella makers and brick makers and men, young men who'd given their lives for their country...

The problems I had were insignificant... I had three brothers who would take care of me, I would never be homeless or hungry or unloved... I'd be alright, I just had to keep hold of my emotions and my anxious thoughts; I just had to keep calm and rational... *close your eyes, clear your heart, cut the cord...*

"What's happened to your hands?"

I opened my eyes. Rebecca stared down at me as I wallowed like a big pink, red-haired hippo.

"I was in a fight..." I began to sing 'Human' quietly to myself, to keep me focussed.

She was shocked and sat down on the closed toilet seat.

"Thomas, what's happening to you... are you ill? You've got sacked, and now you're in a fight?"

I should have been glad of her sympathy... but strangely I wasn't... I was actually indifferent.

"Perhaps you should see the doctor? Perhaps you need some tranquilisers..." she began to talk about depression, I closed my eyes and tried to clear my heart... cutting the cord was more difficult.

She went away and came back with a cup of tea, which was kind... then she asked if I could finish in the bath because she had to shower... she could have showered as I lay there... but never mind, I got up with difficulty because I was stiff and sore in different places... falling over in the snow last night, sleeping on some steps... the fight...

I wrapped a towel round me, Rebecca is not a big fan of seeing me totally naked.

"Oh my God, you're covered in bruises! You really were in a fight!" she exclaimed.

"Kiss me better, Becca!"

"What happened? Who was it with?"

"Some kids were picking on an old tramp."

"You beat up some kids?" she seemed even more horrified at that.

"I didn't beat them up, I thumped them and they ran away and then I took the old man to a homeless shelter..." I wanted her to say she was proud of me, that I'd done a good thing...

"Well, I just hope they don't report you to the police... first a man with a gun and now this!"

I went into the bedroom and lay down, pulled the duvet over me, and when I woke up I was alone in the flat.

Tolik, who was born in 1845, died in 1920... within living memory. My father Edward would not have known him, but he must have heard him talked about; for a fleeting fraction of a second, I wished I'd known my father properly, I wished I'd known him when I was an adult, not a small boy, frightened of the shouting man who kept falling over and bumping into things. I realise now he must have been a drunk... it was almost strange that Paul should go into the wine trade with an alcoholic mother and a drunk for a father...

I wondered what my father looked like... I guessed, because my three brothers looked so similar, that he must have been like them. He'd seemed a big man to me, but I was only little... I couldn't remember his face and have no memory of any photos... I don't have many photos of my childhood... there weren't many taken until I was living with Marcus. I appear in his family photo albums, embarrassing pictures of a fat, baby-faced boy with red hair and a permanently self-conscious look.

Tolik's wife Emma, née Wyeth, died in 1921; he was seventy-five when he died, she was seventy-three. Their daughter Emma married Richard Dean, and I wondered if he was connected to the umbrella maker, James Dean, maybe a younger brother of the man her aunt Thirza had married? Tolik's second son, John had married a Maria Mansfield. They moved to Nottingham, and had three daughters, Winifred, Lillian and Beatrice. Families were getting smaller, and the names were changing too.

I was convinced now, that Thomas, Tolik's eldest son, must be our ancestor... there were no other Radwinters from whom we could be descended unless a completely new person arrived in this area with the name of Radwinter... but there were so many coincidences of name... I was convinced, that Thomas who'd been the landlord of the Lark, was the man from whom we came.

Thomas married the Irish woman, Eleanor Quillen, and she'd given Paul his middle name; he is such a dashing and handsome man, I think he must have inherited some of her Irish spirit, and maybe the Irish twinkle in his eye... or was I being too fanciful? I had a note on a bit of paper, and I couldn't remember how I'd found it, that Eleanor was born in Castleblaney in County Monaghan, in 1870. She first appeared in the 1891 census for Strand, working in the Camel Arms Hotel, Strand.

I deviated from following Thomas and his family and looked at Castleblaney; I found the town website, and what a lovely place it looks, near Lake Mucknow, and is almost equidistant from Belfast and Dublin. It is a place which has a strong tradition for music, maybe Eleanor was musical, maybe she had a beautiful voice and that is where Paul's boys get their music from.

My phone bipped. The unknown number. *'Are you alright? I can't believe you did that xx.'* 'Fine,' I texted back, *'more excitement on the way home, tell you later xx.'*

Tell you later? When later? Sometime after Christmas later... some unknown time in 2014 later...?

Thomas died in 1942... 1942! Good heavens, that's hardly any time ago at all! That was in the war! He was... why am I so slow at working out ages, he was seventy-five. Eleanor died in 1951 – the second half of the century, and she was eighty-one. She died eight years before Marcus was born.

I felt as if I was skipping stuff now; I'd been so meticulous when I first started, writing down every scrap of information, and when I looked back at my notes I saw there were pages of stuff about people who weren't even related to us! I guess I worked more quickly now, was able to duck and dive through the records and find what I wanted. It wasn't just me though, record keeping improved as the century progressed.

I looked through some of my scrappier notes, and came across the envelope from the Lark; I scanned all the photos, all the news cuttings, front and back of everything, even the Radwinter drowning mystery.

I started Googling random words, Radwinter, Easthope, drowning...

I don't know quite what I was expecting, but I was shocked to the core when I found it:

A sad fatality occurred near Easthope on Sunday, when a resident named as Mr Thomas Radwinter, and his wife Mrs Thirza Radwinter were drowned off Castle Point. Mr Radwinter from Essex, but resident for many years in Easthope and former landlord of the India Inn, was aged seventy-six; his wife Thirza, had been in poor health for the past year and indeed, had not been expected to see Christmas. Mr Radwinter had taken the boat to give his wife sea air when some sort of accident occurred and they perished in the incoming tide. Their son Tolik who now holds the license to the India Inn, is reported to be inconsolable. Both bodies have been recovered, and they are said to have died in each other's arms. Notice of the arrangements for their funeral will be forthcoming.

I jumped up and stood for a moment then hurried round the flat, to the kitchen, to the bedroom, to the bathroom, restlessly moving… Thomas had died in tragic circumstances…but with Thirza? His wife, Thirza? The mother of Tolik?

I couldn't work out what I felt, shock, horror, mystery… died in each other's arms?

I snatched up my phone and rang the unknown number.

"May I speak to Kylie, please?" I asked the woman who answered.

"She's not here."

"Sorry to have troubled you," and I switched off my phone… drowned? *Drowned?* But Thirza had still been in Essex in 1881, and Thomas had disappeared in the 1870's!

Tuesday, December 24th 2013, Christmas Eve, afternoon

I went back to the 1891 census and looked up Tolik and Emma... still at the India Inn; Paul and Mark were still living at home, aged fifteen and twelve, both at school... and also living at the pub...

I leapt to my feet again... I felt sick, I felt excited, I was shocked...

The door opened and Rebecca returned.

"Becca! Becca! You'll never guess!" I cried before she could even speak.

"Can you help me with all this?" she had bags and bouquets of flowers. "People are so generous, look at all the things I've been given!"

"That's wonderful, sweetheart," I took a couple of plastic bags from her and one of the bouquets.

She always received a lot of gifts at this time of year; she was very popular with the residents, their families and the other staff. She began to tell me who'd given her what and how kind everyone had been, but I was bubbling to tell her my news.

"I've got something so exciting to tell you!" I exclaimed as she put the wrapping paper to one side to see if any could be re-used, she is so economical with things, never likes to waste anything.

"They've given you your job back?" she looked up.

"No... sadly, no, but never mind anyway, you know I couldn't find Thomas?"

"Thomas who?"

"Thomas Radwinter – you know, the first one, who came from Poland!"

"Oh that, I thought you had some proper news, not some person who died hundreds of years ago and might not even be your family."

"But he is, I know he is! I'm sure of it! Anyway, you know he disappeared?"

She cut across me to ask if I wanted a cup of tea, she'd been eating mince-pies all afternoon and was thirsty.

I bit back my enthusiasm... I'd tell her when she was more relaxed, not tired from work. I offered to make the tea and feeling a little deflated went into the kitchen. I wondered what we would eat tonight... in the past she'd made a special casserole from a recipe her gran had given her, it was lovely, with beef, and tiny onions, and brandy and port... Midnight Soup, and we usually ate it late on Christmas Eve and then as soon as it was past midnight we would open just one present from the each other, before going to bed... She's been so busy at work she hadn't made any this year, unless it was in the freezer... I'd ask her if I should take it out and defrost it... but if she hadn't made any I didn't want to sound as if I thought she should have... oh dear, back to feeling nervous of saying or doing the wrong thing...

Perhaps we should go out for dinner... or if she didn't fancy that maybe get a take-away and watch a DVD, or something on TV...

She came into the kitchen with something on her mind, and I asked as meekly and as affectionately as I could if we should eat out tonight, or get a take-away, unless she had some Midnight Soup tucked away somewhere.

"Oh Thomas, I'm sorry, I forgot to tell you... I'm going out with some of the girls from work tonight, just for some cocktails, I won't be late, I promise!"

"But it's Christmas Eve!" I toned down my response but I was angry... and somehow not surprised, in my heart I'd known this would happen.

"I thought you'd be at the quiz," she poured the tea.

I took a deep breath.

"There isn't a quiz tonight, I should have mentioned it... I'll go along to the pub anyway and see the boys... "

She took her cup into the sitting room and I followed her.

"What time have we got to be at the Willows tomorrow? Not too early I hope?" I asked.

"Can you get rid of that ridiculous reindeer... it's broken and it looks stupid."

"It's a brave and noble beast it saved me from certain death!" she had her back to me, looking at the plastic creature... I should have read the signals... maybe I did and just didn't believe what I knew was coming next... "So when do we have to be up and about tomorrow? I take it we'll have our presents before we go?"

"Well, when did you tell Paul you'd be there?"

I was baffled.

"What time is Paul expecting you?"

I was totally confused. She still had her back to me... and then I knew... I could step away from all of this, capitulate, give in...

I put my cup down and went round and put my bandaged hand on the reindeer's neck and looked Rebecca in the face.

"Tell me honestly what you are talking about, Rebecca."

"You're having lunch with Paul tomorrow, aren't you?" she stared at me, and there was the faintest flush on her cheek. "You did ask Paul if you could have lunch with him tomorrow, didn't you? You did tell him I would be at the Willows, didn't you?"

I had an urge to pick up the reindeer and hurl it… I didn't…

… and then it was *'I told you,' 'no you didn't', 'yes I did, are you calling me a liar?'*

"Yes, Rebecca, you are lying. You did not tell me that I wasn't invited to the Willows, you didn't even tell me about Christmas lunch at the Willows, your father did… and you did not tell me to ask Paul if I could spend Christmas with him…"

And then it was total war… nothing was thrown except accusations and recriminations, no-one was struck by anything but angry words and bitter retorts…

It ended with Rebecca grabbing her coat and rushing out of the house, saying she was going to her parents.

Tuesday, December 24th 2013, Christmas Eve, late afternoon

I sat for a long time with my head empty of any thought, my sore hands were shaking and I was trembling. I think after that I went a bit mad… I think I broke down in a strange way.

I went to the Christmas tree and sorted out all the presents beneath it and took out all of mine and unwrapped them. I folded the paper, I put the ribbons and bows to one side and made a pile of presents on the coffee table; I had a bottle of Highland Park Loki from Paul and Ruthie, goodness knows how much that must have cost, and a pretty little box with some shortbread. I had some spotty hankies from one of their boys, a bow-tie from another, a CD by Azalea Banks, and map of Poland from the other two. I had the box-set of 'The Thick of It' from John, and an old photo of The Lark in a nice frame from Marcus and Jill. I had a sweater which I would never wear from Maggie and Phil, some gloves from one sister-in-law and a scarf from the other...

How fortunate I was to have such kind and generous gifts... how lucky I was...

I unwrapped Rebecca's presents to me; there was Family Tree Maker Platinum - 2014 Edition, software to create your family tree, and there was another bow tie... it was red so I'm not sure what it would look like with my red beard, and there was some cologne, Obsession by Calvin Klein; she'd bought me some last year but it made me sneeze and I didn't actually like it very much...

And this is how I went a bit mad... I took all the decorations off the Christmas tree, one by one, and arranged them round the room. I put a row of baubles in descending sizes along the mantelpiece; I wrapped the television in tinsel and tied it in a bow; I took the star and put it in the fireplace, on the mock coals; I took all the little decorations and hid them round the sitting room; I took off the tree skirt and put it on the armchair like an antimacassar.

I took the flowers from the bouquets she'd been given them and arranged them all over the flat, I even put some in the toilet in a rather nice arrangement, the maroons and reds and golds of the roses against the white porcelain, and organized a rather attractive wreath of greenery around the toilet seat... It all looked rather festive, and I organized a similar display of bronze chrysanthemums in the basin and the shower... I ran out of anything to put in the bath but I dribbled some red shower gel of Rebecca's and some green of mine along the bottom in a random but, I thought, rather attractive festive design.

Then I went into our bedroom and took the bag of little gifts 'Father Christmas' had got for Rebecca, and I went to the drawer where she keeps her stockings and tights and found a pair which had sparkly thread running through. I put a tangerine, a walnut and some shiny coppers in the toe and then put all the little things I'd bought her, chocolates, bath bombs, a miniature Limoncello, some La Senza underwear, a tiny book of muffin recipes... I carefully put all the little presents down the leg of the tights, then laid it at the foot of the bed on her side.

I took the bottle of Oh Lola! and sprayed it all over the bed until it was empty, then laid the empty bottle on Rebecca's pillow.

I got my laptop and went on Facebook, and although Jessica was my only 'friend' I was able to find my way to Julie's page because she hadn't set it on private as Kylie had set mine. I found the photo I wanted, downloaded it, cropped it slightly, wrote a caption on the bottom, printed it on photo-paper and when it was dry, put it in the cardboard inner of a kitchen-paper roll. I had to unwind all the kitchen paper but I did it very neatly, and left a pile of it in the middle of the kitchen table. I went through to the sitting room and found a spray of silver bells which had been on the tree and I put it on top of the pile of kitchen paper.

Then I got a bit muddled because I had Midnight Soup in my head, so I found the recipe for it written in Rebecca's gran's handwriting, and tried to find all the ingredients… which I couldn't and we had no meat anyway, so I just left what I'd found on the side, arranged nicely, with some of the bows from the unwrapped presents on top.

I took a big drag on my inhaler.

I'd go to the pub… see if anyone was there… I think there's an extension tonight… I got my coat and sprayed it with Febreze and hoped no-one else would detect the aroma of old tramp, put some things, including my whisky and the picture of the Lark in my backpack and rang for a taxi.

The taxi driver was a jolly sort, an old bloke who whistled and talked about the dreadful state of English cricket to me, sitting beside him in his cab, the reindeer in the back. There was still a lot of snow about and it wasn't very pleasant out, but not too bad… I couldn't face the thought of the 207, and the reindeer agreed, so I splashed out and had the old guy take me to the Lark, all the way from the flat.

The Lark was pretty packed, but no-one minded the reindeer, in fact he was bought several drinks which I looked after for him, not being sure of his age. Leo was there and delighted to see me, and reminded me that he wanted a serious talk with me about food; when I said I was looking for a new job he embraced me and kissed me on both cheeks... he was quite drunk, mind you.

Damian was there too, and he got a little amorous with me, but not in a nasty way, and having told me I was gorgeous and wishing I thought he was, he wandered off to talk to some arty looking students who were in the long part of the bar, leading down to the back exit.

I told Bob how thrilled I was with the pictures and cuttings, and told him that I would bring them back when it was less hectic, and also fill him in on a little of Thomas's history. We were virtually shouting at each other above the racket of the juke box extra loud and everyone laughing and singing.

I kept checking my phone... but there were no messages. At one point I went out into the back yard and looked for a little while at the unknown person's number, wanting to call...

Instead I called Paul; he sounded pretty mellow and then passed me to Ruthie who was so warm and lovely I almost wished I was going to be with them for Christmas lunch.

Which brought me round to thinking about my wife; why hadn't she told me about the Willows, why hadn't she told me properly about the arrangements for Christmas Day? Why had she lied to me?

I didn't ring her but rang her parents who were very pleased to hear from me, and most cordial and friendly. I was tempted to ask to speak to Rebecca, but I didn't bother because it was obvious from what they said that she wasn't with them.

I kept my emotion well away from all of this... it was as if I was very drunk... which I wasn't.

Tuesday, December 24th 2013, Christmas Eve, closing time

I banged on the door of the India Inn, banged until my bandaged fist hurt. Perhaps she wasn't in... The reindeer had no suggestions, so I started singing '*It came upon a midnight clear...*' I knew all the words, I'd been in Marcus's church choir when I was a kid. I'd hated it, the chorister's outfit made me look even fatter; the choir master said I had a good voice, he even wanted me to sing solo, but I wasn't brave or confident enough, and Marcus got cross with me...

I got to the end of the first verse, and someone shouted 'Well done, mate! Nice one! Merry Christmas!' and I shouted back the same. I started on the second verse 'Still through the cloven skies they come, with peaceful wings unfurled...'

Suddenly to my surprise the door of the old pub opened.

I could just make out Kylie peeping into the darkness... and I had a sudden thought... supposing she has a boyfriend? Well, of course she has a boyfriend, someone as beautiful as her is bound to have a boyfriend...

"I just came to say Happy Christmas," I called... how foolish I was, why hadn't I thought it through properly? Because I could no longer think anything through... my mind was as scrambled as my life.

"Thomas? What are you doing?" she called.

I began to back away, apologising and then I bumped into the reindeer, my feet went on the ice and I was sitting in a pile of snow. I must have given a little cry because I landed on one of my many bruises.

She ran across the road looking as slight as a fairy... she was so thin...

"What the fuck are you doing Thomas?" she sounded cross and I began to apologise... a whole life of apologies, more than thirty years of saying sorry, and half the time I didn't know what I was apologising for.

"I came to wish you Happy Christmas, I'm sorry, I didn't mean to intrude..."

She got hold of my arm and pulled me up, amazingly strong for someone who looks so slim.

"I should have realised, about him I mean..."

"Him who?" she was beginning to pull me with her back to the pub.

"Your boyfriend."

"I don't have a boyfriend you idiot!" I turned back and grabbed the reindeer by his antlers and picked up my back pack and let her take me into the pub. She shut the door and we were in utter darkness. I'd imagined it smelling damp and of the river, but it smelt... well, just like an old shut up place.

Something brushed by my leg... a giant rat! But then it meowed... Kylie had my hand and drew me forwards and I left the reindeer by the front door, maybe he and the cat would become friends.

We seemed to cross an open space and then came to a doorway and there were stairs; I couldn't see a thing but Kylie was able to find her way in the dark. Neither of us said anything, but the silence around us seemed warm and friendly. I'd thought this place might be draughty, damp and musty... it wasn't any of those things although it was very, very cold.

We went up the stairs and there was a glimmer of light, and Kylie drew me into a room which must look out towards the wharf.

"There's only the bed to sit on," she said in a rather cool way. "Would you like some coffee, it's all I've got."

"Yes, please, thanks... I'm sorry to have come here like this."

The room was lit by a couple of nightlights in jam jars and I couldn't see very much of it. There was a big bed, a very old bed with brass knobs on the corners, and it creaked as I sat down. There were pieces of furniture which I could dimly make out but not really to know what the room was like.

"Sorry? Why sorry?" she was by what looked like an old fashioned dressing table, lighting something... a little gas stove, like a camping stove, and then she was spooning coffee into a couple of white mugs I could just make her out by the glow of the flame. I was entranced, looking at her, seeing the faint reflection of her face in the old mirror. "Why sorry, Thomas?"

"I have some exciting news about Thomas," I replied.

She stared at me for a moment and then came and sat beside me on the old bed and took my hand.

"Which Thomas are you talking about?" she asked gently. I couldn't reply. She put her other hand to my forehead as if checking my temperature. "I'm sorry I've nothing to eat."

I picked up my backpack.

"Polish salami, and chocolate marzipan... it's Polish as well. And some apple cake, and some adorable shortbread" I her gave the things I'd bought in Dorata's shop and she began to laugh.

"Oh Thomas…" she said. "Oh Thomas…"

She brought the coffee over and found a knife and plates and we had some salami and then some apple cake and then we had some marzipan… it tasted good… when had I last eaten? I'd be losing weight at this rate.

We didn't talk apart from her asking about my hands and being surprised by me taking on the lads attacking old Red. Then she said actually she *wasn't* surprised; it was typical of me to stand up for someone in trouble. Then I asked if she would like some more to eat, and she offered to cut the salami, and we agreed that the cake was very good, and so was the chocolate marzipan.

I asked if I could have another coffee… it was so surreal, sitting in the semi-darkness, whispering to each other about salami and marzipan.

"Can I tell you my exciting news about Thomas Radwinter, Thomas who came from the Ukraine… Його звали Тарас… I learnt that from the book you gave me, his name was Taras… Thank you… Спасибі," I leant over and kissed her cheek. "You know Thomas disappeared… he vanished and left Tolik and Emma in charge of the India Inn?"

"He did, and he sailed on *The Sobraon* to Sydney in 1870…"

To say I was astounded is a huge understatement… my mouth literally dropped open and I stared at her in the semi-darkness… She began to laugh as I tried to speak…

"How do you know?" I asked at last.

"I looked him up… you were wittering on about him, he'd disappeared and he hadn't died… so I looked him up on some shipping lists…"

My mouth must have been opening and closing like a goldfish but at last I managed to get to grips and speak, to tell her what she might already know…"

"He came back and he was living with Tolik and Emma here in 1891," I said at last. "Somehow he met Thirza again, and brought her here to live with their son and his family… I've no idea how… I can't trace anything until…"

I got out my phone and switched it on; there were some messages but I ignored them, didn't even bother to see who they were from. I found the newspaper archive and showed her the story about Thomas and Thirza's drowning.

"I don't think I'll ever be able to find out what really happened," I said. "But I think when Tolik was settled with Emma, Thomas left them… maybe he went to find Thirza then, maybe he just went and took *The Sobraon* from Plymouth to Sydney… but he went in search of his brother who was also called Tolik. He would have been in his fifties then, and living who knows where… but maybe Thomas found his brother."

I stopped and searched my backpack again and took out the bottle of very expensive and very fine whisky which *my* brother had given me. Kylie found a couple of small cups and I poured a little into each. "He came back to England and he found Thirza… there is a certificate of her death… but maybe it was a different Thirza, there were several Thirza Downhams in the area… but he found her, and he brought her back here, and they are on the census for 1891, here, here in this pub… maybe this was their room…"

We looked at each other and then I chinked my little cup against hers and we drank the Highland Park…

"I think she became ill, very ill, and he couldn't bear the thought of being without her again after it had taken so long to be reunited… I think they took the boat, and they rowed out to sea so they could look back to the land where their family were, their son Tolik, his other children and their families, to his grandchildren… I think they embraced, maybe wrapped something around themselves to keep them together, and then I think they slipped into the sea…"

We sat in silence, staring at each other.

"I've found Thomas…" I said.

"Which Thomas are you talking about?" she asked as she had before.

I leant forward and kissed her mouth… "This Thomas," and I kissed her again.

Wednesday, December 25th 2013, Christmas Day, morning

When had I ever, *ever*, been so happy?

I don't know what time we woke, Kylie sleeping across me, her head beneath my chin, my arms wrapped loosely round her. My face was cold but the rest of me was snuggly and warm. She moved a little bit and murmured something.

"Kylie, is there somewhere I can pee? I'm desperate!"

Goodness knows what facilities there were here, no electricity or heating that was for sure.

"The bathroom is next door, they haven't cut the water off, thank God," she mumbled.

I stumbled onto the landing and narrowly avoided tripping over two cats who sneaked into the bedroom. The bathroom looked as if it hadn't been touched since before the war; there was freezing cold lino on the floor, a massive old cast iron bath, a huge old basin with brass taps, and the toilet was one of those with the tank above and a pull chain. It was absolutely perishing, there was ice on the inside of the window, squirled into a fine tracery of delicate patterns.

I didn't care, my heart was light and everything was clear… the fog and the anxiety had vanished, and I could breathe deeply without my chest complaining. I couldn't see into the future, of course I couldn't… I didn't have a job, I had no idea what I might do except I was pretty sure I couldn't bear to do what I had been doing. But whatever, I would find something to do, I'd survive. The flat would be sold, and assets realised, and for a while I would have a little cushion of finance to keep me and Kylie… Me and Kylie… I looked in the speckled mirror at myself; a complete stranger looked back… he grinned at me, and then he winked.

I hurried back to the relative warmth of the bedroom and wriggled back under the covers, the cats complaining. Kylie wound her arms round me and I held her, my one arm could go completely round her, she was so tiny. She was as tall as me, but so thin…

"It's Christmas Day," I said. "Do you want your Christmas present now?"

She gave a dirty snigger, and I laughed too. I retrieved my backpack and pulled out the cardboard tube from the kitchen roll; I wished I'd wrapped it in pretty paper but I'd been in such a turmoil last night. We sat up and I arranged one of the blankets she'd piled on the bed around us.

"Happy Christmas, Kylie."

She pulled the photo from the tube; it was the one Julie had taken on her phone of Kylie and me walking into the Oriel. Along the bottom I'd written 'The proudest day of my life'.

"When I walked into that room, and everyone turned to look at us… I felt… I felt… I was so proud to have you on my arm…"

Much later I asked when she would have to go… she looked puzzled. I'd thought she would go to see her sister, to be with her little boy. Her face closed like a flower when the sun goes in and she looked away from me. We were still in bed, it was the warmest place to be and we'd had breakfast of coffee and salami and apple cake, and then another shot of whisky to toast ourselves.

She told me, with some of her old brittleness that she wouldn't be seeing him until the evening… she only saw him at bedtime to try not to confuse him about where he lived and what his routine was. I said nothing, but I thought it would have been better for him to be with her as much as possible… and on Christmas Day, to be without your mother on Christmas Day…

It triggered a memory… If I thought about it I could work out how old I would have been, but I was very young and something horrible happened which I truly do not remember. Marcus and Jill came to our house and rescued me and John, and took us back to their home, their girls were babies, and it was Christmas Day…

I kissed her forehead, and pulled the blankets up so we were in a little cocoon.

"And when do you have to leave, Thomas," she asked, quite sharply.

"I don't have to leave, not until you tell me to."

She sat up so suddenly that she pulled the covers off me. For once I think she was speechless.

"I'll stay with you Kylie for as long as you want me to, and I hope you'll want me for a very long time."

Part of me was as shocked as she was… yesterday I'd been married to Rebecca, Rebecca was my wife… now I was no longer married, and had no wife… whatever Rebecca might think.

She stared at me and a flood of the old emotions came rushing back, like a black wave of horror about to engulf me.

"Do you really mean that?" she asked in such a quiet voice that it was little more than a breath.

"I do mean it, and since this is our first Christmas Day together, what should we do?"

A tear trickled down her cheek, she looked so utterly adorable that I had to pull her to me, and I held as she cried a little.

"I've nothing to give you," she said at last, and now I gave a silly laugh.

"I wouldn't say that… but I do have an idea… if you want… something different… really, really different…"

Wednesday, December 25th 2013, Christmas Day, lunchtime

The door was opened by the man with piercings all over his face; his shaven head was hidden by a Santa hat.

"Wotcha, friend, come in and welcome," he said in an extremely deep voice.

We went into the large hall and the little lady I now know was Monica hurried out to us and greeted us warmly; I'd rung to ask her if the invitation was still open.

"You are welcome to join us for our meal," she said. She had tinsel round her neck.

"Thank you, but is there something we could do to help?" I replied. I was amazed at how in control of everything, including myself I felt. Holding Kylie's hand I felt I was capable of doing anything.

Monica took us through into a largish dining room; the old house had been extended at the back and now accommodated long tables and chairs. The tables were laid with table cloths and decorated festively, and all around were men and women of all ages, from the decrepit and ancient, to the young and haunted. Many had been ravaged by hard times, many had been ravaged by alcohol or drugs… how fortunate we were.

There was a choir of jolly looking ladies dressed in gold and black who were singing á capella, old Christmas favourites but with a bouncy rhythm; the 'diners' who were organizing themselves in their places were trying to sing along and the place was filled with a hubbub of happy voices.

"You don't mind coming here?" I asked Kylie as Monica led us towards the kitchen counter.

"I don't mind where I am as long as I'm with you, sugar-babe," she replied and whispered something very rude and we both giggled.

I was sent into the kitchen and was given a red apron to put on; everyone was delighted with my bobbing antlers, and I set to with carving the massive turkeys and haunches of ham.

The kitchen was frantic with helpers rushing around, making gravy, straining vegetables, wrestling recalcitrant roast parsnips out of the pans and into serving trays. There was a giant man mashing potatoes as if his life depended on it, someone else dolloping cranberry jelly and Cumberland sauce into bowls from a massive jar which must have held a couple of kilos. There were some great big steamers going and I guessed they had the puddings in them.

As I carved the turkey, all the bones and all the juices and gel went into a big pan to be made into soup no doubt. As soon as I filled a serving tray it was whisked away and another put in its place, and then I was wiping my gloved hands and onto the hams.

Monica came rushing in clapped me on the shoulder and told me I was doing a grand job; all was hustle and bustle and happy voices and when I glanced out into the dining room through the large hatch I could see Kylie going round the tables with jugs of drink, a bright red glittery crown on her head... she looked so happy, and was laughing and joking with all the people she was serving;

there was no embarrassment or awkwardness, she was just completely natural. She glanced up as if she could sense I was looking at her, and I bobbed my antlers at her and she lifted a jug in salute.

The choir finished and most of the people in the kitchen rushed out and round the other side of the hatch to take up plates of meat, and the vegetables were piled on in heaps. I was still carving the ham as the dinners were rushed to the diners so they would still be nice and hot... I was nice and hot, and I honestly cannot remember a time when I felt so full of joy. I felt strong, and confident and sure of myself.

I wondered how things were going at the Willows, and I chuckled to think how ghastly it would have been for me. I would have helped, of course I would, but I would have been anxious the whole time that I was doing something wrong or saying something wrong.

"Are you OK, Thomas?" Monica asked. She had a paper hat on and it had slipped down her forehead so it rested on her eyebrows.

"I'm great, Monica, thanks so much for inviting us," I put down my implements and kissed her.

"I thought you said your wife and you would be busy elsewhere," she said.

"Oh, Kylie is not my wife, not yet... I'll tell you all about it sometime... "

She looked a little embarrassed but intrigued then hurried to get some more gravy.

"Monica, I haven't seen Red? Is he not here?" I called as she was busy with the ladle.

"He's not feeling too good, Thomas, he wanted to stay in bed… "

"Can I go and see him when I've finished with this ham?"

The pierced man came a few moments later and said he'd take me to Red, and he led me through a door at the back of the kitchen and what must have been a backstairs when this was a family home in the nineteenth century. The passageways and corridors had many doors, and I guessed the old place must have been divided up into many different rooms to accommodate the 'guests'. There were fire doors and notices about not smoking, and other rules including ones about alcohol and dogs.

We arrived at a door and the man knocked and then stuck his head inside.

"Come on Red, you've got a visitor!"

It was a bare room with two beds with two lockers beside them; there were flowery curtains at the window, and outside I could see it was snowing again.

The old man was propped up on the pillows, the covers drawn up to his chin, with just his grimy old hands and red beard sticking out over the sheet.

"Hello, Red, Merry Christmas."

"Mate! Mate!"

"What are you doing still in bed; you're missing your Christmas dinner."

"I don't know mate, I don't know."

"Come on, I've been busy carving the turkey and ham, there's lots of lovely food!"

The pierced man tried to chivvy him in a surprisingly gentle way.

"Let me give you this," I said. "And then if you want to put it on, you can come down and join everyone, and if you don't then you stay nice and cosy here, and I expect someone will give you some lunch later."

I put a plastic bag I'd taken from my backpack on the end of the bed; inside was the sweater Maggie and Phil had given me; it was lovely and thick and warm, but I would never wear it.

I found my way back downstairs and followed the noise to the dining room. The silver band had arrived and even though the diners were still eating, they struck up and thundered through more Christmas music, so loud that it was impossible to converse but no-one seemed to mind.

A pair of arms snaked round me and I turned and gave Kylie a hug.

"This is the best Christmas ever!" she exclaimed, her eyes sparkling.

"It really is," I said. "It really is!"

Wednesday, 25th December 2013, Christmas Day, afternoon

We got a taxi; Kylie said it was extravagant but there was no other transport, no buses were running. I'd assumed we would go back to the India Inn, but she asked if I would mind coming with her to see her sister... *Would I mind?* I felt honoured, but nervous, excited, but unsure of how I would be introduced, and how I would be welcomed.

Kylie said nothing, but gripped my hand not too tightly as it was still sore, as the taxi edged its way through the vile dusk. I was stuffed with food, had really eaten far more than I should have, and I'd tried to make sure Kylie ate plenty too. We'd sat down when all the other guests were just about finished and many drifting away to their rooms or outside to smoke, even though the weather was so dreadful. We sat with Monica and the other volunteers and everyone talked about all sorts of things, and only afterwards did I reflect that there was nothing personal spoken of, as if we were all anonymous.

Now we crept along towards Hope Village where Kylie's sister Reneasha lived. I had no idea what her situation was, Kylie had asked me once in the yard at the back of the Lark why I didn't ask anything, well she'd asked nothing either, not where Rebecca was, nor what had happened between us... and now I still asked nothing.

Kylie directed the driver for the last little way, his satnav seemed to have gone into a sulk with all the windy streets. This was the new part of the estate, with modern flats and houses; I'd never been up here before, although for a while when I was still with Mum we had lived in the older housing.

"I bet you've never been here before, Thomas," Kylie said in a low voice.

"I used to live on Bottom Hope, when I was with my mum, before I lived with Marcus," I said... how little we knew of each other. "Kylie..." but the taxi was stopping. "I'll tell you later."

She got out of the cab and stalked away as I paid the driver and then I hurried after her. We went into the hallway of a modern block of what seemed to be four flats. It was clean and tidy but as we went up the stairs there was the pounding of music.

Kylie banged on a door and it was opened, and I don't know who was more surprised, the woman who opened it or me.

"This is my sister, Reneasha," said Kylie and her accent had changed, *sistah, Reneashah*. "What's the matter Thomas, did you not think my family might be black?"

I'd assumed they were, but I'd never imagined that her sister was the woman who I'd saved in the shopping mall.

Before anybody could say anything, a small body shot out of the door and clutched Kylie.

"Mama! Mama!" it was little Kenneil.

Kylie lifted him into her arms, kissing him and then he saw me and gave a piercing shriek.

"Kissmuss!" he screeched stretching his arms out to me.

"He thinks you're Father Christmas," Kylie said, struggling to hold him as he tried to get to me.

I took him from her and he clutched my beard again, screaming with delight. She dragged me into the house where the noise of the music was phenomenal. There were a lot of people crammed into the tiny place, singing dancing, and to my dismay, smoking, smoking with this little boy here, and it wasn't just tobacco being smoked, either...

Kylie and Reneasha had gone into the little kitchen area just off the main room and appeared to be arguing. No-one paid much attention to me, but everyone was friendly enough. Kenneil wiggled to be put down but then grabbed my hand and pulled me into another room; it was a small bedroom with one bed and a cot. On the floor was a plastic mat with roads and buildings painted on, covered in model cars.

"Car!" Kenneil held one out to me and I sat on the floor and we played cars.

After a while he got a book; unbelievably it was one I'd had as a child, 'Each Peach, Pear, Plum' by Allan and Janet Ahlberg. I leaned against the bed and he sat on my knee and as I read to him I could hear John reading to me. We looked at the pictures until he got drowsy and so did I, and I settled him in my arms and we both drifted off to sleep.

I don't think we stayed very long, I rather lost track of time... it had been such a curious few days... sleeping in the snow, then sleeping and not sleeping in Kylie's bed, making love to her, and her making love to me... the busy but happy Christmas lunch... playing with Kenneil, sleeping with him in my arms.

I'd found the first Thomas... I just had to do a few more checks to link his grandson Thomas with my family... maybe his son Charles was my granddad, or great-granddad... or maybe...

I felt almost drunk as Kylie roused me, she took Kenneil from me and I could hear her singing to him as she put his pyjamas on, and I stayed slumped by the bed and rang for a taxi as we were going apparently.

"Say night-night to Thomas," and she crouched down with him so he could kiss me. He was barely awake but murmured 'Kissmuss'.

I still felt disoriented as we went back into the main room which was slightly less crowded now; I was the only white person and the only person without a drink, but not for long as someone thrust a glass of punch into my hand... I took one sip and boy, was it strong... but good and I took another long slurp. Kylie was back talking to her sister in the kitchen, and I was reminded of the argument I'd seen them having by the Christmas tree in the mall...

"Hey, man, is your name Radwinter?" a tall man with dreadlocks hanging over his shoulders was peering down at me... and suddenly I recognized him! It was the way he was squinting at me...

"Vinroy - is that you, man? Still not wearing your glasses?!"

It was my friend from school... I hadn't seen him since I was sixteen, but as we shook hands and exclaimed over how good it was to see each other again, the man slipped away and I could see my friend, the boy with corn rows and his glasses held together with Sellotape.

I asked after his brother Fitzroy and he asked after Marcus and we caught up with each other's news. He had three daughters and he worked at Strand Music Centre, teaching kids to play guitar and drums. He called a woman over and introduced her as his wife, she was a teacher too, but at Strand Grammar.

"And you, man, are you married? You got kids?"

"I was married, but no, not now... and no kids... not yet..."

I remembered the names I'd dreamed about Lillah, Tolik, Isabella... just fantasy.

Kylie came over to me, her face stiff with suppressed anger, and a little of my happiness died, had I done something wrong? ...this was my default position, that I'd done something wrong... She greeted Vinroy and his wife sullenly, pulling at my arm because we had to go.

"Hey Kylie, man, are you with this dude?" Vinroy said. "He's my brother, he's a good guy, you're lucky if you've got him!"

"I am lucky, Vinny, I am the luckiest person in the world!" she exclaimed, the annoyance slipping away, and I realised I had to relax... I had to let go of my anxiety, and begin to trust... to trust other people and to trust myself.

"That's odd," I said, "I thought I was the luckiest person in the world!" and I also thought I was right!

And in the night we talked... She was surprised at my dysfunctional childhood; I'd seemed so straight she said... and I guess I owed Rebecca that, and Marcus. She talked about her sister... she found it difficult to believe that I hadn't known Reneasha and her were family, that it was just a bizarre coincidence that I'd been the one in the mall... and the man with the strange tattoo... He was their mother's dealer, and that was what Reneasha had been arguing with him about. Their mother was a junkie, my mother was an alkie...

Kylie and Kenneil had lived with her mother who'd been an addict for a long time, but managed it... until she couldn't... I didn't like to think about either my beautiful girl living with an addict, or her innocent little son... Her mother began to lose control and Reneasha very kindly took in Kenneil, while Kylie continued to live with and try and help their mother... who now owed her scary dealer a lot of money...

My mum had got into debt too with her drinking, and once, not that long ago, I'd overheard a conversation between my brothers about how much money they'd given her over the years, even when they weren't earning a lot themselves…

Kylie and Reneasha and their mother's social worker got Mrs Pemberton into rehab at a place in Weston-super-Mare which was how Kylie had ended up in the squat and why she was so desperate; her money went to pay back the dealer, pay Reneasha for Kenneil's keep, and pay for his day-care. Reneasha wasn't in a great job, she had her own two kids, but she too tried to help their mother.

"But now I've got no job, I guess I'll have to go on benefits and have him with me… I wasn't happy really with him being there… Reneasha's a good girl, but she has her own kids, they've been sleeping on the sofa so Kenneil can go in her room… But I don't like the smoking, and the noise, and all the people… They're good people… But it's not what I want for him…"

I said nothing, just let her talk, feeling her breath against my skin, her fingers twisting a curl of chest hair… Rebecca had wanted me to have a body wax, but I'd refused… my skin is too sensitive anyway…

I waited until I found the right moment… if it was the right moment…

"Kylie, I love you, I love you very much… I don't want to impose but if you want… then maybe we could find a place for us and for Kenneil…"

"I haven't asked you, Thomas… but what about your wife?"

"In the past... all in the past. If you'll allow, my life is with you, with you and Kenneil."

Thursday, December 26th 2013, Boxing Day morning

Boxing Day. The snow had come from the north and was all up the windows. We had a little giggle over whose turn it was to get up and make coffee... I lost, I think, but I didn't mind.

I was standing, wrapped in a blanket, shivering as I waited for the water to heat in the saucepan on the little camping gas stove on the dressing table, the two cats Martin and Gordon, weaving round my bare ankles and I switched on my phone and was surprised to see the number of messages waiting for me. I ignored those from Rebecca and looked at the series from Paul and Marcus.

"Oh, God!" I exclaimed.

I took the mugs of black coffee back to Kylie and showed her one from Paul. *Where the fuck are you, bro, seriously worried that I haven't heard from you.* There was similar but more restrained messages from Marcus.

"What should I do?" I asked her... the last few days had been a kaleidoscope of highs lows, madness, total sanity, love... joy... love... I'd not even bothered to get in touch with my brothers... I was struck by guilt and shame.

"Take that look off your face!" she snapped. "You've a right to take time out... Be pleased that they love you and worry about you... but don't feel guilty. You're an adult!"

She was right... I guess. I called Paul and he answered before I'd have thought it had time to ring. There was a torrent of expletives and then he took a breath to ask where I was and was I alright.

"I'm in heaven," I said and Kylie smacked my arm but only gently. "Sorry, Paul, I'm fine really I am, sorry I've not rung you, it's been a bit hectic."

"You're sure you're ok, Rebecca wanted me to call the police…"

"*The police?!* Why? The police?" I was astounded.

Rebecca had rung Paul last night wanting to know what time I would be home, assuming that I'd gone to him on Christmas Eve. Everyone had been mighty shocked that I wasn't with him, or with Marcus, and had begun to get worried when my phone was switched off. They were especially worried because of what I'd done at the flat, with the Christmas tree and the decorations.

I apologised again and told Paul I was in Easthope… his silence showed how surprised he was.

"I'm in Easthope with Kylie," I told him. Her face was a picture; Paul could not have been more surprised than she was … I think she'd thought I'd want to keep her a secret. I grinned at her and blew her a kiss and I pulled her to me, holding her as I told Paul we'd been to the night shelter yesterday and helped with Christmas lunch there, and then we'd visited someone.

"When you say you're with Kylie…" Paul said slowly and I could hear Ruthie murmuring in the background.

"I mean I'm with Kylie, she is my new life," I nearly said 'wife', and I had a little giggle.

"Fucking hell…" Paul said. And then "Does Rebecca know about this?"

"No, not yet, perhaps I ought to text her…"

"*Text her?* Thomas, you've been married to her for nearly ten years and you're going to *text her*?"

I apologised, it did sound a bit heartless, but on the other hand…

"I'll ring her…" I really didn't want to see her; I was too much of a coward and thought she might hit me again… I'd hit kids attacking an old man, I'd thrown a reindeer at a madman, but I would never lay a finger on a woman… well, only in love…

"Tommy, are you sure you're alright… you sound… well, are you sure you're alright… come over and see us… come for lunch… "

I wasn't sure about that… spending the day in bed with Kylie seemed much preferable…

"… and can you please ring Marcus… he's as anxious as I am."

I am, he said, not *I was*… he was still worried about me… as if I was still a small kid terrified of my own parents…

He wished me Happy Christmas and told me he loved me, but his voice was not as warm as it had been recently… I told him I loved him but I think he'd switched off.

We lay in the bed in silence and I looked round the room. There was an old wooden wardrobe, it was huge and looked antique. There was a bookcase with maths and economics books Kylie had needed for her degree course. There was the dressing table, and there was a stand, an old fashioned wooden thing, maybe a night stand which had a porcelain bowl set into it, and a jug on the shelf beneath, and I wonder if Kylie washed here when it was too cold to go into the bathroom with the ice on the inside of the windows. I'd taken some warm water into the bathroom and shivered as I washed there yesterday... actually wishing I could shower... it had been so cold, I'd been frozen, my hands numb by the time I went back into the bedroom. Kylie must be hardy, she didn't seem to notice and certainly didn't complain. She kept the cats because, like me she was afraid of vermin... the poor girl, my poor girl...

There was a wooden chest, there was a chair, and that was it. There was a rug on the floor which looked modern if not new, but there were no curtains at the windows which were the old fashioned sash-type, which rattled like anything when the wind swung round. There was extremely faded floral wallpaper, which looked as if it had been stuck back up in places... but the room was dry.

We couldn't continue to live here... it might be rent free but it wasn't good enough...

I realised that neither of us had spoken for a while...

"What are you thinking?" I asked.

"Ring your other brother..." she said and her voice seemed distant. "And then ring your wife."

I stroked her shoulder, her skin was so soft, and traced the shape of her shoulder blade and then followed the bumps of her spine. I ran my hand over the smooth curve of her hip, over her rounded buttocks...

I rang Marcus. I think Paul must have rung already him because he didn't sound shocked to hear from me.

"I've been so worried, Thomas," he said, and I felt guilty and awkward. "Which is ridiculous, I know," he went on. "I should stop thinking of you as a little boy. It was just that last time you visited, it was so lovely to see you, but you were so very unhappy, you seemed desperate... We were going to talk about it, weren't we, you said you were worried about your future and worried about Rebecca... why don't you come and stay for a couple of days. Bring Rebecca too if she would like to come."

Oh fuck... Paul had told him I was all right, but that was all...

He asked again about Rebecca, was she being supportive as I'd lost my job... I shivered at the memory of the foul row we'd had, her alarming rage...

"I have to tell you, Marcus... I know you'll be angry with me... but I've left Rebecca..."

I was treated to another shocked silence... if my two brothers weren't grey already then I would have turned their heads and beards ashen today.

Kylie got up and stalked naked from the room.

"Would you like to come up here for a while... I can come and get you, where are you at the moment?"

"Marcus..." my chest was beginning to feel tight, and I sat up in the creaky old bed. "Marcus... I have to tell you that I have found someone else... I love her... and when this mess is sorted out..." I ground to a halt.

"I see..." he said at last as if he was very tired. "I see... You're not a child Thomas... I love you very much and I have to trust you. You are a good man... a good... man..."

"Thank you, Marcus..."

He said goodbye quietly, and we rang off. I lay back. I remember Kylie saying... way, way back, that I was an awkward glt and would blurt things out without thinking...

I could have handled things with my brothers so much better... I shouldn't have mentioned Kylie... I should have let the dust settle with Rebecca...

Without thinking too much about it I rang Rebecca.

I don't know what I was expecting... She'd been worried, I'm sure, she's a kind person really even though she hasn't been kind to me recently.

"Where are you?" she practically screeched. "Where the hell have you been? And what the hell did you do to the flat? I've been out of my mind with worry!"

"No you haven't, you've been out of your mind with guilt!" I spoke loudly and coldly. I wasn't going to get drawn into one of her stupid arguments where the ground constantly shifted beneath my feet as she moved the fucking goalposts all over the pitch.

She was shocked. "What do you mean? Where are you? What are you playing at?"

"I'm not playing at anything, Rebecca; I've decided that I can't live with you any more, I don't want to be in the flat, and I don't want to be with you."

It was cold, it was callous, it was brutal. She screamed, she literally screamed so even though I held the phone away from my ear I could still hear her.

She stopped for breath and I said "Can I speak to Smithy?"

There was utter silence and then she rang off.

I knew she'd been having an affair with Smithy for some time... I'd pretended to myself so completely, convinced myself so utterly, that I was almost surprised to hear myself say it. All those late nights working, all the times when she couldn't answer her phone, going out on so many Christmas 'do's' when the staff of the Willows was so small.. Oh Lola.

My phone rang. Not Rebecca but John ringing from Italy... Paul had been in touch with him, John congratulating me, John delighted, John happy that Kylie and I were together. I looked up, she was standing in the doorway, naked and shivering, so lovely, so truly lovely.

"Just a minute, bro, tell her that," and I held the phone out to her. She took the phone, and sweet John had her smiling within a few minutes and when he rang off, I told her to get dressed as I was taking her out for either breakfast or lunch.

Thursday, December 26th 2013, Boxing Day, late morning

I was back to being in my state of bliss; we were warm and we were sitting so close together that I thought I could almost feel her pulse. We were in the Armenian café and stuffed full of wonderful food and we each had a glass of Ararat brandy which Vekan had poured for us. The café was full but we were squished together by a little table and I had my laptop out and we were looking through the birth records... and it was heavenly to have someone so interested, and so intelligent, pointing things out, asking things...

I chased the dates for Thomas's three sons, Charles, Walter and Horace... 1892, 1893, 1894, and I commented that he hadn't wasted much time once he'd married Eleanor... I looked at Kylie dreamily, Isabella, Lillah, Tolik... sisters and a brother for Kenneil...

"Well, come on, let's see when they married and who, let's see if this Charles is your grandfather," she nudged me back to the present, or rather back to the past.

Charles Radwinter married Sophia Carragher, in 1911... He was only nineteen, even younger than I was when I got married; she was twenty-three, she'd been born in 1887... and their first child, Charles Henry was born in... 1911. So that explained that!

"How old are you, Kylie?" I asked... she was twenty-three... "I'm nearly ten year older than you..."

"So? I'll be twenty-four in three weeks if that makes it better!" she seemed irritated.

"I better start thinking about how we can celebrate it then, hadn't I?"

I looked back at the census when Sophia had been living at the Lark, pregnant with Thomas's first grandson... she too was Irish, like her mother-in-law, Eleanor Quillen, and she too came from Castleblaney... family friend, or just family? Another thing to explore another time. Charles and Sophia had another son, Arthur in 1913, and two more sons, Michael and David in 1919 and 1921... after the war, and I remembered the notes I had found about Thomas giving thanks that his sons had survived the war.

Charles's brother Walter married in 1919, but he and his wife Frances had no children, and the youngest brother, Horace married Annie in 1915 and they had one child, a daughter, Irina.

Charles junior was born in 1911, and following the pattern his father had set, he married young in 1931, Helen Donnelly (another Irish girl? Was she also from Castleblaney?) and Charles and Helen had three children... Edward, James, and Angela... my father, my uncle and my aunty...

I had it... I had the line, from Thomas Radwinter/Taras Radwinski and Thirza Downham, to Tolik and Emma Wyeth, to Thomas and Eleanor Quillen, to Charles and Sophia Carragher, to Charles and Helen Donnelly, to Edward and Sylvia Magick and to me...

"Guess what?" I said to Kylie as I filled in the last little bits on the family tree I'd constructed on MyTimeMachine. "I love you, Kylie."

"Stupid git," she grinned... her teeth were perfect, she had dimples when she smiled... I could kiss her right there... "What's that little man with the peaked cap?"

He was a little purple symbol which showed I had mail... a message from Dominick in South Africa.

Hi Thomas! Hi cousin! Great to be in touch. I hope you and your family have had a great Christmas – do you have children yourself, Thomas, I have two a couple of lads called Brent and Bailey, they're fine kids. I wonder if we could exchange emails, then I can send you some photos! I'll let you have more details of our family when things calm down here after the holiday!

Regards,
Your cousin, Dom

"This is so exciting!" I said and we clinked glasses.

"You've still got a little purple man," she pointed.

I had another message:

Hey there; I see you have listed the name Radwinter... my name is George Radwinter, and I believe my ancestors came from England in the nineteenth century. My g g grandfather was Cazimir Radwinter and I believe he came from a place called Easthope in England. Do we link? Regards, George R.

"And do you link?" asked Kylie.

"This is surreal! Yes, Cazimir is Thomas's uncle… not the first Thomas, but Thomas who had the Lark - Cazimir and his brother Taras went to the States… I can't quite remember when… Cazimir was not much older than Thomas, he was born in… 1863, and Thomas in 1867… oh my goodness!" we chinked glasses again.

My phone rang. It was Paul. He surprised me by apologising, apologising for his reaction when I'd phoned this morning. In turn I apologised again… I should have got in touch, but I'd been in a bit of a turmoil… He brushed my words aside; would Kylie and I like to come round for a drink this afternoon. He and Ruthie were going out later, but he really would like to see me… and the boys would like to see me…

"I've just had some really exciting news… someone in America has contacted me… he's another distant cousin!"

"So are you coming round for a drink?"

"Yes… yes, we'd like to…" I hoped Kylie would like to… she said nothing but pointed to the little purple mailman I had another 'postal delivery'.

Hi, my name is Chanday Radwinski and I am keen on tracing my Radwinski roots; I believe that my ancestor Tolik Radwinski came from England and I see you have Radwinski as a name of interest to you so I'm wondering if you know of Tolik? Thank you and happy Christmas from Oz,
Chanday.

"Another cousin?" asked Kylie... yes another cousin... "No more purple postmen," she observed.

I really wanted to take her back to Easthope and make love to her again... but... but I ought to go and see Paul and Ruthie, *we* ought to go and see Paul and Ruthie...

My phone rang again and with a sinking heart I saw it was Maggie, Rebecca's mother. I answered it in dread, not knowing what I would hear, anger, upset, blame...

I felt sorry for her; she'd always been very kind and even loving towards me, and now she was heart-broken and unable to understand why I'd so suddenly decided to leave Rebecca. This was not a conversation I was prepared to have over the phone. She was very emotional, almost distraught. I calmly told her that I was certain of what I was doing, no, there would be no reconciliation, there never could be and I didn't want one. She should talk to Rebecca, I said. I didn't apologise, but kept it short and finished it firmly and, I hope, cordially.

I looked at Kylie and she looked at me.

"I take it you're the bad guy," she said after a moment.

"I am... and nothing I could ever say would explain otherwise..." it was quite traumatic... I would never be anybody other than the man who broke their daughter's heart... and I daresay after a suitable period Rebecca and Smithy would... or maybe they wouldn't and Rebecca would be alone...

"That's fine by me, sugar-babe, I never did like goody two-shoes," Kylie took my hand. "Are you sure about this, Thomas, about us?"

"Yup, and if you're not I'll just have to find a way to persuade you!" I spoke lightly but my heart was very heavy.

I liked Maggie and Phil, they'd been very generous to me… When in my foggy way I'd been thinking about the state of my marriage, in another lifetime when I'd been so unhappy, I'd never once thought about the effects of it failing on other people… Rebecca's family, her grandparents, her cousins, her aunties and uncles… all of whom had liked me and tried to be family to me too…

"Thomas!"

I glanced up; it was Amelia and Andrea, the wives of my cousins Tony and Max… I blushed as I remembered what I'd overheard them say about me… but I stood and embraced them and then introduced them to Kylie who had her tough expression on.

"Kylie, this is Andrea and Amelia, my cousins' wives… they are Radwinters too… Andrea and Amelia, this is Kylie, my… "

There was a gap and the two women looked at us with suppressed amazement, Kylie looked as if she wanted to fly at me and bite my head off…

"This is Kylie my fiancée… Rebecca and I have split up… Kylie and I…"

It was hard to tell which of the three women were more astonished.

Kylie looked as if her eyes were going to pop out of her head, and later I replayed her expression and chuckled over it… adorable, Amelia and Andrea had called me adorable, Kylie was truly adorable.

"I haven't said 'yes', yet!" she stuttered as if she was furious.

With an exaggerated sigh I stood up, courteously moved my two cousins-in-law aside and then knelt in front of Kylie and looked at her with what I guess Andrea and Andrea would call my 'puppy eyes'.

"Kylie, I adore you, I love you, please will you do me the honour of accepting my offer, Kylie please will you say you will marry me?"

"Say yes!" someone shouted, and I glanced round. I'd forgotten that every table was full and the whole cafe was looking at us.

"Please say 'yes', my knees are killing me on this hard floor!"

"Get up you twat!" she shrieked. "Of course I'll bloody marry you!"

I made a big deal about getting up as if my back or my knees were bad... in actual fact the floor was hard and my back was a bit achy after two nights of sleeping with Kylie...

There was a terrific racket and Kylie kissed me full on the mouth so passionately that I had to sit down before I embarrassed myself. Andrea and Amelia kissed me and kissed Kylie... and I remembered what they'd said about Rebecca... It was suddenly mad and strangers were shaking my hand or kissing me or kissing Kylie and people were ordering drinks and the place was suddenly like a party and all I could do was sit and grin like an idiot and stare at Kylie who seemed to have stars in her eyes.

Thursday, December 26th 2013 Boxing Day, afternoon

It was early afternoon by the time we were waiting in the bus station for a bus to take us to see Paul and Ruthie. I'd rung him again to say we were coming and he was back to being warm… even so, I knew once all the fuss had died down I would have some tough conversations with my two oldest brothers.

I'd dithered all my life, drifting into whatever people had advised me to do, being so anxious to please, to be loved, to be safe, that I'd not always made the best choices… for myself or other people. Now for the first time I'd made a decision, I had chosen what I wanted, and I had been honest with myself.

I loved Kylie, she said she loved me… she said she'd fallen in love with me the first time we met… which considerably surprised me because no-one, no-one had ever fallen in love with me before. I'd been courteous and respectful, she said, I'd looked her in the face, and I'd been nice to her… and I had a sexy mouth… I blushed greatly at all this… I'd never ever suspected, never even dreamed… she found this hilarious and that was when she found I was very ticklish… which was horrid… well, sort of horrid… well, sort of not when Kylie tickled me…

I wasn't deceiving myself that our life together would be easy. Kylie is a very strong person, a tough person, and I think when we began to share our histories, I will find out about some hard things she'd endured growing up… but I also think she will be surprised by things I went through. I'm mild-mannered and speak properly and have good manners… but that doesn't mean I didn't suffer as a child…

Yes, now I can be honest and say I did suffer as a child, I had an awful childhood, saved by my brothers, particularly Marcus. He'd done so much for me, had been like a real father to me, even though he was strict, he was loving and had high expectations.

I realised too that I was a strong person; I could stand up for myself, and even more I could and would and did stand up for other people. Maybe that was what had prompted me to go into law, aged eighteen and confused and ill-informed about lawyers defending the weak and doing good… I ended up conveyancing and writing wills…

Our two tramps were wandering about; it wasn't snowing today but the wind was bitter, and I wasn't surprised that they wanted to stay in the bus station.

They came over and sat with us, the little old man was really wandering in his mind, I couldn't make sense of anything he said; he sang to us from time to time and then his words were clear, but he kept forgetting them.

Red had a terrible cough, but was pleased with his new jumper, the one I'd given him. I was a little surprised that he realised it was from me, he'd seemed so vague yesterday.

"What's your name then, mate?" he asked conversationally. Kylie had taken some of my money and bought us all a hot chocolate; I'd had rather too much Armenian brandy and wine and I needed to be sober and sensible when I talked to Paul. "I knew a bloke called Radwinter once, he was my mate, mate. We were banged up together."

What did he mean?

"Prison, mate, we were in prison… long time ago now… kept myself clean since then… well a bit of vagrancy, a bit of drunk and disorderly… you know mate, disturbing the peace.."

A Radwinter in prison! When I'd told people about exploring my family history several people had commented about skeletons in the old cupboard! I wonder what this Radwinter had done… and I wondered where he fitted. I was intrigued.

"Raddy were older than me, good bloke though, mate… like you a good bloke," he broke off to cough hideously and then drank some chocolate. "Your bloke, pretty lady, he's a good bloke your bloke!"

She agreed and I pressed old Red to tell me more about my criminal connections… because obviously Raddy and I must be connected, I just hoped not too closely… I didn't want any more to do with guns.

He'd been in prison with Raddy in the seventies…

"Got let out on his birthday he did… remember it as if it were yesterday… "

I asked what Raddy had done; Red told me it was armed robbery… that didn't sound very nice… I didn't want to be related to someone who'd done an armed robbery, and I remembered the man with the gun in the mall. He'd been Kylie's mum's drug dealer… good Lord…

"Nah, Raddy were a car-man, mate, he were the driver, that's why he got out after seven years… got out on his birthday, fifty he were, half a century… we went to celebrate in the Centurion, halfway there, Raddy said… he was good to me old Raddy… wonder what happened to him…"

It was fascinating talking to the old tramp... this was a life I couldn't imagine. I'd been to school with some rough kids, especially in junior school, but armed robbery, going to prison... Perhaps I'd led a sheltered life. He was beginning to get muddled now, talking nonsense, and he slipped a bottle from his pocket and took a pull on it. I wanted to tell him not to, but it was none of my business.

I asked Red what Raddy's first name had been. Eddy, name's Eddy, but that was Red's name. The old tramp had gone to sleep, curled up on the bench next to Kylie; his mouth dropped open and I could see he had no teeth... I wondered how old he was... probably not as old as he looked.

The bus would be here soon so I took the empty cardboard cups and dumped them in the rubbish. We got our things together, shook hands with old Red and he thanked me again for the jumper, and called me 'Raddy' and we went to get our bus.

Kylie seemed quiet and I wondered if she was anxious about meeting Paul again, in these new circumstances... but no, she said she was fine. She took my phone and was playing about on it, looking at all the things we'd found out this morning, all the loose ends we'd tied up as we ate our Armenian breakfast... 'our', 'we', little words which meant so much.

Tom seemed on permanent door duty, he flung it open as he usually does, hugged me as he usually does and hugged Kylie... which was odd because I never remember him hugging Rebecca; I think she was always a bit stiff with him because she wasn't his godmother... just as well really, considering the new situation! I guess he must have met Kylie when she came with John to Paul's party last week... but even so... it seemed really nice and welcoming.

Django was in the hall and he seemed pleased to see Kylie too and he launched into a conversation which referred back to the music he and his mates had been playing last week, and suddenly he'd grabbed her arm and was pulling her upstairs saying something about the album he'd been telling her about and what did she think of Wretch 32.

I was consumed with jealousy, he was a young, slim, good looking guy who could play music... I stood feeling hot and fat and silly – and I mentally lurched back to that night when I'd come to meet Ruthie...which had been when all of this started... and now here I was again, dithering in the hall... and it was a total rerun because Paul came out of the kitchen on a cloud of gorgeous smells and embraced me, kissed me and pulled me in to see Ruthie who waved her oven gloves at me as she put something on a cooling rack.

Otis and Luke were there, busy eating but when they saw me they immediately asked if Kylie was with me, and then they too vanished upstairs so I was left with my brother and his fiancée. I had new eyes now, and I saw this had all been engineered so Paul could talk to me; I wondered if Ruthie would leave too, but she put a plate in front of me laden with golden delicious things.

"I hope I've done them all... falafel, spanakopita... um kibbe and... heck, tiropita, oh yes and kreatopita..." I must have looked puzzled but then it came back; I'd texted her when John and I had been in the Lebanese restaurant... she'd been interested in doing different things... "I'm sorry I've neglected you, Thomas, I've used all your ideas, and I've got some Easter stuff which I'm going to be trying after New Year... and I'd like you thoughts on Valentine's Day!"

Valentine's Day... I blushed a fiery red and concentrated on the spanakopita I was eating still warm... mmmm, nutmeg...

Paul sat at the table and poured me a large glass of something gorgeous, and unlike when I was at his party and I'd just poured it down my neck, I sipped it slowly and appreciatively. Ruthie and he chatted on about nothing much, how busy they'd been, how well everything was going for them...

"Have you spoken to Marcus recently?" I asked. "Did he tell you about my job?" They looked blank. "I am surplus to requirements... I will receive a great package and fabulous references, and a generous settlement, blah blah blah, but basically I have been made redundant." They were both shocked. "The good news is," I continued trying a tiropita... divine, buttery, flaky, yummy... "I have traced the family back all the way to 1815... That's great, isn't it, a direct line!"

"Are you alright, Tommy?" Paul asked. "Rebecca is very worried about you..."

"Is she? Well that will be a first. Sadly for her, maybe, it's too late... I've left..." I wanted to try a kibbe, but I just had to have another tiropita.

"Yes, you said... earlier... "

"Paul, this hasn't just come out of the blue... I have been miserable for months, she's treated me like shit, she's sleeping with another guy, and really... well, I don't actually like her that much, I certainly don't love her... and do you know, I think maybe I never did."

Paul looked so serious that I couldn't meet his gaze. There was silence in the kitchen and I just concentrated on eating the mezze Ruthie had put in front of me... concentrating so hard that in fact I didn't register that Paul was talking to me. He put his hand on mine, stopping me taking another bite of a golden kibbe.

"Rebecca thinks you're having a nervous breakdown," he said.

I looked at him for a moment; I'd never seen this expression on his face before... I began to sing *'I can see clearly now...'*

"Tommy, stop it!" he spoke harshly and I looked at the floor... had he had it retiled? I couldn't remember this pattern... maybe the whole kitchen had been redecorated and I'd not noticed... I looked round at the cupboards and units trying to work out whether they were new.

"I'm sorry, Paul," I apologised. "No I'm not having a nervous breakdown... things aren't right at the moment, but soon they will be. I've lost my job, and that has been a terrific shock, I feel... rejected, upset, hurt... and disappointed that they hadn't the courage to discuss it with me before they told me. Things have been going wrong between me and Rebecca for a while, I married her too young, maybe, and we have become different people, although maybe we always were... I'm the baby of the family, and have been immature and silly... but suddenly I feel, I feel..."

I came to a stop. Paul had wanted to interrupt me but Ruthie had her hand on his arm and he let me speak.

"I was very flippant about Rebecca... but our marriage really is over. It was something I overheard Andrea and Amelia saying... Rebecca and I have nothing in common; I have been loyal and faithful to her since we were married, but some months ago she began to see someone else... she didn't know I realised... I never said anything... I suppose I properly realised the state of things after there was that incident in the shopping mall... you know about that?"

Silently Ruthie reached for a newspaper, Strand Argos special Christmas Eve edition... and inside was another report, this time naming me... *'Modest hero, Thomas Radwinter...'*

"Rebecca wasn't proud of me, she was angry that I'd got involved..." I stopped again. "I know it seems as if I jumped out of Rebecca's bed and straight into Kylie's arms... I've worked with Kylie for two years, and never realised... But she is one of the most honest people I know, she's brave, she's strong, she's lovely... and she picked me up when I was on the floor in a heap... I love her, Paul, I really do... and my future is with her... don't know what I'll do for a job..."

I took another spanakopita... were they my favourite or did I like the tiropita best?

"I'll give you a job, Tommy," Paul said. "You can work for me... I mean it; I need a guy like you with your talents..."

"And Kylie can work with me, I'm starting a new business and if she's been working in a solicitor's office for two years then she'll have what I need," Ruthie said softly. "... and you've given her a great reference..."

Crying is so annoying, and I seem to be doing a lot of it at the moment... I think I'm broken... but I know I will be fixed. I sobbed in Paul's strong arms, Ruthie disappeared and it was only much later, when I'd been out for a walk with Paul in his back garden, and cooled my burning face with snowflakes that we went back to his welcoming house.

Thursday, December 26th 2013, Boxing Day, evening

Paul dropped Kylie and me in Easthope; none of us said very much, she held my hand so tightly. He and Ruthie got out of the car to hug us and then drove away. I suggested the Lark… it would be warm in there, and light, I could look at Kylie.

I'd forgotten, she would want to go and see Kenneil, he'd not been mentioned and I wondered what my brothers would say about him… wondered what perspective they would have on the situation; I was about to say that she should have asked Paul to drop us in Hope Village… but maybe she didn't want him to know where her family lived…

So it was much later when we got back to the Lark; we'd trudged through the snow to Hope Village, and slipped and slithered our way up to the flat where Reneasha lived, and then slipped and slithered our way back down an hour later… how could Kylie bear to spend so little time with her son? I barely knew him and I didn't want to come away.

The flat was empty apart from Reneasha and her two sons, teenage boys who glared at me and barely spoke. Kylie tried to get Kenneil to call me Thomas, but he was fractious and just called me Kissmuss and clung to me wanting me to put him in his pyjamas and clean his little teeth and read a story. Reneasha knew who I was, she recognized me from the shopping mall, but she said nothing, and it was rather an awkward atmosphere.

It was quiet for Boxing Day evening in the pub, but perfect for us. I asked Bob the landlord if there was any food, he said there were some turkey sandwiches, brilliant, I said, and I told him that Thomas Radwinter, former landlord of the Lark was indeed my great-great-granddad.

We sat near the fire and got the laptop out again and I filled in all little bits we hadn't finished earlier.

"I'm sorry I got so emotional at Paul's" I said as we looked at the 1841 census again. "It's going to be hard for a while, sorting out everything... I ought to ring Marcus again... and I'd like you to meet him properly, if you don't mind..."

"Ring him now," she said, not looking at me, any more than I was looking at her, but pressed so tight against me. "And if you can bear to, you ought to ring your wife... I'll go and sit at the bar if you want."

I rang Marcus, he was so loving over the phone that it almost set me off again. It was a repeat really of what I'd told Paul, but with me in more control. I ended up by telling him about the last links I'd made, that our grandfather Charles was the son of another Charles... and the fact that we were sitting in the Lark right now... and yes, I added, I'm with Kylie.

He asked if she was the *'young woman'* who'd asked me for money for the old tramp... and I remembered that he'd said she would be a good friend to me, *'extraordinary'*, I think he'd said. He was silent for a moment, then asked me to come and see him soon, asked again if I was alright, said he loved me, and said goodnight.

Kylie smiled, and I kissed her and had a sudden surge of desire so strong that for a moment I could hardly breathe and she asked if I needed my inhaler...

We messed about a bit more on the computer and then Bob came with the turkey sandwiches and some mince-pies, so it was quite a bit later when I told Kylie that I needed her beside me if I was to ring Rebecca, if she could bear it. She made a funny face and I rang my wife, my ex-wife...

Rebecca was very calm; she'd maybe spoken to her parents, maybe they'd advised her... maybe she'd had second thoughts... She asked me when I was coming home. I wasn't, I told her. She asked me if we could meet, I said I would rather not at the moment. She suggested I met her parents, maybe I replied. She said she'd rung my brothers but they wouldn't tell her anything, so could she go and speak to them, to give them her side of the story. That stumped me... I said I was very sorry, but I had no interest in her side of the story, I'd seen it unfolding over the last few years and I'd had enough. I didn't say I was very sorry about anything else... Even when she asked if I still loved her and I said I didn't, I didn't say I was sorry about it.

She burst into tears and it rather irritated me; I asked her what her plans were and she stopped bawling to ask what I meant. I actually meant what were and Smithy's plans but instead I said I'd be in touch and just said goodbye, rather coldly.

Was I cruel? Yes.

Kylie reached into my pocket, got my wallet, went to the bar, and bought us a couple of rums... I don't actually like rum, except when I tasted it, it tasted of her kisses...

"Let's go shopping tomorrow," I said, when she was sitting beside me again, our hands clasped. I'd put some underwear in my backpack and a t-shirt... but I'd now run out of clean things... how did Kylie manage to always be so smart and neat? She told me she showered each day at Reneasha's when she could, and took her washing there, she couldn't afford the launderette.

Perhaps we should look for a flat tomorrow... I didn't say that to her, I didn't want to hurry her, or try and take over her life, but I was beginning to struggle with one freezing room and an even more freezing bathroom at the old pub.

"Maybe we should buy the India Inn," I said, burying thoughts of my former life.

"Well, it is for sale," she said jokingly.

"Is it? What? Is it really?" I sat up... I liked the old building, it had an elegance to it in an ordinary, homely way.

"Yes... yes it really is... I've been dreading someone buying it...You can look it up and see, Jacobs Homes and Property are selling it."

"Really? It really is for sale?"

I suddenly had such a surge of optimism that I had to kiss her... but only a brief peck, I didn't want Bob to be telling us off... I remembered the first time she'd kissed me...

"I think we'd better drink up and go back," I said, feeling all hot and tingly.

"Oh yes, why's that then?" she grinned at me... and it was the first full on happy look she'd given me since this morning in the Armenian café.

"Just so you can show me you really do want to marry me... I don't want to go wasting money on an engagement ring tomorrow if you're going to chicken out!"

"Chicken out... what sort of word is that?" and we both burst out laughing.

"Hello, Thomas."

"Marcus!"

My brother stood looking down on me and I felt about nine years old, and for a moment terrified that I'd done something wrong and he would be cross... He was never cross in a shouty or violent way, but in a sad and disappointed way... But what was he doing here? What did he want? He looked very tall and thin in his tightly buttoned coat, the long scarf wound round his neck; he looked very pale and very cold.

I stood up and received a hug, and he held me really tightly for a moment, more of a Paul or John hug than the usual Marcus embrace.

I introduced him to Kylie and they shook hands, each looking very wary... if Marcus ever looked wary.

"As soon as you said where you were I had to come and see you, make sure you're alright," he said and I thought his voice trembled slightly, but there was a lot of noise as more people had come in so I was probably wrong.

"Let me get you a drink, Marcus, please..." I said after we'd stood looking at each other for a few moments.

I hurried to the bar and asked for a couple of beers and a coke and Malibu for Kylie. It took longer than I'd hoped, there was a crush of people, some of whom knew me and greeted me warmly, trying to chat, then the barrel went off and had to be changed. I kept glancing back at Marcus and Kylie, wondering what they were talking about so earnestly... surely he wasn't trying to tell her to... tell her to...

I began to wheeze and pulled out my inhaler... I was using it far too much... maybe something was wrong with me... maybe my body was giving up on me as well as my mind... felt dizzy... things began to flash in front of my eyes, or maybe they were just inside my head... Rebecca screaming at me, Rebecca hitting me, the man pointing a gun at me, hitting the lads, old Red, Raddy, the wind blowing me into the wall opposite the old pub...

"You alright Tom, mate? You look a bit pale..."

Bob put a couple of pints down in front of me.

"Fine Bob, lack of ale makes me pale..." I was going crazy, even *I* thought I was going crazy...

I couldn't bear the thought of losing the peace and happiness, the calm and joy I'd felt, safe in Kylie's thin arms... couldn't bear the thought of it being snatched away from me.

I pushed through the friendly crowd, I could see Marcus and Kylie talking, but it seemed to be her talking, him listening... was that a good thing? Should it make me worry more?

The pool players stopped me to wish me Merry Christmas, then the Long John Silvers were there trying to chat, someone caught my arm, Damian and he kissed me on the mouth but I actually didn't care, I had to get past him to get to Kylie, to get to Marcus...

They both looked up as I eventually got to them and I knew, just knew they'd been talking about me.

I sat down making some jovial remark, feeling very hot again and my hair was sticking to my forehead... I should get it cut... and I remembered the big pink kiss Kylie had left on my forehead once before.

"Are you alright sugar-babe?" Kylie asked.

"I was just thinking about gin... there's some sloe gin behind the bar, well, I was thinking you could flavour gin with anything, couldn't you? But I mean what about curry spices... not curry powder I don't mean... but like cardamom and coriander and fenugreek, real seeds not the powder, and chilli of course and if you put just a little turmeric in it would be an amazing colour wouldn't it?"

Marcus looked anxious and totally perplexed, Kylie put her hand on my mine and I thought she was shaking, but it was me who was shaking.

"Or you could do a Thai version, couldn't you? That could be sensational... coconut and lemon grass and Kaffir lime leaves and coriander...Or a Moroccan version... wouldn't that be amazing for Christmas? That would be just amazing, or mince-pie flavour... Christmas pudding!"

I stopped because I thought Kylie was going to cry.

"... or vodka... flavoured vodka... but that's very popular... Polish... Russian..."

"Tell me about all the Radwinters you've found. Kylie tells me that the pub where the first Thomas came is just near here," Marcus spoke gently.

I looked into his blue eyes beneath his wild grey eyebrows and I began to calm down a little. I locked my fingers through Kylie's and began to tell him, in a more rational way, I think, about the line of men and women, stretching from 1815… and gradually I began to relax and be more normal.

"So I have the link from Thomas to Dad!"

Marcus thought about this… perhaps I shouldn't have mentioned our dad.

"My father was not a bad man, Thomas, he was weak and I wonder now if he may have had a psychological problem which these days would be diagnosed as something like Attention Deficit Disorder… and neither was Mum a bad person… but together… together things went wrong… maybe they should not have married each other… I don't know where he is now, I don't even know if he is alive or dead."

Maybe Rebecca and I should not have married each other… Kylie took some money from my wallet and went to the bar… I craned my neck to watch her…supposing she just walked out, supposing she walked out and went back to the India Inn and I banged and banged and banged on the door and she wouldn't let me in?

"Thomas, *Thomas* … I have to tell you something," Marcus looked very severe. At some point in my erratic childhood I had an old illustrated Bible and one of the prophets, Elijah, maybe, looked a little like Marcus, but Marcus was kind and loving even if he was severe and strict.

Was Marcus going to tell me I'd made a mistake? Had Kylie told him something and now he was going to tell me. Had my ancestors come all the way from Lviv just so I could sit in this pub and be told…

Kylie sat down beside me and slipped her slim hand into mine.

"Thomas, I think you might be shocked to know that I have built my life on a lie."

Shocked? … Where had this come from?

"No-one knows this, no-one who is still alive…"

I had a flash of memory of his disapproval when I told him I was looking at the family tree, poking about he'd said, *not happy poking about*… what did he think I was going to find? The criminal Radwinter who'd been in prison with old Red? …unless… unless… that criminal Radwinter was closer than I'd imagined, I mean very close, like our Dad… Dad was not a bad person Marcus had said, but…

"I once told a lie, not just told it, but lived it… and that lie had profound consequences… profound… "

"Go on," said Kylie in a rather cool, tight way. I looked at her.

"You see Thomas when you were born Dad was not here… not around, he was away… had been away…"

In prison! Oh my God! Well, it might not be nice to think about Dad being a criminal… but Red said he'd been a car-man, just the driver…

"In fact, he was sent to jail… he was in prison… he was sent to prison in 1974 and he came out of prison in 1981."

1981… 1981… But I was born in 1980… My world began to crumble… Edward Radwinter is not my dad… I'm not a Radwinter… not Thomas Radwinter…

Kylie took my face in her hands, looking into my eyes…

"Wait," she said to me. "Go on," she said to Marcus.

"You were born in 1980, Thomas... I was twenty, I was doing my theology degree, I was training to be a vicar..." he stopped again.

"Go on," said Kylie, "Go on."

"I fell in love... She was on some sort of exchange programme... she was from the USSR... she was so beautiful, her name was Tomochka... Tomochka... We had a child, a little boy... she had to go back to the Ukraine and so ... and so..."

"And so I don't understand..." I felt sick, I felt drunk... I looked at Kylie.

This seemed ludicrous, to be having this conversation in this pub, in the Lark full of beery people... but in a sense where else could it have happened?

Marcus looked bereft of words, he suddenly looked old...

"Marcus is saying that he and Tomochka had a child, a baby boy... she didn't want to take him back to the Ukraine, maybe she couldn't... Marcus was studying to be a vicar... so your mum took the baby, she looked after him, like my mum did with Kenneil... the only thing is Kenneil knows I'm his mama... you don't know who your real mama is, but your real dad is here."

Shocked, I jumped up and looked round the pub, looking for an old tramp with piercing blue eyes.

"Sit down, Thomas, you twat, Marcus is your dad."

He had his head bowed, I'd never seen him look like this before, he looked... he looked... as if the weight of the world was literally on his shoulders. Marcus wasn't like this, Marcus was certain of things, Marcus was sure about things... Marcus didn't look beaten by anything...

"The first time I saw him I could see he was your dad," Kylie said… *the old geezer with the beard? I thought he was your dad…*

I sat down. "Say that again…"

"I don't know how to say it in Ukrainian, your mother is called Tomochka, Marcus is your dad, your real dad…"

I felt very dizzy… I'd been on a roundabout at a fair once and when I came off I felt so ill, and Marcus had picked me up and carried me through the crowds, holding me tightly until I felt better and could walk on my own again…

I remembered Marcus coming to parents' evenings at school, reading my reports, coming with me to my interview at Strand Uni… being there for my graduation… Marcus picking me up when I was lost in a crowd like little Kenneil, holding me when I was sick from the merry-go-round…

"Томочка моя мати, Маркус мій батько… that's how you say it in Ukrainian…" I said… I looked at my hands, they were shaking.

Marcus lifted his head to look at me… I didn't have the Radwinter blue eyes, I didn't have the chiselled good looks, high cheekbones, high forehead… maybe I had Tomochka's colouring, maybe I had her eyes… maybe her family were plump with red hair…

"I haven't said her name for over thirty years…" and his voice did tremble.

"Is she still alive?"

He shrugged and we sat in silence.

"Does Paul know... about you and me? And John? Does he know? And Jill does she know that you're my... you're my...?"

Marcus shook his head.

In the bar round the corner a group of lads began singing to the jukebox; it was the Killers again, 'Human'. The lads sang lustily, their signs were vital, their hands were cold they were kneeling, seeking an answer...

We didn't speak but the pub was full of noise, happy people, people enjoying themselves, friends, brothers, fathers and their sons for all I knew... we sat in our silence listening to the laughter, and the singing.

"Are you very angry with me, Thomas?"

"All my life," I said, but I think I said it in my head so I started again. "All my life I wanted a real dad, all my life... but I had one, didn't I? All my life my dad was with me looking after me, caring for me, loving me... All my life you've been there for me, haven't you, Marcus?"

"I have, Thomas... I loved you from the moment you were born and the nurse put you into my arms. I only ever wanted what was best for you, and tried to do what I thought was best... But I failed... when I look at the girls, Sarah and Paula..."

"My sisters..." I have sisters... "You haven't failed..."

I took his hand and he gripped mine so tightly. I pulled Kylle to me and kissed her warm cheek...

My name is Thomas Radwinter, I am the eldest child of my father Marcus Radwinter, and he is the eldest son of Edward Radwinter, the eldest son of Charles Henry

Radwinter, who was the eldest son of another Charles, the eldest son of Thomas Radwinter, the eldest son of Tolik Radwinter, the eldest son of Thomas Radwinter, born Taras Radwinski and maybe the son of Cazimir... Cazimir of Lviv in the Ukraine...

I am Thomas Radwinter.

...and next...

Wednesday, January 1st 2014, New Year's Day

"Look, Thomas, look!" Kylie was rubbing the snow off a lop-sided gravestone; I was chasing Kenneil, pretending I was going to throw a snowball at him, he was squeaking and laughing, even when he fell in a big pile of snow.

I hoisted him up. "Come on, little man, let's go and see what Mama has found!"

Kylie was standing beside the gravestone in her bright red coat; she'd only let me buy it for her from John Lewis's in Strand because it was in the sales, and even then told me she was keeping an account of all the money I was 'lending' her. She stood in her new red, fur-lined boots, pointing at the gravestone she'd cleared.

I stood beside her and put my arm round her shoulders. The inscription was faint, but etched with snow it showed up well enough.

'Sacred to the memory of Thomas Radwinski Radwinter, born 25th September 1815 of Radzivilov Russia, died 10th November 1893 and to the blessed memory of Thirza Radwinter, born 3rd March 1825 of Radwinter Essex died 10th November1893. Beloved parents of Tolik Radwinter, and of his brothers and sisters. "In death they were not divided"'

"Why do you think Paul asked me to look for the family history?" I asked her after we'd stood in silence for a little while, Kenneil contenting himself with poking my beard.

"Paul knew that your dad, I mean Raddy, was in prison when you were born, and he was probably cute enough to know Sylvia couldn't be your mum... Whether he thought or knew anything about Marcus..." she stopped.

"I think he set you off on this journey knowing what you would find… and I think he told John to be there for you."

"It's so strange… Marcus still feels like my brother, and Paul and John, they feel like my brothers too, not uncles… It hasn't changed anything…"

"It's changed you."

"No it hasn't, you've changed me!"

She mouthed 'twat' at me, not wanting to say it in Kenneil's hearing. He wriggled and I put him down and he ran around again, so full of energy.

I put both arms round her and leant my head against hers, and looked at the gravestone; the sun was shining and it sparkled off the snow and the lichen looked like gold dust.

"You've found Thomas," Kylie said.

"I've found Thomas."

Thomas's family line:

Cazimir Radwinski
|
Thomas Radwinter b 1815 né Taras Radwinski m Thirza Downham b1825
|
Tolik Radwinter b 1845 Radwinter, m Emma Wyeth b 1849
|
Thomas Radwinter b1867 m Eleanor Quillen b 1870
|
Charles Radwinter b 1892 m Sophia Carragher b 1887
|
Charles Henry Radwinter b 1911 m Helen Donnelly
|
Edward Marcus Radwinter b 1931 m Sylvia May Magick b 1936
|
Marcus Edward Radwinter b 1959 & Tomochka
|
Thomas Marcus Radwinter b 1980

THE RADWINTER FAMILY

Children of Edward Radwinter and Sylvia Magic

Marcus Edward Radwinter, b 1959 Strand, m Jill Edwards
Paul Quillen Radwinter, b 1965 Strand, m Susan Jones
John Magick Radwinter, b 1973 Strand m (1) Eleanor Marple (2) Fiona Roberts)

Children of Marcus Radwinter and Tomochka

Thomas Marcus Radwinter b 1980 Strand

Children of Marcus Radwinter and Jill Edwards

Sarah Radwinter b 1984 Strand
Paula Radwinter b 1986 Strand

Children of Paul Radwinter and Susan Jones

David Django Radwinter b 1995 Strand
Luke Dylan Radwinter b 1996 Strand
Samuel Otis Radwinter b 1998 Strand
Tom Bowie Radwinter b 2000 Strand

Children of Sarah Radwinter m Philip Johnson

Joan b 2009 Strand
Phyllis b 2010 Strand

Children of Paula Radwinter and Jacob Porter

Paris b 2011 Strand
Boston b 2012 Strand

Available on Amazon:

The Radwinter stories:

Radwinter	(Radwinter I)
Magick	(Radwinter II)
Raddy and Syl	(Radwinter III)
Beyond Hope	(Radwinter IV)
Earthquake	(Radwinter V)

The Easthope stories:

Farholm
Lucky Portbradden
night vision
The Double Act
The Stalking of Rosa Czekov

Lois Elsden has also written:

Flipside
Loving Judah

You can find Lois at:

https://loiselsden.com

https://loiselsden.co.uk

https://Facebook: Lois Elsden - writer

https://Twitter - @locoimloco

... and you can read her blog on WordPress

... and as part of the Moving Dragon Writes blog on WordPress (as Somerset Writers)

Printed in Great Britain
by Amazon